TILL DEATH DO US PART

BLURRED LINES

BELLA DI CORTE

Editing by: Alisa Carter

Cover Designed by: Emily Wittig Designs

For my other half

According to Greek mythology, humans were originally created with four arms, four legs and a head with two faces. Fearing their power, Zeus split them into two separate parts, condemning them to spend their lives in search of their other halves.

— PLATO, THE SYMPOSIUM

Love is a serious mental disease.

— PLATO, PHAEDRUS

INTRODUCTION

Dear Reader,

When I realized how much I enjoyed writing criminal worlds, one thing I was determined to do was explore different aspects of them. Even time periods.

For example, The Fausti Family (who we will connect with again in these pages) are a royal criminal family. They rule Italy and govern all our dangerous worlds. The Gangsters of New York are set in...New York. That series feels rawer and more unforgiving.

Till Death Do Us Part is the first book of mine set in Chicago. I couldn't wait to dive in and experience an entirely new world. How would the Outfit stand apart from the Five Families of NY? I also couldn't wait to explore the city and meet the cast who would make this book come alive for me. Including Chicago's long history with the mob.

I hope I did it all justice.

This book...it made a permeant mark. Even after spending weeks with Felice & Roma, I can't seem to get over them. Their love and connection haunts me, but in the best way. I find myself wanting to visit and stay with them, returning to this story and what it holds within its pages.

A love between two very different people; a connection that's only heightened by their differences, instead of being hindered by them.

If you've ever been tethered to another person while trying to make it to the finish line (trying to figure out how to win together), you'll get this comparison once you read this story.

If not, hopefully you'll experience it once you start to read: the odd but exhilarating sensation of trying to make two bodies work together when you need one to win.

In this book, it's a matter of reconnecting, according to Plato, and winning at the game of life. Starting out as two, but somehow merging back into one and becoming even stronger.

I'm still so in love, and I hope you'll fall just as hard for the story beyond this intro. I hope, like with all my books, this book will feel like coming home. A comfortable place to land when you need it the most.

It is for me. I hope it becomes the same for you.

Much love,

Bella

P.S. If you're new to my books, you can find more information on The Fausti Family (**which you do not have to read first**) on my website.

PROLOGUE

FELICE

From the way the light hit her in the club, she seemed to be severed in half by lightning, as if she had a storm in her soul that had manifested in the atmosphere around her. Half of her was in shadow, the other half lit up. The sharp, jagged line split her down the middle. Behind her, circles moved in and around each other, as if some invisible wind pushed them in different directions. The music rumbled the walls and floor like thunder.

She danced alone, eyes closed, face content, her body going with the flow of the song. But that presence around her kept everyone at arm's length.

The scene was one Plato had described years ago. It was almost out of context, given where we were and the times, but true all the same. We all start out as circles, but we're severed in half by a thunderbolt, punished by the gods we're trying to emulate. We scatter, from one end of the earth to another, always searching for the half that makes us whole.

Plato claimed that, if we didn't force our steps, instead going with the flow, the stars would lead us back to our other half.

Destiny.

Fate.

Whichever word you use to define the hidden power that controls what will happen in the future, it was working in this building between us.

I'd never searched for anything in my life. I'd always just gone with the flow of it. If a red light took a few extra minutes to turn green, I waited patiently. Same with traffic. If something stopped me and made me late, so fucking be it.

A second or two could change the course of destiny.

As I took a drink of my whiskey, I was convinced the jagged half of her was my other half. It was the reason all these boys, besides one, kept their distance. They felt my presence all over her.

Now, don't get ahead of yourself.

This was more than love at first sight.

This was a completion of something that started long before this moment ever did. It went beyond this time and place. I felt the area where she'd been torn from me heal. An instant connection, even though her name had never crossed my lips and I'd never touched her skin. I'd never given her a thought outside of this second.

I'd never felt the impact of a violent crash before this moment.

A crash that made me whole instead of killing me, even though the fusion was going to be a fucking painful process. And if something belonged to me, especially something as vital as my other half—it was mine.

Every breath.

Every choice.

Every step.

Delivered me to this moment.

To her.

"Roma Corvo," I whispered into my glass.

She belonged to me.

Felice Maggio.

Not even a thunderbolt, or death, would be able to separate us again.

CHAPTER 1

ROMA

I should have known better. Drinking on an empty stomach would only make me feel woozy and sick at the same time. Or maybe my sister, Lolita, should have known better and gotten me to eat before we went out to Jupiter, a club she'd been itching to visit. But at least we had made it to an all-night diner, where we were trying to get somewhat straight before we went home.

I mean, I'd had alcohol before. A sip of champagne here. A glass of wine there. But never to that extent. It felt like my head and body were disconnected.

Being the youngest sister out of five girls, I'd always been treated like the baby, but this felt different. This felt like my older sister was throwing caution to the wind for both of us, not watching out for me. But that night, I should have been watching out for her.

Lolita's girl's night out was her way of coping. She was running from a future that was advancing on her. The thing about our family? We were all arranged to marry men we'd never met. It was our father's choice. He believed in keeping alive a tradition stemming back to Italy. Our parents' marriage was arranged, and my father felt it was the only way for his daughters too.

The Corvo sisters.

Isabella

Talia

Alina

Lolita

And me...Roma.

The easiest way to remember our names and the order of our births was to remember the first letters of our names put together spelled ITALY. Except my parents replaced the "Y" with a city. Not too many Italian names start with the letter "Y."

Some of us were relieved that we didn't have to decide. Others, like Lolita, were not so happy about it. Especially since she fell for a guy she met while in beauty school. Ben was his name, and he'd gotten a haircut from her.

Our father was traditional in one sense, but in another, when it came to school and jobs, he was okay with whatever we wanted to do or be. The timing of our marriages was mostly ours to choose too, unless we took forever to pin down a date.

This was Lo's night to end Ben's chapter of her life and begin a new one. She was set to meet her fiancé next week. What made it somewhat easier for her was that Ben totally flipped when she broke it off. He said things to her that made me want to knock his block off.

"Five nuggets." Lo counted them and pushed them closer to the edge of her plate. "I'll bet you five of my precious veggie-saurus nuggies that those guys over there—" she chucked her chin toward a group of guys in a corner booth who kept shooting glances our way "—would be doing the dino mating dance if it was still in style."

My eyes roamed to their table. A guy with dark, curly hair held my stare for a second before turning back to his friends.

That was nothing new. Guys looked at me, but most of them never approached me.

My sisters always told me I was intimidating for a woman, though my parents had always called me warm. My skin had a Mediterranean olive hue, and my hair was chocolate brown. My eyes matched my hair, but instead of being welcoming, my sisters said they were shrewd. Something about not hiding the rejection if the guy wasn't up to my standards. According to them, no man was good enough.

It really didn't matter, though. That part of my future was already planned. So what if the guy I'd built in my head probably didn't exist? He would always just be a fantasy because my husband was already picked out for me.

I shook my head. "Not even the most outstanding mating display could make him my type."

She flung a fry at me. "You are so picky."

The crinkle cut potato landed on my plate. I ate it, going back for more. Even though my stomach felt like it was turned inside out, the more food, the better. It was starting to take the edge off.

"I can be picky if I want. It's not going to do me any good, but I can still have opinions."

She grumbled something about her freedom being taken away. In our culture, family was important, and we just didn't go against our parents. Since our mom had died, we especially didn't want to break our father's heart by rejecting something he'd planned for since his children were born. The guilt would be too heavy to carry around for the rest of our lives.

"It's really not so bad, Lo," I said. "It takes all the pressure off. It's no longer your responsibility to find the perfect match. Babbo will be responsible if you kill him."

"Funny, Y," she said, calling me by the nickname my family stuck me with because my name was supposed to start with that letter. She turned her face toward the table full of guys, not shy about staring. "If you could build your perfect mate—"

I grinned and rubbed my hands together, knowing it was a bit evil looking. She laughed and pushed her plate closer to me. I nabbed one of her veggie nuggets.

"Tall, dark, and handsome. Except for his eyes. Green. Green eyes. Wears suits but is comfortable in a T-shirt and jeans. Has a soft spot for me only. The rest of the world—" I shot her the bird, but I meant that was how he'd feel about mostly everyone and everything but me.

"You saw him."

"Saw who?"

"The guy watching you dance at Jupiter."

"Um...no. What guy?"

"No shit. You didn't see him? Eye color can't be confirmed, but the rest...spot on."

"You didn't tell me?"

"How was I supposed to know you had an idea of this *perfect* guy in your head?"

"Fair. But I do and you asked."

"Yeah, but I expected a general picture, not for you to build him like a car." She tucked a strand of rainbow-colored hair behind her ear. She loved colors, and the entire wheel seemed to work for her. The vibrancy made her eyes pop and shimmer like glass.

"Muscular and fast," I said. "If we're summing him up in terms of a vehicle."

"In bed?"

"Rough, sometimes a little freaky, but nothing that'll send me running, and can be romantic when the mood calls for it. But what do I know about that? The closest I've come to sleeping with a male was in kindergarten, when we had nap time."

She grinned. "A dinosaur?"

"Carnivore," I said, no hesitation. "Brings up your last question. As fierce as one in bed. His mating display? *Hot.*"

"And here you don't eat meat." She shook her head. "I'm going to wish Babbo luck with your arrangement. The guy at Jupiter didn't even seem real—that's how fine he was."

"What about you?" I asked, changing the subject. How

terrible would that have been to have seen the guy in my head, meet him in the flesh, and then he be forbidden to me?

She shook her head, taking a sip of her drink. "It would be too depressing to design and build a husband, then have him be a total dud. It's almost like going to a car dealership and finding the perfect ride. Then...the price."

"*Waaa...waaa...womp.*" I made a losing noise because I was just thinking the same thing.

"Exactly." She looked over at the table again. The guys were laughing, their eyes pinging from each other to us. "I have a wild hair. I feel like I need to do something...drastic."

"Like?"

"Like experience a man that's not my husband."

"Lo," I said, but she refused to look at me.

"I wouldn't go that far with Ben. It would have hurt too much, you know? To experience something life-changing and then have to give it up. But just one night, no strings attached...*my* choice."

That was fair, but not supposed to happen. Even though it was modern day, our arrangements were traditional.

She turned to face me. "I mean, look how gorgeous you are. It doesn't seem fair you can't shop around before you live happily ever after with Babbo's choice."

A heavy breath escaped my lips. I was sure it was still one-hundred-proof. "You can say no, Lo," I whispered.

She wiped her eyes, glitter smearing on her palm and face. "We're the only two left. None of our sisters said no."

Right, because our identities were tied to our family, and we knew the consequences: we would lose our father if we denied him this. We no longer had our mother. Even if she was still alive, she had agreed with him. She loved the idea of arranged marriages for us because their love had been like a fairytale. Our father would die a lonely man without us. That was how perfect they were together. No one could measure up to her, or what they shared.

The sadness in Lo's eyes made them hard to meet. I turned my attention back to my plate. Snatching my hand, she said, "Fuck it," and hauled me up.

The two guys who drove us watched our every move, but they didn't intervene when Lo started to talk to the table full of guys. She asked them if they were from Chicago. It seemed like they were just coming from a club in the city too. Friendly conversation that put no one on edge.

Besides, where would we go? We had chaperones.

It seemed like one guy was chattier than the rest, though. I could tell he was into Lo. A minute or two of back and forth went by, then Lo slowly moved her eyes to the bathroom and whispered, "Meet us outside in five."

Chatty Guy nodded, and we headed toward the diner's bathroom after she made a show of saying goodbye. I noted as we made our way that Curly Locks refused to look at me again.

"Lo!" I hissed at my sister as her ass hung out of the bathroom window. She was trying to climb through to get to the parking lot. We were ditching our escorts, but she didn't even give me the plan. She just dove.

"Just get your ass through the window, Y. We don't have time to discuss this."

"Looo!" I was in no shape to climb through. My heels were high, and the alcohol buzz was still going strong. All this together added up to disaster. My sister had to catch me before I high-fived the parking lot with my forehead.

Instead of her steadying me, though, we both went down. We started laughing so hard, we couldn't get up.

"Bish!" She slapped at me, cracking up. "You look slim, but you must weigh a ton! It's gotta be your height. What are you? Six feet of solid bone?"

"I'm five seven, thank you very much. What are we doing, Lo?" I sighed and finally sat up, knocking some parking lot rubble off my legs. "Why are we out here without our babysitters?"

"I had a connection with the guy in the striped shirt. I'm

doing it, Y! I'm taking charge of my V status. I might commit my life to someone out of duty, but...tonight is all mine. I hear opportunity knocking, and I'll be damned if I don't answer it. This is for *me*."

Before I could respond, shadows started to move toward us. The guys from the table had converged and were grinning down at us. Lo grinned back and offered her hand to the one in the striped shirt. She needed help standing.

He yanked her up so hard, she made a breathless sound, then went to say, "What the f—?" But the breath was knocked out of her when he punched her in the stomach.

I didn't even have time to scream.

Curly Locks had my hair in a death grip, and he was using it to drag me toward a darker area of the parking lot. Once the shock wore off, adrenaline kicked in and I started to fight. I was no match for him, though, and before I knew it, the world went dark.

CHAPTER 2

FELICE

One of the earliest memories I had of my old man was him taking me to a park where a couple of kids were playing. It was Chicago in early winter, and the snow hadn't fallen enough to keep the ground from being slick. My old man was supposed to meet someone there for business.

I stood next to him, watching as two boys hurled a football back and forth. One missed the throw, and when he ran to get it, he slipped and hit his head.

"Blood," I'd said, pointing.

My old man looked away from the kid and down at me. "What you said?"

"Blood," I repeated.

"I don't see no blood." He narrowed his eyes at the kid.

A second later, a pool of red blossomed underneath the kid's head. The other boy glanced at us before he and my father went to check on the kid who had slipped. He had a split on the back of his head that needed stitches.

It was late when we left the hospital. The kid's mom had to be called at work, and the entire process took time. I remembered the streetlights hitting my old man's eyes as he drove his big black Cadillac. He wore a dark suit underneath a thick coat, and his hands were still stained with the kid's blood. Wasn't the first time I noticed the same stains on him.

"How'd you know the kid was bleeding?"

I stared at the profile of his face and then shrugged. "Smelled it."

"Smelled it," he repeated. I couldn't tell if he was curious or shocked.

"It smells like a wet penny would taste to me, but saltier." I thought about what I always assumed was his cologne until I made sense of what it actually was. Blood. I shrugged again. "There's no mistaking it."

"No," he said, and his voice took on a softer tone, almost as if he was thinking while answering. "There's no mistaking it when it calls to you because you're a carnivore, John. Just like me."

Rarely did he or any of his friends call me by my given name, Felice. They called me the English equivalent of my middle name. John. In Italian, it's Giovanni.

Even years later, the carnivore in me scented the smell of blood before I even made it to the hospital room. Between the strong antiseptics usually permeating the air, the metallic, salty smell lingered. Except this time, it smelled a bit sweeter to me, almost like lingering perfume.

A group of men I recognized hovered outside of a door. They all wore dark suits and grim expressions. They were speaking in hushed tones, oblivious to the medical staff hustling around them.

Tommaso Russo, who was the boss of the Outfit, wore the grimmest expression of all as he listened to the conversation. He was in his mid-seventies, on the verge of retirement, but was still as sharp as his custom-made suit. He'd seen and done a lot in his life, so if something brought him out of his bed at this hour, it must have been dire.

Cassio Ricci, who like me was one of the closest men to Tommaso, used the wall to brace himself, hand in his pocket, staring at the ground. His eyes were vacant of his thoughts. He'd

called me as I was leaving the nightclub. He told me the boss
wanted to see me and where to go. That was all it took.

The men all got quiet as I approached. Cassio snapped out of
whatever he was thinking and met my eyes. Tommaso stepped
forward and took my hand before kissing each of my cheeks.

"John," he said. "We have a situation."

My eyes held his before he turned some and motioned with
his chin toward Emanuele Corvo.

Corvo was speaking to a doctor, and for the first time in
however many years I'd known him, he looked disheveled. His tie
was loose and snaking around his neck. His white hair stuck up all
over his head. He kept taking his glasses off, cleaning them on his
shirt as if the world was smeared and he couldn't get it clean.
Without the round-framed spectacles, his eyes looked beady and
tired.

"John," Tommaso said again, demanding my attention.
"Emanuele's two daughters were attacked tonight. It's not
looking good for either of them." He took my hand and
squeezed.

That squeeze spoke the words he didn't have to. I'd take care
of it. But surprising both of us, I was the one who cleared my
throat and spoke.

"Which daughters?"

Tommaso stared into my eyes, trying to dig for information I
refused to give. "It's past my bedtime. Cassio will fill you in on
what we know." With that, he turned and headed toward
Emanuele with five guys in tow. He squeezed the man's shoulder,
whispered something in his ear, and then left the building.

"Coffee?" Cassio asked, holding up an imaginary cup.

"Which daughters?" My eyes fixated on Emanuele, who took
a seat, ran a hand through his hair, then hung his head.

"Miss Iridescent and Miss Illinois." He smirked when I
looked at him. "Miss Iridescent, Lolita, always has different color
hair. She's a colorist at some popular salon in the city. The other
one—she's the youngest—was Miss Illinois a while back. Roma.

Guess she didn't want to compete after that. She quit. Everyone thought she had Miss Universe potential."

"How serious?"

He sighed. "Lolita is missing. Roma is in critical condition. Dr. Corvo usually has men with them when they go out, but they ditched them, and here we are."

"That's all we know?"

"That, and there was a group of guys at the diner. There was some harmless flirting from across the room. The girls stopped to talk to them before they headed to the bathroom. Maybe the sisters knew them; they hopped out the window to meet them in the parking lot. Didn't take them long to beat Roma half to death and get out. The bodyguards said they were only gone about ten minutes when they found Roma outside. The guys left their table not even five minutes after the girls disappeared into the bathroom."

We both grew quiet as two men bypassed us and headed toward Emanuele Corvo. One of the men was older, and the other one was much younger. The older man took a seat next to Emanuele, speaking to him in a hushed tone, while the younger one took a position with his back against the wall, studying his phone.

"You all right, John?" Cassio asked.

I didn't answer. The older man was my paternal grandfather, Alfonso Maggio, and the younger was my father's brother Jack. Jack was younger than me, but older than Roma. It was no surprise they were kissing Emanuele Corvo's ass, even though what they should have done long ago was beat it.

If it wasn't for Tommaso, Emanuele would be dead.

Emanuele Corvo was a famed physician who invented a life-saving heart device and a pill to erase some of the damage, but he refused to save my old man. Said the damage to my old man's heart was too extensive. But Tommaso? Who had just as much damage? Emanuele had saved him, which was why Tommaso felt indebted to him.

Alfonso and Jack were still the heads of the pharmaceutical company my great-grandfather, Giovanni, had started, and they had purchased Emanuele's life-saving device and pills for the market.

Kissing Emanuele's ass wasn't limited to the company. Everyone knew Emanuele was traditional when it came to his daughters. The older sisters were married to men Emanuele had chosen for them. It would be no different for the younger two. I wasn't sure who had been chosen for Lolita, but an arrangement between Alfonso and Emanuele was in place.

Jack and Roma would marry.

The daughter of a legendary doctor married to a pharmaceutical mogul's son? For them, it couldn't get any better or be more perfect.

That was why I'd been at Jupiter. I went to see and fuck the woman Jack was going to marry, fucking them over in the process.

Jack's eyes swung to mine, as if he heard my thoughts. He'd been at the nightclub earlier, one of the boys watching her while she danced. She might not have known who she was going to marry, but Jack had known he'd been watching his future wife. He liked what he saw. There was no doubt he'd claimed her.

"Poor bastard," Cassio said. "He's going to lose his wife before he even has her."

"Yeah." I fixed my suit and headed toward the two guards who were supposed to keep her safe. "Poor bastard."

Not because he'd lost her before he ever had her. But because she'd always been mine.

CHAPTER 3

FELICE

I was getting impatient. It'd been two weeks, and she was still in a hospital bed, letting fucking machines act as her lungs. Her face was unrecognizable. She was patched up like a rag doll that had been torn to shreds by a feral animal.

It took five or so minutes to take perfection and come close to killing it.

Killing her.

With every beep of the machines she was attached to, reality slammed me in the face. She was hanging on by a thin thread of life. The thought of never looking into her eyes, so she could make the connection, made my chest feel hollow.

I took a deep breath and sat in the chair next to the bed. Her hands sat there, one on top of the other, over her chest. My hand reached out and took hers. It was soft but cold.

The door started to open, and I took my hand from hers before whoever it was entered. I didn't bother standing or looking, not until a throat cleared. It was two of Roma's sisters, Isabella (the oldest) and Lolita. Isabella pushed Lolita in a wheelchair.

"What are you doing in my sister's room?" Isabella stepped in front of Lolita, about to charge me, but Lolita took Isabella's hips in her hands and peered around her.

"It's okay, Isa. He's a friend of Tommaso's."

We hadn't had much time to talk, Lolita and me. Not after I headed a massive manhunt for her. She was found at an ex-boyfriend's place. He'd arranged the entire attack. He was pissed that Lolita had broken up with him for the man Emanuele had chosen for her to marry.

The ex's original plan had been to save her from a fate neither wanted, but he'd been waiting outside the diner, and he wasn't happy when his friend called him and told him Lo's plan. He'd lost his mind when he thought she'd wanted his friend, and the plan turned violent. The ex was out to punish her for playing him, and his friends were all for it.

Lolita had paid with the loss of sight in one of her eyes and the fading bruises she wore around her throat. He was in the middle of strangling her when I'd walked in. If we would have been a minute later, she'd be six feet under and not breathing.

Isabella's eyes narrowed. "Friend or not, what are you doing in my sister's room?"

"Isa," Lolita said, her voice firmer. "He's the one who..." She refused to say more.

It took Isabella a second, but the pieces must have clicked. "You saved Lo?"

I offered her my hand. "John Maggio."

She took it and squeezed. "Thank you. We really appreciate it, but it still doesn't explain why you're in my sister's room. *This—*" she nodded toward Roma "—sister's room."

"Checking on her progress," I said.

"She's getting better." Isabella sighed, looking at Roma with an almost maternal concern and warmth. "But not fast enough."

"Isa, give me a minute," Lolita said. "John will bring me back to my room in a few."

Isabella looked between us and then left, but with hesitance.

"My sister...Isa...she's the oldest. After our mom died, she claimed that role. She feels like she has to manage our lives. She has two kids of her own, and she can't tell the difference between them and us."

"Isabella doesn't know me, and after what happened..." I shrugged. "Can't blame her."

"I don't. Not about this." Her eyes moved away from mine and locked on her sister's form in the bed. Tears ran down her cheeks. "I just wanted to have some fun, you know? I'm sure it's public knowledge the Corvo sisters have arranged marriages. I didn't mean for this to happen. I never thought—" She stopped abruptly and took a second to compose herself. "I never thought he could hurt me like he did. He seemed totally harmless."

"People can be deceiving," I said, realizing how gullible she seemed.

Emanuele arranged their marriages, their futures, but I knew he didn't totally shelter them from the world. Or they wouldn't have been at Jupiter, the nightclub, the night Ben decided to take fate in his own hands and play Russian roulette with it.

Her head turned, and she met my eyes straight on. "Are you deceiving, John Maggio?"

"You tell me," I said.

"You look dangerous, like you could unplug my sister and not even lose sleep over it."

"I'd lose sleep over it," I said.

"So cold, but so warm," she muttered, almost to herself. "I know you're not in here *just* to see if Roma is doing any better. I remember that night. Every second of it. I remember you being at Jupiter. You were watching her dance."

"The entire place was watching her dance."

"True." She wiped her cheeks. "But there's something different about you. The night you showed up and saved me, I was so confused. I thought maybe I was hallucinating. I still can't believe it when I look at you. Y—that's what we call Roma— described you to me before the attack. She had this image of the perfect guy in her head. It was you. Physically."

"Maybe she saw me."

"No. She would have totally flipped out and told me. She was surprised when I mentioned you—just a fine guy who was watching her dance. Roma is the most beautiful girl I've ever seen, but her looks *are* deceiving. She's not into what most people would think she is.

"She doesn't mind dancing by herself, or eating alone, or settling in for hours to read about creatures that went extinct millions of years ago. Then again, she doesn't mind trying new styles of clothes or makeup. I...I would always convince her to be my test doll, to try new looks and hairstyles..." Her hands came to her face, and she started to cry into them.

She wasn't being loud. She was holding back for her sister's sake. But her shoulders shook with the intensity of what she was feeling.

Isabella came back into the room, standing by the door. "I think you should go," she whispered.

I took another look at Roma, fixed my suit, then headed for the door.

Isabella called my name, stopping me before I walked out. "You look like Jack."

He was standing close to the nurse's station, waiting for Isabella to let him in the room. Our eyes met.

Isabella must have been eavesdropping on our conversation. She was making a point. So was I.

"Jack looks like me," I said and left.

CHAPTER 4

ROMA

It seemed like the night from hell continued to haunt me. From the moment I opened my eyes, weeks after the attack, I kept going in and out of consciousness. It reminded me of the night that left me helpless in this hospital bed. My head felt disconnected from the rest of me, but I knew my body was in bad shape. Especially when I opened my eyes, and the world was fuzzy and tainted red.

My eyes were bleeding from the asshole who had punched them. When I moved them around, it seemed like liquid lava floating in water. The doctor said I might have to have surgery to get rid of it.

The entire situation tired me out, and I didn't fight against the weights when they made my eyes close.

"What's with all the dinosaurs?"

The voice was deep and warm. I didn't recognize it. I forced my eyes to open and stay that way. It seemed like I was looking through lenses filled with blood, and I could barely see anything. I wanted to blink it away, but it refused to budge. Fighting it gave me a headache.

This man was new to me, though, and it simultaneously made me curious and panicky.

"Who are you?" I croaked.

The man's shape was haloed red by the light, like he'd been washed in blood, and the sun was hitting him from behind. If they had come to finish the job, I was ripe for the picking. The last time I was so vulnerable, I wore diapers.

"Felice Maggio, but everyone calls me John." His hand touched mine, and it was as warm as his voice.

When I moved my hand away from his, he put distance between us, going to sit back in the chair he'd occupied.

"Tommaso Russo is a friend of your father's," he continued. "I work for Tommaso."

I knew who Tommaso Russo was and what he did. He was the boss of the Chicago Outfit. He looked like an unassuming old man, but his job title told a different story.

Babbo had friends in dark places. Tommaso was one of them. We never really spoke about it, but we all knew. Sometimes they would come over to the house. Those were the times he shut his office door to keep us out and to keep them in. Mamma used to say he wasn't to be disturbed.

"Babbo asked Tommaso to send you here? To keep an eye on me?"

"You don't need eyes on you. You're safe. I took care of it."

"You took care of them."

"To a degree." He got comfortable in the chair. The pleather squeaked when he shifted his weight. "Tell me about yourself, Roma."

To a degree? What was that supposed to even mean? It didn't matter. I closed my eyes and sighed.

"I really don't have the energy," I said, "to discuss much."

"Your mouth tired?"

Who was this guy?

"*I'm* tired," I bit out.

"That's an excuse." His voice was calm, smooth, and oddly reassuring, even though he was insulting me. He had the voice of a therapist.

"Wait," I said. "Are you a professional? Are you here to 'talk' me out of this?" By "this," I meant the state of perpetual fear and tiredness that had inflicted me like a sickness since the attack.

He laughed, and it was a nice sound. It was full and warm, like his voice. "I'm not sure what 'this' is, but no, that's not why I'm here. You were right about one thing, though. I am a professional, but not the talking-it-through kind. They'd never hire me to talk someone out of jumping because my job is to do the pushing."

Okayyy. That shut me up for a second. Even though he'd made the comment about "taking care of them," it wasn't as blunt as "my job is to do the pushing." He moved closer to the bed, and his cologne wafted in the air. The scent was manly, and it matched his chemistry perfectly. He could have smelled that way naturally, but I knew it came from a bottle.

I wanted to breathe it in like air.

Maybe my reaction to it was so strong because I hadn't smelled anything but antiseptics for a while. It was like eating tasteless food while on a diet. It all tasted better than it should.

"The first step to getting out of here is making the choice to," he said, bringing me back to his original point. "Moving your mouth counts as exercising muscles."

Maybe I was misreading him, but it almost seemed like he was determined to get me talking again. Not sure why. And I wasn't sure why I admitted this to him.

"Maybe I don't want to get out of here, *John.* My entire world broke into millions of sharp pieces, my trust in humanity included. I mean, my sister never thought he could do that to her, and he took her eyesight."

"And your sense of security," he said.

"For the opposite of a therapist, you're spot on."

"I'm excellent at reading people, *Roma.*" He took my hand again and squeezed. "Get out of here. I have a gift for you when you do."

This time, I enjoyed how warm the short embrace was. It

almost felt...safe. It was strong enough to make me feel it, but it didn't hurt me.

"What is it?" I asked.

I could sense his grin. "You'll have to wait and see, Y." He stood and fixed his suit. Then he headed toward the door, glinting like a ruby. He turned back toward me, as if he had just thought of something. "Your sisters call you Y. That short for Yimenosaurus?"

I laughed, and it hurt. "I'm impressed, but no."

"That's right. You threw off the initials of Italy with the name Roma."

"Hard to find a name that starts with the letter Y."

"Maybe. But I think you were born to break the mold." The door opened a little wider. "I'll be waiting for you to come and get your gift."

"John." I hesitated for a second. "You asked about all the dinosaurs. I've been obsessed with them since I was little. I had no clue why back then. Still not all that sure now. Except...I think it's because I enjoy digging up things that no longer exist, but at one time did. I told one of my professors it was like finding true love, or a miracle. Most people don't think either exists anymore, just like some people don't believe dinosaurs ever did. It feels good to prove them wrong. It feels even better to touch the proof."

"*Molto bene.*" His voice was a bit softer.

He left, and all I could do after was think about the last ten minutes. I'd heard his voice and his laughter. I smelled his cologne. But I couldn't see the features of his face or body through the haze of blood.

Still, I was attracted to him in a strong way. It felt like there was an instant connection between us.

It didn't matter, though.

My father was still my father, and more than ever, he felt if Lolita would have listened to him about the arranged marriage, she would still have her eyesight, and I wouldn't be in this hospital bed.

Felice "John" Maggio was nice to think about, but that was all he'd ever be. A nice thought when the carnivores came out to hunt me in the darkness.

CHAPTER 5

ROMA

October marked three months since the attack. There was no use in dwelling on it. Life moved on. Just like it did after Mamma died. But...I was stuck. Frozen in a pocket of fear I couldn't seem to move past.

I reached for the dinosaur-shaped purse that had been delivered to my hospital room when I was recovering. A T-rex. My sisters were responsible for the balloons sporting numerous dinosaurs decorating the room, but not the purse.

Lolita had handed me a card that'd been tucked inside the carnivore. An address had been written in black ink. Underneath, *John* had been scribbled.

"That wasn't subtle at all," I mumbled to myself, flipping the card over and over. I stared at the ceiling as the doorbell continued to chime.

Halloween night and everyone, including my family, was dressed up. Covered faces didn't inspire trust, so I snuck to my room with a candy apple and slipped in bed. My plan had been to watch TV and ignore the world, but between the chaos going on downstairs and thinking about the man named John, watching a show or movie seemed like wasted time. I couldn't concentrate on it.

I wished thinking of John would lose its attraction. Since the day he introduced himself to me in the hospital, it was hard to get him out of my head. He hadn't visited me again, and I never told anyone about him coming to see me. I wasn't sure if I ever would.

At first, it seemed like my very own secret. Something for me to keep and think about every so often. But the sound of his voice stuck close, and more than the gift he mentioned, I wanted to see his face now that a haze of blood wouldn't make him blurry. I wanted to see if he matched the image I'd created in my head.

I'd somehow given him the face of the fantasy man I'd built. I'd be crushed if he looked anything like Curly Locks.

Sighing, I sat up and grabbed for my candy apple. Isabella was big on Halloween, and she made them every year using mamma's recipe. While I broke into the sweet cinnamon shell, I contemplated going for a ride.

Half of my brain warned me of how foolish it would be to make contact. The other half warned me of how stupid I'd be if I didn't.

Curiosity, or whatever it was, won out. I decided to just drive past his house. He probably wasn't even home. Most of his business was probably done at night. He couldn't push people during the day, right?

Ignoring the thought, I finished my apple and looked at myself in the mirror. I added a black beanie over my hair. Wearing a black turtleneck, black jeans, black leather jacket, and black boots, I needed something to brighten my appearance some, so I reapplied the lipstick Lolita had given me. It matched my nail polish. A mauve brown with pink mixed in.

Not that he was going to see me, but things happen. Best be prepared.

As I headed downstairs into the whimsical haunted house our home had become, thanks to Isabella, my stomach sank. So many people were in costumes. It freaked me out. I held onto the banister and took deep breaths.

These were people I knew. Nothing to be cautious about.

Before I could run back upstairs, I darted down, slamming into a solid chest. My hand shot out, grabbing a sleeve.

"*Whoa*," he said, putting his hand on my arm. "Where's the fire?"

My eyes fixated on his mask. It was one of those plague uniforms for doctors back in the 17th century. The head was in the shape of a beak. A black leather coat covered him to the neck.

He ripped the mask off, and his dark brown hair stuck up all over the place. His eyes were soft brown, but the rest of him was hard. His features seemed chiseled out of expensive marble. His face was so well-defined and his skin so taut, his cheeks were hollowed. His eyebrows were dark and fierce. His lashes were long and full. He was probably in his late twenties or early thirties.

He was a watered-down version of the guy I'd built in my head.

"Are you okay?" he asked.

His question snapped me out of my staring, and I realized my knuckles were white from squeezing his costume sleeve. I let go of him but held on to the banister. My heart thundered.

"Yeah," I barely got out.

"Good." He smiled. "No costume for you?"

"I'm not really into it this year." I cleared my throat, about to ask him who he was and what he was doing in my house, but Babbo and his good friend Dr. Tito Sala stopped on the bottom floor and looked up at us. Another man stood next to them, but I couldn't tell who it was. He was in costume too.

"Gianni," the man in the costume called toward us. "Let's go."

Gianni held out his hand to me. "The name's Jack. Everyone calls me Jack, except for my dad, who sometimes calls me by my given name."

I looked between Jack and Babbo. Babbo had an odd expression on his face, like he was waiting to see what my reaction was going to be.

"Roma." I turned back to Jack and took his hand. "Nice to meet you."

We shook, then Jack bounded back down the stairs, the mask under his arm, joining the three men. He waved at me as he followed behind them.

The way Babbo was looking at the two of us...

My mind snapped back to reality when I noticed Isabella waving at me.

"Are you coming down or what?" she called.

"Or what," I said when I made my way to her. "Can I borrow your car? I think I'm probably boxed in." I hadn't gone anywhere since the attack. I hadn't left the house unless someone drove me. And I knew everyone had parked behind me as they arrived for the party.

"Where are you going?" Concern weighed down the soft expression that had just been on her face.

"For a ride," I said. "I need to get out by myself for a while."

"Roma—"

"If you're boxed in, I'm sure Lolita or Talia isn't."

My sister meant well, but I wasn't one of her kids. She held my eyes for a few seconds, like maybe I would break and not go alone if the look she gave me was stern enough.

She threw up her hands when she realized I wasn't budging. "My keys are on the entryway table, in the glass."

I grabbed her keys and was about to leave out the backdoor when I noticed three of my sisters sitting at the table. Alina was bent over, digging in her bag. She sat up, handing Lolita a wedding magazine.

"We need to start planning now," Alina said.

Talia rolled her eyes, and Alina caught it.

"If she decides on spring, it'll be here before we know it. Venues and businesses book up."

Was Jack meant for me or Lolita? I left out the front door, not even caring.

I held on to the wheel tighter, willing the heater to do its job faster and regretting not wearing a heavier jacket. Late October almost felt like the beginning of winter. I wouldn't have been surprised if it started to snow, it was so cold. I couldn't remember the last time we'd had snow for Halloween in Chicago. It wasn't normal.

What I was doing wasn't normal either. Creeping on a man who admitted to having ties to the Outfit. Babbo purposely kept that part of his life separate. He didn't want that kind of darkness to touch his family. But it had touched two of his daughters, and it didn't even come at the hands of men who pushed people for a living.

Though Babbo now had ammunition as to why arranged marriages were in our best interests. Ben had proven him right. So what if the practice was archaic? He thought of it as preserving a part our heritage while also doing what was best for his daughters. He knew the families of the men he chose. He knew what the men did for a living and who knew whatever else.

Before the attack, I was all for it. It was romantic, in an old-world way, and I trusted Babbo. He'd made good choices for Isabella, Talia, and Alina.

After the attack, I didn't know how I felt about anything. It set me in limbo, and I didn't know which way was up or down anymore.

Halfway there, I started to chicken out.

A sign for Caffè Bar lit the darkness. I pulled in without planning to, Isabella's tires squealing. Alina and her husband, Gino, owned a few of the coffee shops in Chicago. His brother owned ones on the outskirts. Their great-grandfather had started the company. No other coffee or customer service in the area compared. It took less than five minutes to order and get my latte.

Blowing into my cup, I continued, watching for signs as my sister's GPS chirped in my ear. I was so close, my stomach started to churn. The exit was coming up fast, even though I was in control of the speed of the car.

I wasn't sure if I could do it.

Horns blared around me as I crossed over lines I wasn't supposed to and took the exit at the last second, making the toys in the back seat squeak and laugh as they were thrown around.

"Shit," I muttered, setting the cup of coffee in the holder. As I wiped some hot liquid from my jeans, I asked myself, "Am I really doing this?"

Yes was the apparent answer because I kept going.

The world felt too quiet as the toys shut up and I started to crawl down the streets of his neighborhood. I turned on the radio, and Halloween music for kids blared through the speakers. The soundtrack for all the families out for the holiday.

It didn't fit my mood, though. I switched stations, and Tina Turner came on. One of Mamma's favorites. Isabella liked to listen to most of the music Mamma liked. We all did.

It put me at ease, like Mamma was in the car with me, even if the rational side of my brain whispered that she wouldn't have approved of this. She'd tell me to listen to Babbo and go home. I couldn't, though. Not until I saw John's face.

I had to prove to myself that the connection between us in the hospital room wasn't as strong as I felt it was.

Slowly, I slid into a parking spot across from his place and shut the van off. Maybe he'd be handing out candy and I'd get a good view of him from where I was parked. I wasn't sure if men like him even entertained nights like this, but his light was on.

If he didn't answer the door, I'd call him a dud and be on my way. Because only assholes did that to kids.

A stream of little legs ran up to his door and then ran back toward another house. I couldn't see who was giving out the candy, though. I should have brought one of my nieces or nephews as a prop.

That gave me an idea. I got out and followed a pack of kids up to the door. It was dark, and the parents next to me didn't notice I didn't have a kid of my own.

My breath held a second after one of the kids knocked. I continued to hold it after a stunning blonde answered the door. Her hair flowed down her back in beachy waves. Her eyes sparkled, and her lips glistened red. The leather cat outfit she wore seemed painted on her skin. She fixed her ears and looked right at me.

"*Nooo* way! Miss Chicago!"

Miss Chicago? I looked behind me, like she was talking to someone else. All eyes were on me.

"Hahahahaha. *You!*" She pointed at me. "Don't pretend like you don't know who you are. I'd know you anywhere! In my opinion, you're the most beautiful Miss Chicago we ever had." She turned around. "John! Come see. Miss Chicago is out trick-or-treating!"

"I'm not!" I looked around at the crowd staring at me. "I'm *not* out for candy."

"Miss Illinois," a deep voice said from the door.

I automatically turned toward it.

If I could have found my breath and will to move, I would have stumbled back. My entire body felt like jelly. The only thing keeping me upright was his eyes on mine.

Felice "John" Maggio.

Tall, dark, and handsome. Except for his eyes. Green. Green eyes. Wears suits but is comfortable in a T-shirt and jeans.

If he were a car, he'd be a muscular and fast one.

No doubt about it, he was a carnivore. It seemed fitting that I'd seen him through hemorrhages in my eyes. I'd seen right through him.

Blood called to him. Made him hungry and feral.

He was Jack on steroids.

All angular features and a jaw strong enough to carve hollows from his cheeks. His hair was darker, and he sported stubble. It made the color of his eyes pop. He was older than Jack, judging by how his face seemed to be set, like he'd relaxed into his skin. A rock that's mature enough to accept that its burden in life is being a rock.

He was the guy I'd built in my head—physically. I wasn't so sure if this version would have a soft spot only for me. He was a heartbreaker, and I assumed he didn't discriminate between them.

The world seemed to have stopped for a second, and then the barrier was breached. Sights, sounds, and smells came back to me.

"I'm not sure what kind of candy Miss Chicago would want, but..." Leather Cat was searching through her cauldron, picking packets up and dropping them back in.

"I'm not here for candy," I said to her, staring at John.

The look in his eyes said what I didn't have to. *She's here for me.*

I hoped he read the response in mine. *Now that I've seen what a heartbreaker you are, I'm out.*

A man who looked like that and was a gangster? I might as well open my chest and hand him my heart to destroy.

I pulled a kid toward me. He tried to shrug out of my hold, but I held tight. "He's here for candy, and I'm with him."

"Mom!" the kid screamed.

We both looked down the street. The kid's mom was talking to a group of other parents. She narrowed her eyes at the sound of panic in his voice and started to rush toward us.

I pushed the kid forward. "Get your candy, Timmy."

"I'm not Timmy—"

"That's right. You're a superhero tonight!"

"Oh." Leather Cat giggled. "My bad! I thought *you* were out for candy."

I shook my head, then took off for my sister's van. The little boy's mom stopped me before I could get there.

"What's your issue with my kid, lady?"

"Nothing," I said. "I thought he was my nephew. Timmy. I got lost from my family and so many kids have the same costume."

A few of the parents stood around her, like they had her back. They watched me until I got in the van. I tried to start the engine, but it kept cranking without starting. I was starting to get frantic. My sister was notorious for forgetting to fill up her tank. Last Christmas, I'd even given her a gas can as a gag gift because it was a running joke in our family.

It didn't seem so funny now.

No matter how many times I tried to start the car, it refused. It was drained. I held on to the wheel and set my forehead against it.

A knock came at the window. I turned my head a fraction and met a pair of green eyes set in a tan face. His hair was black and slicked back. It seemed as soft as silk. It glinted in the night like spilled ink. He smiled at me, his perfect white teeth shocking in the night.

It was the first time I really noticed what he was wearing. Black turtleneck and black slacks. He looked like he had just stepped off a runway in Italy, except he was more rugged, like he wouldn't mind hunting and killing his food. Getting his hands dirty and his teeth stained with blood. Which made him seem more real and extremely dangerous.

Oh damn. We matched—our clothes. If we stood next to each other, it would be hard to tell where he began and where I ended.

He opened my door, and I held onto the wheel even tighter.

"In the neighborhood?" He lifted a thick brow.

"No," I said, being honest.

Our eyes held for a second before he nodded. "You came for your gift."

"If by *gift* you mean to check you out, then yeah."

"You've seen me before." Something about his tone was odd, like he said one thing but meant another. Like he knew I'd never seen him in person before, but I *had* seen him.

How could he know the only time I'd seen him was in my head? Because I'd *built* him.

No.

There was no way he knew that. I was creating something out of nothing.

"No," I said. "My eyes were full of blood."

"Your eyes are clear now?"

"Crystal," I said.

He lifted his arms and turned around. "What you pictured?"

A hard wind blew, scattering dead leaves and kicking up the scent of his cologne. I breathed it in, and the butterflies in my stomach felt like they were being pushed around, too, by some invisible force between us.

No, I wanted to say, *my imagination didn't come close to reality*, but instead I said, "Somewhat."

He grinned and slid his finger down my face. The touch was soft enough to linger, but he applied just enough pressure that I knew I hadn't imagined it. His finger smelled strongly of his cologne. "All healed, Dino."

I closed my eyes, and my breath trembled out. The feel of his touch sent my pulse running. "Dino?"

"From the Ancient Greek δεινός. *Deinós*. Meaning: terrible, awesome, mighty, fearfully great."

That sobered me some. I opened my eyes and met his. "I know it means dinosaur, but I'm not sure how to take those adjectives."

"That's how I'd describe you."

"Terrible?"

"On my stress levels." A second or two passed before he stuck his hands in his pockets. "You look healed on the outside."

He saw me. Saw past the physical wounds that had closed, but not the ones modern medicine couldn't touch.

"Somewhat," I whispered.

He ran his finger down my face again, but this time he lingered. He reached into his pocket and pulled out his phone. The light from the screen lit his face, making the hollows of his stubbled cheeks seem even deeper. He sent a text. A second later, my phone chimed in my purse. I dug around for it and pulled it out.

Unknown Number: Tomorrow morning, 5 sharp, Dino. Be ready for me.

"You sent me a text when you're standing right here?" I asked.

"Easier than you having to memorize my number this second."

"Right," I said, saving his information in my phone. I probably sounded as muddled as I felt.

"Roma."

"Yeah?" I looked up, blinking. I'd been concentrating on saving his info, taking my time. The intensity between us felt like pressure building, and I wasn't sure how to release some of it. One idea was to reach out and touch him, to make sure he was truly real, but I couldn't do it. I wasn't forward enough.

"Memorize it. It's the only number you'll ever need." He glanced to his right when the sound of a car grew closer. The headlights lit him up. "You'll be followed home."

I opened my mouth to tell him I'd run out of gas, but he'd already shut my door. He casually strode to the sidewalk, hands in his pockets, watching as two guys in suits got out of the car stopped in the middle of the street.

One of the guys filled the tank while the other one watched. The one who watched knocked on the window a minute or so later and made a motion for me to try the motor. It turned over and I put the van in gear, pulling out. I watched John fade into the distance, the car close on my bumper behind me, but I knew it was only an illusion. He wasn't going anywhere.

Fantasy had turned into reality, and he was more than I'd ever bargained for.

CHAPTER 6

ROMA

Mamma used to say that when you're young, you don't feel the cold. My sisters and I would try to leave without a jacket even with the first signs of snow. Mamma would stop us and tell us to put a coat on. *"Playing outside is not worth getting sick over,"* she'd always say.

Yesterday must have been the day I started to feel the cold. I couldn't seem to warm up. I stood on the sidewalk, huddled deep inside my long coat, trying to stop the bone-deep chill from making my teeth knock together.

Or maybe it was nerves.

Felice would be picking me up at any minute. I'd texted him last night and told him to meet me at the Museum of Prehistoric History instead of at my house. It was always filled with people, my sisters especially. The museum wouldn't raise any suspicions because I worked there.

My watch lit up with a text message.

Hayden Burton: Are you coming back soon?

Turning a fraction, I checked the building. Hayden Burton was the director of the museum. He'd been sending me emails along the same lines. I'd taken some time off because of the attack, but I was ready to get back to work. I had a degree in paleontology at only twenty-three. I'd started college at sixteen, dually enrolling while in high school, and dedicated myself to my passion. I loved my job. I missed it.

I raised my watch to respond with speech to text, letting him know I'd be back on Monday, but a Range Rover with tinted windows pulled up to the curb in front of me. I put my wrist down and made a mental note to respond to Hayden later. Felice had stepped out of the car and was making his way toward me.

A strong gust of wind made his long coat flutter. It made my heart do the same thing. Darkness had cloaked him last night. Daylight, no matter how dreary, brought him to life, and all those gorgeous features couldn't be hidden.

His hair was slicked back, every strand landing in the perfect spot, and his jaw was covered in dark stubble. His clothes, a suit underneath a designer coat, were impeccable. The way his cologne hung in the air made me think he'd stepped out of a warm shower not long ago.

He walked with confident swagger around the car and onto the sidewalk.

His eyes met mine before he leaned over and kissed my cheek. "Roma," he whispered as he pulled back.

"Felice," I managed to get out.

Maybe he liked the way I'd said his name. His eyes lowered and heated for a second before he took my hand and led me into the street. He opened the driver's side door for me.

"What are we doing?" I asked.

"You're going to drive me."

Before I could protest, he picked me up and sat me in the driver's seat, shutting the door after. The interior of the car smelled like cold air, fresh coffee, and him. It made my head swim for a second.

He slipped in on the passenger side and shut the door. He fixed his suit, then told me to put my seat belt on. He did the same.

"I always wear my seat belt," I said, strapping in.

"*Bene.*" He nodded to two cups of coffee from Caffè Bar sitting side by side in the holder. "One for you."

"*Grazie.*" I refused to go, though. He wanted me to drive him. Why? Only one way to find out. I asked him.

"Just drive." He nodded toward the road, picking up his cup and taking a sip.

"I have no clue where we're going."

"That way." He nodded ahead.

Smart ass.

I hit the gas and pulled into traffic. At the same time, Felice grabbed for the *oh-shit* handle above the door. Someone laid on the horn, whipping around me when I did. I gave them a little wave. They might have given me a rude hand gesture, but I refused to take my eyes off the road.

"My car is much smaller," I said as way of an explanation. My gas pedal was more reactive to my foot. It seemed like I had to apply more pressure to this one to get going.

Felice said nothing until he started giving me directions when he needed to. When he directed me to turn at the last second, his grip on the overhead bar turned white.

"You can't tell me at the last second," I said.

"Three blocks away. Don't consider that last second."

"That wasn't three blocks."

I felt his eyes on the side of my face, and I was positive if I would have met them, he would have challenged me with a look. Instead, I pretended to concentrate on driving.

A few blocks away, I noticed a group outside of Victory Gardens Theater. Everyone was bundled up, facing a woman who talked while she gestured around.

"I wonder what's going on there?" I chucked my chin toward the scene and slowed down.

Felice glanced at the crowd and then at the road. The direction of his eyes turned mine forward, and I slammed on the brakes before I bumped the car in front of us. Felice was clutching his coffee cup when I looked at him again.

"Mob tour," he said.

I almost laughed, thinking he was making a joke, but there was nothing humorous about his face.

He tapped on the window once with a knuckle, which I took as the same as him pointing out of it. "This used to be called The Biograph Theater. John Dillinger, head of the Dillinger Gang, was ambushed and killed here by FBI Agents. My great-grandfather was there when it happened."

"When was this?"

"Sometime during the early 1930s. During the Great Depression."

"Was your family involved in...what you are?"

"Both sides, but more prevalent on my mom's side."

Maybe I needed to take one of these tours. I wasn't all that well versed in mob history.

Silence fell between us as I continued to drive unless he had to give me directions. A few minutes later, he directed me to turn into a parking lot. We were at a warehouse. He pointed to an open spot.

His head came forward a little when I hit the brake, and he groaned. Or maybe growled. It was hard to tell. It was somewhat muffled, like he was trying to hide it.

"That one was on me." I lifted my hands. "These brakes are sensitive."

He held out his hand for the keys after I shut the ignition off. "Who taught you how to drive?"

I took a breath and grabbed for my coffee. "Mostly my mamma. Why?"

"You're a fucking danger to the roads." He stepped out and shut the door before I could argue. He smoothly moved to the driver's side and opened my door. "You need a tank, but I can't imagine the destruction if you had one."

He took my free hand, like it was the most natural thing in the world, leading me to a side door. I couldn't help but notice how warm and big his hand was. It engulfed mine.

It took me a second to focus on what he'd said and to stop focusing on how my hand felt in his and how, when he touched me, my pulse raced. "I resent that! My driving is fine."

"Fine?" He laughed, and it was sarcastic to the bone.

"Yes, *fine*. Good, actually. Better than good. *Excellent*."

"Who gave you a driver's license? Someone with a death wish?"

I pretended to laugh. "You're such a wise guy."

He was, so I shut up.

"I take it back," he said. "Not someone with a death wish. A man."

"What does the sex of the teacher have to do with anything?" I refused to move, staring up at him, while we stood on the outskirts of the warehouse.

"You look in the mirror lately, Dino?"

"What a crummy thing to imply." I huffed past him when he motioned me in with his arm.

He followed behind, setting his hand on the small of my back. I could feel his warmth against my skin, and I shivered. Maybe he felt it. The pressure increased, and so did the heat.

It felt better than it should have. I told myself it was because the inside of the warehouse seemed much colder than it had outside.

The front area was separated from the rest by particle board that resembled stained wood. A man at the reception desk nodded at Felice and buzzed us into the back of the place. It was open, with men in white aprons and hairnets walking around. Some of them were loading sides of beef onto trucks backed up to the openings of the warehouse.

"Where are we?" I asked.

Felice said nothing as he led me to another area. This one felt even colder. My breath turned into clouds as I breathed out, and I huddled deeper into my coat. I pulled my hat down some and took a sip of my coffee, but it had cooled down and was almost cold.

We stopped when we came to a password-protected door in the back. A red light on the wall blinked after Felice put in the code. The lock *clicked* and we were allowed through.

Was he taking me ice skating? Because that was how cold the air was. But deep down I knew he wasn't the kind of man who took a girl ice skating or gave her sweet gifts. He was a carnivore, like the dinosaur purse he'd given me, and it wasn't in his nature.

I sensed something then, but it was too late.

He opened a door to a locker—like a humongous freezer. After we went through a couple of slabs of beef, he had to catch me before either my legs gave out or I bolted. My mind was giving my body opposing orders. I didn't even notice when my coffee slipped out of my hand.

"Roma," Felice's voice was warm and close, but I couldn't respond.

Hanging from hooks that had been shoved up their asses were the guys who had attacked me and my sister. They were slumped over, feet dangling.

"Look at me."

Felice's voice broke through the terror, the shock, and my eyes snapped to his.

"Someone hurts you, I kill them." Felice took the first guy by the hair, so I had a clear picture of what had been done to him.

Was I still breathing? Even my chest felt completely numb as he took turns with each one.

Faces were frozen in screams. Eyes were like glass under cloudy water. The only one who didn't have both of his eyes was Ben. Curly Locks was unrecognizable except for his hair.

"Sick." The word seemed to come from far away, but it was loud inside of my head.

I flew toward the door, a hand covering my mouth. I slipped some but managed to get out right before all the coffee I'd drank made a comeback in a hall trashcan. Or whatever the hell it was. It was filled with what seemed like lard, and it stunk.

I felt eyes on me when there was nothing left in my stomach

and my jaw relaxed. When I looked up, Felice was watching me. He stood with his back against the wall, hands in his pockets. In his fancy suit and gorgeous coat, he looked like a fine business-man, but beneath the clothes, he was something else entirely.

"You did that to them?" I asked, wiping my mouth.

He nodded. "For you. For the sister you love."

"That's what you consider a *gift*?"

"It's a gift that'll earn your trust. Or would earrings made from their blood have been better?"

"You're psychotic." My voice came out shredded and raw.

"Somewhat." His eyes were as cold as the freezer, even if his voice carried summer in the Mediterranean in its tone.

"Take me back to the museum," I whispered.

He nodded and went to touch my lower back again, but I stepped away from him. He stared at my face as the door buzzed open but said nothing. Neither did I. Not even when he dropped me at my car.

Felice "John" Maggio had killed my nightmares and earned my trust—and that scared me more than what he was capable of, because it only made me want to spend more time with him.

CHAPTER 7

ROMA

Friday Felice had given me the "gift."

Saturday, I slept like I did before the attack—solid.

Sunday night I tossed and turned all night. I couldn't stop thinking about Felice.

What he did for me.

How cold and hard his eyes were, but how warm and alive he felt when he touched me.

It was Monday morning, and I was paying for the restless night. I was thankful to be returning to work, though. I needed something to shift my focus because Felice Maggio was burning a lot of mental miles. I even stumbled coming down the steps at Babbo's. I was tired and not paying attention.

The big house held a chill, but the smell of coffee and woodsmoke from the fireplace seemed to make it more comfortable. I headed toward the kitchen, expecting to see Babbo at the table. I found it empty. I made myself two pieces of toast with avocado, then I poured myself a cup of coffee. I took my plate and mug to the sunroom with me.

Besides the kitchen, it was Mamma's favorite room in the house. She could sit in there for hours, especially during spring, when her garden would start to bloom. She'd always have a cup or glass of something with her, along with a book. She'd always tell us, "If you have access to a book, you can't complain about being bored." That was why the sunroom had a small library.

Lo was sitting on the sofa with a mug of her own, staring out the windows. It was a depressing sight because the garden was dead. The prettiest thing about the scene was the burnt colors of fall decorating the trees and ground.

What was even more painful was how Lo and I had gone from being tight to having miles of distance between us.

On the surface, everything seemed normal. We made small talk, ate together, even if in silence, but I could feel the separation. When those assholes had broken us, they had damaged our relationship. We were the only two left in Babbo's house, and that bonded us. But it seemed like ever since the attack, she blamed herself, and she didn't want to face me.

"Hey," I said, taking a seat next to her. I set my plate and mug down on the table, grabbing a soft blanket from the back of the sofa. I got comfortable, settling in. I refused to let her shy away from me.

"Hey," she whispered, but she refused to look at me. She kept looking at the dead garden.

Her hair was drab, and she had dark circles under her eyes.

"You think you'll ever try to bring it back?" I nodded toward the graveyard. It was nothing but wilted and shriveled plants and flowers. Isabella had tried to revive it, but with no luck.

"No," Lo said, and I could tell that was her final answer.

"Me either." I sighed. As depressing as it was, it was Mamma's, and the yard seemed to know that.

She glanced at me and then looked forward again. "Going back to work?"

"Yeah," I said. "It's time."

She nodded, and after a little back and forth about it, we both became quiet. We got lost in the silence we created. It wasn't peaceful. It was almost as loud as our screams had been that night.

The fracture was there, trying to divide us, but we were too hard-headed to let it.

When we'd fight, Mamma would always remind us that we were all we had. It was a guilt trip, but it worked.

"I don't blame you," I blurted, but it came out soft. It had to be said, and I was sick and tired of feeling like my sister was slipping away from me.

"Not even a little?"

I stared at the profile of her face. After I grabbed her hand and squeezed, she met my eyes. Tears slid down her cheeks.

"I don't blame you at all for what happened that night. But I *do* blame you for me being Miss Illinois."

She wasn't expecting that. Her shoulders tensed before she laughed. I did, too, pulling her in for a hug.

Pulling away, but not far, she wiped her face. "I wasn't the only one who pushed you to do it."

"True." I sighed. "That was collective family pressure, but you started it."

"Mamma did! I just—"

"Took it to another level? Yeah, you did."

"You won, didn't you?"

"How could I forget?"

She smiled and it was mischievous, a little more like herself. "Do you really regret it?"

"Sometimes." Like when leather-clad blondes singled me out in a crowd, calling me Miss Chicago.

The story was on the tip of my tongue, but I didn't want to tell Lo yet. How would that conversation even go?

"Soo... I met this guy while I was in the hospital. And guess what? He killed the guys who almost killed us. Then he took me to see them as a gift! Isn't he a sweet carnivore? Oh, and I almost forgot to mention the strangest thing. He's the guy I built in my head. Trippy, I know."

Yeah, that wouldn't work.

She took some of the blanket and we shared it. "No matter

how you feel about it now, you'll always be the most beautiful Miss Illinois in my eyes."

I smiled. She did, too.

Babbo interrupted our moment by clearing his throat. He stood in the doorway with a cup of coffee. Paisano, his Bracco Italiano, came flying past him, jumping on the sofa, coming between me and Lo. We both petted him as Babbo grinned.

He asked us if we were okay in Italian. After we said yes, he wished us a beautiful day, kissed us each on the forehead, then whistled for Paisano to follow him. He was leaving for a business meeting.

My eyes stayed glued to where Babbo had just been standing. "Do you think there's a registry or something to find matches for us? Like did Babbo find Carlo, Joseph, and Gino from a list?"

Carlo, Joseph, and Gino were my brothers-in-law, married to Isabella, Thalia, and Alina respectively. The men seemed tailor-fit to match my sisters, but I never really thought to ask how the mechanics of it worked. I just knew Babbo knew a lot of people, his roots in Italy were strong, and it was always an agreeable situation.

"Our parents had an arranged marriage," Lo said. "Babbo knows how it works."

"Yeah." I took a sip of my coffee. "But we live in a different time now. That was way back when."

"Uncle Tito helps," she said.

Uncle Tito was Tito Sala, a famed doctor for the Fausti family, one of the most powerful families in Italy. Given their professions, Uncle Tito and Babbo became good friends. They knew each other from medical school.

I ate my toast, taking another sip of coffee to wash it down, tempted to tell Lo about Felice. Not about what he'd done, but about how he seemed to materialize out of my head, but she started talking before I could.

"He was right."

"Who?"

"Babbo, about the arranged marriage. I shouldn't have gone after Ben. I thought it was ridiculous, the idea of having my parents choose my husband. I rebelled because I wanted the choice. It's not so ridiculous, Y. I've been doing a lot of thinking after what happened.

"Babbo and Mamma had a dream marriage. It wasn't without its hard times. It wasn't perfect. But there's a legacy of true love it leaves behind. They fell hard for each other. They respected each other and the vows they took. I want that. I don't want what the modern world has to offer now. It pales in comparison. Look how happy Isabella, Talia, and Alina are."

I didn't know what to say. I'd thought I wanted that too. I'd never fought it. But after I met Felice, I felt myself being pulled in his direction. I had no explanation for it, but it was strong. Like a force. And it was one of the reasons I tossed and turned last night. He was forbidden to me.

Even more than that, Felice wasn't Babbo's choice, and he'd never choose a man like him for me. Babbo would never accept it.

My mind drifted, as it had been lately, but I returned to reality when Lo grabbed my hand again. I focused on her face and tried to ban Felice from my thoughts.

"My...guy, he's an artist, Y! Babbo told me. His family lives in Italy, but they lived in New York for years. They moved back when he was old enough to be on his own. He goes back and forth, but he's been into the Chicago art scene lately. He's a *tortured* artist. Has some issues with social scenes. He's reclusive."

"You're excited?" My voice sounded lacking, even to my own ears.

She either didn't notice or didn't comment on it because she went on with gusto. "Yeah, I am. He's like my own canvas. He's already bringing out the artist in *me*. I'll light up his world with all *my* colors!" She closed her eyes, probably dreaming of all the possibilities. Lo was a social butterfly. When she started talking again, her voice was lower. "This feels like a new start, Y. Something exciting coming for me. Something to look forward to."

I smiled and squeezed her hand. "I'm so excited for you, Lo. I can't wait to meet him."

"Me too."

We both smiled.

"What about you?"

I knew what she was asking, but I wasn't ready to answer. I touched my hair instead. "I need something new and fresh too. How about you give me a new cut before I leave?"

"Roma—"

"You only call me Roma when you're mad or trying to get me to see your point. It's only hair, Lo. Do your worst."

My sister hadn't touched hair since the attack. She'd had big plans for her career, and I wanted to see that confidence in her again. I knew she'd lost a lot, but she hadn't lost her life. The assholes who had tried to end us had.

"Come on." I stood and held my hand out to her. I could tell she was on the brink of no, and I wanted to pull her away from it. "I need this."

She stared at my hand, looked outside, then met my eyes. She put her hand in mine and I pulled her up.

CHAPTER 8

ROMA

The air in the Museum of Prehistoric History was cool, and the only way I could describe how it smelled was *natural*. It instantly put me at ease and transported me to a world long gone.

I'd volunteered at the museum while I was working on my degree in paleontology. When a job opening became available after I graduated, the staff thought I'd be a good fit. I was assistant to Hayden Burton and Elsa Lang. She was the Curator of Paleontology.

Because I'd volunteered, I also helped the special events coordinator from time to time. The building was magnificent. All marble, iron, and Pantheon-worthy columns. I'd also fill in when they were down a docent. I loved doing educational things with kids, like field trips.

The museum felt like a second home to me. I could see a future there.

With my bag in hand, I was careful not to spill my coffee as I said hello to Gonzalo, the 27-foot-tall titanosaur who welcomed visitors on the main floor. The giant spread out 120 feet across Wrigley Hall. Gonzalo was molded from fossil bones excavated in

Argentina. Such a beautiful creature. It always gave me a thrill to
see him.

Elsa and I shared an office, and Hayden had his own private
one off it. Elsa was working at her desk when I walked in, Hayden
looking over her shoulder as they discussed paperwork she was
looking over.

Elsa was in her mid-twenties and reminded me of an old-time
movie star. She had long, golden hair that was styled to fit a time
gone by. Her eyes were vivid blue, her features slight and sharp.
She was exceptionally smart and always so nice to me.

"Roma!" She almost head-butted Hayden as she jumped up,
her arms outstretched for a hug. "You look fabulous!" She held
me at arm's length. "Look at your hair!"

I touched the ends. It was much shorter, and it had to be
styled for it to look decent. "You like it?"

"Like it?" She smiled, running her fingers where mine had just
been. "I love it! It makes you look...more mature somehow."

Her face changed after she'd said it. Maybe she regretted using
those words. I didn't want things to get awkward, so I told her it
was just the cut of my hair, then said hello to Hayden. He told me
how great it was to have me back and, thankfully, it was business
as usual after that.

Before I knew it, it was lunch time, and Elsa asked me to pick
up food from The Herbivore. It was a little place down the street
we frequented. They had awesome vegetarian options, amazing
smoothies, and the staff knew us as regulars.

Sometimes when Elsa and I had more time, we'd enjoy the
walk and have lunch together. She was interesting. She was already
a paleontologist, and she was working on her degree in archeology.
Later, she planned on becoming a historian. She'd fly through that
degree because she was a human information sponge.

My phone vibrated with a text while I was waiting for our
order. My sisters and I had a group chat. It was easier for us to
keep up with each other that way, and no one felt left out.

Isabella: Saturday we're having brunch at Babbo's.

Talia: What's the occasion?

Alina: Where have you been? Lo is meeting her hubby-to-be.

Lo: Yeah, what Alina said.

Y: Can't wait.

Lo: Y, send us a picture of your hair.

Isabella: Lo, you're doing hair again?

I took a selfie and sent it with the caption *Lo's work is all Gucci.*

My phone blew up. My sisters all loved it, excited that Lo was returning to her passion. The conversation turned back to the brunch when Isabella started to spam the chat with decor ideas.

Talia sent an eyeroll emoji and said she was out.

I smiled and scooted up in line. Talia was no-nonsense and refused to take part in any type of decorating. I sent a similar text. I really wanted a moment to play a dinosaur game on my phone before I had to get back to work.

"I have another gift for you."

I would have jumped if Felice's hand wouldn't have been on my lower back. He must have felt the shock go through me like a tremor, though, because the pressure and warmth of his touch increased. It burned through the black silk blouse I wore. His hand was precariously close to the top of my ass.

"No offense, but I'm good in the gift department."

He grinned. "No earrings then?"

"Yeah, I'll pass. Have enough of those. Especially ones made of my attacker's blood."

His face turned serious. "Have you been sleeping well?"

He asked the question, but it seemed like he already knew the answer to it. He wanted to hear me say it.

"Honestly, yes. And I wasn't paralyzed with fear as I left the house or walked down the street. I'm not back to business as usual, but I'm not where I was."

I couldn't bring myself to thank him for what he'd done,

because it seemed...an odd thing to be grateful for, but I hoped he heard the relief in my voice.

We moved up a spot and I braved a glance at him. He wore a cashmere black sweater and black slacks. His hair was slicked back to perfection, and his eyes glistened like green gems from all the natural sunlight flowing through the windows.

Even though the place mostly smelled like all the different items on the fresh menu, his cologne floated through it. It was the first time I could place a specific scent. It was citrusy. Not entirely out of place.

He was though.

This was a carnivore of a man amongst herbivores. Maybe that was why he wore it. To cover up his true scent. Not going to catch a plant eater smelling of blood.

The glance turned into more. He turned his head and we stared at each other. He reached out and barely touched the edges of my hair.

"So beautiful," he whispered.

I shivered, and there was no hiding it. "Lo did it before I left for work this morning. I needed a change." I wasn't sure why I felt compelled to explain. Maybe because my pulse raced, my breath felt shallow, and I needed something, *anything*, to say other than the truth.

I'm so glad you're here. I like when you touch me.

Gael, a guy working behind the counter who knew us as regulars, called my name, holding up my bag. I went to take it, but Felice grabbed it from him first.

"I'll take that." I went to grab it from him, but he took my hand and led us toward the door.

"Wait!" I tugged on his hand. "Shit."

Elsa had come in, and she was looking for me.

Felice let me go when we came to a table where a man in a suit sat. Felice set the bag down and started rummaging through it.

Elsa waved when our eyes met. She side-stepped the thick

lunch crowd to get to me. "I needed some fresh air and thought
I'd walk back with you. Food's not done yet?" She looked between
me and Felice. "Oh. I thought you were bringing our food
back—"

"I am."

Her eyes clearly stated she was confused.

"I have to bring this food back to the office." I went to put my
to-go box back in the bag, but Felice smoothly moved it and
handed it to the guy in the suit.

"Bring that back for Ms. Lang," he ordered.

"Wait!" My hand shot out. "That has my dressing and bread
in it."

The guy in the suit handed the bag over. Felice dug around,
pulling everything out. He gave it back and the guy went to wait
by the door for Elsa.

"You know him?" Elsa stuck a thumb at Felice.

"Somewhat." I sighed.

Felice offered her his hand. "John Maggio."

"John," she repeated. It was breathy. Elsa took his offered
hand and gave him her first name.

"Ms. Lang," he said, "Roma is having lunch with me today.
Celso—" he nodded toward the guy in the suit, holding the bag,
waiting by the door "—will walk you back."

"I don't need him to—"

"I insist."

She tucked a strand of hair behind her ear and her cheeks
flushed pink. "Oh. Okay. Thank you." She smiled at me. "See you
after lunch, Roma."

Felice pulled out a chair for me, and I huffed as I sat down.
Elsa had melted for him, and he wasn't even being all that warm.
When he'd said, "I insist," it sounded more like, "End of conversa-
tion." He was used to being the boss, and it was clear.

He took a seat across from me and watched as I prepared my
Mediterranean salad. After I took out the toasted pita bread from

its sleeve and set it on the side of the bowl, I stabbed some lettuce, took a bite, then met his eyes.

"What are you doing here?" I asked after the bite had gone down.

"I came to see you."

"Are you sure?" I asked sarcastically. "I thought maybe you came to see Elsa."

He took a napkin and dabbed at my chin. Then he opened his mouth. Did he want me to feed him? Seemed like it. I couldn't resist, so I did. He nodded in approval, then stood and went back to the counter. He came back with two waters. He opened mine and handed it to me.

I took a sip, hoping it would help my parched mouth. His eyes were intense, and they felt like heat against my skin.

"Get used to seeing me, Roma." He reached across the table, taking my free hand in his. "I'm not going anywhere."

Like it did at the warehouse, his hand engulfed mine. I hadn't been imagining it. His fingers fiddled with the bangles and watch on my wrist. Butterflies rushed my stomach, dancing all around the lettuce.

"If your interest in me is more than platonic...my marriage has already been arranged, or it will be."

"You refuse to break the rules, Dino?"

"When it comes to that?" I set the pita down. "Yes. I don't want to lose my family over what's right anyway."

"What's right anyway," he murmured.

"Ben," I said, hoping the name would be explanation enough. "But he was wrong."

He stared at me long enough that I turned my eyes from his. I concentrated on eating my salad. Getting through this lunch with my sanity intact. This man made me feel exposed, and I refused to lose my heart to someone I couldn't have. It was bad enough he kept me up at night. I couldn't spend time with him and be safe from him.

"You're a vegetarian?"

The question surprised me. I looked up, and he caught a stray piece of lettuce before it fell out of my mouth. He fed it to me, then wiped my bottom lip with his finger. He rubbed the finger back and forth against his lips, like he was tasting the best olive oil money could buy.

"Yes," I whispered, or he might have heard the stuttering of my heart through my mouth.

"My little herbivore." He didn't grin or smile. His eyes grew more intense.

My little herbivore. My heart stopped completely and fainted.

"You don't like meat?"

He was talking to me again. I had to force myself to answer.

"I've eaten it before, but it's not good enough to make the violence behind it worth it. And I don't like what it does to our bodies. My mamma died of a massive heart attack."

"I attended her funeral."

"I don't remember you being there."

"I didn't remember seeing you. I would have."

I nodded. "There were a lot of people."

"She was well-loved," he said. "I went to pay my respects to Corvo."

Again, he said one thing, but I could've sworn he meant another. There was no ignoring the hard coldness behind the sentiment.

"How long have you known my family?" I cleaned my plate, then set it to the side, making a neat pile with my trash.

"Longer than you've been alive."

"How old are you?"

He sat back, eyeing me. "Take a guess."

"You won't be insulted?"

He put a hand to his heart. "That's fucking cold."

I laughed. "It's not that! You just seem…" *Distinguished, but underneath the clothes, so ruthless.* "Mature."

"Forty-one," he said.

He seemed older by the way he carried himself, but not by his physical appearance. I had a feeling he would always look fine at any age. Time would be kind to him. And I quickly did the math —there was an eighteen-year age gap between us.

"You age well." I went to stand, to throw my trash out, but he slipped it to his side. I walked around, to the front of the table, but this only gave him better access. His hands, strong as they were massive, grabbed me by the hips. His touch seemed to be better than cardio for my heart.

"You ready for your gift, Dino?" His eyes were looking up into mine.

All I could do was shake my head. *No, I wasn't.*

He chuckled. It was deep and dark. The sound of it hit me between the legs. A grin stayed on his face as he collected my trash and dumped it. He kept my hand in his, my bag in the other, as we walked back to the museum.

He walked me in, and we stopped underneath Gonzalo. I held out my hand for him to shake. I was going to leave him with a *nice lunch, but I'm booked up for the rest of my life* line, but he derailed my thoughts.

His hand slid down my face, and my eyes closed. I concentrated on every inch of skin he touched. His palm stilled against my cheek, his thumb touching my bottom lip.

A breath or two later, his lips touched mine, and all I could do was stand there and let it happen. It was more of a brush, but it felt like it had branded me for life.

He pulled away before I wanted him to.

He left me standing in the middle of the museum, hand tucked in his pocket, my first kiss his.

It took me a moment to break out of the trance. To pick up my bag from the floor, along with my heart, because it felt like it had fallen at his feet, and head back to the office. It wasn't until I was sitting at my desk, Elsa with a million questions in her eyes, that I realized he'd never given me the gift.

Something told me he hadn't forgotten. I'd find out soon enough.

I didn't know if I felt anxious or excited about it. When it came to Felice Maggio, they were almost one and the same.

CHAPTER 9

FELICE

S he slammed the door to the car, locked it, then stared at it. She kicked the tire a second later.

I grinned.

She adjusted her bag over her shoulder, heading toward the Farmer's Market, her lips moving. She was talking to herself. Complaining, it seemed like.

She was dressed casually in a long-sleeved white shirt, an open front sweater, blue jeans cuffed at the ankle, and tan flats with a strip of black where her toes went. Dark, stylish sunglasses covered her eyes. Her new haircut gave her a more mature look.

Simply put, Roma Corvo was a stunning woman. It didn't matter if she was dressed up or down. She stole my fucking breath —something almost impossible to do.

She stopped at a table with handmade soaps. After chatting with the seller for a second, she handed him some cash and then pocketed the things she'd bought in her bag. She went to stroll forward but stopped, pulling her phone out. A second later, my phone lit up and vibrated with a text.

Little Herbivore: I want my car back, John.

I hadn't answered her since I switched out her matchbox of a car for one of the safest on the market. A Volvo Wagon.

She hadn't even noticed when I pocketed her keys out of her bag on our walk from the restaurant back to the museum. Trying to act oblivious to me wasn't in her favor. She'd probably noticed the cash I set in their place. It was for the lunch we shared.

I wondered what she told Emanuele when he noticed the new set of wheels. Though it surprised me to find out she'd bought a secondhand car with her own money. She was sporting her independence in a way she knew he would be okay with.

Me: You'll call me Felice.

Her fingers flew across the screen. A second later, a response came.

Little Herbivore: Everyone calls you John. That's how you introduce yourself. So, excuse me for following what seems like the norm.

Me: You're not everyone.

That stopped her for a second. Her shoulders relaxed before her thumbs started to pound against the screen again.

Little Herbivore: Seriously, Felice. I want my car.

Me: It's a clown car, and you'll be flattened. You can't drive.

That was the understatement of the century. I never flinched, and up until Roma, nothing made my heart race but the pursuit of the hunt. But her driving was up there with standing on the edge of a pit filled with complaining, talkative people at the bottom. A version of fucking hell for me.

Little Herbivore: It's not a clown car. It's a FIAT!

She moved her sunglasses to the top of her head, pulling her hair back. Her thumbs moved again.

Little Herbivore: How about we make a deal?

Of course, she'd want to make a deal. She was probably used to making them with her old man. Emanuele Corvo did everything for his daughters, including arranging their marriages, but he also gave them the freedom to carve out their own paths in the world. He knew being too strict was only going to make them defiant.

Roma wanting to make a deal with me proved how naïve she

was to the world, though. She should have known better than to even say the word to a man like me.

Me: No deal for your safety.

Little Herbivore: Hear me out. What if you teach me how to drive? And we drop the motorcade!

Even though I'd switched her car out, I still had a man driving in front of her, one behind her, and one on each side. She was forced to slow down, following their leads.

Me: If I refuse?

Little Herbivore: I'll be forced to report it stolen.

I barked out a laugh. I was about to text her back when a guy came to stand next to her. She turned, as if he had just said her name. Her smile came easy at seeing him.

I placed him right away. The guy from the restaurant who had handed me her bag of food. He had a surfer boy tan and wild, curly blond hair. I didn't miss how Roma seemed to fixate on it while he started up the conversation. His hair brought back memories of the guy who'd attacked her. She was squeezing her phone like a lifeline.

My feet started to move toward her when Cassio fell in line with me. He held his daughter's hand while she licked her sucker, barely keeping up but not caring because she was occupied. Cassio's wife had died, and he was raising Adelasia on his own.

I stopped walking, and he did too.

"Is that Miss Illinois? Dr. Corvo's daughter?" Cassio narrowed his eyes. "That's not Jack she's talking to."

Cassio had always reminded me of the Maggios. They had strong genes. Sometimes I wondered if he was my father's son. Even though my old man loved my mom, he had plenty of affairs over the years. But Cassio's old man was also part of the life, and it would have been a death sentence if anyone had ever found out my old man was fooling around with Cassio's mom. It was one of our laws, not to mess with another made man's woman, and it was taken seriously.

I tossed Cassio my keys. He caught them with one hand.

"Where are you going?"

"To take care of business." I nodded toward Roma, who still had her phone in a death grip. While I walked over to them, I sent a text to Celso, giving him orders to bring Roma's Fiat 500 to the market.

Her eyes registered surprise, then relief when she noticed me. I set my hand on her neck, squeezing. Her muscles were tight, but after I touched her, she relaxed and breathed out. It pleased me that she trusted me.

Maybe pleased was the wrong word. It felt too good. I was like an adrenaline junkie always craving to be near her. It was a hunt I wasn't used to, but I was already addicted.

Restaurant Guy stopped what he was saying about fresh seasonal vegetables. A moment passed where no one said anything, and then Roma must have realized he was waiting for an introduction.

She gave him my name as John. She told me his name was Gael and that he worked at The Herbivore. Other than Roma being intimidated by his hair, there was nothing threatening about him. But he must have gotten a different sense about me. He took off right after I showed up, claiming he was meeting someone. Didn't want to be late.

We stood there for a second before Roma turned to face me. A blast of light hit her in the eyes, making the milk-chocolate color shimmer. She slid her sunglasses down over her eyes and pursed her lips.

"What are you doing here?"

"You're sorry I came?"

She hesitated for a second. "If I say yes, I'd be lying."

"Do you trust me, Roma?"

"Yes," she said without hesitation. "But that's not why I'm happy you're here. I could have dealt with Gael and his curls."

A breeze swept by, rustling her hair. I removed a piece from her cheek, letting my finger linger against her skin. She put her hand over mine.

"Admit that you missed me." My voice came out lower and rougher than expected, like it was grating against sandpaper.

The pulse in her neck hammered against my hand.

"I miss *my* car, Felice."

"You're a terrible liar."

"I know," she whispered, squeezing my hand. "But I do want my car back. What about the deal? You can teach me how to drive."

"Your skills are beyond help."

She smiled, and there was some mischief in her eyes. "I catch on quick. Or are you not a capable enough teacher?"

Before I could succumb to the urge to take her home, teaching her all I fucking knew, I took her hand and then hung her bag over my shoulder. "What are we shopping for?"

She stammered for a second, probably at the change of direction in conversation, and finally said, "Flowers."

I led her to a tent full of bouquets. Her eyes scanned a few before she turned to me.

"Do we have a deal or not?" When I hesitated to answer, she blew out a sharp breath. "Why do you care about my driving anyway? You're acting like a T-rex guarding its bone."

Yeah, that about summed it up.

A heavy breath escaped my mouth. "I didn't like how I felt when you were unconscious in the hospital."

She lifted her sunglasses and studied my face. "You were worried about me."

It didn't sound like a question or a statement. It was one of those in-between phrases that could have been either or. I only nodded.

"Oh." The response was automatic and soft, but she held on to my hand tighter.

We left the admission alone, and she shopped for the next hour, placing a huge order for flowers and buying fresh produce. She took out a bag of dehydrated apricots and started chewing on them after her bag had started to bulge.

"Time for lunch," I said.

She yanked at a piece of the flesh with her teeth and nodded. "You hungry too?"

"I can eat."

"I know of this amazing Mexican restaurant not far from here. They offer fabulous vegetarian options."

We dodged foot traffic until we came to the parking lot. Roma sighed when she saw Celso standing next to her car.

"I frigging love that car."

"It's a matchbox on wheels, Dino."

"It's not. It's fun and flirty. It fits me."

"Red your favorite color?" The car was siren red with tinted windows, which gave it a sexier feel, but it still seemed like it could blow over with a strong enough gust of wind. This was Chicago. The fucking Windy City.

"Not necessarily. I just thought it looked hot on this car."

Celso nodded at me and handed over the keys. As he walked away, he made circus noises with his mouth, like when the clowns start to get out of the car. Roma glared at his back, until she shook her head and slid in the passenger seat, still eating her apricots.

The small bobble dinosaur in a boat on the dash started to tremble when I took the driver's seat. It started to sing when Roma pushed the button.

"If you're happy and you know it clap your...oh."

The arms of the dinosaur were too short to reach the oars. She started laughing, probably at the look on my face.

"I even miss my dinosaur, Felice. It was a gift from Lo when I bought Felicia."

"Felicia?"

She started laughing even harder. "My car. Men are not the only ones who name things."

I sighed, turning the key over. I fucking regretted letting Cassio take mine. I felt like I was going to burst through the interior like the Hulk. My feet might even go through the floorboards.

"Wait!" She held up her hands in a frantic stop motion.

I hit the brakes and her head bumped the seat some.

"Sensitive brakes?" She grinned. "Seriously. What's it going to take to get you to agree to give me driving lessons?"

We stared at each other for a beat before the look on her face changed. It became calculated and determined. She unbuckled her seat belt and leaned over some, apricot drifting in the air between us. Her car smelled more like the perfume she was wearing the other day, though. Mandarin and vanilla.

She was fucking sweet.

Her eyes met mine before they closed, and she kissed me. Her mouth was like candied apricot. When she pulled away, she seemed dazed, but I'd never had more clarity in my life.

Game over. I'm done.

"All right." My voice probably sounded to her like it was full of gravel, but to me, it sounded full of surrender. "We'll make a deal. But from here forward, you only make deals with me."

She nodded, turned forward, and grinned.

Fuck me.

CHAPTER 10

ROMA

The house was alive with sounds while everyone prepared for our guests. I wanted to crawl back into my warm bed and steal a few more minutes. Between feeling anxious for Lo and my thoughts constantly on Felice, I was lucky if I got two hours of sleep. I knew how important today was for Lo, though, so I forced myself up. I took a hot shower, then did my hair and makeup.

Since we were doing brunch, I decided on earth tones for my makeup with a long green taffeta dress. It reminded me of Felice's eyes. I paired it with a tan belt, a few bangle bracelets, and a pair of matching closed-toe heels. I spritzed a little perfume on and went in search of Lo.

I peeked my head over the banister, wondering if she'd gone down to help Isabella and Alina. Talia would either arrive on time or be doing something that didn't involve prep work. But when I heard Alina say, "I haven't seen her yet!" I knew Lo was probably hiding out in her room.

I knocked on her door, but she didn't answer. I stuck my head in. "What's going on, Lo?"

She was sitting at her vanity, a robe on, staring at herself in the mirror. She shrugged. "I was just wondering if Babbo told him about my eye."

"I'm sure he did." I stood next to her, fiddling with her hair. "Or Uncle Tito did."

She sighed, looking over the makeup she set out. "I'm nervous as shit."

I grinned. "I would be too."

She was about to come face to face with the rest of her life, not knowing much about this man, except for some basic details.

That gave me pause.

Jack, the guy I'd met on Halloween night, was a watered-down version of Felice. I wondered if Lo was going to marry him, and if she did, would it make things awkward?

"You?" She placed a hand over mine. "You've always accepted this."

"That doesn't mean I wouldn't be nervous. Besides, what if my guy doesn't come close to the guy I built in my head?" Because he had a name, Felice "John" Maggio, and hot blood pumped through his veins.

Her eyes whipped up to mine, then they fell on the makeup again. "I better finish getting ready. They'll be here in less than an hour."

"You want me to keep you company?"

She nodded. "I'd love that."

We squeezed every second out of that hour, and a few minutes past, Talia knocked and let herself in. "They're here."

Lo looked like she wanted to scream. "What does he look like?"

Talia smiled. "Come see for yourself."

This was the part that always made me the most excited. Seeing who my sisters were going to marry for the first time. I had to give it to Babbo. He was three for three so far, as far as success rates went. Not only were my three sisters in happy marriages, but they were physically attracted to their husbands.

We all crowded around the top of the stairs, trying to see him. A group had clustered at the bottom, and introductions were being made.

"That's him," Talia said. "Sandro Di Lazzaro."

He looked like a young, Italian version of Brad Pitt. His hair was sun-kissed and tousled, and his skin was golden brown. I could see him painting in nothing but a pair of old jeans, but he pulled off being dressed up too. He was wearing a long-sleeved button-down with a pair of khaki pants.

"*Whoa*," Lo said, leaving us behind as she sashayed down the steps.

Talia and I laughed quietly as we followed behind her.

Lo and Sandro were introduced, and there was an awkward handshake then hug between them. After, Babbo directed us to the sunroom for brunch.

As usual, Isabella had outdone herself.

The sofas had been replaced with more convenient seating, and a wooden table that could sit fifty was placed in the center of the room. It had belonged to my maternal grandparents and was shipped by boat to Chicago from Sicily. The flowers I'd ordered at the Farmer's Market graced the table, bringing the colors of autumn inside, but the rest was filled with food.

Isabella even arranged for a pancake station. A chef manned it and created them from scratch when a guest ordered. The entire room smelled like cinnamon.

"Subtle," Joseph, Talia's husband, said, coming to stand next to me with a plate. He nodded toward the spread of cheeses laid out on a charcuterie board. Fruits, nuts, meats, and jars of honey were placed in the most optimum spots around the cheeses.

I laughed, grabbing for a dairy-free pumpkin yogurt. "Isabella is nothing if not subtle."

Isabella and her husband, Carlo, owned a farm about eighty-five miles outside of Chicago. The farm had been in Carlo's family for generations. They were known for their Italian cheeses, especially their pecorino. Isabella said the recipe and method to make it were from the old country. She was proud to display all the things that came from their farm. She even had bees, so I assumed that was where the fresh honey came from.

Talia came to stand next to us, searching out the protein on the table. She had been in the Marines with Joseph at one time. He was high-ranking, and so was his father. They were a career military family. But after a couple of years, Talia decided not to enlist again. She bought a gym and began bodybuilding.

"What's so funny?" she asked.

Joseph told her and she grinned.

"This kind of event is like a drug to Isabella." Talia used tongs to snag some Mediterranean chicken kabobs and set them on her plate. "This is kind of odd, though." She chucked her chin toward a stream of people entering the sunroom. "Mamma never did that. Reserve the first hour or so just for our family and his. Everyone arrived at around the same time. Isabella's way reminds me of a funeral."

Since Talia brought it up, I had to agree.

Isabella was wonderful at parties like this, but it was apparent she was trying to fill our Mamma's shoes, except occasionally, she would change things up and do it her way.

She'd always been the one who craved Babbo's approval the most. She glowed when he boasted about things she did. And the compliments flowed like water from him at parties like this.

Joseph nudged me. "You'll be next."

I plastered a smile on my face and filled my plate. The room was filling up, and with all the new arrivals, I knew there was going to be a line around the table. I found an empty seat and took it.

It was hard for me not to think of Felice and wonder what he'd think about all of this. I wondered how it would feel to have him here with me. It was such a sweet sight to watch Lo walking arm in arm with Sandro around the yard, getting to know him and talking about the future they were going to build together.

From my vantage point, I could see he'd slipped a ring on her third finger.

"She seems happy."

"Hmm?" I was lost in thought and failed to notice Elsa standing next to my chair, looking out at Lo and Sandro like I was.

I stood and set my plate on the seat of my chair, hugging her.

Elsa basically invited herself. I think the future historian in her wanted to witness something most people didn't anymore. She said the mechanics of an arranged marriage fascinated her. She really wanted to get inside Babbo's head, but I knew he'd never agree to talk to her about it.

"I'm going to get some pancakes," she said. "Save me a seat next to you!"

Since I was done with my food anyway, I set my plate on the empty chair next to me. More people were arriving. Uncle Tito and his wife, Lola, were talking to Babbo when a group of about four or five arrived.

Babbo was lit up as if he'd eaten a candle, and he was vigorously shaking hands. He kissed the only woman in the group on both cheeks, then took her hand in his. He seemed even more excited. She said something to him and he turned, looking around the room. When he found me, I thought the smile on his face was going to blind me.

"Shit," I muttered underneath my breath. Jack, the guy I ran into on the stairs on Halloween, was in that group.

Jack. He wasn't intended for Lo, which meant...

Triple shit.

He smiled as he walked across the room, coming straight for me. Damn. In the bright light, it was so apparent he was another version of Felice. His features were not as bold, his eyes were different, and he had nothing on Felice's swagger, but he was definitely a version of him. When he was close enough, he bent down and placed a soft kiss on my cheek.

"That seat taken?" He nodded toward the chair with my plate on it and stuck his hands in his pockets.

"I'm saving it for—" I looked for Elsa. She was coming back with two plates all piled with food. "Elsa. We work together at the museum."

"It's okay," Elsa said, catching the tail-end of our conversation. "I can stand."

"Nonsense," Jack said, taking a plate from her. "Have a seat."

"Thank you." She moved my empty plate and took a seat. She situated one of her plates on her knees, then grabbed for her other. As Jack handed it to her, she studied his face.

"Elsa Lang, this is Jack. Jack—"

"Maggio," he filled in for me.

"Maggio," I repeated, certain I heard him wrong. But he thought I was just repeating it for her. He hadn't given me his last name before.

"Nice to meet you, Elsa." He waved at her, seeing as both of her hands were occupied.

"I thought you looked familiar," Elsa said, totally oblivious to my freakout. "You resemble John. I met him—"

"You know John?" Jack's demeanor totally changed. His eyes narrowed and his lips pinched.

Elsa hesitated for a second. Maybe she could feel how hard I was mentally screaming at her, begging for her not to tell him she'd met him through me. She knew the deal with my family. Just like I'd filled her in on the car situation. I told Babbo she was taking a trip to the countryside and asked to borrow my car because it was better on gas.

"I've met John once." She hedged some. "Chance meeting. Are you related to him?"

"Unfortunately, yeah," he said. "John's my nephew. But there's some bad blood there."

There were not enough shits left in the world.

"Nephew?" Elsa casually took a bite of pancake, not giving anything away. "He seems older."

"My father is his grandfather. His father was my older brother."

"Was?" Elsa was digging for me, and I appreciated it.

"He died." Jack looked at me, ready to change the subject. "Can I steal you for a second?"

I looked at Elsa. She shrugged. I looked at Babbo. The entire group, including who I assumed was Jack's parents, were watching us. If the woman with the fancy chignon was his mother, she was much younger than his father. Probably the same age gap between me and Felice.

This revelation was totally overwhelming and unnerving. All I could do was nod at Jack. He offered me his hand as I went to stand. It seemed like he wanted to keep it, but I acted like I needed to fix my dress as I stood. We started walking toward the door leading to the yard.

"So," he said as we stepped outside onto the gravel path. He stuck his hands back in his pockets. "Miss Illinois, huh?"

"That's right," I said, not sure what else to say.

"Impressive," he said. "You don't meet one of those every day."

Or marry one of them, I wanted to say, but held my tongue.

"What do you do, Jack?"

"I'm in pharmaceuticals."

He went on to tell me he was in business with his father, Alfonso, and how much he respected Dr. Corvo. How his family had become good friends with mine over the years. My father trusted his and vice versa. I only added to the conversation to keep him talking. I couldn't seem to find anything interesting to say.

My mind couldn't wrap around this—who Jack was. And how he said there was bad blood between his family and Felice.

I was certain my father was giving me this time to get to know Jack before he came to me with the arrangement. Maybe because I hadn't been the same since the attack, and he thought he was easing me into it. In truth, I was different, but not totally because of the attack.

Stealing a glance at Jack, my body went numb for a second. How could I marry him? He was a reminder of the man I'd never get to have. His nephew. It would be a lifelong hell to look at Jack and be reminded of my feelings for Felice.

The man who didn't numb me but made me feel alive.

What kind of hell had I been flung into?

Footsteps sounding on the gravel behind us made us both stop walking. Elsa and Lo. I introduced Lo to Jack and Jack to Lo. I was hoping they had come to break up our time together. I kept squeezing my dress to hide the fact my hands were shaking.

Lo held up her hand. Her third finger was now adorned with an intricate gold ring that looked like it was made of gilded lace. "He designed it himself for me!"

I grabbed her hand, and her eyes changed. Maybe she felt what was going on underneath the surface. "It's beautiful, Lo." I hugged her.

She took my hand back and looked at Jack. "Would you mind if I steal my sister for a few?"

He hesitated for a second, like he didn't want to. Then he nodded and disappeared inside. He watched me for a second through the glass in the sunroom before Alfonso took him by the shoulder and led him out of sight.

"Keep walking," Lo said.

The three of us walked until we came to the pool house. We went inside and Lo shut the door and locked it.

"What's going on, Y?"

I paced back and forth, worrying my hands. I wasn't sure what to do with them. I had a bad feeling about all of this.

"That's the guy Babbo chose for me to marry."

"Jack?" Lo asked. "Are you sure?"

Elsa had taken a seat, watching us as she pulled grapes from a bowl on the counter.

"Almost positive," I said.

"Oookay. He's close to the guy you described for me, right? We can work with that."

"No!" I shouted, not meaning to. "I can't work with that, Lo."

"Why not?"

"He works for a pharmaceutical company. They test on animals, and...and...insulin is so high! Why is it so high? It doesn't cost that much to make, and the price is so astronomical people can't afford it. It's a major money-maker, that's why! It's awful to do that. To test on animals and to deny people life-saving drugs."

Lo just stared at me. Elsa popped another grape in her mouth.

"What's really going on, Y?" Lo asked.

"Isn't that enough?"

Lo shook her head. "You can talk to him about those things. Maybe try to make a change to his business through him."

"He likes to do the talking," I said. Besides the Miss Illinois comment, which sent alarm bells sounding because of how proud of it *he* seemed, he didn't take a breath to ask me anything else.

"You're hiding something from me, Y."

I looked at Elsa, and she stuffed two grapes in at once. Lo caught it.

"You told Elsa?" Lo looked hurt.

I sighed. "It was hard not to. He showed up at work."

"Who?" Lo took a seat next to Elsa and grabbed the bowl from her.

"John Maggio."

Lo started to choke on a grape, and Elsa beat her on the back.

"You met him?" she croaked out.

"*You* met him?"

Lo looked a little guilty. "Sorry I didn't tell you, Y. You were in the hospital and Isabella took me to your room. He was there, sitting with you. He looked just like..."

"The guy I described to you?"

She nodded. "I didn't want you to be disappointed."

We both knew what she meant. She didn't want the man I dreamed up to appear out of nowhere and I have no chance with him. Because if I decided to marry on my own, I would be giving up my family. Even though my father never pressed the issue, it was understood we would be out of his life if we denied him this. And there was no way Babbo was ever going to approve of Felice. Period. His crimes looked different from Jack's. They didn't fall under the guise of *doing good*.

Lo sighed. "If it's the business side of this that's tripping you up, look at it this way, I'm sure John's is worse."

"No, Lo," I said. "It's different. I know what Felice does, but he doesn't seem to hurt *innocent* people."

In fact, he made sure those assholes never hurt anyone again. I knew Felice wasn't the hero, but he was no villain to me. I couldn't tell my sister that, though. It would lead to the truth of what he did for us. It seemed like delicate information and could only go so far. I trusted Elsa and Lo, but I didn't trust them enough with Felice's future. If they were ever questioned about anything, they didn't know anything.

"Who's Felice?" Lo asked.

"John," I said. "That's his real name, but not everyone calls him that."

"You ever thought about talking to Dr. Corvo?"

Lo and I looked at Elsa. She lifted her hands in a *I had to ask* gesture.

"It was stupid of me to bring up business." Lo spun the new ring around her finger. "I know it's not about that. I'm just trying to find something helpful to say."

"I know."

A knock came at the door. We all looked at each other before Elsa hopped off the stool and went to answer it. Sandro stood on the other side. He smiled when he noticed Lo standing behind her.

"Just give me a few—"

"No," I said, touching Lo's shoulder. "We should go back. This is a day for you and Sandro."

She asked me if I was sure. I assured her I was. Nothing was going to change by us stewing on it.

On the walk back, Elsa hip bumped me, smiling when I met her eyes. I smiled back, but it was hard to do. Lo and Sandro were holding hands as she laughed at something he said in Italian, her body swaying in to his every so often.

They seemed so right, and I couldn't help but wonder how everything had gone so wrong for me.

CHAPTER 11

ROMA

We'd made a deal. Felice would give me driving lessons during our time together. If he couldn't make it, the motorcade escorted me. The entire situation had really pissed me off at first, how bullying it seemed. But after I'd seen his face at the Farmer's Market, when he admitted he'd been worried about me, it changed my mind.

Mamma used to say, "Do not waste people who worry about you. There are not enough of them in the world."

It brought back memories of the brunch and Jack Maggio as I drove to meet Felice. I wasn't sure if Jack was one of those people. I didn't know him all that well, but something told me Jack loved Jack more than anyone. He was good at charming people and being the center of attention.

When he wasn't talking to me at the brunch, he had a crowd around him, always making them laugh. I could count how many words I'd said to him that day. All he needed was a little encouragement and he went off like a rocket.

At some point Lo had passed me and whispered, "Give him a chance."

Truth was, I didn't want to. I wasn't attracted to him. There was nothing that pulled me toward him. My body yearned to be next to Felice's all day, every day. And when he didn't text me or show up when we made plans, it almost felt like something was missing in my life.

It was the craziest thing I'd ever felt, and I didn't understand it, but there it was. I admitted it to myself because what's the point of lying when I felt it? It was like Paisano chasing his tail. It would only drive me mad.

I needed to focus, though. Concentrate on driving only. I was getting closer to the shopping center not far from Babbo's house where I met Felice every morning and where he dropped me every evening.

If anxiety had a scent, everyone around me could've smelled it. It was coming out of my pores, but I wasn't getting rid of it. It seemed to skyrocket when I spotted his car in the parking lot.

Before I even pulled in, he stepped out of his car and held a spot for me. After I took it, he opened the door of my Fiat and took the passenger seat. He engulfed the small space with his physical size and the scent of his cologne. Cold air clung to him, making it smell even stronger. He was dressed in his usual uniform of all black.

God help me, he was heartbreakingly beautiful.

My hands squeezed the wheel, and I took off too fast. I didn't even bother to look at his reaction. I just knew I had to concentrate on keeping it together, to make it to work without any incidents that would cause horns to blare at me. Being next to Felice made the impossible situation entirely too real. And no one could help me fix this. Because there was no solution. I was going to lose someone.

I felt totally alone in the world.

Felice reached out and took my hand, holding it in his.

Whatever music had been playing in the background hadn't even registered until he leaned forward and changed it. He'd told me after the Farmer's Market that the faster the music, the faster I seemed to drive, and the more reckless I became. He'd been playing softer and slower Italian music on our rides. That was what he'd changed it to.

It was a duet with an Italian tenor and an Italian coloratura mezzo-soprano.

Like him, it was heartbreakingly beautiful and somewhat haunting.

I went to switch lanes and stole a glance at the profile of his face. He was staring out of the window, and my heart took off like a wild creature heading to freedom.

He must have felt my eyes on him.

He met my stare and set the wheel back in place. I'd started drifting into the next lane. It seemed like it was only the two of us in the world. Then the invasive sounds of horns shattered my peace, and I snapped my attention back to the road.

The lyrics of the song stuck with me, whether he intended them to or not, and when I arrived at the museum, I rushed to get away from him. He caught me by the arm and started to haul me toward the car Celso had followed us in. It was dark with even darker windows.

"Let me go, Felice!" I tried to snatch my arm out of his hold, but he held tight. I knew I was disguising my true feelings with anger, but I didn't know how to handle this. I dug my feet in a little harder, moving my upper body wildly, and he stopped walking, but he didn't let me go.

We faced off in the parking lot.

"Have a nice time with Jack this weekend?"

"You knew," I breathed out, but it was more accusatory. "You knew he was the guy Babbo chose for me."

"Yeah. I knew Jack was the boy."

"You didn't tell me!"

"Would it have changed anything?"

"Yes! No! I don't know!" I started to lose it. This felt like death to me in so many ways.

It didn't seem like he knew what to do with me. He was at a total loss, if the cornered look in his eyes meant anything. Before I could fight, he lifted me off my feet and brought me to his car. He ordered Celso to take a walk and grab some coffee.

Felice took the back seat, setting me in his lap and holding me, like he'd be my armor against the world.

Shield or not, this felt like goodbye to me. I couldn't win this one. I had to let him go and it was ripping me apart.

After I calmed down, I looked up at him. He stared down at me.

Both of us moved toward each other.

Our lips met.

It felt like we'd crashed into each other, and when we did, the line where he began and I ended became nonexistent.

His tongue explored my mouth. I was hesitant at first, but the more he teased me with his, the more I wanted it.

He started to kiss my face before he met my mouth again. The kiss was getting rougher, and my hands reached out for his body. He was solid, nothing but muscle, but not overly bulky. He grabbed the hem of his sweater, pulling it over his head.

My hands ran up and down his chest, over the stubble on his jaw, while he kissed me so deep, I could barely breathe.

I'd worn a leopard print top with a black faux leather skirt, black stockings, and black velvet, high-heeled booties. His hands explored every curve while he reached down and unzipped my boots. He worked on my skirt next, my stockings, and then my top.

All that was left was a matching lacy bra and underwear. He situated me on top of him, his hand coming to my neck, taking a fistful of my hair.

His eyes seemed to drink me in. His pupils were dilated, pushing most of the green out.

He looked wicked, and I shivered.

He leaned in close to my pulse, inhaling the scent of my skin, as he whispered, "So fucking beautiful." His voice was like sandpaper, but it didn't touch the itch I couldn't find to scratch.

It made me crave more.

He pushed my breasts up until they spilled over the bra, then took my nipple in his mouth and sucked. My hands automatically gripped his shoulders, needing something to hold on to. The pleasure surging in my veins made me feel drunk. I bucked against him, my head tilting back, a moan trembling out of my mouth.

"That's it, Roma. Rub yourself against my cock." He pushed my underwear aside as I started to grind against the bulge of his pants.

It was so big, I thought it might burst through the expensive fabric. It was causing a delicious friction between my legs, and when he pulsed his hips up, sucking and squeezing my nipples, I whimpered into his mouth.

My body started moving faster, harder. I was crazed, like I couldn't get enough.

My body had, though, because it felt like flames licked my skin and pleasure like I'd never felt before rushed me like a hot flash. I came around him with a cry, digging my nails deeper into his shoulders. When the tremors subsided, reality slowly returned, but I was still dazed.

He continued to kiss me, our tongues still searching. The pulse between my legs beat like a hot drum, and when he ran his hand along it, pinching the sensitive nub, almost feeling like a bite, I made a helpless noise and came even harder than the first time.

My skin was sensitive, like no one had ever touched it before.

No one had, not in that way, until him.

He was watching me when I opened my eyes. His hand came to my face, holding it in place, bringing my mouth to his. The kiss was harder and rougher than before. When we pulled apart, I wondered if one of us was bleeding. I tried to break out of his grasp, but it was like iron.

"You're mine, Roma," he said in Italian. "Do you understand?"

His words were like cold iron, too, and I felt them lock me into place. This was supposed to be goodbye. But I didn't think

Felice understood what the word meant, or he didn't care. And I had no clue how to set myself free.

Problem was, being shackled to him felt right, and that worried me the most.

It hit me as Felice watched me walk into the museum.

I'd come close to giving him something I couldn't take back in his car.

If he would have initiated sex, I wouldn't have said no. But so far, he'd only taken things that showed no proof, except for the marks he left behind that only I could feel. And I couldn't stop feeling them.

His touch on my skin was still alive. The pulse between my legs started to drum again.

"Stop thinking about him, Roma," I whispered to myself, feeling like all eyes were on me. It felt like everyone knew what I'd done in the car. I sipped the coffee Celso had brought me, hoping the heat was an excuse I could use for being flushed. I avoided eye contact and rushed into the office.

I came to a sudden halt when I found a guy with a little girl standing next to Elsa's desk. Some of the coffee sloshed out, and I cursed and wiped it on my skirt. The guy reminded me of Felice. Were they related? And why were they all coming into my life suddenly?

The little girl must have been around three or four, and she was playing with a stuffed dinosaur from the gift shop. Elsa was talking to her about it. The guy had been staring at Elsa, but when I walked in, he turned his eyes on me.

"Roma," Elsa said, "one of John's friends is here to see you."

He held his hand out. "Cassio Ricci."

His grip was firm but not too tight. And he might have been a friend of Felice's, but he also seemed like a partner in their shared business.

"And this little beauty is Adelasia." Elsa smiled at the little girl. She smiled back, putting the stuffed animal in Elsa's face, growling some. Elsa growled back and they both started laughing.

I'd never seen Elsa smitten with a kid before. She even refused to do tours for field trips.

"My daughter," Cassio said, bringing my attention back to him.

"She's beautiful," I said and meant it.

He thanked me and then asked if he could have a second to talk to me. Elsa's eyebrows shot up, as if to say, *I've heard that before—a lot over the weekend.* I agreed and set my things down at my desk. All but my coffee. It would give my hands something to do if things got awkward. Or I could throw it in his face if he tried something.

Cassio offered Adelasia his hand, but she turned away from him. He looked like he didn't know what to do about it.

"I can watch her," Elsa offered. "I don't have anything to do right now."

My eyebrows shot up, and she shrugged. She liked the kid.

"I don't usually leave her," Cassio said. "But it might be easier. I'm sure I don't have to imply that if anything happens to her, the same will happen to you, Ms. Lang."

"No implication needed." Elsa saluted him. "I have this."

Cassio told Adelasia he'd be right back and to be good. She ignored him to play with Elsa.

We entered the museum and followed the stream of traffic heading toward all the exhibits.

"I'm going to make this brief." Cassio stopped, forcing guests to walk around us. "It's in everyone's best interest if this thing between you and John stops."

"I know," I said.

He blinked at me. "That's it? No argument?"

I sighed. "No. I'm sure you know how traditional my father is. And over the weekend, while my sister had her engagement brunch, I learned who my father expects me to marry. Jack Maggio."

He nodded. "Jack is—"

"Felice's uncle. I know."

"Felice?"

"That's his name?"

"Yeah," he said. "But no one calls him that. Not even his own mother. Tommaso will occasionally, but it's not often."

Tommaso. The boss.

"Why are you telling me this? Don't you think you should talk to John?"

He barked out a laugh. "That's like asking that big fossil over there to move. Nicely." After a second, he sighed. "This is not going to end well. For anyone. You know this, but it bears repeating.

"Dr. Corvo is good friends with Tommaso Russo. Years ago, Dr. Corvo prolonged Tommaso's father's life. Then he saved Tommaso's with that invention and those pills of his. Tommaso is indebted to him. Dr. Corvo is serious about the arrangements he makes for his daughters. He's not going to like that John's sniffing around you...the daughter already promised to Jack Maggio."

"And there's bad blood between John and Jack."

"Between that entire side of his family. John's old man, Sal, was the oldest. Alfonso, John's grandfather, wrote Sal off before he'd even left John's grandmother for his new wife. His business ties only made things worse."

"Like he has room to judge," I said, thinking about how dangerous pharmaceutical companies were.

Cassio studied my face. "Are you fucking serious right now, Miss Illinois?"

"Yeah." I ignored the Miss Illinois jab and took a sip of my coffee. "His business is not what it seems to be either. I don't like their ethics."

"Well, you better start pretending," he said, giving me a stern eye. "That's your husband's business. His livelihood. Don't go knocking it until, at least, *at least*, after the wedding night."

"I have a question."

He made a go-ahead motion.

"If giving John orders is like asking Gonzalo to move, nicely, why did you come here expecting me to do it?"

"The fossil has a name?"

"Of course."

"Strange. Who names bones?" He shook his head, then shrugged. "I don't know what else to do. I love John like a brother. I don't want to see anything happen to him. It's only a matter of time before he starts making a scene about this. When he does, Dr. Corvo will go to Tommaso, no doubt about it, and Tommaso's hand will be forced. That's what happens when you're indebted. And Tommaso, he's old school. His word still means something. Which means John ends up on the chopping block." He made a slashing motion across his throat.

Maybe my face paled, because he nodded.

"Didn't mean to upset you, but the truth is a cold slap to the face. Thought maybe you could change his mind. And whatever you do, don't tell John about this meeting. He'll put *my* head on a chopping block for talking to you."

He left me standing there, not sure what to say.

CHAPTER 12

ROMA

It was impossible to get any work done after Cassio left. I was in an impossible situation, and I knew before it was over, blood was going to be spilled and life was going to get messy. It already was.

Elsa tried to take my mind off everything by keeping me busy, but I was having a hard time reconciling that some of the best times of my life were going to be mixed with some of the worst. What we did in the car felt so good and so right, but the visit after was a cold slap to the face, using Cassio's expression.

I sighed for probably the hundredth time.

Elsa lifted her eyes from her desk and a stack of papers. "Go to lunch and then go home. Take a few personal days, which will give you an extended Thanksgiving break."

I was supposed to have lunch with some of the women who competed in the Miss Illinois pageant with me. We stayed close and had lunch or dinner every so often to catch up. They were all beautiful, and most people assumed that was all they were, but they went much deeper than the surface. They were passionate about causes and education and the arts and so much more.

Today, though, I wasn't in the mood to be in my own skin, much less be good company to anyone else. And the thought of taking time off depressed me. Then I'd be forced to think this all through when I was sure there was no solution.

"Seriously, Roma, go have lunch, then go home and think about what you want. Not what everyone else wants, but what *you* want."

I knew what I wanted, but I couldn't have him. Not without hurting my family.

As I was packing up my things, Kerry Hall, the events coordinator, came into the office. Her amber silk blouse shimmered against her black skin. Her hair was pulled away from her face, showcasing her perfect features. Her cheekbones were high and defined and her smile was so warm.

She was so striking and elegant, it was hard not watch her every move.

She took the seat across from Elsa and crossed her legs. "Are you feeling okay, Roma?"

I made a so-so gesture with my hand.

"A lot of nasty stuff has been going around." She scrunched up her nose. "I was actually coming to see if you could help me with a gala we have coming up in December. It's for an Italian American foundation. They're raising money for various charities. I expected to see your father's name on the list, but I didn't. One of the yearly beneficiaries is Salvatore Maggio's Heart Foundation. Seemed like something Dr. Corvo would be part of."

I inwardly groaned. "When did they book?"

"In August. Last minute. They weren't happy with another venue."

This had Felice's name written all over it. What was he playing at? Was he going to try to go public with this thing between us at the event? I didn't buy a coincidence.

"So," Kerry said, waving at me to get me to focus. "Can you do it?"

"Roma is taking a couple of personal days before the holiday," Elsa said. "When do you need her?"

"I can handle it until after the break." Kerry turned to me. "But I'd really appreciate your help on this one."

"I'd be working the event?" I asked. "Not just be behind the scenes?"

"Yes, it would be great if you'd be my assistant that night."

"Okay," I said.

"Is that a yes or no? It sounded more like a question." Kerry laughed, probably at the look on my face.

After I nodded, *yes*, Kerry gave me the date, then turned to Elsa.

"Lunch?"

The walk to The Herbivore seemed like a blur to me, and when my friends asked if I was feeling okay, I told them not really and begged off. I sent Felice a text, letting him know I was leaving work early. I blamed it on a migraine, which was true. It felt like the thoughts in my head were pumping weights.

Before he could drive me, or have Celso, I left. I was extra careful on the drive home. I didn't want to give him a reason to steal my car again. After I'd drifted into the other lane that morning, I was surprised he hadn't.

The house was empty when I got home. I rushed to my room and changed out of my clothes. I needed what Isabella called "rags." Clothes with holes and history. A pair of sweats and an old sweatshirt I'd bought in Rome one summer.

The spacious house held a chill, so I added thick socks. I grabbed a bag of kettle corn, eating it as I drifted from room to room, not sure what to do with myself. The sunroom didn't hold the same comfort as it usually did. I ended up in Babbo's office.

It was all dark-stained wood and thick leather-bound medical books. It had an old-world Mediterranean vibe. Most of the house did.

A carved frame with a hand-painted picture of my great-grandparents graced the wall. The rest of the pictures were in silver frames on a shelf.

A picture of my parents on their wedding day. Mariella Basile

Corvo, my mamma, made a striking bride. A black and white of my paternal grandparents. Singles of Isabella, Talia, Alina, Lolita, and me right after we were born. One of all of us together. A picture of my father with each of his daughters on their wedding days. His four grandchildren. Paisano ended the line.

"Roma?" My father had a heavy Italian accent, and it always made my name sound musical. "You are home early. Is everything all right?"

He stood in the doorway, watching me.

"Yes. Elsa gave me a few personal days since the holiday is coming up."

"*Bene.*" He nodded and took his hat off, hanging it on the peg. He did the same with his coat and scarf, but they went underneath. He set his leather bag down in its special spot. He still carried one.

Paisano followed behind him a second later. He'd probably gone to get water before he found Babbo. The dog was like his shadow. I gave him a scratch behind the ear before he got comfortable on his bed.

Babbo motioned for me to take a seat across from him. He sat after I did.

"I have been meaning to talk to you," he said.

The popcorn I'd been munching on made a ball in the pit of my stomach. I wished I'd grabbed a drink to wash it down, but I would have probably choked on it. I'd planned on taking a break from thinking when I got home, but I could sense where this conversation was going.

"Jack Maggio," I croaked out.

He nodded and smiled. "Handsome fella, ah?"

"Yes." I couldn't lie.

"He is successful and comes from a good family. His father has been a friend for many years. I feel the two of you will make a beautiful couple."

There it was.

I'd been feeling as if this entire situation resembled death, but never so much in this moment. I knew it was coming, but when it was confirmed, I felt a piece of my heart shrivel.

My hands held tight to the arms of the chair. The wood had a waxy feel to it, and I knew it would be underneath my nails after I left this room. "Why are you telling me who he is now?"

My sisters didn't know until they were introduced. Not all families did it this way, but my father did.

"You have not been the same since the attack. I wanted to give you time to get to know him. You will trust him that way."

"You didn't do the same for Lolita."

"Lolita is Lolita. You are Roma. I see you as individuals and treat accordingly."

"I need time," I barely got out. "I'm not ready."

His face changed. He was considering what I was saying.

"And I don't want to take away from Lolita's time," I added, letting him hear some of the panic, but hiding a good portion of it. I didn't want to make it seem like I was fighting it, only coming to terms with it.

He nodded after what seemed like the longest minute of my life. "You will take this time to get to know Jack and his family. You will be ready after Lolita's wedding."

He was letting me know without being blunt that he wasn't giving me more time than that. I wanted to say something else, to question his choice, but it would only lead to more questions and him becoming suspicious.

Emanuele Corvo had made it to a point in his life where not many people questioned him. He was considered a genius in his field. The only person I'd ever seen push his buttons or challenge him was Tito Sala, but my father saw him as a mentor. My father looked up to him.

I wished Uncle Tito was here. Maybe I'd have the courage to challenge this. Uncle Tito was a warm soul and a voice of reason. But I wasn't sure if Uncle Tito would do any good. He might talk to my father, but when it came to his daughters and this tradition, Babbo was unmovable.

Elsa couldn't understand why none of us ever stood our ground. Most people who were not brought up in the same ways couldn't. We were raised with certain expectations, and to fail at meeting them meant failing as a daughter. And then to lose our family? The main support system we were taught to value and rely on? It was hard to look that fear in the face and deny it.

"Roma."

My eyes met his. I'd been staring at the purple popcorn bag.

"I do this because I love you. I only want what is best for my daughters."

"I know, Babbo," I whispered. "I'm tired. I'm going to take a nap."

My feet brought me to the door, but my mind didn't register the steps. I stopped before I left his office, my back to him.

The question seemed to come out on its own, even if it felt like I was daring fate. "What if you're wrong? About Jack?"

I refused to face him, in case he'd see the truth on my face.

You're wrong.

He had the wrong Maggio. Jack wasn't the one who made me feel complete. My heart told me so. And Babbo had no idea he was setting me on a path of death by forcing this. I'd always feel ripped in half, knowing my other half existed and I couldn't connect with it for fear of losing my family.

"Sleep, my darling girl," he said after a minute. "We speak nonsense when we are tired."

CHAPTER 13

FELICE

She claimed she had a migraine, but I wasn't sure. The uncertainty of it was driving me out of my fucking mind. Being apart from her put me on edge. If a man made the wrong move, I'd snap his neck. And if whoever was behind this door didn't let me in, there was going to be trouble.

Isabella answered. She didn't hide her surprise, but she wasn't at a loss for words. "I remember you from the hospital. You were in my sister's room." Her voice was laced with suspicion. "John Maggio."

"Good memory." If she took offense to my clipped tone, she took it as she should. I could tell she played by the rules and wouldn't even fantasize of disappointing daddy.

"What do you want?"

Real warm, this one. "Tommaso sent me. I'm supposed to meet with Corvo."

"Dr. Corvo. He didn't mention it and he's not here."

Lolita came up behind Isabella, and her eyes grew wide when she saw me.

"John," she breathed out. "What are you doing here?"

"He *says* Babbo invited him." Isabella's tone implied she believed I'd invited myself.

I would have, but fate was in my corner. Alina and her husband, Gino, owned popular coffee shops in town, and Gino's brother made a deal with the wrong people. He agreed to add prize machines to the businesses. It was a new idea that pushed out slot machines—for making good money quick.

It was a buck for a chance to win free coffee, free pastries, percentages off your bill, points that went toward their app, things like that. Each machine was tailored to fit the busy establishment it went in.

When one of the guys from our crew went to Tommaso with the idea, he approved it right away. Because tailored really meant rip-off. The customers rarely won, and the shops were losing *niente*.

The problem with having them in the coffee shops was, it wasn't our guys who supplied them to Gino and his brother. It was guys from Florida. And they didn't get Tommaso's permission first.

Since I was Tommaso's right-hand man, he sent me to talk to Corvo about the situation. Corvo knew I was coming to discuss it with him. Even though Tommaso usually handled issues with Corvo personally, it was Thanksgiving, and Tommaso loved turkey. He was a fiend for it.

Alina and Talia came to stand behind Isabella and Lolita. They were all studying me like I was studying them.

For being sisters, not much connected them but their last name. They were all attractive, but in their own ways.

Isabella had dark brown hair, bordering on black, and deep curves. She reminded me of a mother hen.

Talia was darker, with black hair and stone-brown eyes. It was clear to see she was the bodybuilder. She had *respect me or else* written all over her.

Alina had auburn hair and green eyes, and she was the thinnest. She seemed to float whichever way Isabella went.

Lolita seemed to have blonde hair naturally, but she changed colors often. She was artistic and marched to the beat of her own drum.

Then there was Roma, or Y, as they called her. She broke the mold. Her hair was on the lighter side of brown, and in the sunlight, some strands sparked gold. Her eyes were the color of milk chocolate, but they would cut a man down to size with a glance.

"If you give me a second, I'll grab my wallet," Alina said.

Before she could turn, Talia stopped her. "He doesn't seem like he's out selling candy, Lina."

"Babbo invited him," Lolita said, but the way she looked at me, it was clear she knew something.

"Then why is he standing outside?" Talia asked.

We all looked at Isabella.

"Babbo didn't mention it to me."

"Corvo didn't invite me," I said. "Tommaso sent me. Corvo is expecting me."

I could tell they weren't used to people calling their father simply by his last name, judging by the different reactions they all had.

"*Dr.* Corvo," Isabella said.

She wasn't going to correct me. In my definition, a doctor wasn't someone who played God and picked and chose who they saved. So, by my understanding of the word, Emanuele Corvo wasn't a doctor.

"I can't get these things untangled!" Roma's voice came into the hallway before Roma did, and when she finally arrived, her eyes were fixed on a string of lights wrapped around her shoulders. She was wearing a headband with antlers on it. "Isa, you'll have to ask Carlo to—" She stopped short when she looked up and saw who her sisters were staring at. "Felice," she blurted.

"I thought he said his name was John," Isabella said, her voice going from suspicious to interrogation mode.

"It is, Isa," Lolita said, her tone almost defensive. "Some people call him John. Others call him Felice. What's the issue?"

"I feel like I'm missing something here." Talia looked between me and Roma.

Alina nodded, but she was still staring at me. "Same. Why are we not inviting John Felice inside? If Babbo knows, let him in, Isa."

Roma's face relaxed when she realized I'd come to discuss business with her father. I'd been to the house on one or two occasions before. Corvo was alone both times.

Four men stepped up behind the women. One of them had a kid on his shoulders wearing a headband matching Roma's.

"What *is* the problem here?" Talia stepped in front of Isabella and invited me in. "My husband, Joe, will show you to my father's—"

I stepped inside, and everyone but Talia and Roma moved back as a unit. I caught it when Lolita grabbed Roma's arm. She seemed frozen to the floor.

I didn't give a fuck about reactions. I took Roma by the arm and whispered in her ear we needed to talk in private, or we'd be talking in front of her sisters.

She walked ahead. I followed her through the house to a sunroom that led us outside. She moved fast, her arms folded in front of her. When she stopped and faced me, her face was as pale as snow. I took off my coat and draped it over her shoulders.

She shook her head and handed it back. "I can't, Felice." Her eyes cut to the left, implying her family might catch her.

"You can't catch cold." I set the coat over her shoulders.

She sighed and a cloud of air blew from her mouth. "Do you understand who you are?"

"I'm the man who would kill for you, but besides that, tell me who I am."

"You're the kind of man my father warned me about. The kind he kept me away from. And now you're showing up at my house."

"Am I scandalizing you, Roma?"

She looked away from me, holding the edges of the coat

closer. Her throat moved. "No, that would be Jack," she whispered. Then she met my eyes. "His business seems worse than yours. But it's not my choice. He looks good on paper."

"It is your choice. It's as simple as saying a word: yes or no."

"Maybe for you." Her voice was soft and full of regret. "My choice isn't simple at all. I'll lose my family, and I don't even really know you. This all might be just physical attraction. Nothing more. I refuse to use my family as stakes in a risky gamble."

"That theory can be tested easily enough."

"I gave you enough of my firsts."

"Not nearly enough. And any man who tries to take more from you will find himself in a meat locker."

"God." She looked up, like she was calling out for answers. Snow fell, and the flecks landed on her face. She let them for a minute. "The sky is drunk."

"Are you?"

She looked ridiculous with lights wrapped around her neck, the headband, and a red nose. But I'd never felt anything so warm before I set my eyes on her. My blood ran cold. And it still did, for the rest of the world.

She smiled, but it didn't touch her eyes. "When it storms, the sky seems angry. When it's sunny, happy. When it snows, I always figured it was drunk. It's cold and disconnected, and it sends all this swaying white stuff down." She held her eyes up for another second or two before she looked at me again. "What if I have sex with you? Would that cure you of whatever this is between us?"

Anger shot through me. It was so hot my ears might've been blowing steam. She must have seen it on my face. She took a step back and held up her hands in a defensive position.

To prove a point, I stepped closer to her until our bodies collided. Her hands hit my chest, but her fingers grasped my shirt. She wasn't afraid of me. She didn't trust herself with me.

She looked up at me, a pleading look in her eyes. It was enough to make me feel emptiness in the center of my chest, like she'd stolen my heart and was keeping it to herself.

"You're a skilled butcher, for a plant eater," I whispered, my voice shredded. "You carved my fucking heart out." I sank my hands into her hair and my tongue into her mouth, searching for the cure, and I found it, but she was going to be the death of me anyway.

Time or place didn't exist when she was close.

She made a helpless noise, and we pulled apart with a violent motion. A motion savage enough to split one into two halves.

"Roma!"

She startled at the sound of Lolita's voice.

"It's nice that John wanted to check on you, find out how you've been doing after..." She looked to her right, where Talia stood in the shadows, facing us. "But Babbo will be expecting him in the office. He's almost home. Isabella called him to tell him John was already here."

"Okay," Roma said, her voice steady. She offered me her hand. It trembled. "Thank you for everything, John."

Her eyes glistened with unshed emotion. I grasped her hand, and she made a breathless noise when I pulled her in.

"Try to stay away from me," I breathed in her ear, not letting her move away. "I'll make the choice for you."

"Time." It was a tortured whisper. "Give me more time."

As I walked back into the house, Lolita ran past me toward Roma. Talia watched me as Joseph placed a hand on her shoulder, suspicion in his eyes as dark as hers.

She stopped me by calling my name. "You took care of those assholes who attacked my sisters?"

I nodded and then didn't know how to react when she thanked me and hugged me. Joseph showed me to the office, shaking my hand before shutting the door behind him. I was regulated to Corvo's office, where he only did business. The rest of the house was off limits to a man like me.

I was never bound by limits, though.

I killed them.

Corvo came through the door with his dog a few minutes after I'd been shown to his office. He hung his hat and coat on the peg while the dog came sniffing around my feet. Corvo snapped at him in Italian, telling him to get on his bed and to stay there.

Even the dog, in his opinion, was too good for me.

Corvo grabbed a bottle of whiskey and filled the glass. He didn't bother offering me one.

I'd been in prisons with warmer atmospheres.

He took a seat across from me, watching me with a cold glint in his eyes. He didn't say anything and neither did I. He had something on his mind. He could go first, or this was going to be a silent meeting.

He drained the rest of his glass and set it down. "Your part in my daughter's life ended. It goes no further." His tone matched the iciness in his eyes. "It was never about my daughter anyway. It was about the favors Tommaso owes me."

"I wouldn't be much of man if I didn't check on her, at least."

"Much of man, ah?"

He meant it to be a slap in my face, insinuating that I wasn't much of one, but he'd have to go for my jugular to get the response he was looking for out of me. I'd learned early on that giving someone else control was a decision. I had hard limits, but I'd memorized them. If a situation emerged that I had never experienced before, I'd act accordingly, adding a line or not. It was that simple.

"That's what I said."

"Your manipulative games will not work on me." His tone was deathly quiet. "I see right through you, John Maggio."

"Good." I sat up some, fixing my suit. "Because I'm not out to prove anything. I don't need any man's approval. Your clear vision will save time."

"Too good for that, you and that family of yours, to be humble about anything."

That family of yours. The organization I belonged to.

"I can't speak for all of *that family of mine*, only for me. I'm man enough not to need validation. I stand on my own two feet. I live life on my terms. I make the rules."

I'd known Emanuele for years, but I never had much to say to him, unless I was delivering a message from Tommaso, and I could tell I'd caught him off guard. He didn't expect me to be so articulate or charming. The change in his eyes, from cold to hot, told me it pissed him off, though he tried to hide it. I'd been in the same room with men who made professional poker players seem like rookies. He was nowhere near as skilled at hiding his reaction as he thought he was.

He loathed me.

Probably because he could sense who, or what, I was.

A hunter.

And his daughter?

An innocent creature, being threatened by my nature.

I got it, but he'd have to kill me to keep me from mine. And if he could see straight through me, like he'd claimed, there would be no true reason for it, except for his dislike of men in my line of business.

He liked what I did for his daughter, though.

I killed in her honor.

I'd always kill for her.

Something he needed to keep in mind.

I'd kill to keep her.

Couldn't have one without the other.

He sat back in his chair, relaxing, probably realizing he'd been primed and ready to jump over the desk to strangle me. "You are no longer welcome here, John Maggio."

I stood, fixing my suit. Tommaso would have to deal with the problem with Gino's brother and the coffee shops. Tommaso wouldn't be happy. He'd talk to Emanuele and then the order would come down to me again. I'd hand it to someone else to deal with. I'd only get involved again if the problem wouldn't go away.

A big fucking waste of time, and to Tommaso, time meant money. It was the one thing he loved more than turkey. It was the bottom line. That was why he liked me so much. I'd always brought in a lot.

Corvo's eyes moved with me as I reached over and grabbed the whiskey bottle and a glass from his setup. I poured myself a small amount and downed it, keeping my eyes on his as I did. I set everything back as he'd had it. All neat and tidy. In order, like he pretended his life still was.

I tipped my head to him, then left.

CHAPTER 14

FELICE

For a second, I thought my eyes were deceiving me, but the sound of Cassio's deep laughter proved they were being truthful.

We were at the museum, doing a walk with the event coordinator, Kerry Hall, when Roma exploded out of her office and went running toward a group of kids. That by itself wasn't funny, but she was dressed in a blow-up T-rex costume, and the short arms were flailing as she ran.

Even Adelasia was laughing, and she wasn't the type of kid who laughed a lot. Cassio felt it was because she'd lost her mom, and she was too young to understand the hurt she felt.

When Ms. Hall noticed, she grinned. "That's Roma Corvo. She's going to be assisting me for the event. Not in costume, though."

Even after I stopped laughing, a grin lingered on my face. My little herbivore was exactly like Lolita had said. Different in such a refreshing way. And the more time I spent with her, the more time I craved with her.

After the scene at Corvo's house, we started our routine again, and I'd agreed to give her more time. It was important to her to keep the peace before her sister's wedding. She said Lolita had been through a lot, with the attack and losing her eyesight in one eye, and she didn't want anything to ruin this special time in her life.

There was no way to be with Roma without causing a war, but I was as serious as a heart attack about making the decision for her if she didn't. And we both knew how serious the heart was. We'd both lost a parent to massive attacks on them.

It always seemed like poetic justice that Corvo's wife died of the same thing that took my old man. Especially since he refused my old man the treatment that could've saved his life. It felt like karma, but looking at Roma, I took it back. Poetic justice would have been Corvo trading places with his wife.

Adelasia started to pull Cassio toward the office, but he was trying to talk her into going on the tour with Roma. She was shaking her head and repeating, *no, no, no.*

"Take her." I chucked my chin toward the office. "There's something in there she wants."

His eyes turned hard. "We're here for the foundation, John."

"What else?" My eyes dared him to say it. He knew me better than to interfere in my personal life, but Cassio knew the situation, and sooner or later he'd try to talk to me about it.

"Fuck, John," he muttered, and then he let Adelasia pull him away.

I turned back to Roma and the group of kids. She was animated about the facts she knew by heart, and she was trying to talk with her hands. The short limbs of the costume jiggled whenever she did.

"She's going to be my wife."

Ms. Hall's stare grew heavy on the side of my face. "Roma?"

"I took one look at her and met the truth. You know when you know." I turned and faced her.

She gave me a blank stare, her mouth open a little. She didn't know how to respond. She didn't need to. I said it so someone outside of my life could be witness to the truth.

"Umm...I don't know if that..." she stammered. "Shall we continue the tour?"

I almost laughed again but stuck with the grin. I was in a good fucking mood.

"Shall we?" I offered Ms. Hall my arm. She took it, but I could tell she was somewhat wary of me after the marriage comment.

She went over all the details she'd discussed with my mother over the phone. The only reason I cared as much as I did was because it was in honor of my old man. The Salvatore Maggio Heart Foundation provided heart-saving medicines and treatment for those who couldn't afford them. It also did screenings, counseling, and maintenance for preventive health.

Our tour ended before Roma's did. She was still talking to the kids when Ms. Hall went back to her office to grab some paperwork. As fate would have it, the teacher announced a break. The kids had to complete some sheets on their own.

Roma's eyes met mine. She gasped when I picked her up and hauled her into the lady's bathroom, the costume's arms flailing and her feet dangling. I locked the door behind me. She had her back as close to the wall as the blow-up costume would allow.

"Hello, Dino," I said.

"You're wherever I go." She was almost breathless. "Don't you ever have to work? Or sleep?"

"I do." I stalked toward her.

Her eyes darted from left to right, but there was nowhere to run. I pushed into the costume, hoping the fucking thing would pop. It was pushing back. I leaned in and kissed her lips. Her mouth tasted like candied apricots from the Mediterranean.

Her eyes slowly opened after I pulled back some. She gazed at me like she was high. "On the surface, you're here to go over the plans for the event, but I have a feeling you want something else."

"Of course." I fixed my suit. "I have a proposition for you."

It looked like she wanted to reach out and fix my collar, but she couldn't. Her arms were trapped. It was the first time I'd ever gotten the sense she wanted to initiate the first touch without having a deal in mind. It did things to me that were hard to put into words.

"I can see it in your eyes." She waddled down the wall some. "You have something reckless on your mind, but you can't pop Herman. He was extremely hard to find, and the kids love him."

"Herman?"

"The dinosaur I'm wearing, Felice."

The grin that came to my face couldn't be stopped. She grinned too.

"I know. I look ridiculous." She glanced at herself in the mirror before she sighed. "But I love teaching the kids about prehistoric times, and Herman keeps their attention."

It wasn't Herman. It was her. Some people shared light with the world. Some people snuffed it out. I was usually the latter, but I couldn't help but be drawn to her. There was no cure for whatever this was between us. I belonged to her, and she belonged to me. It was that simple, though the world was trying to complicate it.

She melted into my embrace when I ran the outer part of my finger up and down her face.

"Your proposition?" she whispered.

Her breath trembled when I moved to her lips. I traced them with a finger, already knowing the shape by heart, then I pulled her bottom lip down, keeping a grip on her chin.

"After the event, spend the weekend with me."

Her eyes popped open. "I can't," she said right away. "You said you would give me—"

"Time. I am." My voice came out hard and my tone was clipped.

"I don't understand then."

"I need more of you." The words came out steady, but they were harder to say than I ever thought possible.

For the first time in my life, I felt a weak spot in me. I'd *wanted* before, but I'd never needed anything or anyone.

I *needed* her.

I didn't fucking care for it.

Especially when I got into bed at night, or woke up in the morning, and it felt empty. Empty of someone I'd never had in it before, but her presence lingered. I couldn't disconnect from it.

"I can't," she repeated. Her tone was regretful, as usual. "How am I supposed to without causing trouble? I mean—"

"You said enough."

She studied me, trying to read past the words. "Enough?" she repeated. "Just enough?"

My suit felt too tight in the shoulders suddenly, and I rolled them to loosen the tension. "Enough."

"Why do I get the feeling you're saying one thing, but you mean another?"

I led her out of the bathroom and toward the kids. The teacher still had them busy. Roma's eyes were on me as I headed back to Ms. Hall, who gave me the paperwork and told me she'd walk me to Hayden's office.

Cassio sat in a chair in the outer office—where Roma and Ms. Lang had their desks—reading a magazine about dinosaurs. Ms. Lang and Adelasia sang some kid's song. When I said it was time to go, Adelasia started to scream. It seemed like she'd formed an attachment to Ms. Lang and didn't want to leave. Cassio wasn't used to dealing with a tantrum-throwing kid, so he picked her up and hauled ass toward the door.

"A minute of your time." I knocked on Ms. Lang's desk once with a knuckle.

She motioned to a chair in front of her desk. "What's on your mind, Mr. Maggio?"

"How do you feel about lying, Ms. Lang?" I sat back in the plush chair and got comfortable. "I'll make it worth the sin."

CHAPTER 15

ROMA

The night of the event, I couldn't stop looking for Felice. I hadn't heard from him since he got me alone in the bathroom and left me with a simple *enough* after he proposed I spend the weekend with him. My gut told me he was up to something. He didn't seem like an *enough, you win* kind of guy when he wanted something and wasn't getting it. And he'd accepted defeat much too easily.

I didn't want to say no, but what could I do? How could I spend an entire weekend with him without raising suspicions? I didn't do a lot outside of my family. Even when one of us traveled, it was usually with someone else. Mamma used to say we didn't have a buddy system but a sister system.

Isabella had me nervous. She was especially suspicious after the night Felice had come to the house. He did have business with Babbo, which was legit, but men in Felice's business never made it past Babbo's office door. Even Tommaso, though he was offered fine whiskey and cigars.

Even in heels and standing on my toes, I wished I'd been born with the neck of an *Alamosaurus*. The crowd was thick. All the men were in fine tuxes, the women in designer gowns. It was a sea of velvets, satins, silks, and sequins.

He had to be attending his own party, right?

When I wasn't assisting Kerry, I kept coming back to the open bar. I figured this might be the easiest place to run into him at some point.

"Looking for someone?"

My breath caught when Elsa set her hand on my waist and came to stand in front of me.

She leaned in and kissed my cheek, then held me at arm's length. "Damn, Roma. You're slaying hearts tonight."

"It's not too much?" I smoothed a hand over the red satin gown I wore.

The top was fashioned like a corset. The sleeves were puffed and hung off my shoulders. It cinched at the waist, had a slit to my thigh, and the hem fell at my feet. I added a simple diamond choker necklace and diamond studs in my ears. Lo parted my hair and slicked it down on both sides, adding a clip-on chignon. My eye makeup was simple, but my lips matched the dress.

"It is and I wouldn't change a thing." She smiled at me. "That's why I've always loved the word *striking*. If we can't strike 'em down like lightning sometimes, are we really having any fun?"

Good. Because Felice Maggio needed to be knocked on his ass sometimes, because it seemed to rarely happen.

"That's why I've been seeing so many dazed men." I smiled back at her. "They've all seen you."

She was wearing a white jersey dress that she paired with a gold lamé coat. She belonged in an old black and white movie.

She struck a sultry pose, and it made me laugh.

Kerry rushed up, and she and Elsa did air kisses on each cheek. Kerry was glowing. Her sequined pink dress hugged all her curves and set off her stunning eyes. I'd told her so earlier.

"Roma, can you remind the band to play some of the requested songs? When I spoke to Mrs. Maggio, she wanted some of her late husband's favorite songs to be played."

"Sure."

She handed me a list with the songs. I only recognized a few of them. The ones I knew were because of Mamma and Babbo.

Mrs. Maggio? This was some of her late husband's favorite songs. Felice had told me his father had died of a heart attack, which was why Felice had probably set up the cause in his father's name. I thought Salvatore Maggio would be proud of his son. The event was a smash, and it seemed like it was raising major funds for all the foundations and charities.

I found the band's assistant and gave her the list, reminding her of the agreement. She assured me the band hadn't forgotten. They had a schedule and were sticking to it. I started to make my way back toward the bar, but I stopped, looking up to the second story. I felt eyes on me.

A man stood close to the balcony, leaning over it, a glass of something in his hand, a woman draped over his shoulder. He was looking right at me.

My heart beat so hard and so reckless, I could have sworn it was going to burst from my chest. I stood rooted to my spot, not able to move. The couple turned and disappeared into the crowd a beat later. I wasn't supposed to drink on the job, but I snatched a glass of champagne from a passing server and downed it. I muffled a belch and grabbed for another.

Call it intuition, but I knew when he'd made his grand entrance on the main floor. The crowd seemed to part for him, hands shooting out from all different directions to shake his.

Felice Maggio created a fine picture in a black tux custom made for his body. His hair was slicked back, and he had dark, sexy stubble for days. His green eyes glinted like haunted treasure.

The only accessory I wasn't expecting was the woman on his arm. It was hard to tell if she was the same blonde from Halloween. Both were statuesque, but this one seemed a little more...refined somehow. Maybe he had one for each occasion.

Her dress was almost sheer and gave the impression her skin had variegated leopard spots. It shimmered underneath the lights. She was gorgeous, and she knew it.

Someone touched my arm. Kerry.

She took the champagne out of my hand and handed it to a server. "Mr. Maggio is here. I'm relieved everything is running smoothly so far." She took a breath. "You okay?"

"Huh? Oh." I turned toward her. "Fine."

She studied my face, not seeming to buy it, but nodded. "When I had my meeting with him, he told me he was going to marry you."

All I could do was stare at her. Then I exploded with laughter. "He was joking, right?"

She shook her head. "I don't think so. Are you going to be uncomfortable around him because of that?"

That's the problem, I wanted to say. *I'm entirely too comfortable around him, even though he makes me breathless and weak.* I held my tongue on that front and shook my head.

"I'm sure he was only kidding."

"One look," she said. "That's all it takes for some people to know."

Know what? I was about to ask, but she stepped forward to take his hand when he walked up to us. He told her how impressed he was with the event and thanked her for all her help. So fucking charming. I almost rolled my eyes, but I remembered who I was—not a child—and stuck my chin up, ready to meet his intense green gaze.

Arm Candy kept her hands on him. She kept rubbing his arm or draping one over his shoulder.

The champagne felt like acid in the back of my throat. When he'd said *enough*, I guess he truly meant *enough*, because he had a backup plan.

"Roma Corvo," Kerry broke through the laser beams I had on Arm Candy's hand. "This is Mr. John Maggio—"

"We've been acquainted." I kept my voice even. "Nice to see you again, Mr. Maggio."

It seemed like the entire world grew quiet as we stared at each other. I couldn't hold his intense gaze for long, though. I flicked my eyes to the left.

"You look familiar," Arm Candy piped up. "Do I know you from somewhere? TV?"

"I don't think so...?" For some reason I wanted her name. I wanted to remember it.

"Margot."

"Roma was Miss Illinois." Kerry gave me a megawatt smile. "She's our beauty, inside and out."

Margot made an *ooh* noise. "Yes! I remember now. *Love* your dress. It's like a gift that needs to be unwrapped!"

"Thank you." I smiled at her. It was so frigging hard to do. It felt like moving my cheeks after they'd been cemented. But it truly wasn't her fault.

Unless Margot knew what was going on between me and Felice, she was innocent in this. Didn't make me want to hurt her any less, though.

"Well, we won't keep you from the gala, Mr. Maggio," Kerry said, throwing some relief my way. "If there's anything you need, we're here. On behalf of our museum, we hope you have a fabulous time."

Felice thanked Kerry in Italian and, setting his hand on Margo's lower back, ushered her to the next group ready to greet them. Or him. Margo was busy keeping one hand on Felice and her eyes on the dance floor.

"You can go, Roma," Kerry said softly. "The party is running smoothly, and I think it will for the rest of the night. I planned for all contingencies, and you helped me secure the rest."

We hugged and she disappeared into the crowd.

I needed a minute to catch my breath, to resolve the feeling of betrayal. Felice expected me to give up my family for...what? A fucking player? Okay. *Yes.* I'd said no to him more than I'd said yes, but it was so risky. Gambling everything I'd ever known for the unknown.

I kept telling myself I couldn't give up my family for whatever existed between us, but then another voice kept shouting that my family shouldn't abandon *me* because my happiness came in a different way than theirs.

Warm hands came to my shoulders when I ran into a chest. I looked up into Cassio's eyes.

"Whatever you do, don't let John see you tonight."

"*Why?*" The word rushed out instead of *too late.*

"Red's his favorite color, and on you...he might hurt someone."

"I'm sure there was a compliment in there somewhere."

He grinned at me. "You're gorgeous, and you know it. But I was being entirely fucking serious. John is a loaded weapon, and you're waving the red flag in a fossil shop."

"I'm working this party. I'm not here for him."

"Define 'working this party'."

"I meant that literally, Cassio. Besides. He's here with someone else. Your worries can be put to rest."

"Yeah, not likely. Even the dead come back to haunt."

I left him standing in the hall, entering a bathroom full of women. Not the most optimum place to iron out my feelings, but I didn't feel like finding Elsa to let me in the office.

By the time it was my turn in a stall, the bathroom had mostly cleared out. It smelled like a department store. As I washed my hands, I stared at myself in the mirror. This jealousy thing was new and ugly, and I didn't know how to get rid of it. I hated Margot's hands on him. I hated the thought of him leading her on the dance floor. I especially hated that I'd be alone tonight while he did things to her to make her scream.

"Damn you, Maggio!" I whispered, but it was more like a curse. I sent Babbo a quick text, letting him know I'd be spending the weekend with Elsa.

He wouldn't be home until Sunday night, and Lo was watching Alina's two kids until Monday. I flew out of the bathroom and went on a hunt for Elsa. She was still at the bar.

"Hey, can you do me a favor?"

"Name it."

"Cover for me this weekend. With my family."

Her eyes glanced at the dancing crowd before she took me by the arm and hauled me toward the office. She shut the door behind her and stood against it.

"John didn't tell you yet."

"Tell me what?"

"He came to me with a deal. Same thing you're asking. I was going to be straight with you, but he told me to wait until tonight. I agreed to his offer. I would have done it for nothing, but my parents' house *really* needs a new roof, and we can't afford it. You know my dad is in the early stages of dementia, and it's been rough. I couldn't pass it up. Anyway. John's sending a crew over to the house this weekend. And we're going shopping." She motioned between us. "That's the story."

"Manipulative bastard!"

He'd planned this all along. He knew Margot was going to send me over the edge and that I'd agree to spend the weekend with him. He knew how jealous it was going to make me. My gut, where Felice Maggio was concerned, was spot on.

Enough my ass.

"*Whoa.*" Elsa held her hands up. "I've never heard you curse like that. Did he bring that woman to the event to make you jealous?"

"I can't be a hundred percent positive, but I told him no about this weekend, and I think he assumed bringing her would make me jealous enough to agree."

"He assumed correctly, the manipulative jerk."

Elsa stumbled a little when someone opened the door. "Visitors are not allowed in here," she said to Jack. Her face didn't hide her irritation at him barging in.

What the hell was he doing here?

"I'm not a visitor," he spoke to her but looked at me. "Well, I won't be soon enough. I'm here to see Roma." He flashed a bright smile in my direction, then winked. He looked back at Elsa. "I was at the engagement brunch. Remember?"

"I remember you." Her tone wasn't all that friendly. She was still clearly irritated he hadn't bothered to knock.

He gave her a dismissive look and met my eyes again. "I saw you rushing from the bathroom. I tried to catch you, but the crowd's too thick and I lost you before I could. Seems like there's always a fire chasing you." He grinned. "Reminds me of the color of your dress."

"What are you doing here, Jack? This is a work party for me."

"We get invites to this every year. John sends them to rub it in our faces, and I usually attend to piss him off. This year, your family got invites. I'm attending on everyone's behalf." He gave the middle finger, like he was giving it to John.

"It's for a good cause," I said, feeling defensive on Felice's behalf.

"My dad tried to have it audited for years, but nothing ever came of it. So, yeah, this event is for a good cause, but nothing else he does is." He waved a dismissive hand. "You don't need to be bothered with details. Isabella told me you were working. She thought I'd be a nice surprise."

Nice wasn't the word I'd use, but I plastered on a smile and nodded.

He smiled at Elsa. "Can we borrow your office for a second?"

Elsa looked at me.

I shrugged like I didn't care, but I hoped she'd caught the words I'd try to imply with my eyes. *Come back in a few and save me from him.*

She must have read it because she nodded subtly. "Kerry is probably going to need you soon. This is a big party, Roma."

"I only have a minute, Jack," I said to him after she shut the door. "I'm working."

He picked up items we had around the office, studying them. Some of them were replicas of fossils; others were dinosaurs carved out of stone. A patron did them by hand.

"Why are you working here?"

The question stopped me for a second. "You do know I'm a paleontologist?"

"Dad might have mentioned it. But why? I mean, this is so manly. I've never known a woman who liked dinosaurs before." He set the whittled T-rex down. "You're gorgeous. You don't need to work. Especially after we get married. You're going to live a life of luxury, not have to dig around in the dirt and stain your nails."

"I live that now," I said. "Being around my passion, for me, is a life of luxury. I'd even like to take a hiatus from the museum and get in some field time at some point."

"I told Dr. Corvo you needed to quit."

"Quit my job?"

He shrugged. "What's the use?"

"What did my father say?"

Honestly, I could sense that about Jack—he wanted a trophy wife. So his honesty didn't surprise me. But I was curious about what Babbo had to say about it.

"We would have to work it out."

"Here's the thing, Jack. I don't think we're supposed to be discussing the terms of our marriage. My father hasn't even confirmed the engagement yet."

"Dr. Corvo told us he did—discuss it with you. It's simple. You're mine."

He started toward me, and I took a step back. His eyes lowered and he was trying to be sexy. My heart beat so fast and so hard, it sounded like a rock smashing against bone.

The backs of my legs hit the desk, and I raised my hands. But I wouldn't be grabbing on to his shirt. I'd be pushing against his chest. "You should go, Jack."

I didn't give a shit if he went back and told Babbo. This was inappropriate. I didn't feel comfortable, and in my father's eyes, I was a naïve girl who'd never been kissed before.

His chest hit my hands, but he didn't push. He stopped. "I'm right where I belong. The moment I saw you, I knew. You were the one for me. You are so beautiful, you almost seem unreal." He looked down at my breasts straining against the tightness of the corset gown. "This dress you're wearing tonight..." He curled his finger and used it to slide up and down my arm. "I love you in red."

It was hard not to look at him, but I concentrated on one of the dinosaur replicas on the other side of the room. If I made eye contact, he was going to kiss me.

He made a strangled noise as he crashed into me. Then his weight was gone. My eyes whipped to where he was. Felice stood in his place. He held the T-rex replica in his hand. His eyes were dilated, and they were reflecting the color of my dress. Blood red.

My mouth opened and closed, a gasping fish searching for breath, until I finally found the words. "He's bleeding." I pointed toward Jack, who was down on the floor.

"He'll live." Felice set the dinosaur back in its place and then fixed his suit and hair. He grabbed Jack by the collar. His head lolled down. "Let's go, or I'm going to kill him."

Felice shut the office door behind us and dragged Jack toward the end of the hall. He left him propped up against the wall. He snatched my hand and led me away from the scene.

When the shock wore off some, I dug my feet in. Felice stopped walking and glared at me. But I didn't think the look was truly directed at me. That was how he looked in the office. I returned the look.

"I'm not sleeping with you."

His grin came slow. "Who said anything about sleep?"

Elsa walked up behind us with Celso. He handed my coat to Felice, who set it around my shoulders, and we left.

CHAPTER 16

ROMA

I sank deeper into the warmth of my coat as Felice navigated the streets in a matte black Maserati GranTurismo S.

It fit the man and his mood.

Unfortunately for him, the dress I wore fit the woman and *her* mood.

"You're a manipulative bastard," I seethed in his direction, crossing my arms.

He sighed, like he was already over the conversation. "You act like a child, we play games like we're children."

"I'm a child? *I'm a child*!" Because I was afraid to lose my family? But the words were stumbling around in my head, and I couldn't get them out. I was too angry.

I'd never felt emotions on such a huge scale before. It was as if he could take every one of them and multiply the intensity of the feeling.

"I helped set you on a path to the truth."

"Did you ever stop to think maybe I didn't want to spend the weekend with you, Maggio?"

He chuckled. "Your actions and reactions prove otherwise. Unless you want to deny those too."

If his laughter had been tangible, I would have strangled him with it. I balled the fabric of the dress in my fists to give my hands something to do.

"Margot," I said. "You brought her to the gala, rubbing her in my face, knowing I'd get jealous. And *I'm* childish?"

"Whatever you feel, your feelings are your own."

"It was manipulative." I took a breath, steadying my voice. "You think you're so much better than Emanuele Corvo. But you're not. You're not giving me a choice either."

I'd always known one day I'd have an arranged marriage. I accepted it. It was just the way things were done in my family. Then the attack happened, and so did Felice Maggio. But he wasn't giving me a choice either. Maybe we both knew what I wanted, but for once, I wanted the right to admit it on my own terms.

His jaw was so tense, if it would have been made of glass, it would have shattered. He gripped the wheel tighter and swerved, cutting across several lanes. I gasped, reaching out for the window as my body pulled toward the passenger door. Horns blared, but he smoothly pulled to the side of the road.

He took a deep breath, then faced me. "Make your choice, Roma."

At this point in the night, I was surprised the corset was holding up. As many times as my heart tried to kick out of my chest, it was a miracle the stays were still tight.

"It's simple. Yes or no."

"That'll be it?"

"*Finito.*"

My gut told me he meant it. Then he'd probably go fuck Margot and I'd be screwed—mentally and emotionally. I'd forever remember this moment and how I *almost* got what I wanted.

I entwined my fingers with his. "Yes." My voice was steady and strong.

He raised my hand to his mouth and kissed it. He set our combined hands on my thigh as he pulled into traffic again and headed toward the unknown.

"That would have been *finito* just for tonight if I would have said no, wouldn't it?"

He grinned and punched the gas harder.

It only took us five minutes or so to arrive at the place Felice was taking me. It was within walking distance from the museum. The building itself was old, with stone friezes probably imported from Italy and hand carved with exquisite details. It was a residential high-rise with what I was sure were specular views of Lake Michigan.

Felice turned in underneath the building and parked. He stepped out of the car and opened my door, taking my hand and leading me to what seemed like an entrance with a private elevator.

While we waited for it, I squeezed his hand.

"What about Jack? I was talking to him when you whacked him with the T-rex. There are going to be questions. *Why did I leave him? Why didn't I get help? Who whacked him?* I was standing right in front of him."

He grinned and I thought it was at my use of the word "whack."

"Did you see me hit him?" he asked.

"No, but..."

"You didn't see anything. You told Jack you were leaving with Ms. Lang, and then you left him in the office. You have no idea what happened to him after that."

"He's going to remember we were talking, and then *boom*. Lights. Out."

"Jack probably has a concussion. Even if he doesn't, stick to the story. Make him question what really happened."

"You're a good liar. So good, it's actually scary."

"Part of my job," he said, and we stepped into the private elevator.

It was a box with mirrored walls and dark hardwood paneling. The numbers climbed higher and higher. To avoid his intense gaze, I concentrated on them. When I finally met his eyes, I wished I could back up a step or two. I felt totally consumed. He was pushing in on my personal space without even touching me.

"What?" I whispered to break the tension.

"That fucking dress," he almost growled before he had me pinned, and his mouth crashed into mine.

For as rough as it started out, the kiss turned slow, then started to grow wilder. I moaned into his mouth. His tongue tasted like bourbon and mint, and his usual scent wrapped around me like a warm winter coat.

His mouth ventured down, and he lifted my chin for better access. He started licking and biting my neck with the same intensity as the kiss. It was like he was trying to eat me alive.

His tongue moved slow and gentle, to taste me, then he'd bite me so hard I'd gasp. His hand came to the slit in my dress and followed it up. Every pass over my skin made goosebumps rise.

"So fucking sweet," he murmured against my hammering pulse. "*Dolce*." His hand slid between my legs. He made a deep sound of approval at what he found.

My panties were soaked.

As he continued to make love to my neck with his mouth, I ground myself against his hand, needing more. I needed the barrier between us gone.

"Open your eyes, Roma," he ordered.

My lids felt weighed down. I blinked against the heaviness, only able to get my eyes halfway open. The look on Felice's face almost had me coming around his hand. His eyes were hooded. He was as consumed by this as I was.

Completely.

Everything he was doing to me, I could see in the mirrors.

"You can deny this all you want, but your body makes you a liar. Look how wet you are for me." He showed me his hand, coated, and then sucked his finger. "Hold on." He placed his hand flat against my stomach and pushed me back until the gold bar railing came to my back.

I used it to brace myself. He ripped my panties and stuck them in his suit pocket. He took a knee in front of me and guided one of my legs to his shoulder. His tongue moved slowly as he parted me with his fingers, but the pressure was insane. Or maybe I was just hypersensitive to him.

The noise that came from my mouth was a loud, shaky, broken sound. I was almost convulsing from how good it felt. The stubble on his face only heightened what I was feeling. I came close to begging him to rip the dress like he did the underwear. The corset was tight, and I needed to be free of it...my nipples ached to be touched.

My hips seemed to have a mind of their own, and I started rocking into him, shamelessly rubbing myself against his face. My breath was coming out in pants.

His tongue started to move faster and harder, and so did I. He started sucking on me, then he bit me so hard I screamed out.

I lost all control. I bucked against his face, so wild to chase the rush. I came so hard my eyes rolled and stars danced.

When I could open my eyes, he was already standing, keeping a hand on my waist. My knees were as solid as jelly.

The door to the elevator had opened to a private entry foyer. I hadn't noticed when.

"My beautiful Roma," he said, moving his lips against my ear.

I closed my eyes and shivered at the warmth of his breath. He smelled like me.

He took my coat and guided me into a space fit for a king.

The penthouse was unreal. Almost as unreal as what just happened to me in the elevator. But what we'd just done had become a lasting memory. This place was solid to the touch.

I knew right away it was the work of an illustrious Italian architect who became renowned for his designs in the boom of the 1920s. He was primarily known for his work in New York, but all his places were coveted. I couldn't imagine this one being any different. Especially since it was probably the only one in Chicago.

Felice hung my coat on a rack. He set his hand to my lower back and took me on a tour.

It was the biggest luxury apartment I'd ever been in. It still had the original walnut wood, and the dark hue of it was stunning against the soft lights flickering from the ornate lights in the gallery hall. Magnificent Italian paintings lined the wall.

The penthouse had all the original details that made it so spectacular; vaulted frescoed ceilings, limestone staircases, a handcrafted stone fireplace, bronze hardware, stone friezes, and hand-carved doors.

Statues had me reaching out to feel what they were made of. The furniture was old-world style, like something straight from a countess's villa in Tuscany.

It was *romantico* and warm in a way only Italy was. I'd traveled with my family a lot growing up, and I'd never been to a place that compared.

Mamma used to say I had a connection to Italy. I could feel my roots there.

As Felice led me through the living room, I couldn't help but look up. The ceiling was coffered and at least twenty feet high. We stepped out through an open door and my breath caught. The outdoor space felt like it had magically transported us to Lake Como.

"This is the east-facing terrace," Felice said, draping his coat over my shoulders.

A fountain, frozen over from the cold, stood as the centerpiece. Grass—actual living *grass*—on the outside of the penthouse crackled underneath our feet as we made our way further out onto the balcony.

Lake Michigan spread out as far as the eye could see. Tiny wisps of snow danced above the water.

"This one is the best for sunrises," he said.

Our eyes met and I smiled.

"I can only imagine."

"Tomorrow morning, you won't have to."

He brought me to another terrace. "This one is west-facing." He leaned over the railing with his hands together.

"Better for watching sunsets." I mimicked his stance.

Chicago's many buildings rose like mammoth shapes in the night and were dotted with light. I could see Navy Pier and the Centennial Wheel.

"This is spectacular, Felice."

The historian in Elsa would have killed to see this place. But even though the history was great, it felt like a home. A home fit for Italian royalty, but a home all the same. It was safe and warm.

I turned to look at the back of the penthouse and set my elbows against the stone. Corinthian columns were lit up by spotlights hidden somewhere in the grass. Wind whipped and snow swirled in the glow. I pulled his coat tighter, inhaling the scent of him drifting in the air.

"Do you like it here, Roma?"

I could feel his eyes on me, but I couldn't face him. I was afraid I might say something I couldn't take back, like, *this place feels safe and warm and like a home because of you.*

When Felice "John" Maggio came to me in that hospital room, it set me on a path to trusting again. I didn't trust the world. It was unkind and ruthless. So was he. But I trusted him despite who he was and what he did.

Maybe it was foolish to believe I was different, but I believed it, even if my brain warned me not to. My gut was on the fence. My heart was already hooked, along with my body.

"I do," I whispered.

His gaze shifted, and I could feel it. It was like he took something important away from me.

His attention.

When I turned, he was looking out at the water. He was unreadable. I wanted to ask him what he was thinking, but I was afraid of the answer. How impactful his truth could be.

"I'd go broke to find out what you're thinking right now," he said.

I laughed. It was like he'd read my mind. But I didn't want to touch the depths of my thoughts. I wanted to keep it on the surface.

"I know what you do, and the money it can bring in, but this place...it's been in the same family since it was built, right?"

"You're cute when you're trying to be polite." He turned to face me, then reached out and slid his knuckle down my cheek. "My great-grandfather, Giovanni, left this place to me. It was his since it was built. He started the pharmaceutical company. At one time, he was one of the richest men in Chicago. He enjoyed spending time with my dad. Thought he was going to be something special someday. Said he had a lot of potential. He blamed Alfonso for ruining him.

"My old man told me Alfonso was the first man to ever look at him with hate and disgust, even when he was a kid. There was no real reason for it. Alfonso played favorites, but he never found one until Jack was born."

"Alfonso and Jack wanted this place?"

"Want. This place means status to them. It's one of a kind. A family heirloom at this point. They fought me for it, thinking they'd drain my resources and I'd have to put it on the market. Tommaso doesn't like Alfonso. He took it personally. They backed off because they knew he was backing me."

"Is Alfonso threatened by Tommaso?"

He shrugged. "Alfonso is not some chump off the street. His father created one of the most powerful companies in history. My business and the men who stand behind me are nothing to dismiss either. After my old man died, there was no one stopping me from killing Alfonso.

"Alfonso went to Emanuele and told him he was worried about what I was going to do. Tommaso is indebted to your old man, but not to Alfonso. Long story short, neither side wanted to start a war but me. It was decided no blood would be shed between us. First one to shed it would be killed, no retribution from the other side. That's when Alfonso found a loophole in the arrangement. He took me to court, trying to wipe me clean so I'd have to sell the penthouse. Making my life hell on the business side. Even though Tommaso appreciated their creativity in getting at me without touching me, he was pissed about it. He took my side on that front, and that's been that."

"Alfonso left your Nonna for his current wife? Jack's mom?" I asked.

"She's wife number three. Two didn't last long. Alfonso's ex-wife, my Nonna Silvia, lives with my mother, as does her own mother. After the fight Alfonso put up for this place, my old man left his share of my great-grandfather's estate to me. He was worried Alfonso and Jack would fight my mother for it."

"Did they? Fight you for your father's inheritance?"

He shook his head. "They fuck with me, but only to a certain extent. They have enough money, but it's mostly about principal. Besides, they're not up for fucking with Nonna Silvia. She has a vendetta."

"The bad blood."

"It's going to get poisonous."

Our eyes met and held. The words he didn't have to say floated between us like the drifts of snow.

Because of you.

I needed to change the subject. Reality was just as Cassio had said. A cold slap in the face. "You said your great-grandfather blamed Alfonso for ruining your Babbo. Salvatore?"

He nodded.

"Why?"

He sighed, and a cloud of smoke blew from his mouth. "He didn't have a supportive family life, so he found a family that would support him. He turned out to be a carnivore, as you would say, like me."

His voice was warm and rough, and the sound of it caused me to shiver. He noticed but must have thought it was because of the weather. He led me back inside and toward his bedroom.

"I left my bag at the museum with my change of clothes," I said, realizing. I was going to change before I left. "Can I borrow a shirt to sleep in?"

He led me to a walk-in closet. Half of the closet was filled with dark suits. The other half was filled with women's clothes.

"Ms. Lang picked everything out for you." He moved his shoulders, almost like his suit had suddenly shrunk. "I gave her your size. Your bag from the museum is in the car if whatever's here doesn't work."

"How do you know my size?" I whispered.

"I'm a man of many secrets, Dino." He winked.

I rolled my eyes and he chuckled.

"Elsa got to see this place?"

"She might have made a spare key."

I laughed. "Better check the rooms. We might have a squatter."

His phone rang and he went to take it, but not before he told me not to change yet. I explored the closet, running my hands over the clothes. Everything still had the tags on, and they were from one of my favorite brands. I made a mental note to thank Elsa. A dresser separated the two sides. I opened the drawers on my side. It was filled with La Perla nightwear and lingerie.

I wondered if Felice spent a lot of time here. It didn't smell like him, and after I went searching for his cologne, I found the unopened box. Maybe he spent more time at the house I'd gone to on Halloween night?

My phone buzzed in my pocket, and my watch lit up. Babbo had texted me back, telling me to text him when I got to her house. Her parents' place was about an hour outside of Chicago.

But the streams of texts were coming from my group chat with my sisters.

Isabella: Roma, did you know someone hit Jack in the head at the museum?

Talia: Does he know who?

Alina: Is he okay?

Lolita: Shit. What did they hit him with?

Y: No. Is he okay?

Isabella: He went there to see you, Y. I told him you'd be working. He has a concussion.

Y: I saw him. We talked for a minute or two in the office before I left. Not sure where he went after. That's terrible.

Lolita: Are you home yet, Y? Should I come home?

Alina: You can't leave, Lo. Who's going to watch my kids?

Isabella: Y, you should crash at Lina's place after you go the hospital.

Talia: I'll meet you at the hospital, Y. Don't want you to go up there alone.

Y: I'm on my way to Elsa's. We're almost there. I planned on spending the weekend with her. Didn't want to be home alone.

Isabella: You have to go up there. He's hurt.

Lolita: Isa, she doesn't have to if she doesn't want to. She's spent enough time in that place.

Talia: Chill out, Isa. They're not even married yet.

Alina: It would be the right thing to do, Y.

Isabella: Elsa's parents don't live that far from me. I'll have Carlo drive me and I'll ride back with you. I'll spend the night at Babbo's.

Irritation and panic started to claw at my chest. Isabella wasn't going to let this go. She was going to try to force me to go to the hospital. I had to stop her trajectory. She was probably changing her clothes as we texted.

Y: No. I'm going to wait. To be honest, I don't feel comfortable just showing up there. I hardly know him. And he was being somewhat pushy at the event. It made me uncomfortable.

Talia: Pushy how?

Y: I think he wanted to kiss me. Not ready for that.

Isabella: You're being ridiculous.

Lolita: You're being ridiculous, Isa.

Talia: I agree with Lo. I'll bend his ass like a pretzel. Don't think I won't.

Y: I'm out for now. Don't want to wake Elsa's parents. Night. *Ti amo.*

I didn't feel like watching my screen explode with texts. Isabella and Alina would form a team, and so would Talia and Lolita. It was usually me and Lolita, and Talia took whichever side she felt was right. This time, she was taking mine.

Before I could turn my phone off, it rang. Babbo. I answered on a whisper. He wanted to make sure I arrived and to tell me about Jack. He asked me a few questions, then said he was disappointed Jack would even attend the event.

"It was for a good cause," I whispered.

He made a dismissive noise and told me he would see me on Sunday. We hung up.

My phone flew from my hand before I could stop it. "Shit!"

"Didn't mean to scare you," Felice said, standing where he wasn't a second before.

"Everything okay?" I breathed out. I was having a hard time catching my breath. The scare paired with how he was looking at me...the stays were straining again.

He was too gorgeous for words.

He'd lost his jacket, and his sleeves were rolled up to his elbows. The first couple of buttons were undone, showing some of his muscular chest. He'd taken his shoes and socks off and was barefoot.

He looked like the king of the penthouse.

"Nothing that can't wait until tomorrow," he said.

"Jack?" I asked, figuring he was hearing about it too.

He said nothing as he stalked toward me. That conversation was over. He stopped when our bodies barely touched.

"Help me undress?" I whispered, running my hands up his chest. His heart kicked against my palm.

His hands came around my waist, and he turned me. He slowly undid the stays, and I breathed a sigh of relief when the dress gave and fell to the floor. Cool air washed over my breasts and nipples, but his hands were warm. His fingertips slid up and down my back, edging right above my ass. My underwear was wherever his suit jacket was.

I kicked off my heels and removed the clip from my hair, setting it on the dresser. I shook my hair, running a hand through it, then turned to face him.

He'd helped me out of the dress, but he'd saved something from it. The stays. He tucked them into his pocket and, lifting me off my feet, carried me to the bedroom.

CHAPTER 17

ROMA

Felice must have turned the lights down low when he'd gone to take the call. The room was dim, the soft lights creating halos.

He set me down on the bed and took a step back.

I looked up at him and got to my knees. I undid the rest of the buttons on his shirt and ran my hand along his chest before I flung it to the floor. I slipped my hand underneath the waistband of his pants, feeling his stomach convulse at my touch.

"You have any idea what your touch does to me?" His voice was deep and husky.

I shook my head, too breathless to say anything.

He moved my hand lower, to the clasp of his pants. I undid them, and he stepped out.

Damn. He was so big, it got caught on his pants. His dick could hold them up, like a coatrack.

A frigging *Giganotosaurus.*

"This is what you do to me." He took my hand and placed it on his hot shaft. He closed his eyes and tilted his head back, pushing himself into my fist.

He looked animalistic as I started to stroke him, taking cues from his facial expressions. Slowly at first, until he groaned, then I picked up the pace. I'd never done drugs, but watching him, I felt like I had.

My nipples ached, and the pulse between my legs throbbed. I needed to taste him, to explore his body with my tongue. He watched me as I moved, his eyes hooded. His skin tasted of salt and something uniquely his. When I came to his dick, I licked him from base to tip, then took him fully in my mouth.

He growled, deep in his throat, and buried his hands in my hair. He kept me in place while he started to pump his hips. Tears came to my eyes, but I tightened my mouth around him.

"Fuck," he ground out, his grip so tight in my hair it was pulling at my scalp. "Your mouth feels good. Take all of me. That's it." He hissed out a breath before he started to lose control, moving like he was fucking me somewhere else.

I didn't know if I could stand it, but I kept going. To make this man lose control made me feel like the queen of this Chicago penthouse. I grabbed his humungous balls and felt them tighten in my hands.

He grunted and pulled out of my mouth, jerking himself until he finished by his own hand. When he opened his eyes, they were even wilder. He went to his pants and wrapped the stays around his hand.

He grabbed my bottom lip with his thumb, then traced down my chin, to my neck, until he circled each of my breasts. I closed my eyes, trembling at his touch. He circled my nipples, soft at first, until he pinched one. I hissed out a breath and bit my lip. A long, slow moan worked itself free when he kissed and teased me at the same time.

The kiss broke, and my sanity with it. The pulse between my legs was ruling me. I wanted him in me, his mouth and hands all over me, at the same time.

"You want it all, ah?"

"Yes, *please.*"

"Get to the head of the bed."

He watched me like he was stalking prey to play with when I

moved. When he had me where he wanted me, he tied me to the frame with the stays. In the hazy light, my wrists looked like they were bleeding.

"Relax, my beautiful Roma. Spread your legs for me."

I did, and he made a deep and satisfied noise in his throat. He climbed into the bed and kneeled over me, his dick jutting out. It glistened, and I could smell him in the air. A sound that was part frustration and part whimper escaped my lips. My hands ached to touch him. I wasn't sure what to do with the pent-up tension.

"I'll fuck you when you're my wife."

He'd fuck me when I was his wife? It was me who said I wouldn't sleep with him. But he'd called me out on the technicality. *Who said anything about sleep?*

"Do we have a deal?" He raked his teeth over his bottom lip.

"Are you going to leave me like this if I don't agree?" I struggled against the restraints, panic taking the place of trust.

"Calm yourself," he said, his voice soothing.

My heart calmed, and so did I at his words.

"This is about pleasuring you," he continued. "But I'm not fucking you until we're married."

"I said that earlier, remember? I wasn't sleeping with you."

"Your mouth says one thing, but your body says another."

"Are you a human lie detector?"

"Your body is mine."

"I do want this," I whispered. *You. All of you.* "Right now."

"After we're married, you'll make an unbreakable vow to me only, and sign it in blood."

I nodded.

He shook his head. "Yes or no, Roma."

A moment passed between us. In his own way, I knew he was asking for a promise of marriage.

"Yes." My answer came out firm.

His mouth closed over mine, and he kissed me so deep, I wasn't sure if he'd stolen my soul when he moved back.

He kissed a path down my body, his mouth warm compared

to the cold air. My skin trembled, and so did the breaths from my mouth. He was hungry again, because he positioned himself between my legs and started to eat me like a starved man. This time he was wild, making grunting noises, reaching up to twist my nipples.

Being tied up made me more vulnerable, but it heightened the experience. I couldn't stop the rush when I came with a loud cry.

My eyes were still shut tight when he untied me and flipped me over, my ass in the air. He used my wetness to rub along my ass cheeks before he stuck his finger inside of me *back there*, while he started teasing the sensitive nub between my legs. I started to push back, needing more. It felt *so* damn good.

My head hung, and I kept moaning and pleading for him to fuck me.

"You're almost fucking breaking me," he rasped out. His touch became rough between my legs, and it sent me over.

I cried out, feeling a rush of wetness run down my thighs from my orgasm. I was so drained I couldn't open my eyes.

He untied me, picked me up, and carried me toward the bathroom. "What did I say about sleeping, ah?"

We didn't sleep the entire night.

CHAPTER 18

ROMA

Felice wasn't understating it when he'd said the east-facing terrace was made for sunrises.

The air was freezing, but the sun was warm as it shed its light over Lake Michigan. It was like a painting coming to life as the shapes and figures appeared with color. The water took on a teal hue, but it was frozen over in some spots. Buildings formed into solid silhouettes, and so did the city around them.

I wasn't sure how long I'd stay out for—the cold was cutting —but it was hard to leave the view.

Felice came up behind me, smelling like a million bucks, wearing a suit that cost a pretty penny. Earlier he'd said, "Business." And it seemed to me it was code for, "I'll be gone for a while."

"Check your messages," I said, as he wrapped his arms around me, breathing me in.

He took his phone out and looked at it. "This is a grocery list."

I laughed. "Foreign, right?"

He pulled me closer and bit my neck. I moved some, giving him easy access to it.

"Whoever stocked the kitchen did a great job, but I need a few more things. I'll make us dinner tonight."

"I'll be home before lunch." He squeezed my ass. "I can't stay away from you that long." He placed kisses all over my cheek and neck, his stubble rough against my skin. "You belong in my bed. Sunrise. Sunset. Every day of my life. You try to walk away from me, from us, this story isn't going to end well. You ever heard of Plato?"

"Refresh my memory." I knew about Plato, but I wasn't sure where he was going with this.

"I'm going to tell it in terms of us. We started out as a circle, you and I, but a thunderbolt severed us in half when we tried to be too much like the gods. This set us on different paths. We constantly searched for each other until destiny led us to each other again. I knew it the moment I saw you. It felt like a thunderbolt hit me again, reminding me of the separation. Reminding me that you are the half I lost."

The warmth of his words clashed with the bitter cold. I held on to him tighter before I walked him to the private elevator. We stared at each other until the door closed. I wasn't sure what to do with myself after, so I made a parfait with dairy-free yogurt. Then I took a hot bath and let the water roll down my back, trying to ease the tension from stress and a long night of having my body worked.

After doing my hair and makeup, I dug around in the closet for something to wear. I decided on a fig-colored long-sleeved bodysuit, a long cardigan of the same color, and a pair of jeans.

It was still early, so I made a cup of coffee and sat out on the terrace again. I called Elsa to check in. I barely said hello when she filled me in on the latest.

"Alfonso Maggio called Hayden and demanded to know what happened to his son. Hayden didn't know what to tell him, except for what I told him. We went to the office to grab our bags, we talked to Jack for a minute before I left you two alone. You met me a few minutes later and we left."

"Felice talked to you."

"He told me to stick to the truth about that part of the night if anyone questioned me about it. He didn't tell me what happened. Hayden did."

It sounded like she'd walked outside. Hammers banged. I asked her how it was going, then thanked her for everything, including the clothes.

"Forget the clothes," she said. "Let's talk about the penthouse instead."

I almost laughed because she sounded almost turned on. I told her where I was sitting, and we got lost in the details for a while. After we hung up, I called Lo. The kids were wreaking havoc in the background while she tried to quiet them down.

"If I ever say I'm ready for kids, remind me of this moment. *Seriously!*" she screamed. "You're both getting coal for Christmas! Damn. They're just like me and you when we were young."

"We were so bad."

We both laughed, and Lolita said we were going to hell for it, or we'd get payback in the form of brats ten times worse than Alina's two. After Lolita gave them cookies to decorate, things became quiet on her side, except for the sound of her doing dishes.

"Has Isa bothered you about going the hospital again?" she asked.

"No," I said. "And I'm not opening our group text right now. I'm on vacation."

"Smart. She's being a pain in the ass about it."

"She's pushing for it."

"Ever since John showed up at Babbo's house, she's been suspicious. Be careful."

"Lo—"

"La la la," she sang. "It doesn't matter to me. When I was thinking about doing what I was going to do, you supported me no matter what. You climbed out the window for me. I'm going to do the same for you."

She would, but it wouldn't be that simple.

"How's Sandro?"

"Nice subject change, but I'm being serious, Y. There's a difference between me and everyone else. You told me about the guy in your head before he appeared. That kind of shit doesn't happen every day. And to have John and Jack be related? It's like something got twisted along the way, but fate is trying to fix it. Do you think that's why I lost sight in one eye? Because if you tell me my loss is not in vain, it'll make it a lot easier for me to accept."

I really didn't know how to respond to that. I was about to say something, though, when Lo started shouting at the kids again.

"Shit. Gotta go, Y. Don't put icing in the cat's fur!" The line went dead.

If Lo's theory was the truth, how shitty would that be if my sister had to lose the use of an eye for me to find Felice?

The night was catching up to me, and I was tired of spinning the wheels in my head, so I decided to close my eyes for a few minutes. It was too cold outside, even in the sun. Grabbing a blanket and taking a nap on the sofa near the fireplace seemed nice.

It felt like I'd just closed my eyes when something tickled my lips. My eyes sprang open. Felice sat on the edge of the sofa, sitting up from a bending position.

"Please tell me you kissed me and that wasn't a bug or something."

He chuckled. "Or something. A big-ass carnivore."

We stared at each other for a second before a sleepy smile spread across my face. "I'm so happy you're home."

He made a pleased sound. "Say that again."

"What?"

"Call this place home."

I had called it home, but what I meant was this was his home, and I was glad he was in it with me. I refused to squabble over technicalities, though. "Welcome home, Felice Maggio."

He leaned down and kissed me again. I understood how all those princesses woke up for it. If it was anything like this, I'd be tempted to fall from heaven for it.

I blinked at him as he pulled away, setting his hand between my thighs.

"Have you eaten?" he asked.

"Not since this morning."

"I got everything on the list and picked us up lunch."

He seemed so proud of himself. I started laughing, getting to a sitting position, throwing my arms around his neck. He set me on his lap, and we started kissing again.

His were rougher. Mine were almost frantic.

I didn't know what was happening to me, but I couldn't seem to control myself around him. I wondered if we would ever have a meaningful conversation again. It was impossible to be this close to him and not need to have my hands on him. I'd spent more time naked than wearing clothes since I got here.

By dinner, he'd worked my body into a ravenous state. I made Mediterranean couscous salad for me, with chickpeas, cucumbers, a medley of olives, feta cheese and a squeeze of lemon. Steak and a potato for him. But I'd barely finished when he carried me back to the room.

It wasn't until Sunday morning he told me he had plans for us, and we'd have to keep our clothes on for a while. I was freaked out a little. If someone saw me with him...

He'd already dressed in a pair of slacks that only upped his sex appeal. He pulled a long-sleeved black sweater over his head. "Get dressed, Dino."

I sighed. I changed into a white placket top with a row of asymmetrical buttons, pairing it with a pair of faux leather pants and boots.

He helped me into my coat, and we left.

CHAPTER 19

ROMA

We went for a short drive around the city, passing The Chicago Theater, then stopping in the Fulton Market area. Felice pulled to the curb and told me he'd be right back. A line stretched underneath a black and white awning, outside of a pick-up window.

He came back with a cup of hot chocolate for me and two boxes of bomboloni, an Italian-style donut rolled in sugar and filled with *crema pasticciera* (pastry cream). The car filled with a warm, sweet perfume, and it danced with the cold scent clinging to his coat.

"I didn't take you for a sweet kind of guy." I took a tentative sip of my hot chocolate through a straw, then moaned and closed my eyes. The presentation was art in a cup. Real chunks of chocolate on top, an actual donut wedged on the side, and whipped cream everywhere else. It even came with a spoon. But the taste? Out. Of. This. World.

Felice glanced over at me before he pulled away from the curb and into traffic. "I've always preferred meat. Until I had something strong enough to get me addicted to the sweeter side." He set his hand between my thighs, and I closed my eyes again, taking slow, deep breaths.

His touch sent an electrical shock between my legs, and the car felt too hot.

It felt like a cold wind had blown in, giving me weather whiplash, when we pulled up to a house I didn't recognize about fifteen minutes later.

I leaned forward some, checking it out. "Where are we?"

"Sunday dinner."

"*With your family?*" I rushed out.

He smiled and used his thumb to wipe the hot chocolate mustache from my upper lip. "It'll be fine."

I hoped Felice was right. Italian Mammas could be very protective over their sons. I flipped the visor and did a once over of my face. I applied more lipstick and fixed my hair.

Felice held my hand and carried the two boxes of bomboloni. Questions rushed my thoughts as we made our way closer to the door. *Will his mamma like me? Did I wear the right outfit? What if I say something stupid? What will she think about the age difference?*

"Something to remember about Nonna Mafalda. She's my maternal grandmother. She has dementia. When she was growing up, her family used to tell her she was Italian royalty. It seems to have stuck with her. Some days she thinks she's a princess, and others she's a queen. She's nice when she's the princess. But when she thinks she's the queen, your curtsy better be good, or she demands violence."

"Violence?"

"She'll call for your head on a platter."

Great. I tried not to obsess over that. I remembered he said his other Nonna, Alfonso's ex-wife, lived with his Mamma too. "Your other Nonna?"

"Nonna Silvia. She's in perfect health, just bitter. She didn't take the divorce well. She's determined to outlive Alfonso and the *puttana.*"

That made me smile. Felice caught it and grinned, holding my hand tighter. Or maybe I was squeezing the life from his after the door opened and his Mamma appeared without Felice having to knock. I felt like I didn't have enough time to prepare for this.

I tried not to fidget as she took the boxes from Felice and kissed his cheeks. She was a short woman with a truly beautiful face. Her hair was black, and she had what Lo called "The Italian Cut." It was shaggy, but also sculpted, with deep waves at the crown and spit curls framing her cheeks. It was probably inspired by Gina Lollobrigida.

She was built like her too. Her curves were apparent. She wore tight black pants with a black sweater adorned with diamond cuffs on the wrists. Her makeup was impeccable, and her jewelry almost blinded me when it was hit by the overhead lights.

Felice introduced us, and before I could say *nice to meet you*, she pulled me in for a hug. Corinna rubbed my back as she told me how great it was to meet me. I responded the same, then she moved out of the way so we could enter the house.

It was older but in amazing condition. It smelled of lemon cleaner, floral perfume, baby powder, and Italian food. Felice hung our coats and kept his hand on my lower back as we ventured further into the house.

Halfway down the hall, Corinna lifted her hand, and we stopped walking.

A woman stepped out of a room off to the right. She wore a crown and held a scepter. A purple velvet robe hung from her thin shoulders. She held her chin up and her eyes looked down on us. She looked at Corinna as if to say, "Introduce us."

"Queen Mafalda of Chicago, I would be pleased to introduce you to John Maggio and his stunning lady friend, Roma."

Felice stepped in front of Corinna and gave a proper neck bow (from the head only), called her "queen," and then handed her a box of bomboloni. She opened them, nodded, then handed them to the nurse in scrubs who stood close.

Then she looked straight at me.

I was mentally prepping myself for this moment. I averted my eyes and gave a small curtsy. Then I gave her a slight smile and held my breath. She made no effort to hide the fact that she was scrutinizing me.

"You shall proceed," she said in a very dignified voice, pointing her scepter at us.

Felice gave me a quick grin, and we followed behind Corinna to the dining room. I was introduced to Nonna Silvia, who was pleasant, but like Felice had said, extremely bitter. It was almost as if she wore it as a perfume. The frown lines around her mouth were severe.

"John told me you don't eat meat," Corinna said, pointing to a couple dishes on the table. Lunch was served family style. "I made those for you."

"Thank you so much," I said to Corinna as she handed me a plate with what looked like a big square of eggplant lasagna.

Nonna Silvia pointed her fork at me. "They say cutting meat from your diet can prolong your life."

I nodded, wiping my mouth, about to respond when she continued.

"I'm determined to outlive my ex-husband. He's a lowlife who left me for a woman half my age. I'm determined to outlive the *puttana* too. She was having an affair with him while we were married, and she knew it. I can't enjoy my life until both are gone."

"That's understandable," I said.

Corrina covered her mouth with a napkin, hiding her smile. Felice grinned as he stabbed a piece of meat.

Nonna Silvia pointed her fork at Felice. "I like her, John."

I'd made it past Nonna Mafalda with my head intact, and I got a compliment out of Nonna Silvia. So far, this visit felt like a win.

"Roma's father is good friends with Alfonso." Felice relaxed in his seat. "Emanuele's arranging her marriage to Jack."

Nonna Silvia's fork crashed to her plate. Corinna looked up slowly from hers. I squeezed my fork. Why did he have to bring that up?

"Your father is Dr. Emanuele Corvo?" Corinna whispered.

I nodded, not sure what else to do or say.

"*Good*." Nonna Silvia's voice was fierce. "Hurt them where it counts, where they can't heal or recover. You wound the Maggio pride, you mortally wound them. That *puttana* too. It's about time someone knocks her off her high horse. Though I have to say —" she sighed wistfully, looking at me "—you'd give her some competition. She doesn't like women who are superior to her."

"John and Roma brought bomboloni." Corrina got to her feet. "I'll put coffee on." She rushed out of the dining room.

Felice stared at the clock on the wall, his face made of stone. No expression whatsoever. His arm was draped over the back of my chair, and his fingers drummed against the wood.

What the hell was he thinking? Why did he have to make dinner so awkward? The mood went from welcoming to tense in the space of those few words he'd said.

I didn't know what to do, so I got up and started clearing the table. Corinna had some of the dishes on a dining hutch when we'd arrived. I brought them back so we could make room for dessert. She came back with a moka pot, small cups with saucers, and the bomboloni arranged on a platter.

When she'd noticed what I'd done, she thanked me. I could tell Felice's news had shaken her, though.

Conversation was slim during *dolce*. Corinna asked me questions about work, but other than that, the table was silent.

Silence was the most uncommon dish at an Italian Sunday dinner.

Felice declined dessert, opting for espresso only. Nonna Silvia decided to take hers in the room with Nonna Mafalda. I almost felt the need to excuse myself to the bathroom. Maybe Corinna wanted to lay into Felice for not telling her before.

I wanted to lay into Felice.

His phone pinged. He took it out of his pocket, checked the screen, and stood.

He kissed me on top of the head. "Business."

"How long will you be gone? I need to get back."

"Not long." His tone was cold, and his words were clipped.

What the hell had him in such a bad mood?

He kissed Corinna on the cheek and thanked her for dinner. A minute later, he was gone.

The table seemed so big suddenly. The house too quiet.

"Mind if I use the restroom?" I stood, needing a moment to myself so I could breathe without feeling like I could hear it.

Corinna pointed me in the right direction. I found my way and was so relieved to be alone. I took as much time as I could without making it seem like I was making number two. Things were already awkward. I didn't want Corinna to think her food was bad and I was taking advantage of her toilet, as Lo would say.

Nonna Mafalda was walking the halls with her nurse when I stepped out.

"You are beautiful," she said to me, smiling. Gone was the curt tone of the queen. "As a princess should be. I'm a princess too. Would you like to see my quarters?"

Her nurse smiled at me, and I took Nonna Mafalda's other arm, walking with them to her room. After a few minutes, she climbed into bed and started to snore. Her nurse said she was on a pretty good schedule, but sometimes she suffered with insomnia. I thought of Elsa and her family. Her father was in the early stages, and I knew she struggled with trying to help her mom and live a life of her own.

Pictures on a table in the hallway stopped me on my way back to the dining room. I picked one up. I was almost positive it was Felice when he was a baby. It was no surprise he was beautiful. Dark, soft hair, parted to the side, gorgeous green eyes, and a smile that could melt ice. Adult Felice's smile had frozen over the warm, except when it was meant for me. I placed the picture back and looked at the row of them.

Felice with who I assumed was his father caught my eye.

"That's Salvatore," Nonna Silvia said, making me jump a

little. "John's father. Your father refused him the life saving device he created and the pills. That's why he's dead."

"What?" I breathed out.

Her eyebrows rose. "You didn't know?"

"No."

"You can understand why Emanuele Corvo's name is not celebrated in this house then. Your father's sins shouldn't fall on you, though. You didn't deny my son." She moved closer to me. "I like you. Don't change my mind."

She left me alone in the hall. I studied the picture again, wondering why my father had denied Salvatore care? Was it because of Alfonso? How ruthless would that be if Alfonso wanted it that way? His own son? And why hadn't Felice mentioned it to me?

"You okay, honey?" Corrina stepped out of the kitchen, holding a towel.

I nodded and wiped my palms on my pants. "Felice was such a beautiful baby."

"My only." She smiled. "I love that you call him Felice. Sal chose the name, but everyone ended up calling him John. The English version of his middle name."

"Giovanni," I said.

She nodded. "You want something to drink? Something else to eat?"

I touched my stomach. "I had plenty. Thank you." I pointed to the kitchen towel. "Could you use some help?"

"Some company would be great."

She turned and looked at me when I started laughing. I hadn't noticed one of the pictures until I decided to take a second look at the baby picture of Felice. Felice and Cassio stood next to one another. They looked to be around the same age. Thirteen or fourteen, maybe. Instead of Cassio giving Felice bunny ears, he was either sticking Felice or the camera the middle finger.

"That's Cassio," she said. "He and John grew up together. I'm pretty sure Cassio is my husband's, but they would have killed him if they found out."

She said it so casually, like it was no big deal. I had to force my feet to move behind her. She told me to have a seat at the kitchen table, but I refused. I told her I'd wash while she put the food away. She set an apron around her neck and then one around mine. She gave me a pair of rubber gloves.

"I didn't know your mamma, but she did a great job with you," she said.

I thanked her and told her Mamma had a massive heart attack.

"I'm sorry to hear it," she said. "I'm always here if you ever need someone. Even if it's just a hug."

The sincerity in her tone touched my heart. She didn't have to like me, after my father had refused her husband life-saving care, but she still seemed to.

"So...Cassio and Felice might be brothers?" I asked to change the subject.

She scraped the veggie lasagna in an empty butter container. "You can take this home. We like meat around here. Oh. Yeah. But remember, this is Vegas' rules. What we talk about in this kitchen stays in this kitchen."

I nodded and lifted my right hand.

She laughed. "I think John knows, but not Cassio. His Pop was a friend of Sal's."

Again, her tone was so blasé. My face must have been transparent, because she tried to hide her *poor naïve child* smile from me.

"I'm sure John's business is no secret to you. You're a smart girl. You've put two and two together. Sal's business was the same. It's just what they do. Though Sal pushed the limits. If I would have known back then, or even suspected, I probably would have made a fuss. She was a friend, you know? I understood the mistresses. But not her.

"I sat at her table and ate dinner. She sat at mine and broke bread and drank wine. It hurt when I connected the pieces. Sal left Cassio some of his inheritance. Cassio assumed it was because his Pop had died, and Sal was a good friend. I've come to terms with it now, though." She looked around. "I forgot the bomboloni in the dining room. The box keeps them fresher. Be right back."

It was hard to put myself in Corrina's shoes. All Felice had done was bring Margot to the gala, and the jealousy turned my insides ugly. How would it feel to know mistresses were a normal part of his life? I wasn't okay with it. It was something I'd have to talk to Felice about.

Corrina came back in and set the platter down on the counter, then handed me my phone. "I heard it going off. It hasn't stopped. Might be important."

I'd left my purse in Felice's car but had tucked my phone in my coat pocket. I had ten missed calls and countless text messages from Lo and Elsa.

Before I could open them, my phone rang.

Lo.

"Y? Y! Why haven't you been answering your phone?"

"It was in my coat pocket, and I didn't hear it. Why? What's wrong?"

Corinna was placing the bomboloni back in the box, but I could tell she was listening.

"Where are you? Never mind. I don't even want to know. But you need to get to Elsa's. Isa showed up at her house."

CHAPTER 20

FELICE

Smoke billowed out of Cassio's front door as he opened it for me. He waved a kitchen towel, trying to fan some of it out.

"I was trying to bake cookies with Adelasia." He stepped to the side to let me in.

"You might want to try again."

"Ma took over. There's no fucking domesticating me. And a little girl likes to bake cookies and decorate them around the holidays. Or so I've been told."

Saucy, a little white dog that had been Cassio's wife's, ran after me, barking as we made our way to his office. He offered me a drink from his wet bar, but I declined, taking a seat on his leather sofa.

"I only have a few minutes." I looked at my watch. "You said this was important."

"Daddy saddled her with a curfew?" he asked as he poured himself a drink.

If that remark had been even a subtle insult toward Roma, I would have taken one of the glass bottles from the shelf and hit him over the head with it. I was already in a bad fucking mood.

It hit me hard after lunch that my time with Roma was

limited. She'd be out of my house and bed in a few hours. The anger I couldn't dispel showed up in the tension in my jaw. Cassio had only said it, though, to lead us into this conversation.

"Don't worry about it," I said, getting the jump on him.

He worked his jaw back and forth. "Don't worry about it?"

"That's what I said."

"You're putting me in a bad spot, John. Corvo is going to go to Tommaso. He already made a comment about you showing yourself to his backyard, talking to his youngest daughter. *Ah—*" he waved a dismissive hand, his voice sounding like Tommaso's "*— he only wanted to check on her.* But Tommaso was pacifying him. I was there for the conversation. Corvo leaves, and Tommaso asks me if I know anything about this. I tell him all I know is that the boss, *him*, sent you in his place on Thanksgiving."

"I'll deal with Tommaso."

"If it was anyone else, especially when it comes to Alfonso Maggio and what he wants, I'd say go for it. Not this time. Not when it has to do with Corvo. You know the deal between him and Tommaso."

"Jack's not getting what's mine."

"Is that what this is about? Giving Alfonso and his son shit, like they've always given you, while also saying *fuck you* to the man who refused to save Uncle Sal? Killing two birds with one stone?"

I'd never put my hands on Cassio before, but I grabbed him by the shirt and slammed him into the wall. Bottles fell and crashed to the floor. So did glasses. Alcoholic fumes bloomed in the air.

His heart pounded against my grip. His nostrils flared. Our eyes were locked. He'd understand what she meant to me, or fuck him too.

My phone rang once, twice, three times before I let him go.

Ms. Lang.

"Maggio," I answered, heading out.

Cassio's mother looked up from icing cookies with Adelasia and looked right back down. I didn't acknowledge her. Even if

Cassio didn't belong to my old man, I had a feeling she had slept with him. It never sat right with me. It was one of the few things I held against my old man. It wasn't fair to my Ma. She thought of Cassio's mother as her sister.

"John?" Ms. Lang's voice rushed out. She was whispering. "We have a problem. Isabella showed up at my house. I'd gone shopping. My mom was outside talking to the roofers and my dad opened the door. You know he has dementia. When Isabella asked for Roma, my dad told her we'd gone shopping. He didn't even remember Roma wasn't there. My mom only caught the end of the conversation and told her where I'd gone.

"Isabella's going from shop to shop, looking for us. Or looking to catch Roma in a lie. Damn. Roma must be the luckiest girl alive. I ran into a friend of hers. Penelope. She ran for Miss Illinois and was runner up to Roma. She's diabetic and wanted to bring light to the disease. Anyway. She's building a house out this way and invited me to check out the land and have a late lunch with her. I left with her. I told her I had to use the bathroom so I could call. Roma's not answering."

"Text me the name of the restaurant and stay there."

We hung up, and Roma called a second later. I told her I was five minutes out and to be getting her coat on. She was waiting by the door, Ma behind her, when I pulled up. She held a baggie Ma must have packed for her. Something in me boiled over when I thought about her not getting to take it home. The tension in my jaw felt like fire.

I didn't even shut the car off. I got out, kissed Ma on the cheek and thanked her again for lunch. Roma did too. Then we left.

Roma was quiet, not really saying much. The feeling from her was colder than it had been outside.

"Where are we going?" she asked.

"To meet Ms. Lang." I gave her the gist of the conversation. "We're going to stop at the penthouse first to pick up your dress and bag."

She nodded. "I talked to Elsa a minute ago."

"I'll drop you at the restaurant. You'll ride back to the market with them. If Isabella sees you, you have an alibi. You ran into Penelope, and she invited you and Ms. Lang to see her land, then you had a late lunch." My voice matched her mood. Chilled.

I was getting sick and tired of the fucking games when it came to her. This entire situation would have pushed me over if it wasn't for one thing: I despised a rat. Isabella was a rat. Nothing I enjoyed more than catching them in a trap.

"What's your problem, Maggio?" She turned to face me, ready to square off. "You've been acting like an ass since dinner! Was that totally necessary? To bring up who my father is?"

"I don't keep secrets, Dino. I'm not a coward."

"I am?"

"Are you ready to tell Daddy about me?" I looked at her, and the answer was clear on her face. "Thought so. You won't ever be truly free until you start making your own rules."

"You know why I can't! I don't want to miss Lo's wedding."

I ticked my mouth, and she made a frustrated noise in my direction.

"You're one to talk about secrets," she snapped. "Your entire *business* is one dark secret. And besides, I'm a woman. I was built for holding secrets. Including yours."

Silence fell between us. Even on the elevator ride back up to the penthouse she refused to look at me. She watched the climbing numbers until we reached the top. She didn't say a word to me as she changed into the spare outfit she'd brought to the gala. She stuffed the dress and her heels in the bag and turned to me.

"*The meek shall inherit the earth*, Felice." The argument must have been playing in her head, and the comeback was late.

"I don't want the earth," I said. "I want you. *Eternamente.*" *Eternally.*

She headed toward the door, and we left. Thirty minutes into the drive, I broke the silence.

"I need you in my bed, every morning, every night, Dino." I squeezed the wheel. "You belong to me."

She took a deep breath and slowly released it. "You're trying to tell me you were an ass because you're going to miss me?"

"That's a simple way of putting it. Remember Plato."

"You truly believe that?"

I nodded. "Nothing else can better explain how whole I am now. And when you leave me, I feel the separation. You're being ripped from my side again."

"Me too," she whispered, locking our fingers. "All of it."

Chapter 21

Roma

Night had fallen, and snow twirled in front of the headlights as Elsa pulled next to Felicia the Fiat.

"Is she serious?" Elsa whispered.

Elsa's headlights had illuminated two figures sitting in Babbo's car, which was parked next to mine. The exhaust spewed out smoke, and the windshield wipers went back and forth, clearing the falling and sticking snow.

I sighed. "Isabella can't help herself."

Babbo turned his car off and stepped out, followed by Isabella and Lo. Lo must have been in the back seat. Babbo's eyes were narrowed, and Isabella stood with her arms crossed. Lo looked pale and like she couldn't get warm.

"What's going on?" I asked after Elsa had parked and I stepped out. "Is something wrong?"

"Where are your bags?" Isabella asked, her tone pointed. "With the gifts you supposedly bought."

"Are you being serious right now, Isabella?"

Isabella ignored Lo. My father's eyes were hard, waiting.

"Here," Elsa said, popping the trunk to her car. She handed me four or five bags.

I had no idea what was in them, but one glance told me it was gifts for Christmas for my family. Elsa must have done some shopping. Felice must have planned for this. Good was an understatement when it came to his level of scheming.

"Have fun ruining my gifts." I handed Isabella a bag.

The bitch actually started rooting through them. She started flinging things around, like she couldn't believe it. I felt bad for her kids. She was like Paisano when he caught a scent. He became obsessed with it.

"Who's this for?" She held up a pink cashmere sweater.

"Lo."

"Sweet!" Lo snatched it from her, holding it against her chest.

Damn, Elsa was good. She always had a habit of studying people, and she had bought gifts for my family that fit each one. The sweater was Lo.

"Enough!" My father shouted when Isabella started going for more. He turned around, ordered Lo to ride with me, then got back in his car, starting it. The high beams hit Isabella before he turned them down.

She stared at me for a second before her words slapped me in the face. "Mamma would be so disappointed."

Elsa squeezed my arm. Lo whispered for me to ignore her and asked for my keys.

Besides the radio playing quietly in the background, Lo singing along to it, the ride was quiet. Isabella's words had hit a nerve, but somewhere between the gala and realizing how out of control Isabella was with controlling my life, I got over caring about what everyone else expected of me.

I refused to exchange my life's happiness for my father's. He had his one true love.

What was so wrong with me having mine?

CHAPTER 22

ROMA

The Gwen Hotel was off Michigan Avenue, tucked away in River North. Hayden had decided it would be a good place to host the museum's holiday staff party because they offered cocktails and curling on the rooftop. The space was decked out with holiday decorations, fire pits, and what looked like a mini area for ice skating but was for curling.

The mini version of a rink had four concentric circles in the center. What looked like weights with different colored handles and smooth bottoms were placed on opposing sides. We were told to separate into two teams. The object of the game was to slide the stones toward the target areas. Each team scored when they knocked the other teams' stones out of the way.

Elsa told me in the Olympics they usually played with sticks and skated on the ice. We stood behind the ice line and slid the stone almost like a bowling ball for this improvised rooftop game.

Kerry, Elsa, and I decided not to play because we were pretty sure our asses were frozen to the sofa. We'd claimed seats in front of a flaming fire pit. I was wedged between them.

"Not even the fire pits help out here," Kerry said. Her hot drink was smoking in its mug, it was so cold. "Who put Hayden 'the competitive one' Burton in charge of this year's party?"

"He d-d-did," Elsa said, shivering. "I d-d-didn't recommend it, but he said it would be f-f-fun."

"*YEAHH!*" Hayden screeched when he knocked the other team's stone out of the way, pumping his fists in the air.

His face was neon red, either from the chapping cold or the glory of winning. He chugged whatever he was drinking in victory, dancing to Wham!'s "Last Christmas."

Hayden was having the time of his life. His team was in the lead, and we all agreed it was only because he seemed insulated from the cold, like a fucking killer whale with blubber. He looked like the kid in *A Christmas Story* who toppled over from too many layers. Most of the mere humans were getting drunk off hot cocktails to stop hypothermia from setting in. He'd reserved a room inside for dinner, but that was in forty-five minutes. We could all turn into ice sculptures by then.

"I need a mask made of *wooool*," Elsa slurred a little, chugging her spiked hot chocolate even faster. "My nose is fwozen—frozem —shit. *Fro-zen.*"

"Are your lips frozen?" I asked, moving mine around. "Mine sort of feel like it. They're numb."

My hot chocolate wasn't spiked, because I estimated drinking one for every five minutes we were out here. They would have to defrost me off the sofa.

A gust of wind blew, sending the flames in the pit swaying sideways, and the three of us did the same, huddling even closer.

"That gust actually hurt." Kerry rubbed the arm not pressed against me. "It feels like cold knives."

My phone went off. The chat with my sisters.

Isabella led the charge, as always, reminding everyone to dress in the pajamas she picked out on Christmas Eve. Mamma took family pictures of us in front of the tree every year, and it became a tradition. Isabella was keeping it alive, along with Mamma's love of the holiday. I never understood where Isabella found the time and energy. She had a husband, two kids, and we were pretty sure another one on the way, and a career at the farm. Yet she found time to decorate the farm, Babbo's house, and spy on me.

Y: Thanks again for ruining Lo's gift, Isabella.

After Isabella cornered me and demanded I show her my bags, like she was my mother or my conscience, the resentment in me only grew. Every chance I got I threw it in her face. It was a childish thing to do, but I couldn't help it.

Alina: There's always Epiphany Eve.

Talia sent an eye-rolling emoji.

Lo sent Talia a clapping emoji.

Lo: Take your pick, Isabella. Coal, garlic, onions, or straw? Because that's what you're getting from La Befana.

Isabella: Get over it already, Y.

"Get over yourself, bish," I muttered.

"Isabella?" Elsa asked.

Before I could respond, Kerry asked me how she was doing.

"You know Isabella?"

"My older sister does. They used to play together when they were little."

Both of Kerry's parents were doctors and friends of Babbo's. I didn't remember Isabella being friends with Kerry's older sister, though. But there was a sizable age gap between us. I said as much.

"They had a falling out over dolls," Kerry said, laughing.

"Dolls?"

"Yeah. One of the dolls was getting married. They had this whole wedding planned. But my sister wanted the doll to marry another doll. Your sister went berserk, saying she had to marry the other one. She said it had been arranged and that was that. They're friends now, but it's a memorable story."

"Sounds like Isabella," I said.

Kerry and Elsa started laughing.

"What?" Smoke billowed out of my mouth.

"We were talking about something funny." Kerry sat her empty mug down. "You were dead serious."

They really started laughing, maybe at the look on my face. I *was* dead serious. Even as a kid, Isabella stuck to the rules and refused to even think about anyone else but her already chosen future husband. She couldn't even let it go while she played with her friend and had a pretend wedding for dolls. I didn't think my response was all that funny, though. They were just getting drunk.

"I'm going to get another—" I began, but Kerry's next words made me go silent.

"Is that John Maggio?" Kerry squinted, looking towards the doors leading outside.

Felice was going to meet me at the hotel. We had plans to go to the ballet after dinner. I assumed he was at "work" until then. It had just been a couple of days, but after Felice told me how he felt about being separated, and after Isabella's stunt, something in me had grown bolder. Getting caught wasn't in my plans, but I refused to not see him or talk to him.

Even though Lo made me solemnly swear to her that whatever my plans were, I'd wait until after her wedding. Traditionally, my parents would wait a few months to start planning a new wedding when we were close in age. Isabella and Talia were barely two years apart, though Talia was more a loner child. Alina was somewhere in the middle, and she was Isabella's shadow. And there was an eighteen-month age-gap between Lo and me. But that was when Mamma was alive. This was new territory with Babbo.

"No," Elsa breathed out. It was almost one-hundred proof. "That's Jack. John's uncle."

"His uncle?"

Elsa explained the situation, and Kerry nodded.

"He looks younger."

"He is," Elsa said, looking at me. Her face became transparent when drunk. It was an *oh shit, look-who's-here-to-rock-the-boat* look.

"Something's going on," Kerry said. "My senses are tingling."

The three of us grew quiet as Jack and three men strode to our table. They were all handsome and built. They smelled like rich colognes, and they had all donned the finest clothes. I hated to admit it, but Jack stood out like Felice did. If I lied to myself and said there was nothing to Jack, I'd be saying that about Felice too. But his looks didn't complete the entire picture. He had nothing on Felice when it came to presence. Felice's intensity made me feel like he was touching me even when he wasn't.

Introductions were made by me first. Jack corrected me when I called him a friend.

"Soon to be husband," he said, shaking Kerry's hand.

"Oh." Kerry paused. She was probably piecing together the situation. What John had said to her, that he was going to marry me, and what Jack had just said. "I didn't realize."

"It hasn't been officially announced yet, but soon." Then he introduced his friends.

I didn't even bother with their names because I was getting sick of Jack showing up and telling everyone we were engaged. I refused to look at him as Kerry, me, and Elsa scrunched closer together to make room for his friends.

Jack took a seat across from me, the flames dancing over his face, when he realized neither Kerry nor Elsa was going to give up their seats.

"Sorry," Elsa said, not sounding sorry at all. "I'm frozen to this spot."

"Same here," Kerry said.

He only nodded, but his gaze stayed fixed on me. He was hell-bent on getting me to meet his eyes. I refused. It seemed symbolic for some reason. Like this situation represented my entire situation. His friends seemed nice enough, though. Conversation was pleasant and flowed.

Then all of them, Jack included, agreed to play the curling game. Hayden was looking for new meat to freeze.

A sigh of relief came out in a cloud of smoke when it was the three of us again.

"Well..." Kerry elongated the word, like she was looking for more to say.

"That about sums it up." Elsa stood. "My bladder is lowly —*slowly*—free-*zz*-zing over. I have to go."

"I'll go with," Kerry said. "I have to defrost."

"What 'bout you, Roma?" Elsa bobbed up and down, either trying to keep warm or trying to hold it in.

"I'll be right behind you," I said. I was going to send a text to Felice. I wasn't sure what I was going to say, but I had to say something about Jack showing up.

I dug around in my purse and pulled out the cell he'd given me. It was separate from my personal in case Isabella ever decided to go snooping. Felice said it wasn't about hiding, but about not giving her what she wanted. I was about to follow behind Kerry and Elsa, still thinking of something to text him on the way, but Jack caught me.

"On your way to the bathroom?"

"No," I said, because it sounded like he intended to walk me. No quiet halls for me and him. "Just needing to stretch my legs. Make sure they're not frozen." I stuck the phone back in my purse.

He rubbed my arms, but I took a step back and set my hands over the flames.

"You seem uncomfortable around me," he said.

"Some."

"Because of what happened at the museum?"

I nodded and wanted to change the direction of the conversation before it headed into territory I didn't want to cross. Like how he'd made me uncomfortable when he went to kiss me. "How's your head?"

He lifted his beanie, his hair going in all different directions, and touched the spot. "I still get a little dizzy, but nothing major. You sure you didn't see who did it?"

"No." I'd only add more if he pressed. I didn't want to take a chance of getting caught in a lie.

"My memories are a little fuzzy, but I could've sworn we were talking and then I woke up..." He shook his head. "Doesn't matter now. You didn't check on me."

"I didn't in person, but I asked my sister."

He winced, like I'd hurt his feelings. "Your sister told me I made you uncomfortable at the museum. I didn't mean to."

"Which sister?" Talia might have threatened to twist him like a pretzel.

"Isabella."

"Did she tell you I was at the museum's holiday party?"

"Dr. Corvo did. He thought I might want to meet some of your co-workers."

Isabella and Babbo were tag teaming now. And Babbo probably wanted him to meet my coworkers so maybe he would reconsider his stance on me working. Maybe Babbo didn't want us to have a major fight over it after we were married.

"Trying to sell you on the idea of me working?" I didn't realize how much of a protective stance I'd taken until the tension in my arms started to burn through the frigid cold. I'd crossed them.

"We're getting married, Roma." The words flowed so easily from his lips. "You're going to be my wife. I have a right to your life."

It hit me in that moment how big of a deal this was. This man thought we were getting married. He'd already claimed me. He thought he had a right to my life and the decisions I made and would make.

"Look." He ran a hand through his hair, trying to tame it. "I didn't mean to make you uncomfortable at the museum. I didn't mean to insult you by suggesting you quit your job. I don't want to fight. We're not even married yet."

"Do you really want to marry me, Jack? You don't even know me."

He looked at me like I'd spoken a different language, but he'd gotten the gist of it. "I have a confession to make. I knew who you were when my dad suggested the idea to me. I knew you'd won

Miss Illinois. I always thought you were beautiful. I'd gone to Jupiter the night you were attacked because I knew you were going to be there. I watched you dance and knew you were the one. I agreed before that night, but after, I couldn't wait to talk to you and spend time with you. Even if you are somewhat intimidating." He smiled.

No, no, no, *nooo*. It was easy to dislike him when I thought he was trying to run my life, but his honesty was endearing, and it made me feel bad. Not bad enough to want to marry him, but sorry that he'd gotten caught up in a no-win situation.

He placed his wool hat over his heart. "I'm not that bad, right?"

I couldn't help it. I smiled at him.

"Right?" He leaned into me some but didn't touch me. "Dr. Cupid made a good match."

"Dr. Cupid?"

He grinned. "Dr. Corvo. My old man calls him that. Says he could make a fortune in the matchmaking business. He's good at it."

I went to respond but closed my mouth on a snap. Felice had come to stand next to Jack and slapped a hand on his shoulder.

"Of all the places in Chicago, I run into my good uncle. Hello, Uncle Jack." His tone was genial, but there was something underneath it that made my blood run cold. He tipped his hat to me. "Evening, Ms. Corvo. Such a beautiful smile you have. Lucky the man who's the recipient of it."

What was with that? *Lucky the man who's the recipient of it.* He sounded like some gent from a different era. I wanted to give him a mean look, but I didn't want Jack to see it and realize how comfortable we were with each other. I left it at a nod.

Jack shrugged him off and came to stand beside me. I took a step to the side because I didn't want Jack to touch me. If he did, things would go from bad to worse. My stomach made an obnoxious noise, and the cold hit me like I was naked out in it. Nerves.

"This is a private office party, John." Jack stuck his hands in his pockets. "You can see yourself out."

Jack's three friends came to stand around us. I wondered if he started carting them around after he got whacked with the stone dinosaur.

Cassio came to stand next to Felice. Two other guys I didn't recognize, along with Celso, flanked him on the other side. They made Jack's friends look like kids.

Felice lifted his arm, pulling his coat back to expose his watch. It was a vintage Patek Philippe. It had belonged to his great-grandfather. I'd seen it at the penthouse. "Rooftop is ours now. But I'd hate to run you off. How about a friendly game before you go?"

"You?" Jack scoffed. "Going to play a friendly game? There's not a game you play that you don't manipulate. Guess you can't help it, though. That's all part of your business. It's what you do."

Felice smiled, and it came too easy. Like when things are going too good and it's only a matter of time before the shoe drops. "I don't need to manipulate games, Jack. Because I make the rules."

Jack didn't have a comeback for that. It seemed to piss him off. His face turned as stony as Felice's usually was. It grew tighter when he looked at me. He was embarrassed that I'd been watching the entire exchange, and Felice had one-upped him. I didn't think it was wise for him to compete with Felice. He was out of his league.

Hayden cleared the air when he shouted, "Time's up! But I could play this all night!"

Felice glanced at Hayden, then met Jack's eyes again. "One game. We can make a wager. And we're on even ground. I didn't make the rules of this game. It just comes down to who's the better player."

Jack seemed hesitant. He looked at me again, then nodded. "All right. What's the wager?"

"Lady's choice." Felice looked right at me.

"No." I put my hands up and started backing away. "You two

can hash it out. Our time here is up anyway, and I'm going to dinner. Good night."

Kerry and Elsa's faces were almost pressed to the glass, looking at me from inside. Instead of coming back outside, they must have decided to watch the show from primo seats.

The entrance to the hotel wasn't but a few steps from the rooftop, but I was out of breath by the time I made it inside. The soothing warmth of the hotel came in second to what was going on outside.

Some of the staff from the museum were coming in for dinner, but some of them decided to stay to make up the teams. Hayden raised his arms to the sky, like he was thankful for another forty-five minutes of ice time. He went to stand on Felice's side.

Jack wasn't paying attention. He pulled his phone out, and it seemed like he was texting. Or maybe he was Googling "how to win at curling."

"Now that we know you're good, we're going to grab some food," Kerry said, squeezing my shoulder. "El needs to eat."

Elsa nodded at me, but it seemed like her head was bobbing on her shoulders.

After they were gone, I pulled out the phone Felice had given me and sent him a text.

Me: I'll meet you at the ballet.

I'd grab a bite with Elsa, change in the bathroom, then have plenty of time to text Felice to let him know where I'd be parked.

My Carnivore: No.

"No?" I repeated.

My Carnivore: No.

I looked up and outside of the window. Our eyes met. He looked down at his phone, his thumbs working, and my phone dinged a second later.

My Carnivore: You'll ride with me.

I sighed. He was going to do this to prove a point. I would be leaving with him, no matter if Jack was here or not. And there was no telling what was going on in his mind when he saw me smile at Jack. He'd been watching.

Evening, Ms. Corvo. Such a beautiful smile you have. Lucky the man who's the recipient of it.

Me: Okay.

Not wanting to watch what happened next, I walked away from the glass. About forty-five minutes later, the phone Felice had given me chimed in my purse.

My Carnivore: Cassio will follow you and Ms. Lang. You drive.

Like I'd let her drive when she couldn't even get the word *steak* out without hissing the "s" sound. I huffed at the phone because of his insinuation and because his curt message meant he was going to work and would be late (or not show up at all). I told Elsa it was time to change, pulled her up, and we hightailed it to the bathroom so Jack couldn't catch me leaving.

───────

Celso was leaning against my car, his arms crossed, when Elsa and I made it to Felicia. He made clown car noises from his mouth as he searched the interior.

"Is that really necessary?" I asked.

"Boss says so," he said, doing a thorough search.

"I'm talking about the noises," I said.

He grinned at me but stopped making them, then walked over to a Lincoln idling nearby, Cassio behind the wheel. Cassio gave me just enough room to put her in reverse and drive forward. He made a motion that I took to mean, "I'll be following."

It was ridiculous Felice had him following me. The Lyric Opera House was only a few minutes from The Gwen. But I gave him a thumbs up and we left.

Elsa closed her eyes and relaxed in her seat.

"Feeling okay?" I asked.

"You ever drink so much you get numb, but all your problems

keep knocking on the door, reminding you that they're there? Let me just say, if you haven't, I don't recommend it."

"The food didn't help?"

"A little. I think I stopped slurring after *sss*teak."

A couple of beats of silence fell between us, but her thoughts seemed loud. Maybe she needed to air them out and set them free.

"You're worried about your parents?"

She blew out a heavy breath, opened her eyes, and sat up. She held her hands up to the vent. "My parents. Money. My life. Money. What's left of me, guilt takes. My dad is getting worse. My mom struggles to take care of him while working from home. She's burnt out because of the stress. And here I am in the city, living it up."

"You help. A lot."

"As much as I can. I'm thinking of giving up my apartment, quitting school and the museum, and moving back home. I can't seem to catch a break lately." She stared into the side mirror, like she was hoping it would have all the answers to her building problems.

Elsa lived in an apartment in China Town. It was small, but she said it felt like home. She loved her landlords and the area. I knew she struggled to keep up with everything, including finishing her latest degree while helping her parents.

"I know that guilt," I whispered. "Mine is different, but I get it. It's not easy to want a life of your own while also needing to help with family. If you give to one, you're neglecting the other."

"I figured you'd see me," she said.

"I do."

She sighed. "Mind if we talk about something else?"

I brought up the ballet and asked her if she'd ever been. We were going to see *The Nutcracker*. She told me she'd been once when she was around seven. She returned the question, and I told her we went almost every year.

"One in particular stands out the most to me, though. The year before Mamma died, she planned a trip to New York for all of us girls and her. It wasn't *The Nutcracker*, but Scarlett Fausti was the lead. My sisters and I were excited because it was a surprise that we were going to see one of her performances. Tickets to her shows sell out. It was a magical trip."

"I've seen snippets of her performances online," Elsa said. "She's got real talent. But her marriage to Brando Fausti sometimes overshadows her career."

I didn't say anything. I had a feeling Uncle Tito had gotten the tickets for Mamma. He was married to a Fausti, so he knew them personally.

Elsa reached in the back seat and snatched her bag. She dug around for a second before she hooked her phone up to my audio system. A second later "Tiny Dancer" played. We both started to sing along.

The impact of another car crashing into Elsa's side made me scream. The sound of metal screeching and groaning sounded like it was coming from inside my head as we flipped over three or four times, everything not belted down hitting us, before the last flip had enough momentum to right us. My shoulder hit the window, then I was slammed back into the seat, and it seemed like I'd forgotten how to breathe.

The dinosaur Lo had given me was still on the dash, his heading bobbing maniacally, the song slurring, dragging, like a record that was about to give out.

I looked over at Elsa, but she was out cold. Her head was bowed, and blood dripped from somewhere. Snow flew inside her shattered window.

My hands squeezed the wheel but trembled at the same time. I couldn't stop staring at them, until I heard a horn. It sounded like it was coming from a tunnel. A glaring light hypnotized me for a second.

I hit the gas, but a delivery truck coming for us on Elsa's side clipped us. We went spinning, and I lost control.

The building came up fast, and we crashed.

CHAPTER 23

FELICE

The look on baby-boy Jack's face when I left the rooftop was fucking comical. All we'd put up were our watches, both from our inheritances, and I'd won. But he was suspicious. The wager wasn't high enough, though both time-pieces were collectable items, and he thought I was conning him somehow. His stake didn't need to be high. I'd already won the woman he was positive was going to be his wife.

My mood darkened when the memory of her smiling at him hit me like a truck. Jack could be a charming little asshole when he wanted to be. Some people thought he was my son.

I wasn't sure where to put this feeling I was having a hard time fucking identifying.

Was it jealousy?

I let that sink in for a second.

It was.

I'd never felt it before.

Roma Corvo was bringing out foreign emotions in me, and they threw me back and forth between love and loathing.

If I stood with this feeling too long, I was going to turn around and find Jack. Find a creative way to have him beg for his life. The thought satisfied the dark thoughts, but my life was never run by thoughts. It was run by actions, and I didn't plan on taking any that would lead to his demise. Ending his life meant ending the game.

We were just getting started, in my opinion, and Jack was being used as a pawn.

I had no doubt Gramps Maggio and Emanuele Corvo had a chat with Jack after the incident at the museum, which was why he started bringing an entourage with him wherever he went. Alfonso wanted to keep him swathed. Corvo wanted him to wine and dine Roma, so to speak.

One thing I couldn't take away from Corvo was that he knew his daughters. He probably schooled Jack on how to salvage what he'd been fucking up. Which was why he was backtracking his stance on Roma working at the museum. Corvo knew if Jack pushed the issue, the marriage would be on a fast track to the end before it had even gotten started.

What none of them ever saw coming was me. The train they wouldn't be able to stop.

Jack could try every single trick in the book, until he was down on his knees begging, and she'd never belong to him. He might never admit it, but he knew he was on the losing side. Just like he knew he was going to lose the rooftop game.

Most men instinctually know if they've won a woman's heart. It's the ones who know they've never had it to begin with that start to hide her away from the rest of the world. Can't keep her if she has too many options. Which was why Jack didn't want Roma working.

My issue was not the same as his. I didn't have an insecure bone in my body. But fuck me if it didn't burn me deep when she smiled at him.

I parked in front of Tommaso's house in North Riverside, about thirty minutes outside of Chicago. The man had made millions but lived in a modestly priced, multi-family house. His place was three stories, separated into three units. He claimed he rented them out. It was just another way for him to prove a legitimate source of income. He was old school and kept his riches buried in the walls and under the tomato plants in his wife's garden.

While the car idled, I called Cassio and had a quick conversation. I wanted an update on Roma. I stuck my phone in my pocket as I walked up to the house. I knocked and waited underneath an old white lattice awning. His wife opened the door and invited me inside.

The house was immaculate but hadn't been updated since the 1950s. It was plastered with floral wallpaper, and the kitchen and bathroom countertops were all Formica. The furniture was covered in plastic to keep it looking "new."

Tommaso sat on the sofa watching television, a blanket draped over where he sat. I checked my watch. It was just 7'o'clock, and he was ready for bed. He invited me to take a seat across from him in a chair. The plastic crinkled underneath my ass and legs.

His wife offered me something to drink, I declined, and she left us alone.

He yawned but didn't bother to cover it up. "Seven o'clock and it feels like midnight." He turned the television low, then grabbed his phone. He had a flip. No text messages. No pictures. *Niente.* "Got a call from Emanuele. Alfonso Maggio's boy told his father you showed up at some party for his girl's work. Emanuele's not happy about you pursuing his daughter. She's been promised to Alfonso's boy."

I didn't say anything. I let him continue.

"Emanuele told me to stop you."

Told. Not asked. That was a fucking risky thing to do, ordering Tommaso Russo to do anything. "Told" and "ordered" meant the same thing to him. He'd be asked, but never bossed, even if he was indebted.

Our eyes locked.

My phone rang, cutting through the silence.

"Answer," he said in Italian.

My chest felt so tight, my heart didn't feel like it could beat. This man was a master at word play, and he probably got creative after Emanuele had called him and insulted him. I forced myself to answer, but my jaw was too tight to speak. I didn't have to.

Cassio. Breathing heavy. Rushing the words out. *Roma. Elsa. Car accident. The first car flipped them over, but it flew past, then the delivery truck clipped them.*

I hung up, not seeing anything but red. Her blood spilled. The scent of it. Not being there to protect her from it.

"Emanuele didn't say how to stop you. When you order me to do something, you better be specific."

What Tommaso had done was a warning to me and a fuck you to Corvo. Tommaso might have owed him, but Emanuele wouldn't boss him. Yet he took care of the problem. I burned with hate for Tommaso for what he'd done. I felt a cold burn for the man who called himself her father for involving a man like Tommaso Russo. Emanuele wasn't dense, and he knew how Tommaso could be.

"John," Tommaso stopped me before I could leave. "Emanuele has a right to feel as he does. Do some research. Find out why."

My phone was clutched in my hand. One day, it would be his throat in its place. "You are not even welcome past the office in his home," I spoke in Sicilian, my voice almost strangled.

Tommaso turned back to the television and turned it up. The men who lived upstairs were in the shadows, watching and waiting.

CHAPTER 24

ROMA

I'd be going home tomorrow, but the doctor wanted to keep me overnight for observation. I had a concussion. I also had a broken nose, whiplash, and some bruising and cuts. I was told Elsa was still being taken care of. More than once I heard we were both lucky to be alive.

The room was dark, and I kept going in and out. I saw my father sitting in the chair in the corner. Alfonso and Jack were next to him when I woke up again. The next time, it was my sisters with Babbo.

When I woke up again, a lone figure sat in the chair, head in his hands. He was unmistakable to me.

"Felice," I breathed out. The relief in my voice was apparent.

"Dino," he said, his voice husky. "Your driving could use some finesse, but you saved yourself and Ms. Lang."

"I learned from the best," I whispered. "Even if I take a sting-like-a-bee approach and you take a float-like-a-butterfly one."

He laughed softly and I grinned, but it hurt. It hurt because I wanted Felice to stay the night and take me home the next day. I wanted him close because he'd become the definition of safety to me. But I knew that wasn't possible.

As if he sensed my feelings, the bed dipped and he pulled me close, kissing my head. I held on to him, not able to let go.

The entire situation made me angry and sad. And I was shaken.

In my dreams, I still felt the world turning upside down, all concept of control lost. I heard the groaning of giving metal and the screeching of tires. The smell of Elsa's blood had clung to the cold surging through the broken window, and it wouldn't go away. It was probably from my bloody nose, but I couldn't stop smelling it.

He cradled me in his lap while I clung to his shirt. I must have fallen asleep. I knew the moment he placed me back on the bed, covered me with a blanket, tucked something soft in next to me, and kissed my lips.

I felt like a part of me was ripping away.

My eyes felt heavy, but I forced them to open. "Felice?" I called out.

Silence met me in the darkness.

He was gone.

CHAPTER 25

ROMA

I was hiding from my family. I did the whole Christmas morning thing, but then decided to take my coffee and sit in the sunroom. Though it was more like an ice room. Snow had piled on the glass, and it was like sitting inside of a snow globe.

I didn't even bother grabbing a book or playing the dinosaur game on my phone. I was thinking of Felice and how I hadn't seen or heard from him since the night he came to visit me in the hospital. The phone he'd given me was gone, and he wasn't answering his phone or responding to texts.

I thought about paying him a visit at one of his places, but apparently he didn't want to talk to me. All I had was another dinosaur he'd left me. It was like the first one, and tucked inside was a card with four words written on it:

I'm always with you.

I'm always with you? Yet he refused to see or answer me. Maybe because he was shaken from what had happened? And Felice Maggio didn't seem like a man who knew what to do with feelings he wasn't used to.

Case in point. A couple of days after the accident, the man

driving the delivery truck was found dead with a bullet in his brain. That was something Felice could do something about. But vulnerable feelings? He had no clue how to kill them.

I took a deep sip of my coffee, closed my eyes, and set my head back. A few minutes later, the sofa dipped, and I opened my eyes.

"You can run but you can't hide," Lo almost sang. She shook her shoulders. "How does the new sweater look?"

"Like it was made for you," I said.

She smiled. "Want me to do your makeup and hair?"

"I'm good."

"I can make those bruises disappear." She ran a hand softly over them, and I closed my eyes. "Or maybe you could just rest today. You seem like you need it."

"Roma!"

My eyes snapped open, and my body jerked at the shout. Isabella stood in the doorway with her hands on her hips, a dishtowel in hand, giving me a disapproving look. She was all dressed up and had an apron on.

"Get upstairs and get ready. Everyone will be here soon. Do you want Jack to see you like that?"

"Umm, I'm pretty sure he's going to see her like that every morning, Isabella," Lo snapped. "Women do sleep. They're human too."

"That's not what I meant," Isabella clapped back. "She just looks extra tired."

"You would be too, if your car flipped and then you crashed into a building!" Lo shouted.

"Excuse me," Isabella used her parenting voice. "Was I talking to you, Lolita?"

"Doesn't matter. I'm talking to you."

Isabella rolled her eyes and tried to grab my arm. I yanked it back.

"Don't you dare fucking touch me!"

Isabella sucked in air. "What did you just say to me?"

She was daring me to repeat it. I did, extra loud. Alina and Talia came to stand in the room.

"You're not Mamma," I said. "Let me refresh your memory. We shared the same one. I'm not your kid. You have two of them, those brats fighting over a toy in the next room." I really didn't mean to bring the kids into it, but there it was.

Besides, we all called them brats to their faces. They only laughed.

"The only brat in this house is you," Isabella said, balling the dishtowel in her hand. "Hurting Babbo like you do. Making Jack feel like shit."

"Yeah, about that. Stay out of my business. Or if you like Jack so much, maybe you should marry him."

"Stay out of your business? Since when do we do that?"

"Since today," I said.

She gritted her teeth. "Make me."

I snatched the Ho-Ho-Ho throw pillow off the sofa, jumped up, and whacked her in the head with it. Her perfectly styled hair went flying. The room went quiet. She took a second, fixed her hair, grabbed another pillow, and whacked me back.

Tears sprang to my eyes because of my nose.

We started hitting each other with the pillows, screaming as we did. I couldn't hear her over my screams, and I doubted she could hear me over hers. Paisano barked and was trying to bite the pillows.

Lo tried to grab me, and Alina tried to grab Isabella, when we started to hit with our hands. But we were both crazed. My only thought was to hurt her like she'd been hurting me. They couldn't grab our arms.

"Enough!" Babbo boomed.

We instantly stopped, and the room fell quiet. Stuffing from the pillows floated in the air. It was hanging from Paisano's mouth.

Babbo glared at us. Some of the guests stood behind him. It

was mostly our family and in-laws who came over. Occasionally friends did, especially if they had no one else. Mamma was big on not being alone on holidays. Jack stared at me. I crossed my arms and stared back. Babbo turned and left. All the guests but Jack followed him.

Isabella crumbled after she caught the disappointed look on Babbo's face. She looked at the room and started to cry, but it was angry.

"Look what you've done!" she hissed at me, gesturing around. Her hair was standing up all over the place, and her lipstick was smeared. "You know why we call you 'Y'? Because we have no clue *why* Mamma and Babbo didn't stop after Lo."

"Isa," Carlo whispered, reaching out for her, but she slapped his hand away and stormed out of the room. He followed her, and so did Alina.

Talia removed a piece of fluff from my hair. "Don't listen to Isa. You know she has a wicked tongue when she gets mad."

"Doesn't change the fact that she's a bitch." Lo shook her head.

I thought about hiding out in my room all day, but I wouldn't give Isabella the satisfaction of not having to see me.

Jack caught me before I went up the stairs. He ran a soft finger down my nose. "You okay?"

"Yes."

"Your sister seemed so sweet. Now I'm not so sure."

"If you fake everything around her, you'll be good. She doesn't do well with the truth." And she was probably pregnant. With her first two pregnancies, she'd go berserk over something as stupid as a dropped cookie. All things considered, I was surprised all my hair was left intact.

He didn't know what to say to that. Neither did I.

"Hey, you want to take a ride?" He stuck his hands in his pockets, turning toward the door. "We have time before we eat. And two kids—niece and nephew, I think—need batteries for games they got. Maybe we can find an open drugstore."

"I need to get dressed first. I'll be down in fifteen."

He gave me the biggest smile, heading into the kitchen while I went to get dressed. I hadn't driven since the accident. My car was totaled, and I wasn't ready to replace her yet. But I agreed to go with Jack for only one reason. I was going to ask him to drop by Elsa's place.

She was almost positive she wasn't going to make it home, and I didn't want her to be alone. And after the fight with Isabella, I was motivated to move out of Babbo's house. Elsa could use a roommate to help with the rent and expenses. It seemed like an ideal situation.

After we found a drugstore that was open and bought the batteries, we headed to Elsa's.

"You're quiet," Jack said.

I was. I was watching as Chicago passed by, lost to my thoughts.

"Seems like a nice time to reflect." I nodded to the window. The world was so cold and so quiet.

"That's usually what I do before the new year."

I turned to face him. "You reflect?"

He looked hurt. "I do have some depth."

"I didn't mean to imply otherwise, but I just didn't take you for that kind of man."

He shrugged. "I reflect, then drown the year in a bottle of something strong. Time for a new start. Out with the old, in with the new."

And...there it was. Probably the theme to his life, including women. It would take the right woman to knock him on his ass. It wasn't me. I didn't care enough to go near him with a sledgehammer.

"I actually know the perfect woman for you," I said.

"You?" He grinned.

"No, not me. A friend of mine. Penelope. She was runner up to me during the pageant. She went on to win Miss America and then Miss Universe after I dropped out."

After seeing Penelope recently, I realized she and Jack would make sense together. He'd fall in love with her the moment he saw her, and she was passionate about the things she believed in. She'd challenge him.

If it worked out, maybe I'd give Babbo a run for his money in the match-making department.

"Why did you quit? You had some real potential." He whistled. "Unbelievable, though. My wife's trying to set me up with another woman."

"I'm not your wife, Jack."

"You will be." His face was set. "Is it a secret why you dropped out?"

I sighed and gazed out the window again. He wasn't going to let it go. "I really didn't want to do it to begin with. Mamma and my sisters thought it would be fun. I didn't think I'd make it, but I did. It didn't seem fair that my heart wasn't in it, and I won."

"That's right. You love digging in mud and finding bones. The total opposite of beauty pageants and girly stuff."

I said nothing else because it was a waste of my time. If he couldn't make the distinction between what I did and playing in the mud and finding bones, he might as well see me as a dog.

We were silent for the rest of the drive. Even as Jack walked me to Elsa's door, we both seemed lost to our own thoughts. But I was wishing he would have waited for me in the car.

It didn't matter anyway. She wasn't home.

On the ride back to Babbo's, I sent her a text checking on her. She texted back that she was able to make it home and hoped I was having a nice time with my family.

Me: How do you feel about a roommate when you get back? Me.

It took her a few minutes to answer.

Elsa: Please don't take it personal, but I'm in limbo right now. I'm not even sure if I'm going to be staying.

I didn't take it to heart. I understood Elsa had her own issues, and she didn't need mine darkening hers. My family would be a non-stop problem. It would be a complication she didn't need in her life.

Still, I couldn't help the sigh that escaped my lips, fogging up the window and distorting my view of the world.

CHAPTER 26

ROMA

It had been two months since I'd heard from Felice. He'd cut off all contact, and it staggered me.

Every day I felt like I was making my way through an ice-packed haze. Life moved around me, but I felt frozen in time. I was clinging to the night in the hospital room, constantly wondering what had changed between us. Wondering why he hadn't even bothered to check on me, or even tell me what the fuck was going on.

I'm always with you.

The words felt like a lie, and I was owed more than that.

Elsa was my only connection to Felice's life through Cassio, so I asked her to speak to him, since I knew they were in touch about Adelasia.

Cassio agreed to talk to me in January, but it was February, and still no Cassio.

Hayden came out of the office and asked me how everyone was loving the special exhibit for Valentine's Day. It was all about the mating rituals of dinosaurs.

"A hit," I said, looking over the roses on my desk. Jack had sent me a huge bouquet of them that took up most of my desk. They were all in shades of red.

Jack. Even the thought of his name made me sigh in tiredness. I expected him every day because he'd been showing up ever since Christmas. The ride we took seemed to give him an unnatural amount of momentum. He'd meet me for lunch (*surprise!*) or come over to the house for dinner.

I'd shut Isabella down—we hadn't spoken since our fight—but Jack smoothly moved into her place.

Everyone was happy in the Corvo household but me.

Hayden brought up Lo's wedding in May. It was being held in Italy. She'd invited him, Elsa, and Kerry. Hayden couldn't attend, but he was pulling replacements from the staff to take our places while we were all gone.

"I'll be gone for her bachelorette party too," I said.

"That's right. Elsa mentioned it. Martha's Vineyard?"

Lo didn't want to go clubbing or anything like that. She just wanted a long weekend with the girls out of town. Our parents had a summer house there. She loved it and had put me in charge of the plans.

I nodded and Hayden said it wouldn't be a problem. He'd always been flexible with my schedule. I wasn't a major player here yet. I was basically Elsa's assistant, and she mostly had me doing things to make her life easier.

"Where is Elsa?" he asked.

"She went to check on the exhibit." She was leaving the office more and more after the accident. She'd say she needed a break, or she was going to check on something. Hayden was starting to notice.

"Does she seem a little...off to you lately?"

She did, but I didn't want to confide in Hayden about my worries for Elsa. I knew what was going on in her life, but maybe Hayden didn't. And I wasn't sure that was all it was, family issues. I just had a sinking feeling more was going on, but I couldn't put my finger on it. "I think she's just trying to recover from the wreck."

"So scary what happened to you two. It was probably someone texting and driving."

"Maybe." We never found out who was driving the first car that hit us.

"There's Elsa!" Hayden's voice was too high and excited, like he was trying to make her feel better by being happy to see her.

"Where's Roma?" she asked.

I lifted my head over the roses. Cassio stood next to Elsa. Adelasia was between them. I stood completely and fixed my black cardigan dress.

"Do you have time for a walk?" I asked Cassio.

"A short one." He sauntered over to my desk and plucked the card from the roses. He roared with laughter. "'Roses are red, violets are blue, I hope you don't think I'm stalking you,'" he read aloud.

That poem was hand-written on the card. Jack had put "*ha ha*" underneath and that he hoped to get to know which color rose was my favorite one day.

"Give me that." I snatched it out of Cassio's hand and stuck it back in the bouquet.

"I'll take Adelasia to see some of the new exhibits," Elsa offered. Adelasia's head bobbed up and down and she grabbed Elsa's hand.

Hayden's voice met our backs as we all walked out together. "I guess we don't work around here anymore..."

Elsa and Adelasia went in one direction. Cassio and I walked with no true destination. We ended up at the mating exhibit.

"Dinosaurs getting it on," he said, almost fascinated, hands tucked in his pockets. "That's something you don't think about every day."

"Unless you're studying it." I had. Their mating rituals fascinated me.

"Takes all the fun out of it. The romance. It's too scientific."

"We're talking about prehistoric creatures. They no longer exist."

"I wouldn't want someone studying my moves when I'm dead and gone. I'm too good to be studied. I'd be responsible for a baby boom."

He watched the screen for a second, listening to the proper English inflection describe a mating ritual. The voice went on about "scraping," and how meat-eating theropods used fancy footwork displays to attract mates, like the way some modern-day ground nesting birds do. The screen switched to the T-rex and how they used visual and vocal sounds.

"Just think," he almost muttered to himself. "We go extinct, what will some future species think are our mating rituals today? Poles and a strip club? Computers with porn? That digital movie channel and chill? *Roses are red, violets are blue, I hope you don't think I'm stalking you.*

"Humans have gone backward. What a bunch of lazy chumps the men in this world have become when it comes to romance. I bet scraping was a real romantic thing to do. This thing says some of the marks were found today. They must have really dug those talons in. And vocals? I bet that T-rex crooned like fucking Dino Sinatra." He gave a roar that went up and down an octave.

"What's going on, Cassio?"

It took him a second to pull himself away from the screen, and then he looked me in the eye. "You know it's for the best."

"That's not what I asked."

"The accident." At his words, his face turned cold and hard. He was one of the first ones on the scene, and I could still remember him talking in my ear, telling me help was on the way and we were going to be okay. "It was no accident."

"I don't understand."

"Just what I said. It was a warning to John." He lifted his hands. Started backing away. "That's all I'm gonna say. Forget I even said it."

How could I forget when his words punched me in the gut? Only three people would want to send a warning to Felice And one of them was my father.

The day dragged after Cassio left. I couldn't stop replaying his words over and over. I kept wondering if me seeing Felice was enough of an insult to Emanuele Corvo that he risked his daughter and her friend to send a warning. But it was hard to believe. Especially after he started sobbing in my hospital room, kissing my hand.

Was it all an act?

Babbo wasn't a crier, though. He had this extremely medical way to assess situations, especially when it came to the sick.

What Corinna had told me about him, how he had denied Sal Maggio care, had thrown me for a loop too. My father was a quiet man, and he liked things a certain way in his family, but I'd always been told what a caring physician he was. I was told he'd go above and beyond for his patient's care. Some of his patients even called him an advocate.

This was all not adding up to me. And why hadn't Felice mentioned the situation between Sal and Babbo? Did he think I wouldn't believe him? Did he assume I'd defend my father because he was my father?

There had to be some explanation as to why Babbo did what he did. But I wasn't going to get answers from Babbo. I already knew that. And what would I say? How would I even start the conversation?

Felice had disappeared on me and had never told me what happened in the first place.

It had only been an hour since the last time I checked the clock. I thought about going home, but what would I do there? It was just so hard to concentrate when my mind constantly tried to figure out what was going on.

Hayden came out of his office. "How about we order in? My treat."

Elsa didn't say anything, and Hayden knocked on her desk, asking if anybody was home.

"Hah?" She looked up at him.

He repeated himself, and we all decided on a place to order. Lunch was nice, but it seemed like we were all distracted and finding it hard to focus. The day seemed to go by faster after lunch, and I realized I didn't want to go home. I was dreading it.

I texted Lo to see if she wanted to do dinner, but she had plans with Sandro. She invited me along, but I didn't want to be the third wheel. Kerry had a date, and I had no clue what was going on with Elsa.

She asked me if I was ready to go when it was time. I'd been driving Mamma's SUV, but Talia had borrowed it because they bought a new house, and she wanted a bigger vehicle to cart boxes. That morning, Talia had dropped me off, and Elsa offered to take me home. She said she was heading that way anyway.

We walked out of the office together, then Elsa slowed to grab her keys out of her purse. I stopped so abruptly that Elsa ran into my back. She caught my shoulders before I toppled over. A brand-new Fiat 500 Sport was parked next to Elsa's car. It was the same color as Felicia, and the windows were tinted. I could see a dinosaur on the dash, though.

I turned to Elsa. She threw a set of keys at me, then lifted her hands. "Cassio told me to give them to you. You want me to wait?"

"No," I said. "I'll be fine."

I got in the new Fiat. The new car smell was strong, but I smelled my carnivore underneath it. I even had to adjust the seat to accommodate my shorter legs. There was another plush dinosaur purse on the passenger side, this one with a rose in its mouth. A card was tucked inside:

Dino,

This car can't be traced. It was paid for in cash, but it belongs to you. You earned it with your finesse, even if you sting like a bee. Make sure you sign all the legal papers in the glove box.

I'm still with you.

Felice

I tucked the note back inside and pulled out of the spot.

I slammed on the brakes.

A moment of panic seized me. Felice had been right. The car was a matchbox. But I thought about what Cassio had said. *The accident? It was no accident.* It had been planned. Carried out as a warning. No one had tried to hurt me since. But I was dying a little every day. And so, I hit the gas and got over the fear, because another one had pushed it out of the way.

This one made my heart stop cold.

I might never see Felice Maggio again.

CHAPTER 27

ROMA

"I still get *Jaws* vibes whenever we come to the beach here."

I adjusted my oversized, square vintage sunglasses and turned to face Lo. We'd finally made it through winter in Chicago and to Martha's Vineyard for her bachelorette party. Our parents' summer house was in Edgartown. And I had to agree, it still gave me *Jaws* vibes too.

"Want to get drunk, shut the lights out in the pool tonight, and watch the movie while we swim?" Talia wiggled her eyebrows.

"Raincheck," Lo said, going back to her hair magazine.

"If I have to wear this—" Talia motioned to her bathing suit "—I want to have some fun."

Lo wore a white bathing suit that said in pink letters, "Wife of The Party." The rest of us had pink ones with white letters that said, "The Party."

"Don't blame me," Lo said. "Y picked them out."

"And you love it." Talia threw a piece of popcorn at Lo's head. She caught it with her mouth. "I do! It's Gucci!"

Lo was glowing, and it wasn't just because we were on the beach. Sandro had lit something in her not even a cold, hard wind could snuff out. It was deep inside of her heart, and she was guarding it. Her happiness made the sun on my face feel warmer.

Isabella and Alina walked up. They threw shade over us with their big sunhats.

"We're hungry," Isabella said. "Everyone ready to take the bikes back and grab a bite to eat? Lexi and Eve are heading toward the bikes now."

Alexius "Lexi" Liu and Eve Garcia were Lo's friends from beauty school. Lo was opening salons in Chicago and Rome, where she planned to split her time. Lexi and Eve were going to help run them both.

"I'm starving." Talia stood, knocking sand from her legs. She tied a hot-pink sarong around her waist and slipped on matching flip-flops. She grabbed her bag and stood next to Isabella and Alina, waiting for us to move.

"Go ahead of us and grab a table somewhere," Lo said. "Text us where. I need to pack my things up, and so does Y."

They went ahead of us.

Lo hit the brim of her floppy sunhat out of her eyes. "Still no word?"

I looked down at my leg and picked at a piece of sand. "No."

I'd confided in Lo about everything, even the accident that was no accident. We both went back and forth between disbelief and wondering if Alfonso was behind it, but her wedding was so close. I didn't want to ruin this time for her. We'd occasionally bring it up, but since Felice was out of the picture, there was nothing else to talk about.

"Jack?"

I sighed and stood, slipping on my cut-off jean shorts and flip-flops. I started packing up my things, and Lo started doing the same. We headed toward where we'd left our bikes.

"I can't marry him, Lo," I whispered. "I just don't know how to break free from Babbo's expectations without breaking...completely."

She nodded. She understood what I meant. Giving up my only parent wasn't going to be easy.

"Jack's so much like John, and he seems to care for you, but he's a...another version of John. Not the same vibe at all."

I'd been playing my part. Showing some interest in Jack, but not to the degree he wanted. He thought it was going to take time, and after we were married, we had our whole lives to fall in love. But I'd never love him. And if someone was ruthless enough to send a warning to Felice the way they had... If I didn't play my part, what would happen next? Would they kill Felice?

"You okay?" Lo asked.

I shrugged. "Remember the conversation we had at the diner after going to Jupitar? You were right. It's harder to dream and lose than not to dream at all. If Felice had never come into my life, I wouldn't know what I was missing."

"Do you love him, Y?"

"Yes," I whispered. But love felt like a simple term for what I felt. It was what Felice had said. Plato.

She grabbed my hand and squeezed. She knew I was in an impossible situation. She had been in it before, but it had been wrong. Sandro was right for her. But that didn't make me believe Jack was the one for me. My heart had decided on Felice before I even had a say.

Probably to change the subject, Lo asked about Elsa. She'd declined the invite to the bachelorette getaway, claiming she couldn't leave the museum, *so much to do,* though she was going to be covered. I really had no clue what was going on with her lately.

Lo's phone pinged, and she started laughing. She showed me a picture of Sandro in his art studio, shirt off, raggedy old jeans on, barefoot, sticking his tongue at her. Underneath the picture was a text with how many days until the wedding. He was counting down. She sent him a selfie and drifted after. She was almost flighty with happiness. Was she in love with him already?

Talia texted the name of the restaurant as we got to our bikes. Lexi and Eve were waiting for us. They chatted with Lo about the new salons as we headed toward the restaurant. I fell back some. I couldn't escape the feeling I was being watched. I could feel eyes on me.

I stopped and looked around, but no one on the street was paying attention to me.

Lexi waved me forward. I parked my bike and told them to go in ahead of me. I wanted to find my lip gloss in my bag. After they disappeared, I dug my phone out and checked it. I had a text and selfie from Jack. Either Babbo or Isabella had given him my number. I studied his face, so like Felice's, and wondered how fate could have gotten it so twisted.

I was trapped in a nightmare. The car was flipping, and I was screaming for Felice. Even though his name was coming out, it felt like I was being strangled while trying to cry. Sort of like limbs made of lead in a dream. He never came for me.

"Roma!"

The dream was slow to fade, but when it did, Lo was shaking me awake.

"A-*l-l-l*-right. I'm a-*w-w*-wake."

"Are you okay?" She stopped shaking me.

"Yeah." I sat up. "Just a bad dream."

"About the attack?"

"No. About the car—" Not accident. "Impaling."

She looked at the open door, then rushed out, "I still get them sometimes about the attack. It's always the moment Ben punched me in the eye. Then he started to strangle me."

"I'm so sorry, Lo," I whispered.

"Me too, about everything."

Everything covered a lot of ground. We both knew it. She took a seat on the edge of the bed and studied my face.

"You look tired. You want to stay in tonight?"

After we got back from lunch, I decided to take a nap. We'd been going nonstop, and we'd been eating and drinking the same.

"No. The past couple of days just caught up to me." I smiled at her. "Besides, this is our last night before we're on a plane to Italy and you're a married woman. We *have* to do this. Let's get ready."

About two hours later, we piled into Babbo's Land Rover and headed toward a reservation-only French restaurant. We had all decided to get dressed up. I wore a hot-pink sleeveless dress that was ruched at the waist, had a thigh-high slit, and fell to my ankles. I paired it with a pair of open silver heels.

Lo's sequined silver dress sparkled against the lights, her veil and sash whipping in the wind.

"I'm getting married!" she shouted. "Here comes the bride... all dressed in white!"

A couple people started clapping and hooting. We all started laughing. The wine had started before we left. Since Isabella was pregnant, she was the designated driver. We must have consumed bottles of wine at dinner. The place didn't have vegetarian options, so I opted for crab cakes. They practically melted in my mouth.

We headed to a dive bar in Oak Bluffs, only about fifteen minutes from Edgartown, after dinner. Lexi popped a champagne top out the window, and we all toasted. We downed the entire bottle while still in the car. By the time we got to the bar, we were all swaying into each other.

We were way overdressed, but like Elsa was known to say, strike 'em down.

The place was packed. The live band already had the crowd dancing. Drinks flowed, and almost everyone was on the dance floor. I stood at the bar, trying not to laugh at Isabella sticking her ball of a stomach out and back. Alina was doing hand movements around it.

A hand slipped around my waist. I stiffened for a second before I stepped away from him and turned.

"Jack?"

"That drunk already?" He grinned.

"Possibly."

He laughed, and his teeth were shocking white in the dark bar. He wasn't shaving and was growing his scruff out some. It made my stomach uneasy. It reminded me so much of Felice. Except Jack's style was all wrong. It was more on the preppy side. That aside, he could be Felice's son.

The thought really didn't sit right in my stomach.

"Don't worry," he said, holding his hands up. "I just stopped by to tell you my dad is flying us all to Italy in the private plane tomorrow."

I nodded. "How do you always find me?"

He shrugged. "I have a sixth sense when it comes to you."

"Or a snitch," I muttered.

He laughed again. "Isabella emailed a copy of the itinerary you put together to all the husbands. I responded and told her I'd be arriving tonight. We're all going to fly to Italy together." He leaned in close and whispered in my ear, "You're still the most beautiful woman I've ever seen."

He left with his three-man crew in tow.

I was having fun until Jack showed up and reminded me why I hadn't been. He was knocking on my mental door while I was trying to forget. Elsa was right. It sucked.

"Ohhhh nooo." Lo danced up to me. She was like a disco ball, she was so lit up, all her beautiful colors on display. "I am the ruler of this trip, and I have banned getting pouty on this night." She waved her beer at me and made a *poof* noise. She set the drink down, then slowly started to bring her hands up.

"Don't!" I said, trying to step away from her, but Lexi, Eve, and Talia pushed against my back. I was trying not to laugh, either, but it was impossible. "Put those things away, Lo!"

Lo made her fingers into guns and was doing a dance with them. She was making a ridiculous duck face and then pointed her guns at me.

"*Bang!* You're it. That's right. Come dance with sissy!"

Next thing I knew, we were all doing the gun dance and

singing. We were dancing around each other one second, and the next, I somehow got lost in the crowd. A man with body odor that smelled like Limburger cheese wrapped his arms around me and yanked me into his front.

"Get off!" I tried to remove his fingers, but they were like claws.

The night of the attack came back to me, and I planned on fighting as hard as I did then. But I remembered how strong Curly Hair was. I was no match for him.

A second later, Handsy Guy released his hold. I turned around and came face to chest with Felice.

Handsy Guy was down on the floor, everyone dancing around him. I had no idea what had happened, but he was out.

Felice seized my hand, keeping it behind his back as he navigated us through the crowd. He stepped on the guy's face as we left.

Once we were out of the bar and down the street some, I dug my heels in. He stopped and turned to me. I tried to extract my hand from his, but he held it in a grip that stopped blood flow.

His green eyes were crazed above a sea of black stubble. He looked almost gaunt under the streetlights. His black T-shirt hugged his chest but was loose around his waist. His jeans hung some but were not baggy. When he ran a hand through his hair, his stomach muscles tensed, and I could see the deep V imprint of his hips.

"Finally graced me with your presence, Carnivore," I said. "How nice of you. I know I should feel honored, but all I can feel is pissed."

I was probably slurring, but my brain couldn't compute if I was. I'd drunk too much, and the shock of seeing Felice had me staggering.

Being this close to me again seemed to make him stumble too.

Right into me.

Our bodies collided, my palms smacked against his chest, and we hit the building behind us. His mouth crashed against mine, and neither of us could resist the thirst. We both drank until we were drunk off each other. It was a high like no other.

Our lips made a violent noise when we parted, but I refused to let him go. I sank my claws in, and he wrapped an arm around my waist, leading me to a dark, fast car parked at the curb. He hit a button on the key fob, it started, and the lights turned on by themselves.

The interior flooded my nose with the intensity of...him. I cracked the window and the Atlantic rushed in, but it did nothing to cleanse his scent.

I sent a private text to Lo while Felice walked over to the driver's side.

Me: Please cover for me.

She didn't text me back until Felice had pulled off.

Lo: I saw you leave with Jack. Got it.

She sent a winking emoji.

We said nothing to each other for the fifteen-minute drive back to Babbo's house in Edgartown. Felice parked down the street.

He opened my door for me, and we walked up to the house together. I got the key out, and he opened that door for me too.

As soon as we were in my room, he kicked the door shut behind him, locked it, and flung me on the bed. I bounced and reached for him as he climbed on top of me. His mouth impaled mine, his tongue deep, as he slid his hand down my leg, removing the heels. His hand came back up and removed my underwear.

I moaned and pushed into his touch when he started to stroke me between the legs. I was being so loud, it was echoing inside of my brain.

He was here and so solid underneath my hands. So real.

He broke the kiss and grabbed his shirt by the collar, yanking it over his head. His hair went in all different directions. Wild. But nowhere near as feral as his eyes. They belonged to a hunter. A carnivore.

"Put your hands on me, Roma," he ordered, his voice husky.

I did, running them up and down his chest, lightly clawing him. He closed his eyes and seemed to melt into my touch. Until his mouth was on mine again. My lip burned, and he sucked the split, then licked the blood. His tongue traced the shape of my mouth before I touched his with mine.

He flipped over to his back, setting me on top of him. He lifted the dress and flung it to the floor. It had a built-in bra, so I was naked. I set my hands against his chest, lifting some. He kicked his boots and socks off, then slid his jeans and boxers off. I came down slowly, and when his dick slid between my legs, we both groaned.

I started moving faster, harder.

He made a noise that echoed the starved hunter, right before he takes his first bite.

My breath came out in a *whoosh* when he flipped me on my back, parted my legs, and positioned himself at my entrance.

"I'll sign my vow in blood to you," I whispered. "Right now."

I could see the indecision in his eyes. He wasn't a man used to losing control. He was on the verge of snapping. I could feel the tension in his muscles, trembling like a wild animal about to escape his restraints.

"You will be my wife first," he said in Italian.

"Does that mean you won't disappear on me again?"

He slid a hand down my face. "No one is moving me out of your life, my little herbivore. Not again."

My little herbivore. My heart gave a tender sigh that escaped my mouth.

I nodded and tilted my head into his palm. He kissed my mouth, my face, down my chin to my neck, until he reached my thighs.

He licked them up and down, and when he hit my center, I started to wantonly rub myself against his face. The vibration of his groan made me come around him in a violent spasm. I felt a surge of heat all over. Like he'd lit my skin on fire in the darkness.

He didn't give me time to catch my breath. He was kissing me again. He growled into my mouth when I reached down and stroked his dick. He sat up, taking me with him, and set his legs over the edge of the bed. He put me between them.

"Put my cock in your mouth, my beautiful girl."

I licked my lips, looked up at him, and did. He was engorged and felt like he was growing harder in my mouth. The feel and taste of him, hot and salty, made me moan.

He caressed my head, hissing out a breath, watching me. "Fuck. That sweet, beautiful mouth. Suck me." He groaned when I moved up and down, swirling my tongue over the tip.

He pulsed his hips up and my eyes started to water, but his reaction to what I was doing to him was only encouraging me. I started moving faster, sucking harder, swirling my tongue. His grip on my head held me in place.

"Your mouth feels this good. That sweet pussy." He started to lose control, like he was imagining fucking me.

My legs were spread some, and I was throbbing, aching.

"You feel it. You're so fucking wet. You need me to fuck you. Fill you up until I can't go any deeper."

"*Mmmm*," I let out a long, low, strangled moan.

"Fuck," he growled out. "Fuck."

Our stares were locked. The intensity in his eyes had turned into green fire. The connection between us seemed to set him off even harder. I was barely keeping up with how fast and hard he was moving. He groaned and went to pull out, but I kept going, holding his stare.

He lost all control and exploded.

I licked my lips, and a small grin came to my face.

His eyes were lowered, but his face was somewhat narrowed. "You're fucking wicked for a woman who doesn't crave blood."

I did crave something. The look in his green eyes. Because those intense looks and stares were mine. There were depths and places inside of him that he only allowed me to access.

The rest of the world was locked out.

Chapter 28

Roma

I'd fallen into the arms of ecstasy and let it carry me away to sleep. A loud bang, however long after, ripped me out of it and made my entire body jump like it'd been shot.

My eyes flew open, my hand automatically grabbing for the warm body next to mine. Felice squeezed my hand. He pointed at my door.

"Y," Lo spoke to it. "You in there?"

"Yeah." My voice was hoarse, and I had to clear my throat.

Laughter came from the other side.

"Get some sleep! We're leaving tomorrow."

"I know," I muttered.

The house went mostly silent after that. And the truth punched me in the face. Felice was in my father's house with all my sisters. What the hell were we going to do in the morning?

"Relax." He moved his mouth softly over my temple. "I'll be gone before anyone sees me."

I looked at my window.

"No," he said, reading my mind.

I sighed and held on to him tighter. The *"I'll be gone"* part of his answer caught up to my mind. "When are you leaving?"

"In an hour or so."

"I don't want you to."

Our eyes met in the darkness.

"You ready for what comes next if I don't?"

I looked away from him. "No. It'll be war. I can't do that to Lo right now. It wouldn't be fair to her."

He sighed. "I'm not fucking used to this."

"To what?"

"Waiting for what's mine, now that I have it again." He set my hand over his heart. "You break me."

"You break me too. You stopped talking to me and coming around because someone tried to hurt me. The accident that wasn't an accident at all."

He squeezed me to him so hard it was hard to breathe. It always felt like he was fusing us together.

"Was it—" I had to take a deep breath. "Was it Babbo? Alfonso? Jack?"

He met my eyes. "Tommaso."

I lifted some, leaning on my elbow. "Your boss?"

He nodded. "Jack had texted Alfonso at the museum's party. He told his old man I'd showed up. When Emanuele called Tommaso, he told him he wanted me stopped. No one tells Tommaso to do anything. You ask him, or he gets creative."

"He tried to kill me."

"No. The delivery truck wasn't supposed to be part of the deal. The first car was the warning."

"How can you direct the outcome of a car accident, Felice?"

"You can't, but he doesn't give a fuck. In his mind, he did as Emanuele told him to. He didn't get a specific order, so he sent the message in a way he knew would get through to me and Emanuele. We brought the problem to his door. He fixed it on both sides."

"His threat worked. You stayed away from me."

"You wanted me to ignore it?"

I didn't say anything.

He took my chin in his hand. "I'm not worth your life, Roma."

"Am I worth yours?"

"We're talking about you, not me."

"What if I cut you off? What would you do? Your—" I felt weightless and then breathless as he flipped me over and took my wrists in his hands, pinning them to each side of my head.

"You fucking leave me..." he rolled his teeth over his lip. "I've tasted your blood, and it's in my system." He came down and licked the split on my lip. "I'll find you."

"Your absence in my life felt like a painful wound that refused to heal, Felice. You were ripped from *me* again. Remember Plato. It takes two to complete the circle. I feel the same way you do if you leave me. I can't be whole unless we're together. I can still function, but only at half capacity."

"Fuck," he said, releasing my wrists. He turned on his back and stared at the ceiling again. "I've always been told I was heartless. Makes sense now. The entire thing went to your half."

I started laughing. He set a hand over my mouth, but he was grinning. I bit him and his eyes lowered before he started to kiss me.

"What are we going to do, Felice?" I breathed out when I could catch my breath.

"We're going to Italy," he said. "Everything after is up in the air."

"You're going to Italy?"

He tucked a piece of hair behind my ear. "I have business to take care of."

"Business," I murmured. I stared at his heartbreakingly gorgeous face, wondering how many secrets he was keeping from me, and would always keep from me. I knew it was the nature of his business, but I wanted in on his life. "You didn't tell me Babbo denied Sal care."

"What goes on between me and Corvo is between us." His

tone was final, and I knew his words were too. As final as any last words spoken.

"Well then," I whispered.

He chuckled, but it barely had any breath to it. "You drank a lot of wine tonight."

"It's not the wine. This all feels like a dream. You're here."

I remembered Lo after Sandro had sent her the text. She was delirious with happiness. Even the thought of Felice got me that way. The thought of him leaving made me feel torn in half.

He pulled me to him so hard, I gasped. "I am always with you," he said in Italian, kissing my face.

"Didn't feel like it." I yawned. "When you were gone, you were gone."

"Sleep," he whispered in Italian, moving his lips over my temple.

A few seconds later, I couldn't keep my eyes open. I fell asleep in his arms. What seemed like seconds later, but was probably hours, he dislodged himself from my hold and got dressed.

"Will I see you in Italy soon?" I whispered.

He kissed me slowly and tamed my hair down. "*Sì*." He went to stand by the door, watching me.

"What?"

He did the dance we'd been doing at the bar earlier. "I'm always with you, Roma."

"In Edgartown? While I was biking to the restaurant?"

"The entire time."

A smile I had no control over came to my face. It was probably goofy as shit. He left me like that.

I listened for any noises in the house, like screeching from Isabella or a tackle from Talia, but the house was silent. A few minutes later, a phone chimed. It was a different sounding alert than my usual. A phone sat on the bedside table. The one he'd given me before.

He'd sent me a text:

My Carnivore: I'm out.

I had weeks—no, months—full of text messages from him. He'd sent me texts every day we were apart. He'd comment on my clothes (he loved me in red) or how being apart from me felt like he was being severed in half again. He sent me Plato quotes or snippets of poems. I laughed at all the funny dinosaur memes and jokes.

Me: I'm in. For the rest of my life.

I couldn't stop yawning. The night had caught up to me, and I was ready to be on the plane to Italy already. Though I was a little on edge. What if Isabella brought up me leaving with Jack last night in front of Jack? What could I say? I decided to take an Uber home and Lo got it wrong?

We were waiting at the private airport, getting ready to board the plane. Isabella kept looking between us, a smile on her face. Jack was texting someone and laughing with his friends.

He looked up at the noise my roller carrier made when it went flying sideways. A man wearing an official-looking windbreaker hustling to get inside almost knocked it over. A few seconds later, a bunch of FBI agents stormed through the airport, drug-sniffing dogs with them. The head agent showed the woman behind the desk his badge, and she went to get whoever was in charge.

Our party moved closer together, watching the drama unfold.

"What the hell is going on?" Lo said.

"Doesn't seem good," Alina said.

"*Wow.* You're so observant, Lina," Talia said, sarcastically. She laughed at the look Alina gave her.

Isabella grabbed her son before he could tap one of the agents on the leg. Carlo hauled him up and set him over his shoulder, holding their daughter in place by her head.

"That's our plane," Jack said, adjusting his carry on over his shoulder. "Let's get out of here."

We all followed him out, but we were stopped by an agent. We couldn't board. The plane was being grounded indefinitely.

"What?" Jack roared. "You can't ground us. Do you know who this plane belongs to?"

"I do," the agent said. "And it doesn't matter if it belongs to a king, it's not going anywhere."

Jack called Alfonso. He'd left with Babbo two days before. A heated discussion ensued. Jack was almost wild with anger.

"Go talk to him." Isabella nudged me. "Maybe you can calm him down."

I didn't think so, because I had no idea what was going on, but I decided to give it a try when he ended the call. He was glaring at the agents guarding the steps to the plane and the ones who were boarding.

"Everything okay?" I asked.

"What do you think?" he snapped.

"I was just asking." I held my hands up.

"Try asking a question that's not a waste of oxygen next time."

The only thing wasted was my breath and time on this asshole. Talia felt differently.

"Who the hell do you think you're talking to?" She rushed over, her carry-on roller flying behind her. "You're not going to talk to my sister like that."

"Shit," Joseph said, grabbing her by the shoulder before she got in Jack's face.

"What's going on, Jack?" Isabella asked, but I could tell she was surprised by how he'd spoken to me. Her tone had turned hard.

"Drugs. Apparently, the captain was transporting them. Or so they say." He waved a hand toward the plane, even though I knew he meant the agents. "This has John Maggio written all fucking over it. Do you see what he's doing, Roma? How he's coming between us?"

He went to take a step toward me, but Joseph stepped in

front of him. Jack was almost unhinged. It was like he was having an adult-sized temper tantrum.

"I know you're pissed about the plane, but take it someplace else." Joseph stood like a wall in front of him.

Jack ran a hand through his hair, cut around us, then stormed back into the building. His friends followed.

"What are we going to do now?" Lo asked.

"Did you call and cancel our commercial tickets, Y?" Alina asked.

I shook my head. "Jack sprang the private plane on us at the last minute. I forgot."

"Sweet!" Lo hauled ass toward the building. "Everything's going to be Gucci!"

"We'll have to rush to make it," Isabella said. "Let's go."

Five hours later, Lo, Talia, Joseph, Lexi, Eve, and I boarded a plane at John F. Kennedy International Airport. Everyone else took the next flight out.

It was a new airline, and it had fancy first-class seats.

"Seats" were understating it by miles, though. More like private cubbies complete with recliners, lamps, and privacy curtains. I couldn't wait to plug my ears with music and go to sleep. Waking up in Italy always felt like a gift to me. It felt like coming home.

With Felice there, I might never leave.

I got comfortable, getting all my stuff in order. I couldn't fall asleep before takeoff like Lo could, but I was preparing to knock out soon.

Take off went smoothly. I placed an order for a drink and then took out the phone Felice had given me, going through all the texts again.

"*Mi scusi,*" a familiar voice said to the stewardess. It came from the cubby across from mine. The man ordered red wine.

The stewardess fixed her hair, even though not a strand was out of place, and batted her long lashes at him. "Of course, sir."

My mouth snapped shut when he met my eyes.

"Miss Corvo." He tipped his hat to me. He was dressed to the nines in a suit. Just like an old-time gangster.

Who the hell dressed like that on a flight anymore?

Felice Maggio, that's who.

When the attractive stewardess came back with his drink, she almost purred, "Mr. Maggio." She bent over, setting his drink down, offering him a glimpse of her cleavage, but his eyes had never left mine. She left without another word.

"Carnivore," I finally got out. "I guess it was a coincidence we ended up on the same flight."

His eyes were intense on mine. "If we go down, we go down together." Then the heat seemed to melt some, and his grin came slow. "Your cubby or mine?"

CHAPTER 29

FELICE

I let my presence be known in Italy, so it was no surprise when the call came through. I'd been waiting on it.

"No," I said. "Not at your home."

Emanuele Corvo wasn't accustomed to the word no. But I wasn't indebted to him. I made my own rules. And I refused to meet Emanuele in his home, allowing him to insult me by keeping me locked in his office, like an ugly animal hidden behind his bars.

"Where do you suggest then?"

I gave him the name of a restaurant in Florence, not too far from both of us. Lolita's wedding was being held at a *castello* in the hills. I wasn't staying too far from them.

He gave me a time and hung up.

I'd picked the place, a *trattoria,* and he'd set the time. If that allowed him to take some of the control back, so be it.

"Should I drive, boss?"

I nodded to Celso, then told him to be ready in an hour. I took a shower, cleaned up my face some with a razor, and then dressed in a dark suit. Celso had the car waiting when I stepped outside. Fredo sat next to him, riding shotgun. I slid into the back seat.

Cassio texted me on the ride. He kept me updated on things

in Chicago while I was gone. Tommaso thought it was a good idea that I disappeared for a while when I'd suggested it. He encouraged me to find a wife to forget about Corvo's daughter. "Plenty of fish in the Mediterranean Sea," he'd said.

He had no idea a different Corvo daughter was getting married the same week I'd decided to disappear in Italy. After what Tommaso had done to Roma, Emanuele refused to involve him in our issue. He knew he'd come close to having his daughter killed. He wanted me punished, not Roma.

I made sure Tommaso was on the same page, as far as forgetting about my relationship with Roma, before I entered Roma's life again. Tommaso never forgot, but the issue between me and Emanuele was nothing but plastic underneath his ass while he tried to watch television. He didn't want to be bothered with it.

This issue had nothing to do with Tommaso or our business, so Emanuele had no right to involve him in the first place. Now that Emanuele regretted his decision, Tommaso was blissfully ignorant to my real reason for coming to Italy.

To bring the woman who would be my wife back to Chicago with me.

My presence in Roma's life made Alfonso and Baby Boy Jack nervous. They were putting pressure on Emanuele to stop me.

Emanuele was feeling enough pressure on his own. Never in a million years could he have foreseen this: someone like me being his son-in-law, never mind his daughter marrying a man he didn't choose for her. He'd almost made it with all his daughters going through with the arrangements he'd negotiated. Roma would always be the one who got away from the tradition.

Celso slowed the car as we approached the *trattoria*.

It was in the Piazza del Carmine in the heart of the Florentine Oltrarno. The district was known for its trendy bars and artisan shops. Roma had been frequenting the area with the wedding party. She'd gone to the Palazzo Pitti earlier and was having dinner with Elsa.

The area was too trendy for me. I enjoyed eating at places that looked questionable but had the most authentic food. But I'd be close to wherever she was.

People moved in streams in front of and around us. The place was packed. Maybe the hype about the Florentine steak would prove to be true. I was still skeptical, though.

"Expecting more company, boss?" Fredo stared out the window.

Alfonso and Jack were on one side of Corvo. Dr. Tito Sala was on the other. Dr. Sala was a physician to the Fausti family. They were like royalty in Italy. Their roots spanned from North to South. They claimed they were Italy. And with Alfonso and Jack in tow, the meeting place seemed right.

Palazzo Pitti was a testament to the riches of the Medici family. Alfonso and Jack thought they were the modern-day fucking thing.

"Yeah," I said. "I expected them."

There was no way Alfonso and Jack were going to skirt out on this meeting. Alfonso might even threaten me with a steak knife before the meeting was over. Then I'd be sticking it in his heart. As for Dr. Sala, he was known to play peacemaker between warring families. He was also known as a matchmaker, even better than Corvo.

I'd met Dr. Sala a time or two, but never really had a chance to talk to him. He visited Tommaso every now and then.

Fredo opened my door for me and came in with me while Celso went to park. I told him to wait at the bar. The smell of an open flame and meat grilling on it made my mouth water. It'd been a while since I'd last eaten.

My party was already seated outside. The Basilica of Santa Maria del Carmine and the Brancacci Chapel could be seen from the grounds. When I approached the table, the only man to stand and shake my hand was Dr. Sala. I introduced myself to him again, but he remembered me.

"I am still all here." He pointed to his temple, grinning a little.

"Rarely do I forget a face or a name. Even at my age. Have a seat, Felice." He motioned to the seat next to him.

Dr. Sala sat at the head of the table. Emanuele sat next to him on the other side and across from me. Alfonso sat next to Emanuele. Jack next to Alfonso. Guess my uncle didn't feel comfortable being that close to me.

Alfonso went to start the meeting, opening his mouth to speak, but Dr. Sala made a motion with his hand.

"Let us look over the menu first, Alfonso. I am hungry. Plenty of time to talk after we order. But I will be staying for dinner no matter what happens. It is too beautiful of a night and a view to let it go to waste over a difference of opinions."

Alfonso made a disagreeable noise in his throat. Jack huffed and crossed his arms. Emanuele stared at me but looked away when he knew I wouldn't be looking away first.

The server came and took our orders. Dr. Sala and I both ordered the Florentine steak. I grinned, though, when I noticed they had a vegetarian menu. My little herbivore would love this place. The rest of the men all ordered strong drinks and nothing else.

"Unlike Tito, I'm not going to prolong this meeting," Alfonso said. "So, I'm just going to cut to the chase. Stay away from Roma Corvo."

"Or what?"

We all got quiet as our drinks were delivered. Once the server left, Alfonso took a deep gulp of his and slammed the glass down.

"Or it's going to be war," Jack said, puffing his chest out.

"Between whom?" I swirled my red wine around the glass.

"Me and you, that's *whom*." Jack motioned between us.

"Roses are red, violets are blue...I guess it'll be a war between me and you." I grinned before I took a drink.

Jack shot up out of his seat like his asshole had been shocked. He went to point at me, but Alfonso squeezed his hand and brought him down to the chair before he lost the finger. "Sit," he ordered.

"This is bullshit," Jack said. "He only wants her because she's mine."

I pulled my sleeve up some, looking at the time. "If Jackie boy wants to throw a tantrum, let him do it at home. Or on a stage. I'm not wasting my time on schoolboy theatrics."

"Where did you get that watch?" Alfonso chucked his chin toward it.

Alfonso's eyes had widened, then narrowed when he noticed it. It was the one Jack had put up as a stake in our rooftop game. Alfonso recognized it.

I looked at Jack. "You didn't tell him?" I ticked my mouth.

"How'd he get Pop's watch, Jack?"

"He won it in a game."

Alfonso looked like he wanted to slap him. "What did I tell you about gambling with men like him? Men who manipulate the rules?"

"Manipulate the rules." I leaned back so my food could be placed down. "It was a game of curling on a rooftop. Simple as that."

"What will it take for you to go away, John?" Alfonso turned to me. His cheeks were as red as my glass of wine. "Name your price."

"You can't afford it."

"I can afford anything."

"Not this."

"I learned the rules of these manipulative games you play from Sal. I refuse to play them because there is no winning for no-bullshit men like me. So cut to the fucking chase already, if you can manage it."

"You can't afford this because it doesn't have a price."

Alfonso was about to explode, but Emanuele lifted his hand, staring at my face. "He's talking about Roma."

I cut into my steak, salivating when the blood drained from the meat. I hacked a piece off and let the flavors flood my mouth, the red wine upping the taste. "I am talking about Roma." I wiped my mouth on a napkin. "So this has nothing to do with money, which means you've already lost."

Alfonso didn't know how to respond to that. His face reminded me of Jack's when I'd told him I didn't have to manipulate the rules because I made them.

"Emanuele." Alfonso turned to him. "We have an agreement."

"Yes," Emanuele said. "We do. You and Jack go get the car. I'll meet you out front in a few minutes."

That left the three of us.

Dr. Sala had been quiet the entire time, cutting his steak into small pieces, enjoying each bite. He was almost oblivious to the tension coming from the other side of the table. He was fucking serious when he said he meant to enjoy his meal and the view, but I knew he was absorbing every word of our conversation.

He seemed like a thoughtful man—a man not easily crossed, even if he was as slight as a bird.

Some of the most ruthless motherfuckers I'd ever met were men who looked like they gave quarters to kids in the neighborhood to buy candy back in the day.

"What made you interested in my daughter?" Corvo asked.

The question took me off guard, but I hid it well. Especially since I knew it wasn't sincere. "I want her." I gave him a simple answer to a much more complicated equation.

"You want her," he almost mused. "I will have a talk with her about this—what you *want* her for."

"We all have secrets, don't we, Doc?" My words were not in direct response to his, but in response to his threat.

Corvo drained the rest of his glass, told Dr. Sala he would see him at his daughter's wedding, then left.

Dr. Sala sopped up the juices left on his plate with a piece of bread. He drained the last of his wine. Then he ordered dessert and espresso. The server asked if I'd like anything, and I told him no. I finished eating in silence while Dr. Sala started on his apple cake.

"You made a valid point tonight, Felice." Dr. Sala wiped his mouth. "I only hope Emanuele caught it."

"What point was that?"

The world wasn't a place I put much value in, but this old man was growing on me, and he'd hardly said a word. Maybe because I felt he was truly open to listening to both sides. He didn't seem to have an agenda either way, just working toward the common good of whatever was on the table.

"There is no price on love." He set his fork down, wiped his mouth again, and drained his glass. "There are also no rules when it pertains to claiming it, or one road to get to it."

"I made the first point, but not the second."

He laughed. "Perhaps not, but that is what I got from the conversation." He squeezed my shoulder. "How about a walk, ah? We will get to know each other better."

I agreed, and we left together. We talked as we walked, but in the back of my mind, I'd put together what Corvo hadn't said but had implied.

He was going to have a talk with Roma about what I wanted her for, which he'd said. He was going to plant a seed of doubt inside of her head, which I inferred.

He was going to try to turn my better half against me.

Chapter 30

Roma

"Piazza della Signoria," Elsa said in awe, looking around. "I think the piazzas are some of my favorite places to be in Italy."

"Wait." Lexi adjusted her bag on her shoulder. "I thought Lolita said this was Palazzo Vecchio?"

Elsa explained it was also known as Palazzo Vecchio, and in true Elsa style, she dove into the deep history of it. It was one of the most important squares in Florence, she said. She went on about the Uffizi Gallery and how it had been designed for Cosimo I de' Medici, who had been the Grand Duke of Tuscany in the 1500s.

We visited the impressive statues, Elsa giving us the history on each one.

She told us all about the excavated ruins underneath the palazzo, which revealed a lot about the Roman and Bronze eras, even a theater.

She animatedly went on about the bonfires of the vanities, where art, books, music, sculptures, etc. were burned for being sinful. There was a plaque for the man who instigated it, who received the same fate.

I knew all this already, but Elsa became alive for the past. It had been a long time since I'd seen her let go this much and enjoy life without being reminded of her responsibilities back home.

It was kind of odd because I had no idea where it came from. The sudden change. It made me wonder if something with her situation had changed, and she hadn't told me. I held out for it, even made subtle comments, but she didn't seem to be in a sharing mood unless it had to do with the history of the piazza.

We went to the Gucci Museum next and then decided on lunch. We chose a place with al fresco dining, and right as we sat, Babbo walked up. He greeted everyone and asked if he could speak to me alone.

I had no idea what about, and it put me on edge. But Felice hadn't been in contact with me since we arrived in Italy. And none of my sisters saw Felice on the plane. So, it couldn't have been about that.

Unless...he was about to ask me for a date to announce my engagement to Jack? Lo was getting married in just three days. Maybe he wanted to hash out the date now and announce it after her wedding, while we were in Italy. We had a lot of family here.

He offered me his arm and I took it. We strolled along the piazza, the conversation easy. When we stopped in front of a bakery, my stomach rumbled. I hadn't eaten since earlier, I'd done a lot of walking, and I was anxious. I knew he hadn't asked me to take a walk with him to find out if I was having fun. I always had fun in Italy.

"Roma," he said, his accent heavier since we'd arrived. "We need to speak about Felice Maggio."

"What about him?"

"He is a handsome man, but he is not a good man. He has wanted me dead since I did not take care of his father. Tommaso has stopped him all these years."

"Why didn't you? Take care of his father?"

"Tommaso ordered me not to."

"Why?" I breathed.

"I do not like to concern you with these things, but I feel you need to know the truth. Salvatore Maggio, John's father, was having an affair with another man's wife. This is not allowed by their laws. Tommaso found out right before Salvatore had the heart attack. Put yourself in Tommaso's shoes."

"But you're a doctor," I said. "Why would it matter what Tommaso orders you to do?"

"I worked for them from time to time. This means, we do not always do what we want, but what we're told to do."

"What are you saying?"

"I am saying, you are engaged to Jack Maggio. Do not only forget about John. Run from him. I am not sure what he has told you, but his intentions are not true. He's out to hurt me through you. He will use you to get back at Alfonso and Jack as well. There is bad blood there. It is a dangerous game, my darling girl. You will only get hurt."

I had no idea how to respond to that. I remembered Corinna's face when she found out who my father was. I remembered how satisfied Nonna Silvia sounded when she told Felice to hit Alfonso and Jack where it hurt, their pride. I also remembered Felice saying whatever went on between him and my father was between them.

"You don't know him," I whispered. "He's not—"

"I know him," Babbo said. "Do you, really?"

I knew Felice could be cunning, but that was something I knew about him too. He never hid who he was. A dangerous carnivore. But the dark parts of his life had mostly been hidden from me, except when a big black sedan literally rammed my car in the side and could have killed me and Elsa.

"Be careful of your next steps, Roma," he said. "You are naïve to this world. I only want to protect you from it." He leaned in and kissed my cheek. He offered me his arm again. "Let's get you back to lunch. You look pale."

The next day, I took a ride with Talia into town. With the number of people and activities at the *castello*, it was impossible to be alone. And when I'd try to sleep, thoughts of what Babbo had said kept me up. I always found it harder to think clearly at night. It was like the truth of the problem was hidden in the darkness. Maybe if I could walk by myself for a while, I could work out my feelings.

"You've been quiet," Talia said, glancing at me from the driver's seat. She refused to let me drive, stating she didn't want to fly off a hill in a car without wings.

"I just have a lot on my mind."

"A lot as in...Jack and John?"

"What do you know about John?"

"Babbo filled us in. He told us about their history."

"Oh." He'd told them so they wouldn't side with us, or him. They would agree he was just using me to hurt Babbo.

"Lo wasn't there," she said. "It was just Isabella, Alina, and me."

All of us knew Babbo loved us, and in individual ways, but it was no secret Lo wasn't one of his favorites. Neither was Isabella, but where Lo did her own thing, Isa chased after his love.

"Let me guess. Isabella was the first to say, *aha! I knew it.*"

Talia grinned. "No, that was Alina. She thought she was getting the jump on Isabella. You know how Alina wants to be Isabella, so she tries to impress her. But no, Isa didn't comment on what Babbo told us about John. She brought up how Jack treated you at the airport."

"Really?"

"Yeah. I told Babbo I was about to twist him into a pretzel."

I laughed a little. "I don't think Babbo cares. He just wants me with anyone but Felice."

"Felice, huh?"

"Everyone else calls him John," I said.

"Nice. You must have special privileges." She smiled, then after a second or so, her lips pinched. "Do you think it's true, though? What Babbo told us? You have to admit, it has a ring of truth to it. I'd want revenge on the man who could've saved my father but didn't."

No was on the tip of my tongue, but I couldn't bring myself to say it. The theory did make sense, but then again, it was only a theory. Or maybe Felice wanted to hurt him and have me for honest reasons at the same time. I even thought about why Felice hadn't killed Babbo to avenge Sal. But it was no secret Tommaso wouldn't have allowed it. If what Babbo had said was the truth, Tommaso gave the order not to save Sal.

"Something to think about," was all I could say.

"By the way, I asked Babbo if he'd ever been in the car with Jack during traffic. He told me he hadn't. I told him he should. And if he ever decided to go public with a match-making business, he should start adding that to his checklist. You want to test a person's true temperament, stick them in bumper-to-bumper traffic on an empty stomach. You'll get the truth."

"You tested this out on Joseph?"

"Yeah. He turns up the music and sings." She went quiet for a minute. "For the record, I want you to be happy, Y. Whichever direction that takes you."

I thanked my sister, then we talked about a bodybuilding competition she had coming up until we arrived in town. It was nice to chat with her, but what I was really after was some solitude. I didn't want to make small talk or have a direction to go in. I just wanted to...be.

Talia wanted a new pair of heels, so she went in one direction, and I went in the other. We planned to meet for lunch, then head back to the *castello* after. I loafed around, grabbing *caffe e cornetto* (coffee and croissant), and listening to the locals talk while I checked out fresh produce. I could always tell the locals because their "c" sounds were soft. *Cheese* sounded more like *heese*. Or *coca* was *hoha*.

All the while, though, I kept thinking about Felice and what Babbo had told me. If I confronted Felice about it, I had no clue if he was going to tell me the truth or not. And if he was honest and told me he wanted to hurt my father, but still had feelings for me?

That still made me a toy to be played with, didn't it?

"Oh shit!" I stopped short when a motorbike jumped the curb and came to a stop right in front of me. I was about to go off on the driver when he lifted his helmet.

"Get on, Dino." He held out a black leather riding jacket.

It was the first time I'd seen Felice since we arrived in Italy. He looked fine as hell straddling the sleek Ducati. He wore a leather jacket, a tight white T-shirt underneath, dark jeans, and black boots.

Even though I had my reservations, I couldn't stop myself from taking the jacket and getting on. It was a tight fit. The pillion seat didn't really feel like a seat at all. My ass stuck out. He had an extra helmet hanging from the handlebar, and he handed it to me. I slipped it on and wrapped my arms around him.

He revved the engine and took off, weaving in and out of traffic, until the city dissolved into the countryside, and he really hit the throttle. We were going so fast, it almost seemed like we were flying. I held on to him even tighter as we made turns and the wind whipped against us, taking any sense of time with it.

He turned onto a long drive, Mediterranean cypress trees lining the path upward. He slowed when the land opened up and we came to a golden villa with wooden teal-green shutters.

Felice parked and helped me off. I removed the helmet and jacket, handing it back to him. While he removed his and set them back on the bike, I sent a text to Talia telling her to go back without me. Felice would drop me later. He was no longer a secret, so I didn't need to lie.

I smiled when I noticed Felice's hair. It was sticking up all over the place. Mine must have been too because he tamed it down with his hands. Then he pulled me in for a kiss. It went on for so long I had to pull away, or I wouldn't have enough oxygen to keep going. He always kissed me like we were about to say goodbye.

If I would have known that was his intention, it would have

made me anxious, but I always got the feeling it meant the opposite. He just kissed me with the intensity of whatever he felt for me.

"You're not staying too far away," I said when I could catch my breath.

He took me in, like he was seeing me for the first time in months. "If you're not next to me, you might as well be on Venus."

I nodded and looked away. I needed more time to catch my breath, and I couldn't when he was looking at me that way, like he wanted to absorb me into his skin and carry me around.

He turned my face back, and I couldn't understand the look on his. Some of the intensity was gone. It was almost like he was wary of my thoughts.

"You have something to say, Dino?"

It was eerie how he seemed to know I was holding back from him. I didn't know what to do, whether I should come clean about the conversation with Babbo or not. I wanted Felice's truth, but I wasn't sure I was ready for it.

"What would make you say that?" I asked.

"Your eyes are guarded," he said, studying them.

"That's nothing new. I've always been told I have mean eyes, or shrewd eyes. It's the reason I'm unapproachable."

"Not mean or shrewd. Guarded. There's a difference. And the reason why you're unapproachable is because all the other challenging males smell me all over you. Always have. You carry me with you."

"Okay, guarded. But they've always been guarded."

"Not with me."

I didn't turn my face away from his, but my eyes. "What do you want with me, Felice?"

He was quiet for so long that I finally looked at him. He was staring at me, his face hard and his jaw tight. When my eyes met his, the look softened, but something had pissed him off.

"*Ti amo*, Roma," he said. "You've always been mine."

He loved me?

Before I could respond, he took my hand and led me into the villa. Celso was inside, along with a man I thought was named Fredo.

Felice nodded to an envelope on the kitchen table. It had Mamma's name on the outside. Inside, a picture of a man in his early twenties, maybe taken in the 70s or 80s, and two certificates.

"This is not possible," I said, reading over the marriage certificate. It listed Mamma's name and the name of a man I'd never heard of before. "Mamma had an arranged marriage with Babbo."

I said the words, but the certificate from a church in Mamma's hometown proved my parents hadn't told us the entire story. Neither one mentioned this man or a first marriage to us. I looked at Felice and slapped the paper down on the table.

"So what? Maybe she made a mistake she didn't want us to know about."

There was more to this, though, and we both knew I sensed it. The other certificate glared at me. Daring me to deny its presence. It was a death certificate with the name of Mamma's first husband on it. He'd died while they were still married.

"Okay," I said, my voice forceful, but trembling. "Are you going to tell me my father killed this man?" I shoved a hand at the certificate, then crossed my arms over my chest.

Felice nodded. "But let's get this straight. This has nothing to do with your Mamma."

"How can it not?"

"She either chose to marry the first man or he forced her. Either way, he abused her. Your father fell in love with her when he went to Sicily with Dr. Sala. She was in bad shape. You can imagine what happened after that."

"Babbo killed him so he could marry her."

Felice nodded again. "He made it look like an accident. He's good at that."

"Why are you telling me this?"

"Because if you think you can change his mind about me,

forget it. There's a reason why he despises men like me. Your Mamma was married to one, and he'd almost killed her because she put her dress over his suit coat."

Men like me. Men who belonged to the mafia. I glanced at the man in the picture. He had a stony expression on his face, like it was unmovable.

"You're not him," I whispered.

"I am, but I'm not." He studied my face. "Have you tried telling Emanuele that?"

Yesterday's conversation echoed in my ear:

"You don't know him," I whispered. "He's not—"

"I know him," Babbo said. "Do you, really?"

No, but I didn't really know my father either.

"Why did you tell me this?" I asked again.

Felice took a step forward, and I took a step back.

He nodded toward me. "That's why."

CHAPTER 31

ROMA

Lolita was a married woman. And it seemed as soon as her wedding was over, everyone turned their attention to me, asking me countless questions about when it was going to be my turn. At the post-wedding brunch the next day, Jack stood up, tapped his glass with a spoon, and announced our engagement. He tried to slip a ring on my finger, but it was too tight.

I thought it was symbolic, but he didn't seem to care. He told me he would get a new one to replace it in the next couple of days. I didn't say anything, only made an *uh huh* sound, because I was going to have a talk with Babbo. I refused to marry Jack.

My stomach turned when I looked at him. When I looked at Alfonso and his wife too.

Then there was Felice.

After what happened, I could tell he was on edge. Babbo too. It was as if they were both worried about what I'd believe about the other.

Lo popped her head into my room at Babbo's villa in Tuscany, giving me a wave that showed off her wedding rings.

"I thought you were supposed to be packing for the honeymoon?" I asked.

"I have time. We're not leaving until tomorrow." She pointed out the window. "It's so dreary. I'm so happy the rain held off until after the wedding."

"You looked stunning, Lo. Everything was so beautiful."

She smiled, and I almost expected the sun to start shining. "I'm so happy, Y."

"Me too."

"Are you really, Y?"

I opened my mouth to respond, but Isabella popped up behind Lo. "We have something to cheer you up. Follow me. And Lo, bring your beauty case."

We all went upstairs and into what we always called the church room. It had low beams and a stained-glass window. Mamma's simple wedding dress was placed in the center of the room, hanging from one of those dress forms. All my sister's gowns were around it, displayed the same way. Mine was there too. She'd seen all our dresses before she died. She helped us design them.

I walked over to it and ran my hand along the material. Lace and satin. It was a classic ballgown with a beaded bodice. Back then, it seemed to fit me. I wasn't so sure anymore. It seemed too young, for some reason. Like the girl it belonged to was naïve to the world and how cruel it could be. It seemed innocent.

"Try it on," Isabella said, coming to stand behind me.

"No." I let the dress go with a sigh.

"Come on, Y," Isabella nudged me. "Let's see if you're the same size, or if it's going to need alterations."

"Yeah, and who knows when we'll see you in it," Alina said. "You don't seem ready to marry Jack yet."

All my sisters looked at me, like they didn't know what was going to happen. Like they might miss seeing me in it. They probably would. I didn't plan on marrying Jack, and I refused to turn my back on Felice. I loved him, even if I was uncertain of his motives. And I couldn't imagine spending the rest of my life without him.

"Okay."

Lo did my makeup and hair while we talked about Mamma and their weddings. After Lo was done, Isabella helped me into the gown while Alina set the veil in my hair. Talia stood back and took a picture.

"Damn, Y," Lo said. "You're too perfect."

I turned to look at myself in the full-length mirror and accidentally hit the vanity. A deep *thunk* followed by the sound of glass shattering made us freeze.

"Shit," Alina said, stepping away from the shattered handheld mirror.

"That's really bad luck," Talia said. "That paired with the rain..."

"Good thing you're not getting married today." Lo glanced at the window. Heavy droplets were sliding against the windowpane, coagulating as more rain fell.

"I thought rain was supposed to be good luck?" Isabella straightened the veil.

"Maybe rain," Talia said, looking in the same direction as Lo. "But this is storm weather."

"Let's show Babbo." Isabella pointed my shoulders in the direction of the stairs. "He wanted to see."

"He knew we were doing this?" I asked.

"He suggested it."

I wasn't sure why, but that threw me. It just didn't seem like him to initiate something like a dress-up session. I took my time coming down the stairs, even though I was barefoot, my sisters all around me. Isabella walked ahead of me. Lo walked next to me and sang *here comes the bride*. Alina and Talia made sure the train and the floor-length veil didn't get messed up.

"Who's that?" Lo asked before I could.

"I was going to ask you the same thing," I said.

Babbo stood at the end of the steps. A burly man with a shaved head stood next to him. I couldn't figure out the look on

Babbo's face. Pissed? Worried? I took a deep breath but caught an unfamiliar scent in the air. Blood.

"Roma," Babbo said when I made it down the stairs. His white down shirt had a red blossom on it. It was sticking to his skin. "This is Mr. Crawford. He works for the Maggios."

"Alfonso and Jack?"

My father nodded. "It seems we will have another wedding today."

"Whose?" I knew the answer, but I breathed out the question anyway.

Mr. Crawford pointed a gun at Babbo. "Yours."

***

"Get her shoes." Crawford nodded at me but gave Lo the order.

She squeezed my arm before she rushed up the stairs.

"You knew about this?" I barely got out, staring at my father. I was pretty sure Crawford had shot him, but physically he looked fine. It also looked like the shirt had clogged the wound.

"Two hours ago," he spoke to me in Italian. "I was to convince you to have a change of heart. I knew you would not."

"You tricked me?"

"I prefer the word persuade," Mr. Crawford interrupted. "And if Dr. Corvo is not enough persuasion..." He kept the gun trained on Babbo while he showed me his cellphone. It was a picture of Felice's Ducati with him on it.

"That should make you happy," I snapped at Babbo. I knew he wasn't the mastermind behind this, but somehow my anger flew out at him. "Felice out of the picture. You getting what you want."

"It does," Babbo said. "But I am sorry it is happening this way. I wanted you to have the same experiences as your sisters."

"You'd still want me to marry an asshole like Jack after what's happening right now?"

"I refuse to allow you to marry Felice Maggio."

"I have them." Lo, coming down the stairs, lifted a pair of white tennis shoes.

"That's the best you can do?" Crawford asked.

She made a face at him. "What did you expect? That she'd have a pair of heels to match?"

"Put them on her, smart ass," he said.

Lo did. She gazed up at me, trying to communicate, but all we seemed to be saying to each other was: *what the fuck are we going to do?* I had no doubt Crawford was not riding solo. He didn't seem like a stupid or careless man. He also came on a day when all the men were out. They were invited by the Maggios to visit Maremma, a coastal town in Tuscany known for the *butteri*. Basically, Italian cowboys.

Felice.

I had no idea if Crawford had done anything to him. I doubted it, given who Felice was and who he belonged to. Even if Felice was untouched, my cellphone was in the church room. And Crawford seemed to be a creature with hidden eyes all over his body. There wasn't a move we made he seemed to miss.

"Try it, bodybuilder Barbie," he said to Talia. "I'll blow daddy's head off in front of all his precious daughters."

Isabella grabbed Talia's arm and yanked her toward her. Alina took her other arm. Talia showed no fear, and she was going to try to take Crawford out. I didn't want to see my sisters get killed, or even Babbo.

I stepped up. "Let's go."

"Glad you're finally coming to your senses." Crawford nodded toward the door. "Walk."

It felt like a short walk to the end of a plank. Crawford ordered Babbo and my sisters to follow me. He followed all of us. When we got outside, a strong gust of wind almost tore my veil off as rain pelted my face. The ground was saturated, and the Tuscan mud was already staining the pure white fabric of the dress.

Two cars with tinted windows waited outside. My sisters were ordered to get in one car; Crawford, Babbo, and I took the other. I was sandwiched between the two. Two men sat in the front seat. Babbo stared out of the window while Crawford gave the men directions. We were headed to a remote church somewhere in the countryside.

I glanced at myself in the mirror. Black streaks of mascara cascaded down my cheeks. My hair was sopping wet, along with my veil and dress. I'd be less than perfect for Alfonso and his son. I took perverse pleasure in that. It was the only thing keeping the blood in my veins warm.

Besides Crawford shooting off directions and the sound of rain and windshield wipers, the ride was silent. I wasn't sure how long the trip took, but it only felt like seconds. This was where I'd be pushed from the plank and into my doom.

The church was set in the center of a field. We'd have to walk to get there. Crawford ordered my father to take my arm, while my sisters carried the train and veil. One of the driver's finally came up with a genius idea and held a black umbrella over my head. This felt more like a funeral procession, but Jack's smiling face killed the mood.

"I know you're pissed off," he said when we were almost face-to-face, "but you wouldn't give in any other way. You won't be sorry. You'll realize one day this was for the best."

"You're right," I said, keeping my tone even, though I was trembling. "I won't be sorry. *You* will. Are you going to keep me locked up, Jack? Because that's the only way you're going to stop me from killing you."

"You don't mean that. You're just mad."

I glared at my father. How did he ever think this buffoon was perfect for me? He sighed.

Alfonso came out of the church. "We're ready to get started."

"I wonder how these pictures are going to look?" I said to their backs. "The trophy wife all soiled in her wedding dress. Are you going to be able to show them off? Because I positively *can't* wait."

"We're having a big wedding in Chicago," Jack said. "This is just to satisfy the arrangement."

"Are you going to force me down the aisle again? Because that's the only way."

"I can be persuasive," Alfonso said.

"How persuasive are you going to be when Felice finds out about this?"

"Felice has no say here," Alfonso snapped at me. "He can't touch me, and I can't touch him. There's an agreement in place—between his family and mine. I haven't touched him. This is considered business and all's fair when it comes to that."

Oh, another loophole, like with the penthouse.

"You're touching who belongs to him," Lo bit back.

"Quiet," my father snapped at her.

The church was empty besides us and the priest standing at the altar. Crawford and two of his men stood outside. I guessed the two men in the car with my sisters stayed by the road, waiting for any signs of unwanted guests. Babbo took a seat on the first pew, my sisters sliding in next to him.

Alfonso took a seat on the opposite side, all by himself in the pew.

Jack turned to me, but I refused to turn to him. The priest cleared his throat, but I refused to move. Jack sighed, took me by the shoulders, and almost mechanically turned me to face him.

"Hello," he whispered, like we hadn't seen each other in ages, and he was being romantic.

I narrowed my eyes at him.

"I'm not cautious of those eyes anymore." He grinned. "Now I think you're adorable when you're mad."

It was a waste of breath to even respond, and I was having trouble taking those. The priest had already started talking. It seemed like he was talking too fast. He was American. Maybe from New York. I almost wanted to shout at him to slow down some. A buzzing had started in my ears, and he was only making it worse.

He got to the part where the congregation is asked to speak now or forever hold their peace.

"We can skip that part," Alfonso said, staring at my sisters.

"I object."

We all turned toward the voice. Felice stood in the doorway of the church, dripping water and blood all over the floor. He looked absolutely mad. His hair was matted to his face, his eyes were dilated, and he held a gun in his hand. It was aimed at Alfonso.

"Come to me, Roma," Felice said in Italian, but he never took his eyes off Alfonso.

"Crawford!" Alfonso shouted. "Crawwwwford!"

Felice grinned, and blood coated his teeth. "You can go out back and dig another grave for him in the yard once I take what's mine and leave. For his friends too."

I snapped out of my shock and grabbed the dress, about to bolt. Jack went to stop me, but Alfonso stepped in front of him and pushed him back. I collided into Felice, but he was unmovable. He put an arm around me, keeping me close to his side.

"It would be nothing to pull this trigger and kill you, but that would be too easy, too quick. Your pride being this wounded? That's going to be the slow, painful death you deserve. Just wait for it. It's coming."

He kept his arm wrapped around me as we left.

CHAPTER 32

ROMA

Once we were outside of the church, Felice scooped me up, hauled me over his shoulder, and rushed to the street. Celso and Fredo were waiting by two cars. Crawford's two were still parked. I could see the men who drove my sisters slumped over in the front seat.

All my energy seemed to drain from my body, and I did the same over Felice's shoulder.

He had me in his car a few seconds later. He strapped me in and hustled to the other side. He put it in gear and peeled out, Celso and Fredo only a breath behind us.

He glanced at me. "You okay, Dino?"

"Not going to lie. It's been an eventful day, and it's not even over." I looked in the rearview. "Are more men coming to the church?"

"Possibly. One of Crawford's men was talking to someone on his cell when we got there. Crawford was certifiable but good at what he did. I can't see him only having two cars."

"You found me."

"It's always just a matter of time."

We became silent after that. I stared out the window,

watching the world pass by in a blur. I ran over the day in my head and sighed.

"This is not—" *going to end well,* I was going to say, but I didn't feel like hearing the blunt truth confirmed. I already knew it wasn't going to. I went in a different direction. "What's going on now is beyond Alfonso fighting you over a penthouse, but he still feels it's a piece of property. Me. Do you think Tommaso will still be so supportive of your side?"

Felice glanced in the rearview. He was quiet for so long, I thought he'd never respond, but finally, he did.

"Tommaso owes your old man. He's already made his alliance clear. He'll side with him, but he'll try to find a way to keep me before he kills me. If Emanuele keeps the situation between us, it'll stay that way."

I went to tell him what Babbo had told me—that it was Tommaso who'd ordered my father not to save Sal. But I wasn't sure if Babbo was telling me the truth or not. And what if I told Felice and he went after Tommaso? There was a coldness in his voice when he talked about his boss after what he'd done to me. I didn't want to push Felice over the edge. He still looked maniacal.

I looked down at my dress and had a feeling the state of it reflected my face too. Felice's hand covered mine, and he brought it to his lips. His warm breath fanned over my skin, and I shivered.

"Where are we going?" I didn't really care. I just didn't want to separate from him again. Lo's wedding was over, and my promise to her had been kept.

"To Sicily," he said.

"For what?"

"To get married."

"What if I say no?" I breathed out.

"You're not saying no," he said.

"Hypothetically."

"I turn into a monster with no sense of right and wrong, only what I want, and make you my wife anyway."

"Oh. You turn into Jack."

"Difference between Jack and me, I know you want me too."

It was the truth. I couldn't argue with that.

The veil tugged at my hair and was hurting my scalp. I carefully took it off and set it in the back seat as delicately as I could. I tried not to think about it being ruined. Mamma had helped me design it. It had more sentimental meaning than anything. I sighed and stared out the window.

Somewhere along the way, I crashed. I hadn't slept so hard since the weekend at the penthouse. When I started coming to, I felt my mouth hanging open. I snapped it shut and sat up some.

Felice held my hand in his, leaning over to my side some. Our hands were in my lap.

"How long have we been driving?" I asked.

"Five hours."

"How long will it take to get there?"

"Another five, give or take some."

I yawned. "Are we going to stop soon?"

He glanced at my face. "You still tired?"

"A lot has been going on since...the moment I met you."

He brought my hand to his mouth, placing kisses all over my fingers. He swerved at the last minute and turned into a gas station. His last-minute turn was so smooth it almost made me jealous.

He found a spot and pulled in. I was trying to figure out how I was going to use the bathroom in the humungous dress as he made his way around and opened the door for me.

"What?" Felice held out his hand to me.

I took it and he helped me out, closing the door. We stood there.

"It's just...I have to go pee."

He looked at me as if to say...*and what's the problem?*

I answered the look on his face. "Problem is, I need help with the dress."

"Taking you out of that dress isn't a problem." He grinned.

"No, but peeing in front of you is!"

He roared with laughter. "You're embarrassed to take a piss in front of me?"

"Pee. Women pee, Felice. Or go number one."

"You go *number one* on me when you come."

He said it so causally, like we were talking about the weather.

"Are you being serious right now?"

He nodded. "Google it."

I was speechless as he led me into the *benzinaio*. The attendant working looked like he wanted to congratulate us, but the sad state of my face and dress probably stopped him. I probably looked like a waterlogged piece of paper after it's dried out. Felice looked a proper mess, too, but it only upped his *don't fuck with me* vibe.

People would only respect him more and think I needed help.

Such is life, as Mamma would say. I sighed.

Fredo met us inside, handing Felice a bag. Then he went back outside and moved Felice's car and started pumping petrol. Celso was filling up their car.

"I brought you a change of clothes," Felice said once we were in the bathroom. He locked the door behind us. "I'll help you out of the dress and then you can go number one." He laughed.

I rolled my eyes and turned around. His hands were warm as he released me from the dress. The material felt cold against my skin from the rain and from the cool air.

"Where did you get this?"

"The dress? Oh, before Mamma died, we picked it out together."

"*Mi dispiace*," he whispered, placing a soft kiss on my shoulder. "*Lo renderò migliore.*"

A tightness formed in my chest and throat at his words. *I'm sorry. I'll make this better.* He carefully took the dress from me while I put on the warm clothes. Sweater and sweatpants that was his. It was all oversized, but at least I had my tennis shoes, even if they were stained. I did my business. He did his.

As he washed his hands, I noticed bloodstains on the waist-band of his jeans.

"You're bleeding." I rushed to him and lifted his black shirt, which was crusty with dried blood. He had a clotted wound on his left shoulder. It was shaped like a gulley, the skin completely torn off.

"A bullet grazed me." He shrugged.

"Any closer to your neck…" I couldn't even finish because that was exactly what he would have been, *finished*, if the bullet would have hit the vital pulse in his neck.

He grinned at me through the mirror, like I was cute. "Almost doesn't count when it's me, Dino."

I shook my head. "It counts to me."

"*Bene*," he said, turning to face me. "That's the only time they count. When I'm collecting wounds and scars meant for you."

All the blood felt like it drained from my face and all energy from my body. He caught me before my legs gave out.

"When was the last time you had something to eat?"

I couldn't remember. The entire day before Crawford, except for the time with my sisters in the church room, seemed like a blur.

I shrugged. "Not sure."

"You'll eat." His tone was final.

Celso and Fredo met us in the station after they finished filling the cars. Between the four of us, our bags were loaded when we left with food, drinks, and first-aid items.

Felice made a deal with me when I kept arguing about cleaning his wound. I ate, and then I could clean it.

Some Italian gas stations had better food than some restaurants back home. I'd gotten a caprese sandwich, and Felice had gotten one packed with meat. We ate pistachio donuts after and drank coffee. Then he pulled to the side of the road and let me clean his graze. He still made a fuss about it at first, but I thought it was for show. He seemed to like my hands on him and the attention.

Somewhere along the way, I crashed again. When I woke up, we were an hour out from Taormina, Felice said. We stopped at another *benzinaio*.

Felice stood outside of the bathroom this time, and when I came out, he was on the phone. He was talking to someone in Sicilian. He hung up before we got in the car again.

"Have you ever been here, Roma?"

"No," I said, trying to see the town from the car window. It was too dark. Only specks of light gave the area some definition. "I've been to Sicily, to Palermo, to visit Mamma's family, but not to Taormina. But I know things about it. It's on the coast, right?" After he nodded, I went on.

"Mount Etna is somewhere over that way." I pointed in one direction. "The Ionian Sea is probably over that way." I pointed in another. "D.H. Lawrence and Truman Capote were inspired by it. It has Medieval streets and a Greek theater, which is second century, I believe. There's also a castle around here. Elsa's interested in its archeological bones. There's a Neolithic necropolis. A Stone Age cemetery on the premises. She told me about it once. But we're about an hour away from Taormina?"

He nodded. "Did you Google that too?"

Okay, so he was right about the *number one* thing. I had Googled it.

"Google might know everything, but I read about Taormina in a travel book once. Lo and I talked about visiting the beaches one summer. Elsa filled me in on the castle. Is Taormina where your family is from?"

"Some. I have family all over Italy."

We slowed when we came to a *castello* nestled in the hills. It was lit from the ground up. Crawling vines spread up the apricot-colored exterior, tall palm trees swayed in the sea breeze, and lush Mediterranean foliage lined the walk to the opening. It didn't seem to have doors, but a path leading deeper into the *castello*.

I was willing to bet a citrus orchard surrounded us. I could smell it in the air. This *castello* was a fortified farm.

Elsa was in my ear. I could almost hear her excitement over this place. This was the one she'd gone on about when Lo and I were considering a visit to Taormina.

A man and a woman met us and brought us to a different side of the property, Celso and Fredo trailing behind us. Grand windows overlooked the courtyard, climbing hydrangeas clinging underneath. The furniture was all antique, the walls exposed stone, the floors terracotta, and the bathroom all tile.

"This place is beautiful," I whispered. "Are we getting married here?"

"Are you ready to become my wife?" Felice wrapped his arms around me, pulling me so tight against him, I almost couldn't breathe.

I closed my eyes when he started to kiss and suck on my neck. He bit me and I sank my nails into his arm.

"Answer me, Roma."

"Yes," I whispered.

"Are you ready to sign your name in blood?" He reached around and squeezed me between the legs. He didn't hurt me, but I felt it through the layers.

I sucked in a breath and sighed it out. "Yes."

He started to massage me through the sweatpants, and I felt like I was melting into his arms. "*Bene*," he whispered in my ear, picking up the pressure and pace. "You're beautiful. So fucking beautiful." He sucked on my earlobe, and I shattered in his arms. He hadn't even pulled my pants down.

It felt like all the blood had drained from my body, and I had no energy left. I wilted in his arms. He kept me upright.

"Take warm baths, go for long walks around the property, eat well, *rilassarsi*." *Relax*, he'd breathed in my ear. "You're going to need your strength."

My eyes sprang open, and I whirled around after he let me go and was heading for the door. "Wait! Where are you going?"

"Business," he said.

"You're leaving me here alone?"

"I'll be on the grounds. You're safe."

This was a huge place. I had no idea how to even leave. I would have to trust him completely.

Did I? With my safety...

I nodded. "How many days do I have to prepare? To relax?"

He grinned. "A week."

He left me alone and shut the door.

CHAPTER 33

FELICE

I'd been up all night, having a meeting with my great-uncle and all his people. Decisions went through Sicily first before they moved to the states.

Whenever Tommaso retired or died, and I took his place, I wanted the agreement with Alfonso terminated.

He wasn't going to keep fucking with Roma and have no consequences to pay for it. If he fucked with her, he fucked with me. And if I offed him now, Tommaso might sprout a wild hair and take it out on her instead of me again. Him ordering her car to be rammed was still fresh in my mind.

My great-uncle listened to and absorbed the information. He didn't give me a definite answer at the end of our meeting, but I wasn't surprised. Sometimes it took him time to come to a decision.

We all stood when Dr. Sala and his two great-nephews by marriage, Rocco and Romeo Fausti, appeared with Mario, the man who took care of the property. Mario used his hand to motion to us, and the three men approached our table. We all shook hands, and my great-uncle decided to stay longer.

I'd met Rocco and Romeo before, but I didn't know them that well. The important thing to remember was, even if all decisions went through Sicily, the Fausti family knew about them. They didn't involve themselves in petty shit, but when things really went south, they'd show up. Other times, they liked to share a meal and talk.

I invited them to have a seat and we all sat around the table. We were in an open area of the *castello*. Every so often a breeze would sweep through. I could smell the citrus orchard and the sea. Something else tangled in the air and was getting stronger with every footstep. Roses.

All the men stood when Brando Fausti and his wife, Scarlett, walked up to the table. I hadn't met either one, but I knew them by reputation. Roma had told me all about Scarlett when we were supposed to go to the ballet.

Scarlett Rose Fausti was a superstar in that world, and somewhat of a legend in ours. Supposedly she could feel what other people couldn't. I didn't put much stock in it, but because of it, she became a target in our world.

Brando was Rocco and Romeo's oldest brother, and he had eyes hard and dark enough to be made of stone. They were accessing me, trying to decide if I was going to be a problem for him or not.

"If you all will excuse me," Scarlett said, stepping away from the table. "I'm going to tour the grounds."

"Scarlett," Brando called before she could get too far. He didn't say anything else, but I could tell there was a warning beneath her name.

She waved at him, and with two men in tow, started for the back of the *castello*. My eyes narrowed against the shaft of light she was walking into. When I leaned some to avoid the glare, I saw Roma bending over, fastening the ties of her sandals.

She was glowing in an airy white dress, her hair braided. When she looked up and our eyes met, she smiled at me, and the heart everyone claimed I didn't have melted in my chest.

She gasped when she noticed Scarlett standing there. "Oh my God—I didn't—Scarlett Fausti?"

Scarlett apologized for scaring her, and after a minute or so of talking, they walked away together.

"This *castello* have a history?" Brando asked. "Dangerous men who might have lived here at one time—and are dead now?"

"Dead *or* alive, *fratello*," Romeo said, a shit-eating grin on his face.

"I believe it does, nephew," Dr. Sala said, adjusting his glasses. He brought up the same thing Roma had. About the Neolithic necropolis.

"Fuck me," Brando said, looking toward where the women had disappeared.

I had no fucking clue what he was talking about, but I thought maybe it had to do with what I'd heard about Scarlett Fausti. I took it more seriously after Brando's reaction.

Mario's wife Virna, along with a couple of her assistants, delivered breakfast to the table. Romeo was laughing at Dr. Sala because he tucked his napkin in his shirt like a bib. Romeo told him he was going to get him a personalized one with his name on it for his birthday. He slapped Romeo on the back of the head and told him to behave.

Brando and I met eyes from across the table and grinned.

I stopped Virna before she could walk away. I asked her in Sicilian if Roma had eaten breakfast.

"*Sì*," she said, topping off my coffee. She told me what Roma had and said she'd cleaned her plate. She'd taken a long bath after and then changed into the new clothes I'd gotten for her.

"*Bene*," I said.

Brando Fausti was looking at me again. He wasn't totally at ease around me, but I could tell something had shifted. He might not trust me, but he must have gotten the feeling I didn't want his wife for any purpose.

Conversation was casual as we ate. After, business was discussed again. My great-uncle brought up the agreement with Alfonso, and Dr. Sala nodded thoughtfully as he went over the finer points. Sometimes it was hard to tell what was on the old doctor's mind.

My great-uncle got a call and decided to leave. Brando stood and went to find Scarlett. Dr. Sala asked me and the other two Fausti brothers to walk with him.

We stepped out of the covered area and into blinding sun, but the salty breeze was constantly circulating fresh air through the citrus trees. Dr. Sala made a comment about Mount Etna and how the soil was rich because of the volcano.

"The best lemons and oranges in the world," he said.

We were all listening to him, but my eyes were on Roma. She was in deep conversation with Scarlett. Brando leaned against a tree, watching his wife.

"She is hard to look away from," Rocco said, meeting my eye. He nodded toward Roma. "Her beauty hypnotizes the eye. She is one of the most stunning women I have ever seen."

Dr. Sala looked between Rocco and me, adjusting his glasses again. They had turned dark in the sunlight. At Rocco's words, Romeo looked in her direction too but didn't comment.

I agreed with Rocco in Sicilian, but I said she was *the* most stunning woman I'd ever seen. He caught the subtle difference between his assessment of her and mine. Rocco Fausti had a wife, but they had an open relationship. He was always on the hunt for another woman to seduce, but the hunting ground he was gazing at belonged to me.

A second later, he met my eyes and grinned. He slapped Romeo on the back and the two went in the opposite direction.

"My nephew has a poet's heart," Dr. Sala said, watching them walk away. "A romantic heart."

"And ruthless blood," I said.

"Same for you, ah?"

"Everything but the poet's heart."

"More romantic then." He grinned.

"Romance doesn't have a place in my life," I said.

"Sure it does!" he almost boomed. "Ruthless and Romance

are not at war. In fact, my brother-in-law, Marzio, who was a poet and a true romantic, likened them to rivers. He said eventually they would both belong to the same body of water, but they began as separate streams and took different paths to it. There is no reason you cannot bathe in both."

"Something to think about," I said, sticking my hands in my pockets.

We'd started for a crude road that led deeper into the orchard. He turned and faced me.

"Emanuele wants you to bring Roma home."

"No. He's welcome at the wedding, but she's with me now."

His eyes turned serious and thoughtful. He nodded. "He fears you will hurt her. Do you give me your word you will not?"

"I'd cut my heart out before I'd lay a hand on her in anger," I said.

"I believe you, Felice Giovanni Maggio. Emanuele will not, even when I give him my word, but I do. Do not make me regret it. I do not make it a habit of keeping those. *Rimpianti.*" Regrets.

We stared at each other for a second before he reached into his pocket and showed me Roma's phone.

"Her family wants to speak to her. Do not deny them this."

"Her choice."

"I'd like to speak to her before I go."

I nodded, but I wanted Dr. Sala to bring back a message for me. I spoke in Italian. "I vowed to never lay a hand on my heart, but I will not hesitate to kill anyone who tries to take her away from me. It will be war, even on my wedding day."

"That is fair," he said with a small one-shoulder shrug, and we made our way back.

CHAPTER 34

ROMA

From the time I'd arrived at the *castello*, the staff spoiled me. Especially Virna, who, with her husband, ran the place. She'd taken Scarlett and me on a tour of the grounds and then asked me questions about flowers and food choices for the reception.

"It's just the two of us," I said. "We don't need much."

"*Signore* Maggio insists."

Scarlett shrugged. "If *Signore* Maggio insists..." She wiggled her eyebrows at me.

I couldn't stop the smile. She was...a whirlwind of grace and roses. She was everything I thought she'd be, but so much more. After the tour, we'd talked for a while, but then Uncle Tito brought me my phone and asked me how I was doing. I asked him if he knew what had happened, how Alfonso and Jack sent Crawford to force me to the church.

"Emanuele told me." He sighed. "He did not want things to turn out this way for you."

"I know he means well and only wants what's best for me, but this choice is not his. It's not mine either."

He took me by the chin. "Fate made the choice."

I nodded. "What feels like a long time ago."

He kissed me softly on the cheek, squeezed my hand, and told me he'd see me at the wedding. Around fifteen minutes after he left, Scarlett and the Faustis with him, Elsa showed up with Cassio.

"What are you doing here?" I barely got out, hugging her.

She looked around. Felice and Cassio were standing off to the side. Cassio didn't look happy, but Felice was staring at my face, gauging it. I smiled at him. His face softened, and so did my heart.

"John. He brought me here." She smiled at me. "I wouldn't have missed this for the world."

"Was Hayden okay with you missing work? I know you don't have any sick time left and—"

"John took care of everything." She wrapped an arm around my neck and pulled me toward the property. "Lo told me about your dress. I know your mom helped you design it. I'm so sorry. Do you need a new one?"

That was something I hadn't even considered.

"Yes. I do. But." I turned to look at Felice. He was still watching me. "I don't want to leave and have something happen. Alfonso and Jack..."

"We'll get one. What about your sisters?"

I pulled out my phone. I must have had over fifty texts from my sisters, between our family chat and individually. My chest felt too tight to read them all. I sent one to our group chat.

Y: I'm with Felice and I'm okay. Wish you were all here, though.

It was a bit cryptic. No one knew we were getting married yet. But I felt compelled to say it. Even though my sisters could be major pains in my ass, having them around always felt like keeping Mamma close. When we came together, her presence felt stronger.

Elsa pulled me closer and started asking questions about the wedding and the *castello*.

Between wedding plans and Elsa's desire for information on the property, it seemed like the days went by in a flash. I found myself standing in front of a full-length mirror in a silk robe with frastaglio, makeup scattered around, my new gown hanging from the bathroom door, still covered up.

I'd given Elsa a description of what I wanted. The designer had seven dresses similar in style. I asked Felice to choose his favorite. I still had no idea which one he chose. I took the dress down and unwrapped it. I grinned. He'd chosen my favorite. A formfitting, long-sleeved, vintage lace design with a high neck. The veil hung next to it. I took it out of the bag and had to sit down for a second.

It was the veil Mamma had gotten made for me. It was perfectly clean.

A knock came at the door. I opened it, expecting Elsa to be on the other side.

Lo held up her bag of tricks, tears in her eyes. "If you think you're getting married without me, bish, you—"

She couldn't even finish. I pulled her in, Alina and Talia all getting in on the hug. When we broke apart, they all filed in. Isabella stood by the door, looking unsure.

"Thank you," I said to her, my voice breaking, "for coming."

Tears rushed down her cheeks as she wrapped me in her arms, kissing my cheek. "You're my baby sister," she whispered. "I love you."

"Okay," Elsa said, coming in. "We need to turn this beauty into a bride."

Lo was already setting up her station. Alina and Talia were all over the place, helping wherever. Isabella went straight for the gown and veil.

"Babbo?" I asked, knowing the answer but asking anyway.

Lo shook her head, then Talia asked if the wedding was being held at the *castello*. The reception was, but Felice was unmovable about getting married in church. It was an hour from the *castello*, in Taormina. It was next to a clock tower and facing Piazza IX Aprile and the Ionian Sea.

We took three separate cars. Lo, Elsa, Celso and Fredo were with me. The square was pedestrian only, but the bridal car was allowed. I tried not to think about Babbo not being next to me. Lo held my hand the entire way.

"Mamma is here with us," she whispered. "I feel her."

My throat was too tight to answer her, but I hoped she was. I wanted her here with me.

The car slowed in front of the church. I'd never seen it before. It was of baroque style and made of Syracuse stone. White roses and baby's breath lined the railings and were displayed in massive stone vases for the wedding.

My wedding.

I took a deep breath and stepped out, Fredo offering me his hand. The scent of the sea was strong in the air. A tender breeze touched my skin, fluttering my veil.

My sisters and Elsa fussed over me, Scarlett appearing out of nowhere it seemed to help them. They all went inside a minute or two later to take their seats. A double staircase led up to the entrance. Uncle Tito fixed his suit as he came down one of them.

His smile touched his eyes when he saw me. He took my hand and kissed it. "You are a vision." He offered me his arm. "You would have been the muse for poets, musicians, and artists of a different time. Of a more romantic time. But I suspect you will play the muse in your husband's memories until his candle burns out."

"*Grazie mille,*" I whispered, kissing his cheek. I looked down at our linked arms. "Is this okay?" I didn't want to cause trouble between him and Babbo.

"He will thank me for being here one day." He sighed, patting my hand. "Life is too short, ah?"

Life was too short. That was why I couldn't deny myself this happiness. My father had it with my mother, was still clinging to it, and I wished he would want that for me, however it happened. But he was too tied up in his preconceived ideas about "men like" Felice and the life he belonged to to want the same for me. I came to terms with his reasoning, but I loved who I loved.

I'd take the chance of winning life with Felice instead of

worrying about losing before the game even started. Besides, arranged marriages and mob ones had about the same statistics. They were final.

Scarlett came out again. Uncle Tito blinked at her. When the sun hit her pink dress, she reminded me of a rose petal when light goes through it.

"It's time," she said. "John is close to walking his bride himself."

I took a deep, cleansing breath and squeezed Uncle Tito's arm. I nodded when he looked at me. He turned my veil down, and we walked up the stairs arm-in-arm.

The congregation stood when we entered. Candles swayed with an invisible breath, and the entire world faded. Our eyes held, and Felice seemed to pull me forward, closer and closer to his side.

Face to face, I smiled at him as two tears slipped down my cheeks. His thumbs barely drifted over them. As we turned toward the priest, Felice set his hand on my hip, bringing us closer together, making us one, and we vowed till death do us part.

The *castello* was filled with burning candles, white roses, and baby's breath, along with a lot of people I didn't know. Felice introduced me to most of them, but then I'd catch a face or two I didn't have a name for.

Corinna didn't seem to know all of them either, but she sat at a table with family she hadn't seen in years, laughing and carrying on. Nonna Silvia had a relaxed smile on her face the entire time. It was the kind of smile a dead person who had the last laugh would wear. Nonna Mafalda stayed in Chicago with her nurse.

Felice wasn't going to invite Corinna, because of my father, but that was Babbo's choice, and it wasn't fair to Corinna. I could tell she was happy to be there. When the dancing started, she was the first one up. Lo followed behind, then my sisters and Elsa.

Felice sat at a table with my sister's husbands. They were all drinking and laughing, except for Felice, who stared at me.

He had been the entire night. He was pulling me again, the intensity of his eyes saying what words didn't need to: *be prepared to make a vow to me in blood tonight.*

The look went straight between my legs, making heat creep up my neck. My skin felt so hot, the delicate pattern felt like it was branding me. I pulled at the lace some, trying to cool myself off. But I wasn't catching a breeze or a break.

The butterflies in my stomach were hyped up on euphoria dope, and it seemed like they kept dropping my heart into my stomach, only to rush it up again. Like little adrenaline junkies.

It happened again when my husband left the table. He plucked a flute of champagne from a server and dropped an apricot in it. The golden liquid started fizzing.

I empathized.

The closer he came to me, the harder my body seemed to hum with pent-up sexual tension.

"Mrs. Maggio." He slipped an arm around my waist, joining us at the hip. His warm hand on me made the butterflies faint, losing all control of my heart. He held the champagne to my lips, offering me a sip. "*Dolce nettare degli dei.*"

Sweet nectar from the gods, he'd said.

"It is good," I breathed out.

"Not the champagne." He offered me more. "*Le tue labbra.*"

Your lips.

I set my hand over his, the new ring on my left hand glinting when the soft candlelight touched it. The center pear-shaped stone was draped between two interlacing diamond ribbons. The band was encircled with more diamonds. The center stone alone had to be over four carats and was set in platinum.

Uncle Tito had put me in touch with the Fausti family's jeweler, and he created a bespoke band for Felice. It was thick platinum with a Mobius Strip design. His eyes had lowered when I'd slipped it on, like maybe he wasn't expecting me to claim him too.

I wasn't expecting our wedding date to be tattooed around his finger in Roman numerals. "This goes deeper than flesh," he'd said. "It's tattooed on my soul."

He offered me the entire glass, and after, tipped the flute so the apricot could flow into my mouth. I bit into the sweetness of it along with the alcohol it had absorbed. Before I could swallow, Felice pulled my mouth to his. I opened to him, offering him some of it. His tongue swept through my mouth, but went so deep, I had to hold on to him.

My head felt flighty, and I couldn't breathe. I had to break the kiss.

My eyes rose slowly to meet his. He was not only heartbreakingly beautiful, but there was something hauntingly sorrowful about him. If he ever left me, those intense eyes would follow me for the rest of my life. They had when he'd stopped coming around.

He sat the empty flute on a table. He set his hands on the sides of my face, cradling it. It was a trick of the candlelight, but flames burned in the depths of his irises when he looked at me. His kissed me softly this time, the tingle lingering as he led me to where everyone was dancing.

A slow, sensuous song started to play, and he showed my body how to move with his. I'd never danced with a man this way before. My husband seemed to know how to move my body better than I did.

My husband. A smile I couldn't control split my face. I wrapped my arms around his neck, tilting into him, as a faster song started to play. The hot summer night, my vows, but most of all, Felice Maggio had set me free.

Between cutting the cake while fireworks exploded in the background to dancing into the deepest hour of the night, it seemed like we drifted through it together, fused as one.

It reminded me of what he'd told me about Plato. Each step was directed by fate if we let go and went with the flow. Every decision led us to each other and the freedom of this moment—of saying yes to it.

As he carried me to our suite, I lay back in his arms. If he gave me a push, I felt like I could fly.

Tension shot through my veins and grounded me when we entered our room. Candles had been lit, the bed turned down, a single red rose set against the pillow.

Against the rich, creamy fabric, it reminded me of a blood stain.

Felice set me down on my feet and circled me like the carnivore he was. I stood still, only my eyes moving with him.

"My little herbivore," he breathed, brushing the hair from my shoulders. "Even if we're different, we both still bleed the same color."

He was about to prove it. I closed my eyes, my body trembling as he started to slowly undo the buttons of the dress. He slipped it off my shoulders, kissing and licking from one side to the other. He tilted my neck to the side and sucked over my pulse.

When I made a breathless noise, fisting the fabric so tightly my knuckles turned white, he lowered the dress to the floor. I stepped out and he picked it up, throwing it over an ornate chair. Underneath the dress, I'd worn a sheer white bodysuit with embroidered tulle over the breasts.

He ran his finger under a strap, taking his time to lower it. He did the same to the other side.

The room was warm, but my nipples were stiff. They ached to be touched, to be sucked like my neck. He palmed both of my breasts, lowering his head, taking a nipple in his mouth. He licked first, then started to suck so hard my uterus felt like it spasmed. I sank my nails into his shoulders, moaning. The floor underneath my feet didn't feel steady.

He pulled away and I whimpered, reaching out for him again. He buried his hand in my hair and pulled my face toward his. His tongue plunged into my mouth, and it felt like he was setting my soul free.

Drowning in this moment. Giving him my last breath. He'd carry me around forever since we'd been tangled somehow.

Our lips moved together as we stepped toward the bed, unable to break apart. Every piece of clothing shed was a lost inhibition. He set me close to the headboard, kneeling over me, his dick jutting out. It swayed and bounced when he moved. He took the rose from the pillow and slowly ran it down my body, between my breasts, over my nipples, over my thighs and between my legs.

I sucked in a breath, trying to savor it.

"You are so fucking beautiful." His eyes seemed to inhale me, feeding the intensity.

They felt like twin flames against my skin, making me sweat. It pooled between my breasts and coated my thighs. The candlelight made it glisten. He licked his lips, parted me, and started to eat me like *dolce*. He sounded like a starved man, the vibrations of his mouth making me reach out. My hands found the headboard and I held on, pulsing my hips up and down against his tongue.

"So fucking hot and wet for me." He groaned long and deep, and my entire body went off, moving faster against his face. The orgasm that ripped through me made me convulse.

He yanked my body down and started to kiss me again. I could taste myself on his tongue. I was whimpering and moaning into his mouth. Something existed between us that was even wilder than him. It possessed me down to my core. He sucked on my bottom lip before he pulled away.

He took in my body, his eyes so greedy. "All mine," he said in Italian, raking his teeth over his lip. "Roma Maggio."

"Yours," I barely got out, "Felice Maggio."

I closed my eyes and wrapped my arms around his neck as he situated himself between my legs. I sucked in a breath and bit down on my lip when he started to stretch my walls.

"*Rilassarsi.*" His breath was warm and husky in my ear. "*Rilassarsi.*"

My body had tensed, and tears streamed down my cheeks. He was stretching me to what felt like my limit. But I listened to him and relaxed, opening myself to him, as he moved in and out, not going all the way in.

It felt so good, I couldn't control the noises from my mouth.

I cried out in pain when he breached me, trying to arch away from him. Cold fire burned deep. I almost wanted to push away from him; he was so big I felt like I couldn't breathe. But it felt good too. A rush of warm desire was flooding my blood, driving the cold out.

"*Shh*." He ran his nose up and down my cheek, breathing me in. "You were made for me. You can take all of me." He slowly slid in further.

I made a garbled noise in my throat. He set his mouth over mine, bringing me from my thoughts and into him, *us*, only.

He pulled out, and instantly, I felt empty. He started to kiss down my body, and when he got to my thighs, he ran his nose over them, breathing in the scent of blood like he was a fiend for it. His tongue flicked against me, and he groaned deep in his chest.

"You know what they say about a man who tastes his woman's blood? He'll be addicted to her for the rest of his life, under her spell. You called to me from the moment I found you. I remembered. Your blood was mine. Created for me. Yours feeds mine, and mine is hooked, demanding yours only. Our blood was meant to be one. Like us."

He reached over and opened a drawer on the nightstand. He pulled out a knife and handed it to me.

"What am I—"

"Right here." He made a slice across his heart with his finger. "Mark me."

"Felice..." I wasn't sure if I could.

"Do it, my little herbivore," he ordered.

With a quick slash of my hand, I nicked him. Blood welled up and he groaned, entering me. I dropped the knife, trying to catch my breath. But the cold fire had gone, and in its place was nothing but hot blood made of desire.

"Fuck. That's it. Move with me. Take all of me." He set his head back, his eyes closing, his mouth parting.

He looked feral.

I wanted him to feast on me for the rest of his life.

He gripped my hips and pushed in even deeper. A sound erupted from my chest that sounded like a mixture between a cry and a loud moan. He couldn't go any deeper. It sent my pulse into overdrive. It felt so damn good.

Over and over and over, he drove into me with a delicious tempo. I wasn't sure what he was doing, but he was driving me higher, higher, and higher. He'd taken my pleasure and cornered it, not letting it run away. It was his. It was unlike anything he'd ever done to me before. Because it was deep inside of me, whatever he was controlling.

He seemed to know it. That he'd reached me from inside, making me orgasm this way.

I didn't know how to push back against it yet. Couldn't.

I screamed out as I came around him, convulsing. I tightened around him like a fist, and he growled deep in his throat. He started to move faster, harder, until he went off like a gun. It was violent and the most beautiful thing I'd ever seen.

This dangerous man controlled by my touch.

He gazed down at me until I started to almost squirm underneath him. He kissed me until I was dizzy. Then he pulled out, going for the nightstand again. He pulled out a piece of paper. Something that looked like a certificate.

He took my hand and rubbed it between my legs. He rubbed his hand over the cut I'd made on his chest. It was a small nick, already starting to clot. It was enough, though. He rolled my thumb over the paper, like he was taking my fingerprint. He did the same with his but did it over mine. He stuck the paper in the drawer.

He sat quietly for a second, his back to me.

"You can run from me, Roma Maggio." His voice was rugged.

"But you will never be able to hide. Our blood is bound by an unbreakable vow now."

I ran my hand over his back, barely touching him, and his entire body trembled. "*Ti amo*, Felice," I whispered.

He turned to me, took my mouth with his for a long kiss, then picked me up and carried me to the bathroom. He washed our bodies, but no water known to man was thick enough to touch the blood vow.

CHAPTER 35

FELICE

I stared down at the table, my finger knocking against it. The black and white picture glared back at me. My wife at her sister's wedding. Dancing and laughing with Jack. I slid the picture back inside the envelope it was delivered in. It was a wedding gift from Alfonso, but I was sure Emanuele Corvo approved.

Virna came into view, Fredo next to her.

"My wife?" I asked her.

"Still in the room."

She'd gone to call Hayden, then to soak in the tub. She was worried about taking so much time off work, but I had called Hayden before the wedding myself. After I told him the museum was getting a hefty donation in Roma Maggio's name, he wished us the best on our honeymoon and said he'd see her whenever she returned.

"Do you need me to make a call about the villa?" Virna asked.

The villa. I bought it for Roma after she mentioned spending summers in Italy and maybe retiring here someday. I was going to take her to see it later, to move our things from the *castello* to our own place.

My eyes fell on the envelope again. I forgave the smile the first time. This time, Mount Etna sat in my chest, about to erupt. I couldn't deal with this fucking feeling.

If Jack would have been close enough, I would have taken my wife's bloodied wedding sheet and strangled him with it. It would have been poetic justice. Just the perfect amount of romance and ruthlessness. Dr. Sala might have been proud.

What I was about to do might equal strangulation to the men I was about to deliver retribution to anyway.

"No," I said. "But I want two packages mailed today." I looked at my watch. "As soon as I bring them down. Fredo will go with you. Do you have two gift boxes and wrapping paper?"

"*Sì*," she said.

Taking the envelope with me, I walked into our room, the sweet scent of apricot drifting in the air. It was fucking heady, and for a carnivore, I couldn't get enough of it. Roma started to sing, and I heard water splashing, like she was tapping her foot to the beat.

Bypassing the bathroom, I went to the corner, where the bloodied sheets from the night before lay in a pile. Virna took care of the laundry, but those were mine to keep. Or had been. I'd gotten what I needed anyway.

A blood vow signed by the two of us.

I ripped the sheet into three pieces and folded each section into a square. Using the stationary, I wrote two notes to go with two pieces. The other one was for me.

The arrangement between Emanuele Corvo and Alfonso Maggio is now null and void by the power of this blood vow, made between Felice Giovanni Maggio and Roma Viviana Maggio.

I signed off with:

John

A knock came at the door. Virna handed me the boxes and wrapping paper, along with tissue, scissors, and tape. It took me five minutes to box everything up.

I found Virna and Fredo, and instead of mailing the packages by carrier, I sent Fredo home on a private plane to bring them back to Chicago. Once he landed, he was to hire a private carrier to deliver them. I wanted signed confirmations when they arrived.

When I got back to our suite, Roma stood outside of the bathroom, a towel wrapped around her, her hair dripping wet. She held up the ripped piece of sheet.

"Um, what is this?"

"A sheet."

"I know." She smiled. "What happened to it?" She started backing away, holding her hands up. The material dangled like a bloodied flag. "What is it with you and blood? What did you do with the other pieces of it?"

"I'm a carnivore, my little plant eater. We like to tear shit up."

She looked down at herself. "I feel that. Truly."

"But you got one thing wrong," I said.

"What?" she breathed out when her back hit the wall and I had her cornered.

I followed a piece of hair stuck to her neck with a finger. It led me straight to her hammering pulse like a vein. "It's not all blood I want. Just yours."

Her eyes grew wide, her mouth parted, and she looked transfixed. She gasped when I hauled her up, threw her over my shoulder, and carried her back into the bathroom.

CHAPTER 36

ROMA

Felice bought me a villa in Taormina overlooking the sea. Well, I insisted it was for *us*, but he insisted it was a wedding gift for me. He said I insulted him when I'd argue about it. But how was a home supposed to be made of only me when it was the two of us? He relented a bit after that, but he told me I understood the point he was making. I did, but it wasn't a home without him in it. His eyes had softened after I'd said it.

After our last day at the *castello,* I found his moods were unpredictable. He'd stare out at the sea and get a look in his eyes like he was watching a storm brewing when the day couldn't have been any brighter. His movements were stiff, almost calculated. Other days, only the two of us existed in the world, and all was right in it.

We hadn't left the villa in a week. Some days, I was so sore from having so much sex, I'd take numerous baths to soak the aches away. But it never seemed like enough. The pull to be near him was a constant thing and only grew stronger every day we were together.

The days were adding up, and I wasn't sure if I ever wanted to leave.

On whatever morning we were on, Felice told me to get dressed. I was almost insulted.

He narrowed his eyes at me. "You wanted to visit the beach."

"I see it every day from our terrace."

He gave me a blank look, like he wasn't sure what to do with me. I was learning that Felice Maggio had a lot to learn about living with a woman. He reminded me of a dangerous carnivore, trying to figure out the ways of a little herbivore.

I laughed, rolling over, the sheet sliding off me. I stopped when he squeezed my ass, and we were at it again.

We finally made it out of the villa a few days later.

Felice showed me around the city. We walked miles and ate at little places unknown to tourists. We visited the ruins of the Greek theater and had dinner with Felice's great uncle and his family. We picked out new furniture for the villa. We chartered a boat and visited grottos, dive sites, and cliffs. We went swimming on Isola Bella (Isula Bedda in Sicilian, meaning *beautiful island*). We paid a small fee and visited the Nature Reserve.

I'd noticed cable cars during one of our trips. The *funivia*, it was called, and it would take us from the town of Taormina to Mazzarò beach.

Celso and Fredo took their own car. We were one behind. The interior had two metal bars for holding on and a wider one with padding to sit on.

After the door shut, I wasn't sure I wanted to be inside. I'd never been claustrophobic, but as the car climbed higher and higher, the sounds like something from an airplane, it felt like I was having a panic attack.

What if we got stuck? What if the cable snapped? I looked out and down. It was a far fall in a box. We'd probably flip before we hit.

The car shimmied, and I grabbed for Felice. He'd been staring out the window, and he gave me one of those looks—trying to figure me out.

"I don't like this very much," I admitted.

"You're with me," he said with all the confidence in the world. Like his words alone could keep us from plummeting to our doom. "If I didn't feel you were safe, you wouldn't be here, my little herbivore." He sat me on his lap and kept my head tucked underneath his chin. His arms wrapped around me like bars.

I held on, breathing him in, the panic starting to subside.

"Keep your eyes on mine," he said when I sat up some, trying to look down again.

"If we fall, we fall together," I whispered.

He kissed me, shutting me up. The fear faded when his mouth kept my mind busy. We pulled apart when the car stopped and the doors opened.

We trekked down to the beach, where Felice's great uncle owned a hotel, and spent the entire day there. The sun was high and bright, playing across the teal of the sea, white sparks glinting like daytime starbursts in my eyes. The air smelled salty and clean, and I allowed the breeze to sweep me away. Going with the flow like Plato had said.

The scenery couldn't keep my attention for too long, though. I was always swept back to him.

My husband.

Time in the Mediterranean had darkened his skin, and with his black hair and green eyes, he reminded me of an exotic wild animal. A carnivore with sharp teeth and a petulance for blood. His attention, though, was always on me.

Time with him always felt like it moved too fast, and the hot day seemed to melt into a tepid night. Pinpricks of light dotted the beach as we had dinner.

After, I wanted gelato. I ate it slowly, pretending to take in the water, but I was dreading the ride back. I sighed when we made it to the pick-up point. I went to ditch my gelato, not able to stomach it.

"Give it to me." Felice held out his hand.

"Here." I handed it over.

We sat in the box again and the doors closed.

Shit.

I was going to start hyperventilating. Even though the view was stunning at night, with the lights giving definition to the water's outline and the monstrous shape of Mount Etna, it was intimidating. We were swinging by a cable over depths I couldn't see anymore.

"Stand in front of me."

"What?"

Felice nodded in front of him, and when I didn't move, he planted me there himself. I reached out for his shoulders instead of the bars, refusing to let go. I closed my eyes and took a deep breath when his hands slid up my legs. The car was stuffy, and his fingers were cool from holding the gelato.

He inched higher, under my dress, to my underwear. He ripped them off, and I went forward some before he set me back. The dress had buttons. He undid the bottom few, so he could open it just there.

I shivered when the gelato dripped between my legs. Felice took a knee in front of me, and I convulsed when his warm breath fanned against my thighs as he started to lick it off. He lifted my leg some for better access. I felt like I was falling backward, but the rush of adrenaline from the fear, the different sensations, hot and cold, the stickiness and him cleaning me up...it was heightening my reaction. The noises I made echoed inside of the space.

"That's my beautiful girl," he said, sliding his finger inside of me. I could feel him watching my face. "You want me to keep licking your sweet pussy?"

"Please," I moaned out, shamelessly grinding against his hand.

"Open your eyes, Roma."

I forced them open. The car's windows reflected our every move. He started to pump into me, while his mouth came down and devoured me again. He was licking me clean, and when I was on the edge, he bit down and sucked on the sensitive nub of nerves, sending me spiraling into oblivion. I hadn't even caught my breath when he unzipped his pants, his dick springing free, and lifted me off my feet. My legs wrapped around him, and he slipped inside.

We both groaned.

He unbuttoned the top of my dress, just enough to push my breast over the bra. He started to suck my nipple, and, using the bars for purchase, I started to move against him harder. He pulsed his hips up, and I cried out. He was massive, and my body had to stretch to accommodate him.

"You're so fucking wet for me." He growled when he rammed me even harder. "Your pussy knows who it belongs to. Me. All mine, Roma Maggio. For the rest of our lives."

I wasn't sure if the car was trembling from us or the cable. We were crashing into each other, our bodies smacking. My breasts jiggled from the impact, and his balls slapped against me. Sweat coated my body, and I was whimpering. He was working my body as hard as the steep terrain was working the cable cars.

"Fuck," he ground out. "My wife likes to scream. Fuck yes." His breathing was ragged. "Drain every last drop from my cock. You're so fucking beautiful." He sank his hand into my hair and pulled my face forward. Our tongues reached out, touching, before he went deep.

He hissed out a breath when I tightened around him. I couldn't hold back. My body felt like it was about to snap. When it did, I convulsed around his cock, my voice breaking, like someone was shaking me.

An animalistic noise came from his throat, and the sound of it made my orgasm stretch. He grabbed hold of my hips, tilting them up, reaching me so deep, he was blurring the line between pleasure and pain. I was like a rag doll, draped across the bar, holding on during a storm. My body had no choice but to give in again. I was too sensitive.

He cursed, coming hard enough to make sweat from his body splash on my chest.

He set his forehead against mine, our breaths dancing, until his eyes opened. He looked high. He glanced behind me, taking in where we were on the ride.

He kissed my lips and pulled out. He buttoned my dress, then, using my underwear, cleaned me up. He stuck them back in his pocket and zipped himself up. He grabbed my hand and my bag, and a second later, we stepped off the cable car.

"That was actually fun," I said, keeping a hand on my dress so the wind couldn't blow it up. "I'd like to do it again someday."

He wrapped an arm around my neck, kissed my temple, and laughed all the way home.

CHAPTER 37

ROMA

We stayed at our villa in Taormina for another week before Cassio called and told Felice he needed to return to Chicago. Tommaso was having issues with his heart, and he wanted Felice home. If something happened to the boss, I knew my husband was going to take his place.

I didn't know how that would change our lives, just that it would somehow.

It was hard not to stress about it as Felice drove us to the penthouse. It felt odd being back in Chicago. It was such a sharp contrast to the warmth of Italy and our time there. Not that I didn't love Chicago and being *home* with Felice, but real life and the responsibilities that come with were almost depressing to think about.

Especially knowing Babbo and my sisters lived close, and things were never going to be the same between us.

Felice brought my hand to his mouth and kissed it. Maybe he sensed the change in my mood.

We stopped to pick up some takeout at a deli for me, and a deep-dish pizza for Felice at Pequod's, before we headed to the penthouse. I sighed when the doorman told Felice a bunch of boxes had been delivered for me. Of course. Babbo had cleaned out my room, like he'd wiped me from his life. Some of the boxes were busting at the seams. He'd stuffed as much as he could into each one.

For a reason beyond me, I didn't want to face the boxes yet. I left Felice to direct the doorman where to set them while I headed out to the balcony. The sun was just starting to set. Strong gusts of wind blew off the water. If my clothes wouldn't have been secured to my body, it felt like they might take flight.

Even though I wasn't ready to face the boxes, I needed two living things from Babbo's. Romeo and Juliet, my two goldfish. Amanda, Babbo's cleaning lady, was supposed to be taking care of them for me. I didn't want Babbo to stop her from doing it, so I'd asked Elsa to grab them when she got back from Taormina.

I pulled out my phone and sent Elsa a text.

Me: Can you bring Romeo & Juliet to the office on Monday?

A few seconds later...

Elsa: About them...seems Romeo & Juliet, the fish version, had the same ending as the play.

She sent me a picture. Romeo and Juliet's bowl had been tossed in the trash at Babbo's house. The glass was turned on its side. Rocks and their little love cave were left, but no fish.

Elsa: No matter what anyone says, *Romeo and Juliet* is not a romance. It has romantic elements, but that's about it. It's a tragedy. Just like what happened to your fish. I'm so sorry.

"He killed my fishes!"

"Fishes?" Felice came to stand next to me, his back to the water. "You been watching *The Godfather* without me knowing it, Dino?"

"Babbo. He killed Romeo & Juliet!" I was so mad, I wanted to kick something. My foot shot out and hit the stone railing. It burned like a bitch, but it felt good too.

He was quiet for so long, I turned my face to see if he'd heard me. He looked down at me. He wore that blank look again, like...*I have no clue what the fuck is going on in that head of yours. What do I do with you, you little alien creature?*

To his credit, he asked, "Romeo and Juliet were your...fishes?"

"Yes! And he threw them out. Why would he do that?"

"Some people kill whatever represents the hurt to make themselves feel better."

"These were innocent fishes."

"People kill fish for dinner, my little herbivore."

Most people would have said "catch fish for dinner" but Felice was blunt about the truth.

"These were *pet* fish, Felice. Not food. He didn't have to do that."

He pulled me toward him, rubbing my arms. "I'll buy you all the fishes in the world."

Even though Babbo had hurt me, and I was covering it with anger, my mouth twitched when Felice said *fishes*. He caught it and narrowed his eyes at me.

"Still trying to figure me out, Carnivore?"

"It'll be a lifelong quest, I'm sure." He took my hand and led me back into the penthouse. "Time for dinner. Not fish. After, I'm going to fuck you so hard you won't be able to do anything but sleep. Then business."

"Pleasure before business, Maggio?"

He lifted me up and set me on the kitchen counter. I opened my legs and he stepped between them. He ran his hand through my hair and then pulled my head back. I was forced to look up at him.

"You before the world." The conviction in his tone matched the intensity in his eyes. "Doesn't matter who, when, or where."

My throat felt tight. "Kiss me, Felice." My voice was barely above a whisper.

His eyes locked on mine before he moved so slowly toward me, my breaths became erratic. Our lips barely touched. Small tastes. I wrapped my arms around his neck and my legs around his waist. He hoisted me up, carrying me to the bedroom. He set me down on the bed, and taking his time, undressed me. I did the same to him, my hands exploring his body.

His shoulders were wide and his waist slim. I could feel every muscle in his arms. His legs were long and muscular, but nothing about him was overly done.

He leaned over me, kissing me again, until we were both in the center of the bed. He directed my leg up some, and positioning himself, entered me. My head tilted back, my eyes closed, and a deep moan vibrated in the center of my chest. He spoke to me in Italian, telling me how beautiful I was, how he would kill anyone who tried to take me from him, how he would die to keep me.

A sharp ruthlessness existed underneath his words that gave me no reason to doubt him.

It was like uncovering a great monster from thousands of years ago. Layer by layer, not to disturb the bones of the thing. It was to be respected, to be pulled out piece by piece, but put together to create a picture of what existed beyond the surface.

The night I'd told Lo the man I'd built in my head wouldn't care about the world, only me, came back to me through his words:

"You before the world. Doesn't matter who, when, or where."

It seemed like he'd tattooed those words on my heart before he'd ever said them to me. His soul was half of mine. And I wanted them on my headstone someday.

His pace and tempo were causing a flood inside of me. The pressure was immense, and it was pressing in on the ache between my legs.

"Keep your eyes on mine," he said, tracing the shape of my lips with his tongue.

It was one of the most intense moments I'd ever spent with my husband. I let the moment carry me away, and I let go. The orgasm that tore through me was violent. The exact opposite of how he'd been touching me.

The contrast was so fucking delicious. It made me delirious.

He started to move faster, animalistic noises coming from deep inside his chest. "Fuck. Roma." He gripped my leg, pushing into me even harder, until he came inside of me. Even after he was finished, he kept us together.

I was still lost to whatever existed between us, and my nails grazed up and down his back. It felt like madness on the outside, but peace at the center of it.

My stomach made an obnoxious noise. His brow was furrowed when he pulled back and looked me in the eye. Kissing me on the nose, he pulled out of me and went to the closet. When he came out, he was wearing a pair of black sweatpants and nothing else.

He left me in the room by myself, and I closed my eyes, taking a deep breath. He hadn't been rough, but emotionally, it felt like a roller coaster.

It was overwhelming to feel such depths existed, but it was overpowering touching them.

A few minutes later, the smell of warm food wafted in the air, and the bed dipped.

"Sit up, my little herbivore."

"Do I have to?"

He pulled me up by my arm, and I kept my eyes closed. I opened my mouth when something touched my lips. I'd gotten eggplant and zucchini pasta with feta and dill at the deli. I made a satisfied noise in my throat, and he fed me another bite.

I opened my eyes as he was looking down to stab something with the fork. I guided his hand toward his mouth when he held it out for me.

"You try it."

He opened and let me feed him. His face totally shut down before he started to chew.

"No good," he said, forcing the food down.

I exploded with laughter. His face softened at the sound.

"It is good!" I smiled, then shrugged. "More for me." I opened my mouth.

He fed me every bite, even scraped the plate, before we took a long shower. I enjoyed sharing showers with him. He washed me, and I washed him. I moaned when he started to massage my scalp. That led to one thing...and then, the water turned cold. I was too tired to even walk to the bed. He carried me, and I got comfortable under the airy bedspread. It was like sleeping on a cloud.

My eyes must have closed for a few, because when I opened them, he was dressed in a suit.

"Business?" I yawned.

He nodded, fixing his tie.

"I don't want you to leave. We've spent so much time together lately..." Even the thought of him leaving made me feel lonely.

It seemed like he didn't know how to react. Maybe no one had ever cared enough to ask him to stay before.

He had eyes that could easily break a heart—the sincerity in them when he dropped his guard and let me see it.

"I make you feel safe," he said.

"Yes. But it's so much more than that. I want you here. With me. Every morning. Every night. I love spending time with you, Felice," I whispered.

Dressed in his suit, sans shoes, he got back into bed. He pulled me close, and I wrapped my arms around his, sticking my ass into his crotch. I fell asleep a minute later, but jet lag was a bitch. I woke up in the middle of the night.

He was gone.

I fell asleep again, reaching for his pillow and hugging it.

Before the sun came up, he was next to me again. I was clinging to him.

CHAPTER 38

ROMA

The museum had always been one of my favorite places in the city. I loved the building and everything inside of it. Days when new exhibits rolled out were some of my most memorable. Sharing new information with the world about prehistoric creatures gave me butterflies.

Felice, Italy, our wedding, our new villa—they still held me in their warm grasps, though. My love for the museum and the passion for what I did seemed to help ease me back into reality. The transition would have been a hundred times harder if I still wasn't so excited about my career.

Felice drove me my first morning back and walked me in. He was going to ride back with Celso. Fredo was going to be my new shadow. Felice refused to budge on it until the issue with my father, Alfonso, and Jack was settled.

Vows spoken in church and a contract signed in blood seemed everlasting enough to me, but my husband wasn't convinced.

"Have a good day at work, honey," I said, waving at him as I walked away. He'd gone as far as Gonzalo, but his eyes never left me.

When I walked into the office, it felt like hanging up first while the other person hangs on. I wanted to dash out just to look at him again. When he stepped through the door, right after I put my coffee and bag down, I ran into his arms like I hadn't seen him in years.

He grinned. "You're a fucking adorable little herbivore." He slipped my eyeglasses on my face.

Sometimes I spent a lot of time on the computer, so I bought a pair of glasses that had blue-light filtering lenses. I thought they made me look scholarly. They were oversized and leopard print. I must have forgotten them in the car. He'd noticed and pocketed them.

"Special delivery, ah?"

He leaned in, setting his nose against my neck, breathing me in. "You still smell like me."

"I was just in the car with you—less than five minutes ago."

The dangerous carnivore had been playing with his food, *me*, before he let her go.

"Too long."

"Right?" I whispered.

He took my chin in his hand and kissed my lips. "Who would've thought apricots were stronger than adrenaline, ah?"

"Me," I whispered, dazed by his kiss. "They're a superfood. I know. I eat them every day."

His laughter made me blink. His perfect teeth were shocking white against a sea of black stubble.

"Excuse me."

Felice turned me with him, but kept me tucked behind him, to face a guy standing in the doorway. He held a package in his hands.

"Ms. Corvo?"

"Ye—"

"Mrs. Maggio," Felice corrected.

"I've recently gotten married," I said. "How can I help you?"

"Uh..." He stared at me.

"What's your business here, kid?" Felice's voice was authoritative. He wasn't to be fucked with.

The guy, who was not a kid, but maybe in his late twenties, older than me, snapped his attention to Felice. He made another stunned noise before he held the package out.

"A delivery for Mr. Burton," he rushed out. "Mr. Burton said Ms. Cor—Mrs. Maggio—would sign for it."

Felice took the package and signed for it. The guy looked around the office, anywhere but at the two of us, while he waited. Felice had scared the shit out of him. Felice handed him the receipt and set the box on my desk. The delivery guy was gone before Felice had turned around.

I sniffed the air, making a deal of it. "Do you smell that? His sneakers started smoking, he peeled out of here so fast."

Felice pulled a gun from his back and pointed it in the direction the guy had gone in. He made a noise to go with it.

He wasn't fucking around. I didn't blame the guy for burning rubber to get out of here. If I wasn't in love with Felice, I would have run too. To the world, I could see how scary he could be. Razor sharp meat hooks in a freezer, a bunch of guys hanging from them, slipped into my thoughts, and I shivered.

Maybe the delivery guy recognized his name. I'd learned it was synonymous with the Chicago Outfit.

I gasped when he pinned me against the wall. "I'll give you that one Ms. Corvo slip-up. Next time, you'll answer to me, Mrs. Maggio."

"What will you do?" I forced myself to hold his stare. It was like challenging a wild animal.

He smiled, but it didn't seem all that friendly. It was wicked. "Have a good day at work, honey," he said, leaving me staring behind him.

His cologne lingered in the air. I was almost too desperate to soak it in. It was as hypnotizing as the man himself. The smell of him, the way he looked, the way he walked, the way he talked...my entire body yearned to follow him wherever he went.

Hayden walked in, oblivious. He had a messenger bag slung

over his shoulder. "Roma! Or should I call you Mrs. Maggio?" He laughed. "It's great to have you back."

"Thank you for allowing me to take so much time off," I said.

He glanced at my wedding ring and whistled underneath his breath. "Think nothing of it." He scooped his package up and disappeared inside of his office.

It was a little strange he didn't put up a fuss about the time. He wasn't a tyrant, but he would have never held my job before, unless the circumstances were dire. Like when Lo and I had been attacked. He would have expected me to give him a heads up about a wedding, and especially about the time I took for our honeymoon.

"Either you're constipated or thinking really hard," Elsa said, setting her bag down. "Since you eat so many greens, I'm thinking the latter."

We hugged, rocking back and forth, and then headed back to our desks.

"Hayden," I said. "He didn't have a problem with all the time I took."

She grinned. "We were all Gucci here as Lo would say."

I laughed. "As Lo would say."

Elsa asked me about the grand opening for Lo's Chicago salon. We talked about it for a while, then she updated me on everything going on with the museum. Kerry had four big events booked. We had a major donor contribution, and another one was interested. Elsa said Hayden was going to have lunch with the interested party.

Before the day got away from me, I marked a few things down in my calendar.

Lo's Chicago opening was a huge deal for her. I was sure Babbo would have something at his place to celebrate, but I wanted to connect with my sisters. I'd run the idea of having a small party at our house by Felice that morning. He said it was my house, I did what I wanted, but he was fine with it. Elsa's birthday was coming up, and Felice had said that Tommaso wanted to have a reception for us. I wasn't totally comfortable with the idea, but saying no to him was even more uncomfortable.

After I was done, we discussed exhibits and finding a new cleaning company.

By the time lunch rolled around, I was ready to eat. "You want to grab lunch at The Herbivore? See if Kerry wants to go?" I asked Elsa as I dug around in my bag for my wallet. "My treat."

Hayden busted out his office, his messenger bag swinging. "I'd like you both to come with me." He wiped sweat from his brow. "We need to move. Don't want to be late. He might leave."

"The potential donor?" Elsa stood, straightening her dress.

"That's the one."

Elsa looked at me and I shrugged. We grabbed our things and followed behind Hayden. I stopped when I noticed a new plaque going up. The museum honored our most generous donors by having a dedicated tablet placed on the wall if they chose not to be anonymous. This one was fancy, with the profile of a woman's face etched into it.

"Roma Viviana Maggio," I read aloud. "The little Herbivore." I turned to Elsa and Hayden.

Elsa shrugged. "John."

I narrowed my eyes at Hayden.

He looked sheepish but said, "We're going to be late!"

Felice must have donated a nice chunk of money to get the plaque and whatever else he'd arranged. Gears turned inside my head, and all the pieces clicked into place. No wonder Hayden didn't fire me. My husband had greased his palm.

We all couldn't fit into Hayden's Mini Cooper, so Fredo was going to drive us. Besides, Hayden thought of the world as his own racetrack. If someone got in front of him, he thought they were doing it to challenge him.

Hayden sat up front with Fredo as he drove us to the restaurant. It was only a few minutes from the museum, on the 95th floor of a fancy hotel. It had a stunning view. Hayden flipped the mirror and fixed his hair. He was nervous. Elsa and I followed his lead and made sure we checked out before we arrived.

The valet would have parked the SUV, but Fredo insisted we all go in together. Paranoia, or maybe thinking ahead to stop issues before they happened, was something Felice's men all had in common. Fredo didn't trust anyone in the car alone.

"Who knows what they might do," he said when Elsa made a comment about it.

By the time we made it to the elevator, Hayden was almost pacing inside of it. When we stepped out, he searched the restaurant.

"Oh no," I said, turning when I realized who sat at the table waving. Jack Maggio.

Hayden stepped in front of me. "What's going on?"

"I'm not having *anything* with him."

"Mr. Maggio?" He stuck a thumb in his direction. "Wait. Do you know him? I just realized...same last name."

"She knows him all right," Elsa said.

"Is he related to John?"

"Jack is John's uncle," Elsa explained.

Hayden glanced at him again. "He looks much younger."

"I'm out," I said, about to ask Fredo to take me back to the museum.

Fredo was staring at Jack with hard eyes.

"Roma," Hayden whispered. "*Please.*" He held tight to the strap of his messenger bag and almost squeezed the word out. "You have no idea how much money he's thinking of donating. It could change the fate of the museum."

"Why do I have to be here?"

"It would look odd if you left now."

"Wait," I said. "Did he mention me by name?"

He sighed. "You were Miss Illinois..."

"Oh boy. Duped." Elsa turned to me. "Don't run from him, Roma. Show him he's nothing to you, while you make a show of that rock on your left finger. Don't let him intimidate you."

"No, don't," Hayden said.

We both glared at him. He lifted his hands.

"This better be worth it, Burton," I said.

He almost did a little dance but remembered where he was and ran a hand through his hair. He fixed his gold-rimmed glasses, and we followed behind him to the table. Jack stood and fixed his suit when we got there. Hayden made introductions, even though he knew I'd been acquainted with the pompous ass.

"Uncle," I said as I shook his hand.

"Funny." He gestured to the seats around the table.

We took them. Fredo took the seat beside me.

"A lot better than *roses are red, violets are blue, I'm really not stalking you.*"

"Oh." Hayden sucked in a breath, realizing.

"It was supposed to be funny." Jack took a drink of whiskey. "You could cut me a little slack."

"Why? So you can try to force me to marry you again?"

Hayden cleared his throat. "Look at this view! I hope the food is as good. I've never been here before. How about everyone else?"

"Look, you've got the money," Jack told Hayden. He looked at me. "I didn't know how else to get in touch with you. You made a big mistake. Even if you didn't want to marry me, you should have never married John. You have no idea who he really is. Yeah, he's charming. So am I. We look a lot alike. But that's where the similarities end. John only married you to get back at Emanuele and Alfonso.

"Do you honestly think John's timing in your life was coincidental? He was at Jupiter the same night I was. He knew I was there. I'm positive he heard something about our arrangement, and he wanted to steal you from me to get back at us."

I had to hide my true reaction from him. Lo had said the guy I'd described had been watching me dance that night. Who was it? Felice or Jack? Or did she notice them both and couldn't tell the difference because it was dark, and she was drunk?

"Your intentions are pure, ah?" The words came out on autopilot, my mind in overdrive.

"Damn. He's corrupting you already. That attitude." He blew out a heavy breath laced with whiskey. "And yes, as a matter of fact, my intentions are pure. I didn't want to marry you to get back at anyone. I wanted to marry you for you."

"Bullshit. You don't even know me!"

"We would have gotten to know each other. So I love the way you look—that's not a crime. You don't think John hasn't noticed your looks? It's the first thing he noticed about you, sweetie. Trust me. John likes 'em beautiful, just like I do."

"You sent a man with a gun to my father's house—a crazy man who *shot* him—to force me to marry you."

"In all honesty, my dad did that. I have the Maggio pride, but it's nothing like his. I agreed to the marriage, but I've been in the same boat as you. I tried to warn him. His plan was going to send you straight to John if things went south. Here we are."

"*You're adorable when you're mad,*" I quoted him. Not sure why, but that line really stuck in my craw. I wanted to deck him for it. It probably had more to do with timing, but I needed to set it free.

He shrugged. "Well, you are." He took a drink. "I'm serious, Roma. Our marriage is off the table, but I needed to warn you. You seem like a sweet girl who just got it twisted somehow. Chose the wrong Maggio. But Sal was a bad seed. John is a rotten apple. It didn't skip a generation with those two because they're one and the same. Believe me, John's using you to kill Dr. Corvo a little every day. A slow death. He's sick over you marrying John."

Elsa snatched my hand and held it under the table. Fredo stood, taking my arm, leading me out. I went with him, still on autopilot. I'd been trying to ignore the truth since I'd married Felice. I knew I'd broken Babbo's heart, but I couldn't find it in myself to put his before mine.

Still.

It was killing me too.

CHAPTER 39

FELICE

Celso and Frankie waited by the car. I waited behind the bathrooms. They were in a brick structure that kept me concealed in the shadows. Bright lights lit the baseball field but kept this area of the park in darkness.

Jack and his friends were the last out of practice. They were laughing until I stepped out.

"Shit!" Jack jumped back.

"Your choice," I said to his friends, who had lifted their bats like they were going to whack me to death with them. But I'd already pulled my gun and stuck it to Jack's forehead.

Celso and Frankie walked up, staring at them. Frankie took a drag of his cigarette and blew the smoke out through his nose. Jack's friends lowered their bats. I shooed them away with a hand, and they scattered like mice in the darkness. Except for one, who waited by Jack's car.

"What do you want, John?"

A gust of wind picked up, fall in the air, but his sweat and blood were stronger. His pants were torn at the knee, and fresh blood smeared his skin and soaked the fabric.

"You really need to ask that question, *Jack*? It seems rhetorical to me."

"Roma," he said.

"My wife. I'll only say this once, then I'll have no doubt you either weren't listening or you don't give a fuck if it happens again. Either way, not my problem. But it'll be yours. She's not part of this game we play, understand?"

"You're the only one playing her."

I grabbed him by the shirt and slammed his body against the wall. I took a handful of his hair, tilting his head back, sticking the pistol under his chin. "Understand? Yes or no, Jack."

"If I say no?"

I smiled. "You always were a pompous little prick."

"Runs in the blood, nephew."

"Yeah, but I have big enough balls to back up what comes out of my mouth. That gene skipped you and Alfonso. I take care of my own fucking business. Always have." I pressed the gun even harder. "You're a smart boy, Jackie. You understand the difference between yes and no. What'll it be?"

"If you're so fucking big and bad, why the need for the gun?"

"Just giving you a glimpse of the moment before you leave this world if you step over the line."

"You're a fucking asshole, John."

That was his comeback when he couldn't think of anything else to say. And the little asshole was ballsy in the face of a gun, but I knew why.

"The agreement between me and Alfonso doesn't include you," I said. "But even an agreement only goes so far when it comes to my wife. Standing behind lines isn't my thing, Jackie. I'm usually the one tripping them. I'm not your old man. You mean nothing to me. And my trigger finger is getting impatient."

A bead of sweat rolled down his temple. "Get that gleam out of your eye, John."

He'd looked into my eyes and read the intent behind them. I was done fucking around. I'd splatter his blood all over the side of the brick if he didn't tell me what I wanted to hear. It didn't matter to me that his blood resembled mine. He'd be long gone if he was anything but harmless to my wife. Alfonso led him around by an invisible collar.

"I'm out," he whispered.

"That's not what I want to hear. I asked you if you understood—yes or no."

"Yeah," he said louder.

I moved the gun and patted his head. "Good boy."

He swatted at my hand. "Get the fuck outta here with that shit."

"You're not a bad-looking kid, Jack. You got potential. You're just lacking a certain ruthless finesse."

"Fuck you, John." He fixed his hair. "And I'm the pompous one?"

I grinned as I walked away from him.

"Yo, John!"

I turned to him.

"If you get off on tripping lines, why haven't you killed me or my old man yet?"

"The game is too much fun to quit playing now."

They hit me. I hit back harder. Nonna Silvia had pegged them years ago when she'd quoted the verse, *pride goeth before destruction, and a haughty spirit before a fall.* I didn't need to wound them mortally to kill them. Their pride was directly connected to their health.

Jack wasn't lying when he told Roma his pride was nothing compared to Alfonso's. Emanuele might be sick over Roma marrying me, but Alfonso was sick over losing her *to me*. It was more satisfying to watch him writhe and groan while his heart still beat, and he still took in air. If I ended it all, I couldn't hurt him. It would be game over. This way, I could watch him suffer while I continued to win.

This wasn't about business, but something much more personal.

"John," Jack called again, his tone serious.

"I don't have all night to chat, Jack."

"She's going to get sick of your shit, like everyone else *not* in your world. And when she has enough, of you or the games you're playing with us, her old man included, she's going to bolt. It's just a matter of time."

I walked off, not disagreeing. She might. But she could never outrun me—I was her jagged other half.

The rat who'd waited for Jack stood straighter when I moved closer to him. He'd been leaning against Jack's car, the barrel of his bat pointed at the ground, his fist tight around the knob. I mentally labeled him a rat. While Jack had been busy with me, he'd called someone. Probably Alfonso.

He set the bat against the car, raised his hands, and smiled at me. It was a *fuck you* sort of smile. I shot him clear through his hand. He looked down at it, at me, then passed out.

My finger was never so fucking happy.

CHAPTER 40

ROMA

The opening of Lo's salon was big enough to have Chicago press there. Babbo hadn't showed yet, but all my sisters were there, along with Elsa and Kerry. Felice stopped by an hour or two into it. It almost seemed like he showed his face on purpose. Like he knew the articles about the opening would include him.

Chicago mobster tied to the new "it" salon.

My name would be next to his. "The former Miss Illinois, Roma Maggio, who's married to Felice 'John' Maggio, is Lolita Di Lazzaro's sister." I knew it ran much deeper than that, though, and probably so did the journalist. But I doubted the journalist would be brave enough to claim Felice was doing it to let the world know Lo's salon was under his protection. And it went even deeper, or closer to the surface, depending on how one looked at it.

Felice wanted the world to know I belonged to him.

One look at him looking at me and it was no secret. The intensity in his eyes had moved up a notch, almost to insanity level, after Jack's ploy to get me to lunch. Felice watched me like I was running away from him, and he was only giving me a head start, before he caught me with no trouble at all.

I lifted on my toes and placed a soft kiss on his lips. "I'm so glad you're here."

He nodded and touched his lips again. I kissed him harder and longer this time. He set his arm around my waist, pulling me close to his side as we mingled some. I didn't want to stay long. I knew Babbo wouldn't show his face if I was there.

I found Lo and told her I'd see her at the penthouse for the after party. It would be the first time my sisters ever visited me at our home.

Lo fluffed my hair and told me to make a grand exit, a huge smile on her face. Earlier, before the opening, she'd done my hair and makeup. She also did Elsa's and Kerry's. Free publicity from three of the most beautiful women in the city, she'd said.

Felice held my hand, looking out the window, as Celso drove us to the penthouse. Fredo sat next to him, not much to say as usual, but he kept fixing his suit.

We all rode in the private elevator, and after entering the penthouse, I checked in to make sure everything was set. Felice insisted on a catering company, which I suspected might be linked to his business.

"We just need the guests, Mrs. Maggio," the owner said.

We were all good on the food and drinks then—the penthouse was spectacular enough to do the rest.

Felice grabbed me and held me tight, forcing me to look up at him. "*Rilassarsi*," he whispered.

"I am relaxed," I said.

He stared at me until I sighed.

"Okay, maybe I am nervous. I haven't spent much time with my sisters since the wedding. I haven't even seen Isa's son yet. I miss them, and...I'm excited about them coming."

He nodded and kissed my lips. "I know they're important to you."

Something about his tone was...off. Melancholy almost.

"I miss them, Felice," I whispered. "But I'd miss you more. I can't live without my other half. I'm where I belong."

"Fucking heartbreaking." He touched my chin. "I'm out for a while. Business."

I nodded. "Will you be back before the party's over?"

He shrugged, and I knew that was the only answer I'd get. Sometimes he kept odd hours and wasn't around much. Tommaso was under the care of my father, but when something happened to him...I wondered if Felice was going to be gone even more. But he was with me for every sunset and every sunrise. He took what I'd said to heart, and it broke my heart a little.

He was everything my father said he was, but not to me.

"Felice," I called as he headed for the door.

He stopped and turned to me.

"The reception Tommaso's hosting for us. I'm looking for a dress. Any particular color?"

"Anything but red. I'll kill someone."

No red. Got it.

He left, and not long after, mostly everyone started to arrive.

"Are you being serious right now?" Lo looked around. "You live in a Chicago Italian palace!"

"What's the address here?" Talia kissed my cheeks. "777 Easy Street?"

"I'm afraid to touch anything," Alina said. "It's all picture perfect. I'm so glad I didn't bring the kids."

"Not me," Isabella said, checking out the kitchen. "I could cook a mean Sunday dinner in here."

We all got quiet after that. We were together a lot, but Sundays were a given. We would stay home all day and cook and eat together. That would never happen here. My sisters would never do that to Babbo. I couldn't blame them. They were stuck in the middle of us, which felt as bad as total separation. Because I knew the strife between me and Babbo was the cause of our family being torn apart.

Elsa and Kerry arrived, breaking up the awkward moment. I started the tour again, and by the time we were done, everyone started to relax. It was almost like old times, minus Babbo. We laughed and joked and talked about the salon. Lexi and Eve were looking forward to the Rome opening. They loved Italy and wanted to go back.

Most of the women gravitated toward the kitchen to stuff our faces while the men lounged around in the living room.

Lo took a sip of her red wine. "Are we ever going to do the book club we talked about? I've been reading some great ones."

We'd discussed it before the attack, but none of us brought it up again until now.

"Ooh, I'm in." Elsa stuffed her mouth with cake.

Isabella looked at me and then at Lo. "Where are we going to have it? The holidays are coming up and with Babbo..."

"With Babbo what?" I asked.

My sisters all looked at each other, and I felt like such an outsider. We still had our group chat, but it hadn't been as busy as it once was. It was like their lives were separated by a wall. On one side was Babbo. On the other side was me.

"We can take turns hosting it at our places," Lo said, trying to glare at Isabella without me catching it. Lo was never subtle about anything, though.

"With Babbo *what?*" I pressed, staring at Lo.

She sighed. "He's been...depressed, Y. After you got married..."

"It's like he's sick," Isabella said. "We barely see him when we're at the house. When we do, he sits in the sunroom and stares out, petting Paisano. He doesn't eat much. He's lost weight. And he's been visiting Mamma's grave more than usual."

"Mamma must have looked...awful," Talia said. "It must have really scarred him, what he saw. It's like he's seeing you the same way. Like he's still looking at you in the hospital bed after you were attacked."

"I never saw him cry growing up," Alina said. "I saw him crying after Mamma died. And when you two were in the hospital."

I looked away from them, at Elsa and Kerry. They looked

away from me. The semi-normal time we were having seemed to lose all its helium.

"What is this?" Lo snapped. "A celebration or a funeral? No one has died, but we're acting like it. Babbo's going through a hard time. Once he accepts things didn't go as planned and Y is married to who she loves, things will get better. For everyone."

No one said anything, but the looks on their faces were clear. No hope for that. I silently agreed. He was so pissed, he killed Romeo and Juliet.

"The book club," Kerry said, turning the conversation back in the direction it'd started. "I'm down."

"We could incorporate wine," Elsa said. "Drinks and romance books."

"Or margaritas," Talia said.

"It could be the hostess's choice to pick the poison," Alina said. "We pick the snacks for team events when it's our week."

"What are we talking about?" Lexi asked, walking into the kitchen, Eve next to her.

Lo started over, and we didn't mention Babbo after that. But his presence hung heavy over my heart. I took my glass of wine and slipped out, going for the terrace. It was one of my favorite spots in the world. Navy Pier was lit up like a carnival, and my eyes were glued to it.

I jumped and almost lost my wine glass when I noticed Felice standing a few feet from me. I hadn't even heard him.

"When did you get home?" I breathed out.

He stared at me, not saying anything.

"Everything okay?"

He shrugged. "Depends."

"On?"

"Your thoughts. They're far away. Too fucking far away."

"You can't chase down my thoughts, Felice."

"Fuck if I can't," he said, charging toward me with all the swagger in the world. He pulled my body into his so hard, I lost my breath. My mouth opened and he seized it. His tongue grappled with mine, and I was snared not even a second later, being, metaphorically speaking, carried back to a place only he could bring me.

His hunting ground.

And just like that, the rest of the world disappeared.

CHAPTER 41

ROMA

It had been a week since the grand opening of Lo's salon, and the intensity in Felice's eyes never lessened. No matter how many times I'd tried to explain it to him—I needed time to grieve the loss of my only parent, to accept the changes in my life—he refused to truly listen.

He was so focused on what I might do—leave him—that it clouded his thoughts. I remembered how blurred my eyes were with blood when I'd first met him. I couldn't help but think the same was going on inside of his head. He could only see red.

A color that triggered him to hunt. He was constantly in that mode.

I sighed, pushing the thought aside for later. The reception Tommaso and his wife were hosting for us was that night, and I was anxious enough. We were leaving soon. I applied lipstick to finish my face, spritzed some perfume on, and then stood and straightened my dress.

In under sixty minutes, I was going to be spending time with a bunch of Chicago's most notorious men—men my father had desperately tried to keep me away from. They were going to be celebrating the marriage of the boss under the *head* boss, who was my husband.

My feet seemed glued to the floor. I had to force them to move, to find Felice. He was having a drink in the living room when I'd last seen him, but he wasn't there. I found him in the Gallery Hall, almost empty glass in hand, looking at the newest painting on the wall.

One of Sandro's artist friends had attended our wedding. Sandro said his friend had an amazing "party trick" and asked if we would mind him doing it at our reception.

Turned out, this party trick wasn't a party trick at all, but talent at its finest. He'd watched as the photographer took a picture of Felice and me in front of the castle.

The palm trees had been swaying, the air had smelled sweet, of sea and citrus, and hundreds of candles had lined the walkway, along with baby's breath.

Felice had my arm in his, we were side by side, but staring at each other.

Sandro's friend had painted the scene on a huge canvas while the reception took place. He'd given it to us as a gift, but Felice refused to accept it unless he paid for it. The amount was in the thousands. I think he would have paid even more for it. He hung it in the gallery and visited it often. The scene moved him.

"Pretty fantastic," I whispered, standing next to him.

We turned to each other at the same time. Even though I'd seen him earlier, he took my breath away. He was dressed in a black tux, his hair impeccable, those prominent cheek bones on display, along with those sea-green eyes.

The lights highlighting the art did the same to him.

He took my hand, lifted it, straightened my rings, and placed a warm kiss over my knuckles. The diamond bracelet around my wrist shimmered with rainbow colors, like it was in a room full of candles. The thick diamond choker around my neck did the same.

"I figured white's a neutral color," I whispered, straightening the designer gown. It was strapless, made of draped and gathered silk cady. "Not like wearing red in a room full of carnivores." I kept my eyes down for a second.

If I held his stare, we weren't going to be on time. It was important we were. Tommaso and his wife had chartered a yacht on Lake Michigan.

"Look at me, my little herbivore." He held my chin when I did, lightly stroking my bottom lip. "There's nothing neutral about you. You could start a war in church."

"*Grazie mille.*" I set my hand over his wrist, squeezing, recognizing his form of flattery. "Should we get going?"

He held his arm out for me, and I took it. When we got to the private entryway, he helped me into my high silver heels and faux-fur coat. He slipped his black dress coat on, a white scarf around the collar, and we left.

Celso drove us to Navy Pier, where the yacht was docked.

The sun was out, since we were setting off before sunset, but there was a bite in the fall air. The wind whipped off the water, tugging at my dress and Felice's scarf. I burrowed deeper into my coat as Felice led me aboard. He owned every room he walked into. All eyes were on us as we stepped inside.

The yacht was impressive. It even had a dance floor.

Felice took my coat, and a server took it from him, along with Felice's. We were offered drinks. Felice ordered whiskey for him and champagne, with an apricot, for me. Then we made our way to Tommaso's table. Men stood around it like they were guarding gold bricks. I hadn't seen Tommaso in a while, and he'd aged in that time. He was skinnier, but his fingers were swollen. His body seemed fragile, but he didn't appear weak to me.

His wife sat next to him. Felice introduced us. She seemed nice, but somewhat guarded. I thanked them both for the reception.

"My pleasure." Tommaso coughed. It sounded like his lungs were full of fluid. "The wedding in Italy was a surprise. It would have been an honor to be there. Sit." He motioned to two chairs across from him and his wife.

"It was unexpected." I straightened my dress underneath me before I took a seat. I thanked Felice for holding out my chair, and he kissed the top of my head before he sat next to me. He set his arm around the back of my chair, his fingers stroking my skin. A promise of later.

"I invited Dr. Corvo to celebrate with us tonight, but he declined."

I took a sip of champagne. "He doesn't approve of the marriage."

Tommaso nodded. "Your father is old school. He still believes in the tradition of an arranged marriage. I consider him a good friend." He looked at Felice. "I've always thought of John as a son. His father worked for me before John was even born. The situation puts me in an impossible spot."

"Not anymore," Felice said easily. "It's done."

Tommaso looked at the guy standing next to him, as if to say, *do you believe this guy?* He took a sip of his water with lemon and set it down. "I suppose it is." His voice was full of gravel.

"It is. And luckily, a marriage isn't dangerous. It doesn't hurt anyone. Unless it ends in divorce. It's not like a car slamming into another one on purpose." I played with the stem of the flute. "I'm hoping my father will eventually come to terms with it."

Tommaso adjusted his thick black spectacles, like fixing them would make him see me clearer. What I'd said, about the car, was aimed at what he'd done to me and Elsa. It wasn't subtle if it made sense.

"Fun," his wife said, nodding toward the dance floor. "Everyone's starting to dance now that we've left shore."

Felice stood, holding his hand out to me. "Shall we?" When I took it, he excused us, and Tommaso nodded.

He moved us around the floor. "Your mouth is a loaded gun, Dino."

I pushed back a little to gauge his face. "I didn't mean to say it. I was nervous earlier, before we left, and on the ride, but it just slipped out." My heart started pounding and I felt loopy with nerves again. "Is he going to be pissed you told me?"

He shrugged. "Depends on if he cares enough."

"You don't want a man like him caring enough about something you've done, I'm guessing."

He nodded. "You don't want a man like him to know you're alive."

"You're close to him."

"I'm only close to you."

I could bring him to his knees in bed, but he could bring me to mine with his brutal honesty. The conviction behind his words stole my breath, but a small smile played on my lips. I felt like a love-drunk teenager.

He grinned and spun me out when a fast song started to play. We danced, ate, and Felice introduced me to some of the guests. Most of them were probably directly connected, like Cassio, Celso, Fredo, and Frankie, but some of them owned successful businesses in the city. Felice introduced them as "associates" of his.

Tommaso called Felice over. Not wanting to be close to him again, I decided to wait at the bar. Chicago passed by outside the windows, the yacht gliding over Lake Michigan with ease.

I turned toward a voice in my ear. Cassio. He was singing the song playing. He grinned at me when our eyes met.

"Want to show me what you got?" He nodded toward the dance floor.

"Why not?"

He could dance. He knew some fancy steps. I told him so.

"My Ma used to teach dance in the city," he said. "You can't be the son of a dance teacher and not know how to dance."

"I'm sure there's a law about that," I said. "Some kind of penalty if it doesn't happen."

He laughed. "In her book of laws, yeah."

He showed me a few steps, and before long, I had the dance down.

"Are you teaching Adelasia?" I asked.

"She doesn't like me enough. She'd bite my hand and run away."

"Elsa seems to bring out her happy." I knew Elsa watched her sometimes. She never mentioned it, but I was sure Cassio paid her to do it. She needed the extra money.

"She more than likes Elsa," he said. "She's obsessed with her."

I'd noticed it too. Sometimes I wondered if Adelasia's mamma looked like Elsa. Maybe because of the similarities, Adelasia felt safe. Or close to her. It broke my heart. I knew how it felt to lose my mother, and I was older and understood what had happened. It seemed like Adelasia didn't, and she was looking for something to fill the void.

"Stubborn."

"What?" I wasn't paying attention and had missed what he'd said.

"Elsa is fucking stubborn. A real pain in my ass."

"A real pain, huh?"

He released me and stared at my face. "What are you trying to say?"

"Nothing." I held my hands up. "I only repeated what you said."

"Yeah, but the tone. The look. Put together, it's implying." He grabbed me again and we floated. "Out of all the women in the world, Adelasia would become obsessed with her. Everything she does, she does to punish me. And I can't fucking say no because my kid loves her, and Adelasia's been through a lot."

A woman came up behind Cassio and tapped him on the shoulder.

"What?" He turned.

"Remember me?" She snapped her fingers. "Your date."

He looked between us as she folded her arms and tapped her foot.

"Dance with your date, Cassio," Tommaso said, interrupting. "I'd like to dance with this one." He nodded at me.

I was close to saying, *this one doesn't want to dance with you*, but I didn't want to cause a scene. I'd said enough earlier.

Felice had taken a seat at the table and was watching. Cassio bowed out and danced with his date.

The song that played was older, and we foxtrotted to it.

"You look a lot like Mariella."

"Thank you," I said, because I always took it as a compliment. Mamma was beautiful.

He nodded. "I always thought Mariella bewitched Emanuele. I met him a few years before he met her. He was never the same after."

"You were invited past the office before Mamma," I guessed.

He didn't respond, and I let the music come between us. It was probably best if I stopped talking.

"You seemed to have done the same to John." He skipped right over what I'd said and continued his thought. "I'm indebted to Emanuele, but John is the future of my business. If everyone is in harmony with this new arrangement, I'm not bothered by it." He squeezed my hand. "But if I need to, I will move pieces around. Understood?"

"Understood," I said, trying not to yank my hand out of his grip. He wasn't hurting me but sending a message.

"I'm stealing my wife back," Felice said, squeezing Tommaso's shoulder.

"She is a treasure," Tommaso said, kissing my hand.

I nodded, faking politeness like he was. Without him noticing, I wiped my hand on my dress.

Felice took me in his arms, keeping the hand his boss had kissed against his chest. But I could still feel Tommaso's eyes on me until Felice led us deeper into the dancing crowd, turning his back on his boss and shielding me from him.

Wind whipped against us as we stepped off the yacht and started toward the car. The smell of the lake, Felice's cologne, my perfume, and alcohol fumes seemed to cling to the air, even though the gusts constantly swirled them around. We hadn't had much to drink, but it seemed like we were the only ones. Some men were still singing.

Even though Tommaso's warning was still fresh in my mind, I had a decent time.

Another big wind kicked up, plastering my coat to me, and I tucked myself closer to Felice. I wondered how brutal winter was going to be if fall was this crisp.

My eyes narrowed when I noticed a cluster of people up ahead. Judging by their evening attire, they were on the yacht and had left before us. Police stood around cruisers, turret lights spinning, stopping them from leaving. They almost seemed boxed in by law enforcement.

"I wonder what's going on?"

Felice said nothing.

We kept moving forward until a detective held up his badge.

"Felice Maggio?" he asked.

Felice nodded.

Guns were drawn, and we were instructed to put our hands up. I was ordered to stay where I was. The detective with the badge started reading Felice his rights, while a police officer handcuffed him. I didn't catch what the charge was. He didn't resist. They set him against the police cruiser, checking for weapons.

"What the hell is he being charged with?" I shouted over the wind and all the noise. I was ignored, so I shouted it again.

"Don't move," one of the police said, blocking me from getting closer.

Shock had melted, and I was starting to get mouthy. Especially after they put him in the cruiser and pulled off. The entire force seemed to go with him. I was left with the guests from the yacht. The men were mad, shaking their heads and cursing. Tommaso and his wife passed me, surrounded by his guards, or whoever the hell they were.

Cassio came to stand next to me. "I'm going to take you home."

"Felice," I said, nodding toward where the police had gone. "He—"

"I know," he said. Even though I could tell he was put out by the set of his face, he was almost taking it in stride.

I was trembling. "What the hell is this about, Cassio? And what am I supposed to do now? Make bail?"

"This isn't his first ride." He placed a hand on my lower back, ushering me toward wherever his car was. "You have a lot to learn about this life."

"Yeah, and this is a crash course. Do you know what they're charging him with?"

"Could be anything."

I was about to respond, but I shut my mouth and narrowed my eyes. A man I recognized stood away from the crowd, one hand in his pocket, the other holding what looked like a ripped piece of material. It whipped in the wind like a flag.

Alfonso Maggio.

CHAPTER 42

ROMA

A watch.

They had arrested Felice over a watch. The watch he won in a game of curling against Jack. Because it was valued over a certain amount, it was considered a felony. It was also considered a collector's item because of its make and model. Alfonso's father had been a collector of them.

Felice's lawyers had provided footage of Jack handing it over at the hotel. Alfonso had told them Felice threatened Jack to get it. It just so happened Felice had his hand in his pocket when Jack handed it over, which made it look like Felice was hiding a gun. But it couldn't be proved and the charges were dropped.

I didn't think Alfonso cared if the charges stuck or not. He was just hitting Felice back. I remembered the private plane incident and shook my head.

Felice, like Cassio, took the arrest in stride. They even shared a chuckle over it after Felice came home. It was a game they found fun.

I thought of the way the police had pointed their weapons at him, and fun wasn't the first word that came to mind. Because of who Felice was and his history, I'd learned his name was on a list and they always arrested him that way. He would always be considered armed and dangerous.

I thought the game sucked. I felt like another stake that had been added. Another one of Grandpa Maggio's watches.

"You're quiet," Kerry said, handing me a lantern to hang.

We were surprising Elsa for her birthday. I'd convinced Cassio to take her and Adelasia out while we decorated her apartment. Her landlords offered to cook. She lived over a Chinese restaurant. It was her favorite.

"Do you think she'll be surprised?" I asked, not wanting to keep reliving the night my husband had gotten arrested. He thought it was cute—*cute*—the way I had freaked out when they'd arrested him.

"You didn't want them to take me," he'd said, his eyes lowered, like he was high off my reaction.

I really had no comeback for that. No, I didn't want them to take my husband to fucking jail.

"She has no clue," Kerry said, bringing me back to the present again.

"You need another one?" Fredo asked, lifting a lantern he'd put together.

"What do you think?" I examined what we'd done. "Do we need it?"

He tilted his head, almost studying the space. "Yeah. It's not gaudy at all. It could use a little more *oomph*."

He handed it to Kerry, and she handed it up to me. I was on a small step ladder.

"I agree," Kerry said, standing back, checking out what we'd done so far.

"I'm not a fan of screaming '*surprise!*'" Fredo said.

We both looked at Fredo. He was putting together another lantern. He looked up.

"Sometimes my finger gets trippy." He made a motion like he was pulling a trigger. "You come at me like that—I'd shoot first and ask questions later. Then I'd miss out on cake. Probably," he added as an afterthought.

Kerry's cheeks puffed out and I turned my face, not wanting to explode with laughter. If I looked at Kerry, we both would, and we wouldn't be able to stop.

Once we had the lanterns up, I texted Felice.

Me: No surprise parties for you?

His response came back almost instantly.

My Carnivore: No.

I grinned.

Me: I'll save you a piece of cake.

I sent him a heart after.

My Carnivore: Life-long quest.

He sent me a confused face after the text.

Look at this guy, using all his emojis with me. I started laughing, imagining the blank look on his face while he searched for the confused face.

He'd never sent emojis until I asked him why. *They're there to help show emotion*, I'd said. Then he started sending them.

A knock came at the door. Fredo answered it. It was Elsa's landlords, Mr. and Mrs. Chen, with the food. Lo showed up next, bringing the cake. A few friends of Elsa's trickled in over the next fifteen minutes. Hayden was the last to arrive. He'd brought games.

Kerry shot me an eye roll, and we both shook our heads. Games were great unless Hayden was playing. He took all the fun out of them with his unhealthy competitiveness. He even went as far as accusing people of cheating when he started to lose.

I checked my watch. Cassio was going to drop Elsa off in the next fifteen. What Fredo had said about his trigger finger made me somewhat antsy. What if Cassio had missed the part about it being a surprise party? I texted Felice asking him to remind Cassio for me. Felice had strict rules about me and other men. We were never alone, and texting or calling seemed to step over boundaries too.

I had no clue what Felice would do if he ever found out Cassio had come to the museum to see me.

My watch lit up. He sent me a thumbs up.

Me: That one is passive aggressive. Forget it exists.

He sent me another confused face.

Kerry nudged my shoulder. "I don't think I've ever seen you so happy." She smiled at me. "I'm so happy for you."

She pulled me in for a hug, and it was so warm, we must have stood there for a minute or two rocking back and forth. Lo wrapped her arms around us, closing her eyes.

"We're all Gucci here."

"I think she's coming!" Mrs. Chen said, pumping her hands down, rushing to get back in the apartment. "She is walking down the street with her friends."

We all hid behind Elsa's cherry-blossom-tree room screen.

"The lights!" I hurried and flipped them off, the lanterns coming to life with soft light.

If Elsa was really paying attention, she'd see our figures shadowed behind the screen, but I hoped she'd notice the new lanterns first.

The door opened, Elsa said, "What the he—" and we all screamed, "*Surprise!*" And jumped out.

When I did, two strong arms picked me up by mine and set me flush against the wall. Fredo was next to me, mimicking my position, like he was waiting for a bullet to come whizzing through.

"Better safe than sorry." He shrugged, fixing his shirt, though it didn't have a wrinkle.

Someone flipped the lights on, and the hugging started. Elsa was genuinely surprised, but I could tell she'd been irritated before she walked in. It took her face a few minutes to soften. I didn't see Cassio or Adelasia, but I didn't bring it up.

What Cassio had told me while we were dancing, about Elsa being a pain in the ass, made me wonder if they had a tremulous relationship. I could tell she truly liked the little girl, but she needed the money, and Cassio was doing it for his daughter.

Lo set two little speakers up next to Elsa's laptop and started playing music. "True" by Spandau Ballet filled the apartment, along with the smell of amazing food and the sound of everyone talking.

Elsa set her chin on my shoulder while I made a plate of food. "Thank you," she whispered, kissing my cheek. "You and Kerry are the best-est friends a girl could ask for."

"My Charlie's Angels," Hayden said, grabbing a drink from the cooler.

"Okay, Bosley." Elsa rolled her eyes.

He lifted the can in the air. "Who's ready to play some games? *Wooo!*"

Kerry groaned as she came to stand next to us. "I'm not playing."

We agreed, but also agreed the setting was better than negative zero weather, standing on top of a high-rise hotel's rooftop.

"But..." Kerry smiled at us, holding out her hands. "Let's dance!"

I took a bite of my food before Elsa set my plate on the counter, and Kerry grabbed my hand. Lo must have been stuck in the 70s and 80s, because she was playing music from that time.

"I'm going to run to the bathroom!" Elsa said, dancing her way there.

Fredo had been watching us, but his phone must have started ringing. He put it to his ear, his forehead tightening as he started heading toward the door. My heart gave a huge leap, thinking it might be Felice. Sometimes he'd show up out of nowhere. Maybe Felice had called and told Fredo to open the door.

My heart fell a hundred stories when Fredo swapped the phone for his gun. He went to stop one of Elsa's friends from opening the door. Too late. A man stood on the other side with a mask on his face and gloves on his hands. He was dressed in black fatigues.

Before Fredo could get a shot off, the man seemed to blow ashes, or something powdery, in Fredo's face. He dropped like a sack, the gun sliding away from his hand.

The man blew more at Elsa's friend. She went down.

The man's eyes locked on me. He shut the door before he charged toward me. I started taking fast backward steps, not sure where to go.

"Hey!" Hayden yelled.

Every eye in the room turned to the man, and besides the music, there was only silence. Lo was too panicked to shut it off.

The man reached in a pouch hanging from his pants and blew the same stuff in Hayden's face when he went to charge him. Hayden's leg was in motion, and he completely stopped and fell. Some of the stuff drifted in my face, and I immediately lost all my senses. The only thing I could feel was my heart hammering in my chest. The room spun, but the man held me up.

"Where is it?" he snapped in my face.

"Where is what?" I slurred out.

"You know!" he hissed at me. "Tell me. Now!" He glanced behind him, at the door, like maybe he was anticipating company.

"I have no idea..." The music in the background reminded me of pliable mozzarella, stretching, stretching...the words elongating in slow motion.

He shook me, hard. "I know who your husband is, so you will get out this alive, but you will tell me, or your friends will—"

Mr. Chen was creeping behind him, but he sensed it and blew the stuff again. Maybe it was my imagination, but it seemed to sparkle. Mr. Chen hit the ground. Mrs. Chen ran and fell next to him, trying to slap him awake.

"Roma!"

We both turned at the sound of Elsa's voice. The man flung me on the floor. I couldn't even hold my hands out to lessen the impact. When I hit, it felt like every bone in my body cracked. I was seeing the world from a floor view, my cheek to it. I could see Fredo and his gun, but I couldn't move.

Maybe Elsa had noticed it and was running for it. The man caught her by the hair. He yanked her back, and it seemed like her feet were paddling backward. He was yelling at her to tell him where it was, but her voice was muffled, and I couldn't make out what she was saying.

Whatever it was, he didn't seem to like it. He started beating her, and there was nothing I could do to help. There was nothing any of us could do. It seemed like the entire room was dazed with whatever he'd been blowing in it.

The door opened, footsteps pounded, and feet started to move in my central line of view. A set of them stopped and yanked the man off Elsa.

She fell to the floor, her hair saturated with blood. It was pooling and running on the tile, reaching Fredo. The shoes were stepping in it. The masked man seemed to be bouncing between two sets, like he was stuck between two walls punching him. His pouch was on the floor. He groaned and cried out. It sounded as if something was ripping him apart.

Knees hitting the floor came into my view, blocking the scene, before arms hauled me up. "Felice?" I whispered. Something was tied around his face, and it was blood splattered, but I'd recognize those eyes anywhere. They were crazed.

"My little herbivore." He said my name like it held the scariest question known to man.

"I'm okay," I breathed, then passed out in his arms.

CHAPTER 43

FELICE

A knock came at the hospital door. Emanuele Corvo stuck his head in and then entered, holding a hat in his hands. He looked gaunt. Haunted. Exactly the way I looked when I was separated from my wife, and she had to sneak around to keep him in the dark about us. I wouldn't deny him this, though.

I meant it when I said my wife was off limits in this game between me and Alfonso. Emanuele made himself a player when he denied me my other half, pinning another man's sins on me.

Roma was still sleeping. I took her hand, kissed it, then left the room.

Cassio stood with his back against the wall, hands in his pockets. We were both stained with blood. His eyes were far away.

"Any word yet?" I stood next to him, assuming the same position.

"Not yet." He shook his head. "Seems like I've been in this place too many times to fucking count in my life. Every time, it's a woman I'm waiting on."

He'd been here a lot when his wife was sick. He didn't mention it, but I could tell he was thinking it. It wasn't something he talked about often.

"Roma?"

"They're monitoring her, because they're not sure what the powder is, but she's stable. Sleeping. I wouldn't be out here if she wasn't."

"I saw Dr. Corvo go in," he said.

I nodded and left it at that. "What happens next, Cassio?"

He sighed and shrugged. He seemed to be plotting his next steps.

He'd taken Ms. Lang and Adelasia to the zoo earlier to get Ms. Lang out of the house for Roma and Ms. Hall. From my understanding, the relationship between Ms. Lang and Cassio was strictly business. Adelasia never tried to bite her, which meant she liked her, and Cassio desperately needed someone who the kid even tolerated to help take care of her.

Ms. Lang seemed to know how to push Cassio's buttons, though. I had no fucking clue how or why, and I refused to go there. But Ms. Lang had gotten herself into some trouble. It was no secret her parents were struggling. She was an only child helping bear the responsibility of helping them—with money and her father's ailing health.

Cassio had found out she'd stolen and then unloaded a valuable antique on the black market. He'd confronted her about it at the zoo. To sum it up, she told him to mind his fucking business and quit the babysitting gig.

He was pissed about it. A few blocks away from her place in China Town, he pulled to the curb and did some research. The thing she'd stolen was worth more than money to the people who'd been looking for it. It was worth blood in their opinion. They believed it held mythical powers.

Cassio had called me and told me what was going on. He said he had a bad feeling about it.

She'd been wound tighter than usual lately, he'd said. Whatever had been moving closer to her had arrived. He'd walked her to her apartment, and the entire time she kept looking over her shoulder. I was en route to Roma, so we both decided to head there. I wasn't taking any chances when it came to my wife's safety.

Fredo was with her, to deal with Alfonso, but this was a different situation. Cassio said from the research he'd done, this cult blew powder that had the potency to knock over a bull.

Roma worked at the museum with Ms. Lang. Whoever was after her might think Roma was in on it too. There was no fucking telling.

I'd called Fredo and told him to be on higher alert. I ordered him to only open the door for us. We'd be there in a few minutes. We had more men with us. We knew something was wrong when a dazed looking girl ran out of the Chens' restaurant, swaying. She was mumbling to herself.

We knew the shit they used could knock us out, so we covered our faces. We tore the motherfucker apart, but it was too late. My wife was on the floor, out of it, and Ms. Lang had been badly beaten.

This fucking place brought back memories for me too. My wife had been here twice before this time, and all three times had me close to losing my mind. What was left of it.

Cassio sighed. "I'm going to take Elsa to my ma's. Her parents can't take care of her. She doesn't have any siblings. And this is worse than the car incident. The Chens don't blame her, but they're older and worried. Can't bring that shit to their door."

"You're bringing it to yours."

He shrugged. "Adelasia will be able to visit Elsa there. I can take care of this."

"If Burton finds out, she'll be out of a job."

"I'll take the rap for it if he does."

I stared at him until he looked at me.

"Desperate circumstances make people desperate," he said. "She's not the kind of woman who steals for no reason."

He was right. Roma went on about how much Ms. Lang loved what she did. She'd called her a career student, always wanting to learn. She didn't seem like the type to steal, especially something that had such a rich history attached to it, but desperate times call for desperate measures. Those who couldn't understand that had never missed a few meals or bill payments.

"You need to be smart about this," I said. "You're not dealing with average street criminals. This is personal to them."

"That shit knocked Fredo the fuck out." He shook his head. "He's in bad shape."

The doctor was concerned Fredo wasn't responding to treatment. He was in the ICU, hooked up to a breathing machine, having a hard time. The doctor thought he might have inhaled more of it than everyone else, since he was so close to the motherfucker. Until they knew what was in the powder, they were fighting against a guessing game.

Questions fucking haunted me, the unanswered what ifs of the powder's long-term side effects, but if I concentrated on them, I'd hurt someone. The uncertainty of it made something inside of me twist toward her room. I needed to be next to her.

Cassio sighed. "I don't have all the answers yet, but when I do, I'll form a plan to end this shit. She's the only one in the world my kid can stand. Without her, Adelasia might turn into a sociopath or psychopath or some shit." He looked at me. "Like you."

I shook my head at him.

Emanuele Corvo came out of the room, setting his hat back on his head. He didn't bother looking at me as he left.

I slipped back into Roma's room. She was still sleeping. I grabbed her hand, settling in next to her, the twisting in my chest easing.

It was my fucking heart.

CHAPTER 44

ROMA

Felice stuck close to my side as we walked to Navy Pier from the penthouse.

The scene was a representation of our current lives. If I wasn't at home, he was wherever I was. If he had business, I'd have to wait for him to finish before I left. I wanted to get back to work, but he wasn't budging. He didn't feel comfortable leaving me, even with his men.

He wasn't familiar with this enemy, and until he was, I was on lockdown.

We fought about it. He won.

"You're fucking beautiful when you pout," he said, wrapping an arm around my neck, pulling me close. He kissed my temple.

I sighed. Even though Jack had said something similar to me, it didn't piss me off as much when Felice said it. Maybe because timing was everything, and Jack's was always off. Felice and I always seemed to step in peaceful tandem.

A cool gust of wind pushed against me. It was probably the perfect way to describe the moments when the truth hit me. The synergy between us felt so natural, but at times, its power stole my breath.

He nodded toward the Centennial Wheel, the gondolas going around it. "Ever been?"

"No." I shook my head. "But I hear the view is spectacular. I'm not sure about being in that small compartment—Oh." I glanced up at him and caught the mischievous grin on his face. He was remembering the *funivia* ride in Taormina.

"I'm in the mood for some gelato after dinner." He winked at me.

I was still a little dazed and unsteady on my feet. Whatever was in the powder was still causing problems. The doctors didn't foresee any long-term issues, but they said it had to work itself out of my system over time. I was mostly good, and it probably wasn't the foreign stuff in my body that made me knock into Felice. It was simply...him.

He kept me closer to his side, probably thinking I was going to fall. Even when he handed the attendant at the Chicago Shakespeare Theater our tickets, he kept one hand on me.

We spotted Lo and Sandro and headed toward them. After we greeted one another, we entered the theater and found our seats. Lo had been wanting to catch a musical based on a best-selling book. It was about a couple whose differences almost ripped them apart.

Felice's face was unreadable during the show, except when one of the cast members would hit a high note. He'd put his head back and his eyes would grow wide. I had to bite my lip to keep from laughing.

Lo was into it, singing the songs on the way to the restaurant after. We'd decided on a Latin place along Navy Pier. We all ordered, and then Lo asked me to go with her to the bathroom. Felice could see it from our table, and there was no entrance from outside or windows.

She ran into the stall and was going on about the musical while she went.

I fixed my hair some. The wind had run its fingers through it, but not in a sexy, tousled way.

"Wheew, that was a close call," she said, coming to stand next to me and washing her hands. "I held it for the entire show." She grabbed for a few napkins, then asked to use my lipstick. "How's Fredo?"

I dug in my purse, handing it over. "Good now. He's out of the hospital."

"Have you heard from Elsa?"

"I talked to her earlier."

"How is she?"

"She's staying with Cassio's mom." What else could I say?

Elsa was being reticent about what had happened. I knew more than Lo about why that man had showed up and tried to kill Elsa, but it was best if everyone else didn't know specifics. The less they knew about the situation, the safer it was. In general, everyone assumed the man was there to rob Elsa.

Hayden bought it. An artifact had gone missing from one of the museums. Apparently, whoever was looking for it—not the actual owner but a group who wanted it—was visiting the homes of museum workers. But Felice had told me what Cassio had figured out.

It was hard to believe at first, but I understood Elsa's situation, and it was a lot worse than she'd let on. Her parents were losing their house, and with her father's medical bills, I think she snapped and did whatever she felt she had to do.

"That must make her feel safe." Lo puckered up.

"She's not alone," I said, giving a vague answer. I wondered if Elsa was even worried about her safety. She was probably more worried that she might kill Cassio. It didn't seem like they could get along.

"Is she going to move back home?"

I shrugged, taking the lipstick back and applying some. "Not right now. I'm not sure what she's going to do after she's healed. She lost her apartment. What happened really shook Mr. and Mrs. Chen."

"It was fucking scary. He was crazed with that powder. I've

had weird dreams ever since." She fixed her hair. "Have you heard anything from Babbo since he visited you in the hospital?"

"No. I had no clue he even came to visit. Felice told me. I think he wanted to get in and get out without waking me up. Did I tell you he packed up all my things and sent them to me?"

"You did. Did you ever go through them?"

"I wasn't ready, but I need to."

"Hopefully he didn't send you the bloody sheet."

I stared at her. "Did Babbo kill Romeo and Juliet on my sheets?"

She turned to me, studying my face. "This has nothing to do with Romeo and Juliet. Felice sent Babbo your wedding night sheet. To let him know your marriage had been...consummated."

My face scrunched up. "Why...?"

"To let it be known the marriage was final. No one could question it. You're his."

Turning away from her, I flung my lipstick back in my purse. It was mortifying to have my father see the sheets we had sex on for the first time. Felice didn't have to do that to prove anything.

I'd signed my name on the certificate willingly. Uncle Tito had witnessed it.

I'd given Felice my blood and mixed it with his. He had a certificate of that too.

I'd vowed my life to him. As final as my last breath.

What Felice had done went beyond his claim of me. He'd done it for that stupid fucking game he refused to lose. He was no better than Alfonso or Jack.

He studied my face when we returned to the table. His arm settled on the back of my chair, and he went to set his hand on my neck, but I pushed up some. I wasn't even hungry. I ordered a drink instead. Felice did the same.

Lo and Sandro walked with us to the gelato place after dinner, but I refused to get any.

My husband got the point.

The walk home was quiet and cold. The house even more so. I

undressed in the closet and put my nightclothes on, doing whatever I needed to do in the bathroom, then I got into bed.

He stood in the doorway of our room, leaning against it, hands in his pockets, watching me. I turned my back on him, feigning getting comfortable. He was quiet for so long, I assumed he left.

I flipped back over, and he was still there.

Our eyes met.

"You—" he pointed at me "—Roma Maggio, belong to me —" he pointed at his himself "—Felice Maggio."

"I know, John," I said. "I'm another stake in this game of yours. Too bad you can't put me on your wrist." I turned over and closed my eyes, but the ache in my heart refused to let me sleep.

The next morning, after Felice left, I dressed in comfortable clothes, stuck my hair in a high ponytail, and found the boxes Babbo had sent over. It was time to face them.

I moved them around, setting them next to each other. Even though a few were bursting at the seams and heavy, I didn't want to wait for Felice to get home. The building attendant and security guard were downstairs, and so were some of Felice's men, but they were only there for emergencies. Felice didn't want them alone with me.

That was fine. I wanted to be by myself.

I used a box to sit on and started with one that had been on top. It was the lightest. A manilla envelope sat on top of my old bedding set from Babbo's house. Underneath it was the scrap of sheet from our wedding night. The blood had turned black.

Last night, I'd been mortified at the thought. In the daylight, I was beyond mortified to be holding the proof.

How could he have done this to me? Shared something so personal to prove a point. I knew the old tradition was still done, proving a marriage was consummated by the blood on the sheets, but so were arranged marriages. We didn't have one of those.

My hands trembled as I slid the letter out from inside the envelope. Felice had written and signed it.

John

I picked up the material, squeezing it in my hand, remembering.

I held the ripped piece of sheet up. "Um, what is this?"

"A sheet."

"I know." I smiled. "What happened to it?" I started backing away, holding my hands up. I read the intent in his eyes. "What is it with you and blood? What did you do with the other pieces of it?"

"I'm a carnivore, my little plant eater. We like to tear shit up."

Not only did he take pleasure in tearing shit up, but hearts too. He'd ripped mine into pieces, like the sheet, using it as weapon to hurt his enemies. I knew he got pleasure from rubbing me in Alfonso's face, but this went beyond that. This felt different somehow. Like he'd crossed a line I hadn't realized I'd set. Because I trusted him enough not to trip it. It felt like he'd taken a private part of me and showed it to the world for his own gain.

His revenge was aimed at my father too, but in a different way. He did it to let Babbo know he'd claimed me and there was nothing he could do about it. Just like my father had claimed there was nothing he could do to save Sal.

Another truth hit me in that moment. Felice had told me he was at Mamma's funeral. I understood then...he'd gone to show Babbo how cruel karma could be.

I'd somehow charmed a dangerous carnivore, but he was still a carnivore, and he thrived on blood.

I startled a little when I looked up and found him standing in the doorway of the spare closet. But I quickly recovered. I lifted the stained sheet.

"Let's see," I breathed out, but there was nothing soft about it. "My father. Alfonso and Jack. Who else needs to see Roma's virginal blood for you to get a hit in? Is the list long? Do we need to tear up the other fucking piece to mail?" I flung the sheet at his face. "We can recycle that one. My father didn't want it."

The material barely reached him. He picked it up off the floor and had the audacity to hold it like it meant something to him. He was holding it so tight, his knuckles turned white. But there was no stopping the hemorrhage. He'd torn a piece of me that felt like it would never stop bleeding because of his motives.

I loved this son of a bitch. And he was using me.

I stood, dusting off my clothes, and stopped in front of him. He was blocking the door.

"Why did you go to Jupiter, John? Was it because you were going with the flow of things? Or because you were planning to fuck the woman who was intended to marry Jack, *me*, to get back at Alfonso?"

He refused to answer me, but his silence was loud. He'd gone to Jupiter to get to me first. To see what else he could win for his side of this game.

I smiled, but it only cut me deep. "I saw Alfonso with the piece of sheet you sent him. The night you were arrested. I had no idea what it was then, but I know now. He's going to carry it around every time he gets a hit on you. But the only one who's getting hit in this game is me. I expected it from everyone else, but not you. I know who you are, John. You're a carnivore. And I know what you see when you look at me. A weaker creature. And you made me feel safe in that hospital room. But I was wrong. So fucking wrong to trust you."

He wouldn't let me through when I tried to slip past him.

Our eyes met and held, a silent war raging between us.

The intensity in his eyes was at madness level, but I refused to let him ensnare me this time. I couldn't get past the hurt in my chest. It felt like it was suffocating me, drowning me, setting me on fire, stabbing me with a thousand knives. I'd never felt pain like this.

I'd never felt so used before.

He broke first, hoarsely whispering, "*Solo tu,*" before he moved out of my way, but followed behind me.

I didn't care that he did. What was the use in fighting when nothing was going to change this? He could try all he wanted, even moving out of my way to prove he'd only move for me, but there was no taking back what he'd done and why. I sat down on the bed, and he moved around to his side. He opened the drawer in the nightstand and got something out of it. He sent it flying and it landed next to me.

It was a picture of Jack and me from Lo's wedding. The photographer must have caught it. I was laughing at something, and before I could stop him, Jack took my arm. It looked like we were dancing, or in the middle of an intimate moment.

"This?" I held it up. "This is what you sacrificed me for? A fucking picture?"

"Alfonso sent that to me." His voice was deep and full of gravel. "I'm sure your father approved."

"Oh, I see. So you had to hurt him back. You had to kill a part of him to make yourself feel better."

What did he tell me when I'd told him about Babbo murdering my fish? *Some people kill whatever represents the hurt to make themselves feel better.*

"You were smiling at him." He shrugged, like his shoulders had grown and his dress shirt was too tight. "I let it go once. That's over my limit. I was either going to kill one of them with my hands or fatally wound their pride with the sheet. I chose the latter, since I knew you wouldn't take the first choice well."

"I wasn't smiling *at* him! The photographer caught me smiling and Jack happened to be there. I wasn't dancing with him either."

"Happiness is mine to give you."

I sighed, pinching the bridge of my nose. I had a headache. Everything ached. I wasn't sure if he was ever going to understand how much he'd hurt me. Maybe he didn't even realize what he was doing. He was so caught up in the game, I wasn't sure if he could ever quit. When someone hurt him, he struck back even harder. The blood of his enemies transfixed him. It didn't matter if I got trampled and bloodied in the process.

My head felt too heavy, so I plopped back on the bed. He rushed over to me, looking down.

"Go away, John." I closed my eyes. "Leave me alone."

"Call me that again," he said, and I was sure he'd raked his teeth over his lip.

"If I do, you'll what? Spank me? Tie me up? *Hurt* me? You already did that."

I curled up in a ball, pulling the covers over me, refusing to open my eyes. Hours must have passed, and I drifted in and out of sleep. When I got up to use the bathroom and change my clothes, the city was dark, and he was gone.

CHAPTER 45

ROMA

"Get your ass up."

The covers were pulled off me. I pulled them back. They were yanked again.

"Go away, Lo." I swatted at her when she tried to right me.

"You ready, El?"

They didn't even count. They just hauled me up. I blinked at them.

"It lives." Lo shoved a hand at me.

"No, *it* doesn't," I croaked. My mouth felt dry.

Lo took a seat beside me. "What the hell is going on, Y?"

"I'm sick," I whispered.

She nodded. "Lovesick. I get it. But why? Is this over the sheet? We all stopped hearing from you right after. It's been a week, Y. I was going to hurt the security guard downstairs if he tried to stop me from getting in here. John approved us, though. You stopped us." She poked me on the shoulder.

"Yes and no," I said. "It is about the sheet, but not actually the sheet. It's about what it represents." I wasn't giving her more than that. I loved my sister. I loved my friend. But this felt like it was strictly between my husband and me.

Elsa walked over to the windows and opened the blinds. I winced when the light hit me.

"Look at you. You're like the Windy City vampire up in this bish." Lo shook her head and grabbed my hand. "What's the big deal, Y? It's a *sheet*. It was sent. It's done. Time to move on."

Easier said than done. He couldn't heal this if he didn't know how. I couldn't get over it if I kept hurting.

"Besides, remember what Mamma used to say?" Lo pursed her fingers and moved them when she continued. "*L'amore non è bello se non è litigarello. Or a different version of the same point. Amor senza baruffa fa la muffa.*"

"*Love is not beautiful if it does not include arguments,*" I translated. "Or, *Love with no quarrel gets mold.*"

"Do you want your relationship to grow mold?" Lo asked seriously.

Going back and forth with John over me returning to work felt like an argument. This felt like something else entirely.

"Before we really get into the heavy debates, how about a shower?" Elsa headed toward the bathroom. "I'll run the water."

"She's right. It's not fair to argue with you in this state." Lo lifted a piece of my hair. "I'm going to have to find and evict all the rats in these nests. They're probably here for the *moldy* cheese you're growing."

I shoved her hand away and got to my feet. It wasn't like I'd been sleeping twenty-four hours straight every day. Maybe fifteen. But I wasn't always sleeping. I was also thinking and feeling and wishing I could sleep the treachery away.

John was there with me. We wallowed together. Neither of us saying anything. Neither of us knowing how to fix this. He brought me food and drinks and then took a seat in the corner. Just watching. His eyes never relaxing.

I caught Elsa on her way out. She didn't want to meet my eyes.

"I don't blame you," I whispered.

She swallowed hard and thanked me. Then she nodded toward the shower. "Go rinse the funk off. It helps."

It helped me smell and look better, but I didn't feel all that revived.

"You look better, but we need to get you out of here for a bit. Let's grab a bite to eat."

"I don't want to leave, Lo. Besides, Fel—John doesn't want me leaving without him."

"Cassio is downstairs." Elsa closed the fridge. "He'll drive us and go where we go. He offered."

Against my best judgment, I relented. Cassio was waiting downstairs and walked us to his SUV.

He looked at me and shook his head. "What?" He opened the back door for me. "You and John running a race on who's more miserable?"

I ignored him, buckling in. Lo sat next to me. Elsa sat next to Cassio. He pulled out of the garage, and the sun hit my eyes. I dug in my bag and slid my sunglasses over them. They were sensitive to the light. I was getting a headache already. I sighed.

"You need food," Lo said.

"And to talk to John," Cassio said.

"Is that what this is about?" I rushed out. "Are you bringing me to him?"

"It's called an intervention," Lo said.

"Hear us out." Cassio glanced at me through the rearview. "You need to talk to each other on neutral territory."

"We can do that at home!"

"Do you?" Lo asked.

"Home isn't neutral territory. It never is. There's a bed there. Whenever there's a bed—" Cassio shook his head "—forget it."

"What does a bed have to do with this, Cassio?" I asked.

"Everything."

"Forget the bed," Lo said. "But just have lunch with him. You'll never get past this if no words are shared. It's like trying to edit a blank page, right? You can't. So, spill it, no matter how hard. It's a start. You and John will perfect it later."

I rubbed my forehead against the window, closing my eyes. They just didn't have a clue. I'd always be twisted up in whatever John, Babbo, and Alfonso had going. And I refused to be used.

Cassio slowed when we came to a restaurant with al fresco dining. John was sitting outside, his black wool jacket on, dark sunglasses over his eyes. My breath caught. It was like I was truly looking at him for the first time since I'd found out what he'd done. He looked haunted. He sat with a cup of coffee in front of him, but he wasn't drinking it. He was pushing it back and forth, staring down at it.

A tall blonde came out of the restaurant and sat at the table with him. He looked at her and said something. She answered him and then laughed. *Hahahahahaha.* The blonde from Halloween.

"You knew about this." Elsa stared at Cassio. "You knew she was going to be here with him!" She lifted her purse and whacked him with it.

He held a hand up. "You're always busting my balls!" He sighed. "All right. This is a setup. John had no clue she was going to be here."

"I don't understand," I said.

"Neither do I." Lo glared at Cassio.

He glanced in the rearview at me and then pulled off. He circled the block but parked where we could still see John.

"When you refused to answer your phone or see your sisters, Emanuele assumed the worst. He went to Tommaso again. This time he was specific about what he wanted and asked nicely."

"That is?" I held my breath.

"John gone." He cleared his throat. "Elsa. Lolita. A minute alone with Roma."

Lo and Elsa looked at me. I nodded. They stepped out of the car, standing next to it.

"What does that mean, Cassio?"

"Exactly what it sounds like. Your old man wants him out of

your life. Tommaso wants John for his own reasons. He's trying to find a happy medium."

"This setup was supposed to make me doubt John, since we're having some issues. Send me running."

Cassio nodded. "I was ordered to do it and to make it seem real, but I couldn't go through with it. I know how John feels about you. I know how you feel about John."

Sirens wailed in the distance until they closed in on the restaurant. Law enforcement jumped out before it seemed like the cars had even stopped. Weapons were raised, pointed at John. The blonde was screaming, causing a scene. They were handcuffing her because she was fighting.

Lo and Elsa moved closer to the restaurant. I couldn't look away either.

"This is part of it, isn't it?" I didn't see Alfonso anywhere with his bloodied flag, though. This wasn't the usual game.

Cassio shrugged. "I wasn't aware of this. Tommaso wouldn't have called the cops. He's old school and still values the code. No law enforcement. Period. Someone might have rolled on John." He must have noticed the confused look on my face. "Ratted him out for something," he clarified. "Or maybe your old man got with Alfonso and set this up."

"Tommaso wants me out of the picture so he can keep John." I took a deep breath. "If I don't remove myself?"

"John's life will be on the line."

"Take me to my car, Cassio."

CHAPTER 46

FELICE

I t was the first time I'd seen Cassio in eight months. He was waiting for me when I got out.

"Penthouse?"

I nodded.

He pulled off, and silence filled the car until I broke it.

"You tell me."

He glanced at me. "Tell you what?"

"You know. Fucking tell me or you die."

"You're going to have to fucking kill me then. I'm not going to pull something out of the sky to say for kicks."

Cassio could lie, but never to me. I knew him too well. He was lost, but he wasn't clueless.

"You tell me my wife's dead."

He wasn't the one who came to me with the news. Tommaso did. *She crossed over three lines and crashed into a cement truck.*

I refused to see visitors or talk to anyone after that.

"How did it happen, Cassio?"

He looked at me, then turned his face forward. "I don't know."

He was fucking lying to me.

"Take me to her grave." The words were poison-tipped barbed wires. Every time I thought them or said them, they ripped me to shreds and tainted my blood. I was experiencing a slow death, a mortally wounded animal begging for my last breath. Had been since she shut me out over the sheet.

Over the sheet. I got it. But too fucking late.

He kept his face forward. "I don't know where it is."

I raked my teeth over my lip. In a move he didn't see coming, I turned the wheel into oncoming traffic. We grappled over it, the car slightly rocking from side to side.

"Let it go, John! Fuck! You're suicidal!"

Cars swerved around us, horns blared, but there was a big truck hauling ass, and it was not going to be able to stop.

"I don't know if she's really dead or just gone!" he exploded.

I let the wheel go and he swerved back into the correct lane.

"Tell me more."

He ran a hand through his hair. "Everything before you got arrested was a setup. Candy at the restaurant, Roma seeing her with you. Tommaso wanted to make sure she ran, but he wouldn't hurt her this time. Emanuele asked nicely for his daughter to be taken out of the issue. It was you he wanted gone.

"After you were locked up, Tommaso told me she was gone too, but the entire thing was being kept too quiet. It never sat right with me. He ordered me to leave it alone. Ordered me not to see you until you got out." He glanced at me. "You go looking for her, he's going to start something. He wants this dead and buried."

"He already killed me. Nothing more he can do."

"Not true, if she's not—" his eyes flicked to me, then back "—*gone*, gone. He might know where she is. He might do something to her and make it look like an accident. He might get rid of both of you on principal. Fuck. I don't know. Those pills Corvo has him on makes him—" He made a whirly motion against his temple.

"You told her all this?"

He nodded. "I couldn't lie to her. She wears her love for you in her eyes. I was honest about what was happening." He pulled into the parking garage underneath the penthouse and shut the car off. "She didn't run to save herself. She ran to save you. I knew she wouldn't run if it came down to her."

He followed me into the penthouse.

It still smelled like her. Like apricots and vanilla and mandarin. It smelled like my little herbivore. My fucking home.

That thing in my chest twisted tight enough to stop blood flow, but it had no direction to go in to find relief. To find medicine. To find my cure. It was enough to drive a sane man mad and I was never of sound mind. I realized it when I'd found her. She was the good and right side of me. The need to keep her close and protect her only made who I was stronger.

I took a seat on our bed, staring at the shut blinds. The room was dim and cool. I needed a minute to clear my head. My chest was in chaos, though, and it was corrupting my thoughts. My eyes fell on the nightstand. The picture of my wife and Jack taken at the wedding stared back at me. I picked it up, and a note drifted from underneath.

Dear John,

We were doomed from the start. I should have known it when I saw you in my hospital room through a haze of blood. A warning. Or maybe it's just bad luck. A broken glass or a storm on a wedding day. Or both. I don't know. I just know without a doubt I'll love you for the rest of my life, even if I don't want to.

I never would have thought a carnivore and a herbivore could share a soul, but we do. We somehow created an entire world between the two of us. Something just for us.

I'll carry you with me wherever I go.

Eternally yours,

Roma

I crumpled the paper in my fist, her words reaching in my

chest and tearing my heart out. It numbed me for a second before the hole started to fucking throb. I could have sworn the pins and needles against my skin was blood pouring out.

"John? Where are you going?" Cassio went to follow me, but I stopped him.

"Stay here. Or go home."

"If there's going to be trouble, I go where you go."

"Not this time."

He didn't follow me when I left. He knew better. I would have broken his kneecaps if he would have tried to.

There was a man who had retribution coming to him—had been for some time—and I'd be the one doling it out.

The lights were on in the apartments above Tommaso's. Shadows of men moved behind the curtains.

His wife answered after I knocked on the door. It was eight o'clock. She was dressed for bed in a robe and slippers. The porch light highlighted how tired she was.

She moved to the side. "Come in."

I followed behind her to the living room, where the lights were out but the TV was on. She stopped, and I did too.

"I'll let Tom know you're here," she said, shuffling toward their room.

I waited alone, confirmation that the men were upstairs.

His wife came back and told me to follow her. She motioned for me to enter their room. The door had been left open. She told Tommaso she was going to make him something warm to drink and then shut the door behind her. I took a seat next to his bed. He was dressed in pajamas, propped up against the headboard with pillows behind him.

"John." He coughed. His chest rattled with fluid. Nature was taken its natural course, and not even Corvo was going to be able save him. "I expected you earlier."

I nodded. "We hit some traffic."

"Ah. What can you do?" He reached over and grabbed a glass of water from the nightstand. He wet his lips, then handed it to me to set back. Like he was too tired to do it. He studied my face. "You look tired, John. Maybe you need to hook up with Candy. She can help you with that." He winked at me.

Candy, the aspiring porno starlet who was at my house when Roma first came looking for me. Candy had called her out in front of the neighborhood as being Miss Chicago on Halloween. Candy, the leech who Tommaso used to send my wife running from me.

"Where's my wife?" I asked, my tone no-nonsense.

"I told you, John. She—"

"Where's her grave?"

"I'm not sure. Emanuele—"

I ripped a pillow from behind him, sticking it over his face. He thrashed and fought, but he was too weak. He was my wife's car when he had a more powerful one slam into it. When he calmed some, I moved it.

He gasped for breath, wheezing. He went to scream for his wife, but nothing came out but air.

"Screaming is useless. Your loyal men are upstairs. Your wife is making you a warm drink. It's just you and me. Truth is the only thing standing between us."

He went to grab for the water again, but I knocked it on the floor.

"Fuck you," he rasped out. He took a minute to catch his breath, to calm himself. He held his hand over his heart, but his eyes were full of defiance. "You want to know where your wife is? She's buried six feet under, the worms making a meal of her beautiful face." He rattled off the cemetery and where to find her marker. "It's over. Nothing you can do about it now. *Finale.*"

He'd had me in chains before because I refused to allow my wife to become a victim of my life. I'd never seen her as a weak creature, but the world was made of men like me, carnivores who thrived on blood.

I was half of her. I'd be the one standing between them and my heart.

His eyes grew wide when the pillow came at his face again. This time, I didn't relent, and I pressed my weight down on his chest. I was stopping his lungs from inflating and blocking the incidental air.

The moment came when he went completely still. It didn't take long. With what I did and the fluid in his lungs, it took him in less than three minutes. He'd never move again. I put the pillow back where it had been. Relaxed his fingers. Picked the glass up off the floor.

I opened the door and called for his wife.

"He stopped breathing," I said when she appeared in the dark hallway.

She dropped the mug of whatever she had and ran to his side. "Tom!" She slapped at him. "Tom! Call an ambulance!"

I nodded, pulling out my phone. I gave them the info.

"I wasn't here for him!" She fisted his pajamas, tucking herself underneath his chin, crying.

"If it's any consolation, he called your name before he went." Then I left.

R. Corvo.

The rose is beauteous, but time causes it to fade;
The violet is fair in spring,
And quickly grows out of date;
The lily is white, fading when it droops;
The snow is white, melting at the very time when it is congealed,
And beautiful is the bloom of youth,
But it lasts only for a short time.

The plain marker in the cemetery was etched with those

words. Just an abbreviation of my wife's name and a poem by Theocritus.

If her bones were inside, mine would rest next to hers eternally.

I exhumed the grave, which was only a foot or two deep, and came up with a box full of stolen money. There was no casket.

CHAPTER 47

FELICE

Corvo's house was all lit up. The driveway was filled with cars. All his daughters were home, except for one. Alfonso's car was parked behind Lolita's. No doubt he rushed over after he heard the news. Tommaso Russo was dead.

He knew who the new boss was.

Lolita answered the door. She sucked in air. "John," she breathed out.

The other three sisters and their husbands came to stand behind her. Sandro put his hand on Lolita's shoulder, his eyes not so sure about my intentions. I intended to make them clear.

"My wife," I said.

"She's not here." Lolita lifted her hands. "Honest to God. You know I would tell you. She texts me sometimes, but that's it. I have no clue where she is. I miss her, John." Her eyes spilled over with tears. She wiped her cheeks.

I bulldozed my way into the house, Sandro moving Lolita out of the way. The group parted for me when I headed toward Corvo's office.

Talia stepped in front of me. She was ballsy. I always liked her. Joseph stood next to her. He'd make a move if I moved on her.

"I know what you must be feeling right now," she said, her

voice strong. "But I'm not going to allow you to hurt my dad. He's aged since...all of this. His heart is...sick. I can see yours is too."

She saw a crazed man covered in sweat, mud, and blood on the hunt for his wife. I could smell death in the air around me. Had been smelling it since I'd been told my wife was dead.

Corvo stepped out of his office, his eyes narrowed. "Get out of the way, Talia."

I went to move but Talia refused. Joseph had to take her by the shoulders and lift her. I had no problem with Roma's sisters, or their husbands, but I'd move like a fucking wrecking ball when it came to my wife.

Corvo moved when I did. He ducked back into his office. He stood behind his desk. Alfonso and Jack stood side by side, backs almost plastered to the bookshelf. Dr. Sala sat in one of the two chairs in front of Corvo's desk. He was sipping whatever was in his glass.

Alfonso pulled a gun on me. "Come any closer, I'll blow a hole in your chest big enough to see through. I know who you met with in Sicily. Now that Russo's dead, our agreement has expired."

It was, but I had no plans to touch Alfonso and his son again, unless they physically touched me or mine. The game was over. They won. They could take whatever monetary prize and move the fuck on. Even before Roma ran, I'd hurt her because of it. I didn't see the truth of it until she pointed it out. I was threatening Jack for using her, but I'd done the same fucking thing.

I turned my back on Alfonso and Jack, facing Corvo. He pulled a gun on me.

"Get out of my house," he said. There was no bite to his tone. No heat. No coldness. It was void of anything.

He sounded like me.

I lifted my hands. "Check me, Jack."

"Hell if he will," Alfonso said.

Dr. Sala set his glass on Corvo's desk and patted me down. He nodded. "He is clean."

Corvo still held his gun. It was aimed at my heart. I'd hurt his, and his finger itched to retaliate, to send me out of his world for good. *Finale.* But it was only wishful dreaming. We would always be linked to each other through my wife and his daughter. He loathed it.

My hands were still up, and I dropped to my knees in front of Corvo. It was done on purpose and not. After finding out my wife was still alive, I didn't have control of my legs when the truth truly hit me.

A gasp came from outside of the office. The dog's ears raised at the noise.

"Get up!" Corvo ordered. Something in his voice then. That hate he was too numb to feel before.

He'd been going through the stages of grief after I married his daughter, like our marriage had killed her. But like me, he was the only thing standing between him and her.

"Get up!" he repeated, throwing a stone at me from his desk. It hit me in the forehead. "I see what you're doing. You're trying to fool my family, like you tricked my innocent daughter. You used her. You used her to kill me. To get back at Alfonso. You don't love her. You don't know what love is, unless the color of it is green."

I said nothing, keeping my hands and eyes up. I might be down, but I'd still look him in the eyes. He tore around the desk, stopping in front of me, sticking the gun to the center of my head.

"I let your worthless father die." Satisfaction laced his words. "I could have saved him, but I didn't."

"Babbo!"

"Quiet," he snapped at Lolita in Italian, but our eyes never broke. "The mighty Sal Maggio was foaming from the mouth, pissing and shitting himself. I sat there and watched it. I didn't lift a finger to stop the devil from claiming him. How do you like that, boy?"

When I didn't answer, he pressed the gun even harder against my head. He went off at the mouth, sounding like he was talking to his wife's ex-husband instead of me. He didn't see me as an individual man, but as the sins of another. He wasn't yelling, but his voice had grown hoarse, like he was straining to get the words out. But that was all they were. Words.

The only thing that could hurt me in this world was my wife.

"Emanuele. *Enough!*" Dr. Sala moved the gun and held it down. "If he were going to do something, he would have done it by now. I would have. I would have knocked your lights out. And I have never, *never*, put my hands on a woman in malice."

Emanuele staggered to his chair, almost falling into it. He swiveled to where he had a bottle of whiskey and a glass, setting the gun down. He poured some and shot it back. "What do you want, John?" He sighed.

"My wife," I said.

Emanuele shrugged. "She came here before she left, but when she left, she left us both. None of us know where she is. I've looked."

I stood, and Corvo pointed the gun at me again, but he was looking behind me.

"Put it down, Alfonso," Corvo ordered.

I stepped to the side. Alfonso's gun moved with me.

"He's not fooling me with his grand show." Alfonso took a closer step toward me. He was so mad, the gun trembled in his hand. "He's not getting another thing from me! Do you hear me, Corvo? We had an agreement. Roma is promised to Jack, even if she's ruined."

The blast from the gun made the dog duck under the desk. Screams came from the hall and cries from somewhere deeper in the house. Alfonso stumbled into Jack, grabbing for his shoulder where the bullet had struck.

"Next time I'll aim lower and more to the center," I said, my ears ringing. I was probably shouting. "Take my warning and run with it."

Alfonso looked at Dr. Sala in shock. He shrugged. "Must have missed that one." He dug in his ear and wiggled his finger, like he was trying to scratch an itch.

Dr. Sala had patted me down, but he hadn't taken my gun.

"Emanuele." Alfonso moved his hand away, palm covered in blood. "Kill him! Do it now!"

Corvo chucked his chin toward the door. "Get out of my house, Al."

Jack had to force him to move. He bitched the whole way out.

Dr. Sala stood, squeezing my shoulder. He looked at Emanuele. "How about a bite to eat while we talk this over?"

Corvo sighed and stood. "Follow me."

Dr. Sala adjusted his glasses and smiled at me. "My old friend was right about romance and ruthlessness, ah?" He patted my back all the way to the dining room table.

"Hello?" A step. "Hello?" Another step. "Who's here?"

"Turn the lights on, Burton."

"Shit!" Something hit the floor. A book, maybe.

He flipped the lights on.

He blinked at me. His hair was a mess, his glasses smeared with what looked like chip grease. He wore flannel pajamas and was barefoot. I was sitting in a chair in his house, pointing a gun at him.

He fell to the floor, like he'd passed out. I sighed and moved toward him. His eyes were shut, and he was keeping very still. I kept quiet as I stared at him. After a minute or two, he peeked.

"Boo," I said.

"Ah!" He froze, staring at the ceiling, not blinking.

"What the fuck are you doing?"

"I was trying to play dead." He panted. He wasn't taking any breaths before, but he was almost gulping air. "It makes predators uninterested. They don't enjoy dead meat. They like it live and fighting. Fresh. The blood right at the surface to make it juicer."

I pointed the gun at him. "My gun doesn't fucking care if you're alive or not when it's making holes. It only listens to my trigger finger. Where's my wife, Burton?"

He fixed his glasses and stared up at me. "Can I get up?"

I nodded and used my gun to point at the sofa. "Here to there. My gun listens to my trigger finger, but my finger gets an itch sometimes. Don't fucking try me."

He sat there for a second, like he was gaining courage, then a nasty stench wafted in the air as he got to his feet. He cut his eyes to me, then avoided them as he took a seat on the sofa. He slumped down.

"I don't know—"

"Not what I want to hear—"

"Please. Let me finish. I don't know where she is, exactly, but I have a feeling about...what she's doing."

"A feeling is not fact," I said. "I'm hunting those down."

"True, but sometimes it turns into one. Someone accessed my computer right before she left. There's a database for dig sites all over the world. I had a feeling it was Roma."

"How big is this database?

"Huge," he said. "It's loaded with information. Who's funding the dig, who's on the job, what they're digging for, and where."

I rolled my shoulders, the tension in my neck matching the tightness in my chest. "You can access it from your home computer?"

"Afraid not," he said. "Only from the museum."

"Grab your keys," I said. "Let's fucking go."

"No problem." He nodded. "But can I change my clothes first?" He looked down at his pants.

"Get the fuck outta here." I pointed to his room with my gun. He walked backward.

CHAPTER 48

ROMA

"Maggio!"

It took three calls of my name to get me to look up from my phone and peek outside of my tent.

Beatriz. She and a few of my fellow paleontologists were staring at something they found around the roped-off dig site.

She looked up and our eyes met.

"Roma!" She waved. "You need to see this!"

"Be there in a second," I called back.

I looked back down at the picture on my phone, not believing my eyes. My husband in front of my father. Babbo had a gun pressed to his temple. Lo tried to send a video, but reception out here was slim. I hadn't even bothered to check my messages in a few days.

A text was underneath it.

Lo: I know you probably won't respond, but Babbo had dinner with John after this...in the dining room.

Tears streamed down my face, but I hurriedly wiped them off. I composed myself and stepped out of the tent and into the hot sunshine. We'd been at it for seven months in Argentina, after Beatriz and her team's prospecting operation turned out successful. They found fragments of fossils on the surface, which meant there was a good chance there was more below.

There was.

We'd found the remains of an *Argentinosaurus*, a herbivore, and one of the largest land mammals of all time. She was a hundred and twenty feet long, about the size of a tennis court in length. Not far from where she was found, the fossil of a *Giganotosaurus* was excavated.

The *Giganotosaurus* was considered one of the biggest carnivores. It's lesser known than the T-rex, because its bite force was three times less, but it was no less impressive. It weighed around seventeen thousand pounds and measured around forty-three feet.

"Do you see this?" Beatriz nodded to an area further out.

Claw marks I could fit in.

She held onto my arm, and I smiled.

"Foreplay," I said.

"Can you imagine?" she breathed.

"How loud it was when they mated? I suspect *loud*."

Like the exhibit had explained, it was suspected dinosaurs had similar mating dances to birds. They made love and war with ceremony. So much energy and showing off. There was no way they were quiet when they actually mated. Not after all that fanfare.

"*Hot*."

We both started laughing. It brought back memories of Cassio at the museum on Valentine's Day, when he was there for the mating exhibit. I tried not to think about it, though. Cassio only brought me to John, and my heart was barely hanging on as it was.

"Wouldn't that have been something if it was Giganto and Argia?" The words slipped free.

"The carnivore and our girl?"

I nodded.

"I doubt it. They were not built for each other. He would

have mated with her and then killed her. If he did not have her for dinner before that."

"Too many differences," I muttered. My heart sank like a stone. I knew they didn't belong together, couldn't be together, but for a second, it was a pleasant thought.

She gave me a strange look, then gazed at the marks again.

It didn't matter what I was doing, or where I was, John manifested himself in my life. I was starting to think what he said about me never being able to run from him was more than literal. His eyes haunted me. I couldn't escape them, and I didn't want to. But not having him close was the worst of it all. To ache for someone so acutely, knowing they were only hours away—I shook my head.

And what he'd done at Babbo's...my heart throbbed.

"Maggio!"

I whirled around at the sound of my name, keeping a hand to my head. I didn't want to lose my sunhat. Two figures stood in the distance: another paleontologist and, next to him, a man dressed in a black t-shirt and black fatigues that didn't hide his physique.

The paleontologist was pointing her finger gun at him, as if to say, *he's asking for you.*

Beatriz squeezed my arm. "Who is *that*?"

I could hardly breathe. Those intense green eyes were hypnotizing me from across the site.

"Roma?"

"Ye-Yeah. That's." Deep breath. "My husband."

"No wonder you have been lovesick. *Hot.*" She laughed, then narrowed her eyes. "What is he doing?"

He slid one boot against the ground. Then the other. Making his own version of claw marks in the mud. He charged toward me with energy, almost knocking me over when he ran into me. He picked me clear up off the ground, keeping me pressed to him, our lips locked, making a show for all the other paleontologists.

"You fucking ran from me," he rasped against my mouth.

"You fucking ran from me. I thought—fuck. Roma. My little herbivore. My wife."

"Tommaso—"

He didn't give me a chance to finish. He held me against him with one arm, his opposite hand deep into my hair, keeping my head from moving back. I couldn't move my lips from his. Until he broke the kiss to look around.

"There," I pointed. "That's my tent."

"You've been sleeping in a tent for months?"

"Since we found most of her remains. At least now we have a portable potty." I wiggled my eyebrows at him. "Fancy, I know."

He shook his head and set me on my feet. He unzipped my tent, and we slipped inside. He had to duck his head to fit. It was dark and kept out most of the light. No shadows.

I stared up at him, and he stared down at me. He buried his hand in my hair again and set me flush against his body.

"John," I whispered, fighting the desire to set my forehead against his chest and breathe him in.

"That's my fucking limit." He raked his teeth over his lip before he pulled me in for a punishing kiss. His dick strained against his pants, hard against my soft.

He walked me backward until my ankle hit the raised bed. I lost my balance and went to fall, but he caught me and sat me down. He removed his shirt, flinging it to the ground. He removed mine, throwing it on top of his. He took my boots and socks off, tossing them to the side. Then he unbuttoned my shorts, setting them on the growing pile. My plain bra and cotton panties came off next.

He took me in like he was seeing me for the first time. The look in his eyes made me arch toward him, already begging for him to touch me.

"On all fours." He nodded toward the bed.

I did as he said, trembling all over, even though sweat dripped from my body. This time of the day, there was no breeze, and the closed tent felt like a sauna. My breasts felt heavy, achy, and my nipples were hard. The pulse between my legs throbbed.

My body always craved his, but when he was this close...

"Please. Touch me."

He ran a hand over the shape of my ass cheek before it dipped between my legs.

"So fucking wet for me already."

"I've missed you," I barely got out, my eyes closing.

He slipped a finger inside of me, opening me up, stretching me. I moaned low in my throat, pushing against it.

"You want more?"

"*Mmm*...yes. I want you."

He kicked his boots and socks off. Unzipped his pants and pulled them off with his boxers. He climbed on the bed behind me. He set his dick close to my entrance and I pushed back, to take him inside, to have him fill me up until I felt like I couldn't take it.

His hips surged forward, burying himself to the hilt, and I cried out as he groaned. He was so big and so thick, it felt like he was stretching my hips. He pushed me forward, his dick sliding halfway out, my face hitting the bed. I turned my cheek against it.

He ran his hand down the side of my face. "I love you more than life." He gripped my hips. "But this isn't going to feel like it. This is going to feel like the hours and days we spent apart. This is going to feel like all the seconds I spent thinking about you—not being able to fucking touch my wife. This is going to feel like your silence. This is going to feel like me taking back what's mine."

He rammed me again, and a garbled sound escaped my lips. He started fucking me like an animal. Grunting and growling, his hands biting into my hips, sweat splashing on my body from his. I wasn't sure if I could keep taking it, but the pain only increased the pleasure.

I was losing my mind from the back and forth. From the insanity of it. From the intensity of it.

"I love you." *I'm fucking you like my body is at war with yours.*

"We'll never separate again." *Feel that? How much I wanted to kill the distance between us?*

"You're mine." *You hid from me. You hurt me. Even before you ran to save me.*

A long, trembling moan left my lips, and I couldn't hold back. My body gave in to his, and it felt like we went crashing into each other when we came at the same time. I felt the impact deeper than bone.

We both stilled. Trying to catch our breath. He pulled me down on the bed, bringing my back to his front. I could feel his heart pounding. Our bodies dripped with sweat. My hair was soaked.

I turned over and he moved back some, giving me room.

"Felice," I whispered, tucking my hands against his chest.

He closed his eyes. "You fucking ripped my heart out, little plant eater. You're not a part of the world. You are my world. You insult me every time you call me John. You deafened me with your silence."

"You hurt me."

He opened his eyes and stared into mine. "No excuses. I was fucking wrong. I own it. I'll own it for the rest of my life. I'll carry your hurt with me like a scar. It won't happen again. The game is over. I ended it. *Finito.*" He kissed my hands.

"What you did at Babbo's—"

"You're the only one who can bring me to my knees, woman. No man in this world can."

The words hung in the air around us. For the first time since he'd arrived, outside noises started to invade what seemed like our own private world. The dig site was still active. Life was still moving forward. The earth was still spinning. It brought me back to reality.

"Tommaso—"

"He's dead." His jaw tensed, and his eyes turned hard.

I searched his face. "When?"

"Four days ago."

"The day you got out of jail."

"He told me you were dead." He pulled me to him so hard it was hard to take in air. "He dug a grave and put a marker on it with your name. He'd buried a box of fucking money."

I didn't try to pull away from him. I needed to be even closer. I wanted to melt into him. It was the first time I truly understood how someone would want to die in someone else's arms.

He kissed the top of my head. "You wouldn't have been alone. We would have shared that grave. Side by side. Someone excavated us, they wouldn't be able to tell us apart. We'd be like we were from the beginning."

I looked up at him, and he looked down at me.

"One," he said.

"One," I repeated.

"Roma Viviana Maggio. You belong to me. Felice Giovanni Maggio. Not even a thunderbolt, or death, will be able to separate us again."

Epilogue

Roma

4 Years Later

"They who are in love never feel the cold," I whispered, staring at my husband through the car window while snow pelted him. It stuck to his hair and lashes and black wool coat. He was walking toward me, hand in his pocket, the other hand holding a hot chocolate for me, a few of the workers from the bombolone place trudging behind him with boxes in their arms.

It was something Mamma used to say. She had a lot to say, I was realizing as I got older. Her little sayings and quotes and proverbs would come to me seemingly out of the blue, but like John, I knew she'd manifested herself in my life. She was always there with me, sending me the reminders when I needed them the most.

A smile came to my face. Felice narrowed his eyes. I started laughing, and he shook his head, opening the liftgate so the workers could put the boxes in the SUV. Our order had grown exponentially over the last several years.

After we got back from Argentina, I organized a sit down with Felice, myself, Corrina, Nonna Silvia, and Babbo. Felice and his family deserved to know the truth. Sal's condition was hope-less, and even if Babbo could have helped him, Tommaso had ordered him not to. Sal had done something unforgivable in the eyes of his boss.

Laws in Felice's world were different from ones our world upheld. Corrina and Nonna Silvia understood them. Felice did too. He knew Sal was having an affair with a woman who was off limits. They all did.

"At least Tommaso showed mercy on Sal," Corrina had said, dabbing at her eyes. "He let him go naturally."

Ever since, they attended all the family get togethers at Babbo's house. Adding them to the mix, plus all the other in-laws and children...we needed a lot of bomboloni.

It was Christmas Eve, and we were headed to Babbo's to stay until after the new year.

Felice closed the liftgate, handed over wads of cash to the workers, then opened the door to the SUV. The chill didn't touch me. All I felt flood over me when he took his seat was warmth.

I was more in love with my husband than the day I'd met him in the flesh.

He leaned forward and turned the radio down. "Admit it."

"Admit what?" I smiled at him again.

"What the fuck's going on. You've had this faraway look in your eyes, real dreamy like, for days, and you keep smiling at me for no reason."

"Real dreamy like?" I exploded with laughter.

He sighed, blowing hot air out of his nose. My carnivore was getting testy.

"Okay." I lifted my hands. I dug in my purse and held the small, flat box with the photo down in it. "I found a new species of dinosaur. It's half carnivore and half herbivore. An omnivore, but it'll take time to know for sure which eating habits he or she will take."

His eyebrows furrowed. "I'm not following, Dino."

I pulled the box out and handed it to him.

He opened it. His eyes scanned the grainy black and white picture. "This has your name on it."

"Yours too." I smiled even bigger.

He turned to me slowly, his eyes finally understanding the cause of the happiness in mine. He ran his knuckle down my cheek. It was a touch so tender, so full of everything he couldn't say, it made me cry.

"You're fucking glowing." His voice was gruff, the exact opposite of his hand.

"You lit the flame," I whispered.

He leaned in and kissed me. The moment between us froze in time. Maybe that was what made winter special. A memory could be preserved and kept as a mental ornament.

Felice held my hand the entire way, constantly kissing my fingers, a grin appearing on his face every so often, for apparently no reason. We both knew, though. Our blood vow had taken on a life of its own.

He kissed me again before we got out of the car. He refused to let me carry any of the boxes. He never had, though. He took as many as he could carry in one hand, and took my hand in the other, leading us to the front door.

The house was packed. Laughter rang out deep inside, and a bunch of kids whizzed by.

"We're having a brat of our own," he said, probably because the kids nearly knocked the boxes out of his hand.

I exploded with laughter, nodding.

Joseph rushed toward us, grabbing some of the boxes. Sandro offered to help with the rest. He said he didn't want the filling to freeze. Gino said he'd help too. Felice took my coat, hanging it up, before he went back out with them to get our stuff.

Babbo was shaking his head, holding a life-size dancing Santa under his arm in a choke hold. He was mumbling at it. I kissed his cheek, and he tapped my face.

"What happened?" I asked.

"One of those brats," he said, shaking his head even harder, "broke my damn Santa!"

The kids giggled and ran from him.

"That's okay," he called after them. "You're getting onions from Befana. Since you hurt poor Santa and he can no longer deliver gifts!"

One of the kids started crying. He smiled at me, satisfied.

I exploded with laughter. He studied my face.

"You eat a flame, my darling girl?"

Carlo interrupted the moment, letting Babbo know he was ready to assist with Santa's surgery. Felice, Gino, and Sandro came back through the door, arms filled with stuff.

"Come with us, Felice!" Babbo said, trying to use his hands to talk, but only knocking Santa around. "I need an extra set of hands."

Felice nodded, set our bags down, and went to help.

I stared in the direction they went in, so complete, I almost couldn't breathe. Lo met me in the hall and placed an arm around my neck, pulling me toward the kitchen.

"Where you been, bish? My mother-in-law is chasing me around, making not so subtle remarks about grandchildren."

"When is it happening?"

She pushed me away. "Traitor. You're supposed to be my armor."

I started laughing, and she narrowed her eyes at me.

"Are you drunk?"

"No."

"Well, I wanna be. Alina brought this new spiked eggnog. Gino's brother's friend makes it. He's just starting to sell it. It's delish."

The kitchen was packed. People were everywhere. Alina and Talia were on each side of Isabella, backs against the counter. She wore reindeer antlers on a headband with a retro, lacy striped apron tied in a big bow around her waist. Her nose was red. She was sloshed.

"Y!" She waved her cup. "You have to try this!"

I picked up the bottle off the counter. *Agog about Eggnog* was the brand name, written in green, white, and red script, lights weaving around it. A woman was next to the name, holding a glass up in a cheers motion, her humongous boobs on display.

The model was the woman who had called me out on Halloween at Felice's house when I'd showed up. The same woman who was there when Tommaso set up the fake scene and Felice was arrested.

"*Hahahahaha*," I mimicked her laugh.

Lo snatched the bottle from me and poured herself a glass. "Are you sure you're not drunk, Y?"

She went to pour me a glass, but I shook my head.

"Why not?" Alina topped hers off. "It's *sooo* good."

"You have to try it, Y." Talia held her cup out for more. "It makes you feel all warm and tingly inside."

Isabella grabbed Talia and Alina, squeezing their arms. "I don't think Y needs it to feel all warm and tingly inside," she said, her eyes on mine.

"Why not?" Lo looked between us. "You can't feel warm and tingly during the holidays without alcohol."

I nodded at Isabella, answering her silent question.

Isabella screeched and wrapped me in her arms, hugging me. My sisters all got in on the hug.

When we pulled apart, Lo asked, "Are we hugging because of the eggnog? It is that good."

"Be right back." I ran out to the hallway and grabbed four boxes out of our bags. I handed them to my sisters when I got back. "I was going to wait until tomorrow morning, but..." I shrugged.

Lo tore into hers. She held up the light green sweater with cartoon baby dinosaurs on it. "Umm..."

"Read the card, Lo!" Talia threw a date at her.

The fruit hit her in the forehead. She didn't even flinch as she read the card. "I'm going to be a dino-mite aunt?" she asked, squeezing the sweater.

I nodded. "Or a Gucci one."

Lo screamed, wrapping me in a bear hug. We rocked back and forth until Corrina and Nonna Silvia walked in.

We greeted them, and it seemed like the hours melted after that. It was a night to remember, and I needed a minute to reflect. Or maybe to decompress a bit. After everyone left and Felice went to take a shower, I padded down the steps in my warm pajamas and into the sunroom. The ceiling was topped with snow, but outside, it fell soundlessly, collecting on the ground.

A sweet smell floated through the air. It was like a quick breeze. There and then gone. It smelled like Mamma's perfume.

"I'm happy for me too," I whispered.

A more manly scent drifted in, but this time, a figure materialized. My husband. He'd showered and dressed for bed, but the long sleeves of his thermal were pushed up his arms. He didn't feel the cold. I wondered if he'd always been in love.

"Here," I said. "Here is where I planned to tell you about the baby. At midnight."

We stared at each other for a second before he reached out and barely touched my face.

He sighed as he took a seat next to me, wrapping me in his arms. I rested my head on his shoulder, curling up even closer to him. We watched the snow fall, both of us quiet. Then his eyes fell to the glass bottle someone left on the table. The one with the woman from Halloween past's tatas.

"*Hahahahaha*," I whispered.

He grinned. "You remember her."

"She's hard to forget. I bet her name is Candy or something sweet like that."

He gave me a look. I tried to sit up some, but he refused to let me.

"It is!"

He nodded. I laughed, my own laugh this time. I sighed a few seconds later, staring at her picture.

"I didn't believe it, you know. That you were with her that day."

He looked at me, the intensity in his eyes raising to DEFCON 3 level.

"I trust you, Felice. But if you ever decide to start...looking elsewhere, I want you to tell me."

"Fucking tell you," he whispered.

I nodded. "Yeah, so I can start doing the same. We can be like Rocco and what's her name?" I thought for a second. "Rosaria."

"We could never be like them. You're much too gorgeous, and I have better hair than him." His tone was dead serious.

Or I thought he was being dead serious. A shit-eating grin spread on his face when I hit his shoulder, and he pulled me closer. So close, it almost hurt.

"A man even looks at you with the wrong intent, he won't live long enough to give another look."

"You're mine," I said, knowing that covered all bases. He'd said it to me enough times. I'd never really thought about it before because he never gave me a reason to. But our lives were changing. I wanted to be clear on that.

He didn't share. Neither did I.

Our eyes met, and we stared at each other. He nodded and I kissed his lips. He refused to let me move back.

"*Solo tu,*" he said, kissing me even harder. "*Eternamente.*"

Only you. Eternally.

We pulled apart, and it hurt more than it did in the beginning. The longer we were together, the harder it was to separate.

Since that time was on my mind, though, I had something to ask him. "How did you find me? When I left?"

He went through all the steps, including breaking into Hayden's house. "Why ask me now?"

I shook my head. "Corinna brought it up tonight. After she found out about the baby, she said something like, *'I'm glad you got in touch with Felice after you left, and that everything worked out.'* You didn't talk to her after you were released?"

"No. I had other things to take care of. I hadn't seen or talked to her since before they pinched me—the last time."

I fell into him and started laughing. He lifted me up, making me look at him.

"Felice." I sighed. "I told her where I was. She was the only one who knew. I knew Tommaso would never suspect it. My father would have never thought of it. My sisters either. Alfonso and Jack weren't going *anywhere* near Nonna Silvia. Someone had to know where I was." My voice dipped. "You found me anyway."

"Can't separate us. Not even in death." He stood, hauling me up and throwing me over his shoulder. "Fuck. You're getting an onion from Befana since we couldn't fix Santa. I can't believe this shit." He spanked my ass and then stopped halfway up the stairs when I said the next words to him.

"*Ti amo*, my dangerous carnivore."

"*Ti amo*, my little herbivore. The only creature who has ever brought me to my knees. My better half. She who holds my heart."

"One," I said.

"One."

As it was. As it would always be. *Not even in death shall we part.*

About the Author

Bella Di Corte writes criminal romance that will steal your heart. She brings to life stories of men who walk the line between irredeemable and savable, and the women who force them to feel. She's known for her rich world building and strong characters. She's also an International Bestselling Author.

Apart from writing, Bella loves to spend time with her husband, daughter, family, and four dogs. She also loves to read, listen to music, cook recipes that were passed down to her, and take photographs.

Bella was born and raised in New Orleans, a place she considers a creative playground.

Also by Bella Di Corte

The Fausti Family:

Man of Honor

Queen of Thorns

Royals of Italy

Kingdom of Corruption

War of Monsters

Ruler of Hearts

Law of Conduct

King of Roses

The Fausti Family Boxed Set: Books 1-3

Gangsters of New York:

Machiavellian, Book 1

Metamorphosis: A Machiavellian Short Story

Marauder, Book 2

Mercenary, Book 3

Underworld Kings:

Disavow

The Ryan Brothers:

Skin Deep, Book 1 (Harrison & Gigi)

Bone Deep, Book 2 (Lachlan & Clara)

Vice City:

Ruthless Consequences, Book 1 (Brio & Lucila)

Dangerous Obsession, Book 2 (Naz Fausti & Ava)

Made in the USA
Columbia, SC
15 February 2023

12086727R00196